G000268830

Recommendation

'*Entangled Legacy* starts with an intriguing premise on which the foundation of this page-turner is built. Emily and Jack wake up in different respective beds, a considerable distance from where they laid their heads the night before. They receive a letter from a former teacher who has passed away and their lives change irrevocably. They spend the proceeding decades trying to solve a mystery that has affected their lives in myriad ways. Coniston's prose is warm and clear and keeps the reader close. At the heart of the eminently readable novel lies affection to scientific conundrums occasionally reminiscent of Phillip Pullman. But this adventure is ultimately about how human beings react to extraordinary events and how they cope with powerful forces that threaten the cast of characters at every turn. Perhaps most importantly of all, you'll have a lot of fun reading it.'

– *Mark Connors, Prizewinning Poet and Novelist*

ENTANGLED LEGACY

William Coniston

Text Copyright © 2021 William Coniston
Cover Copyright © 2021 Oliver Downs, Matilda Downs, Carl
Moore.

Published by William Coniston,
Wilsden, Bradford BD15 0BE.

ISBN 978-0-9935224-3-7

All rights reserved. No part of this publication may be
reproduced, stored or transmitted in any form or by any means
without the prior written permission of the publisher.

The author asserts the right to be identified as the author of
this work in accordance with the Copyright, Designs and Patents
Act 1988

All the characters, events and organisations portrayed in this
book are fictitious and any resemblance to actual persons, living
or dead is coincidental and not intended by the author.

ACKNOWLEDGEMENTS

My wife, family and friends remain tolerant of my writing habits and give me encouragement, inspiration and constructive criticism. I know how lucky I am that they do and I thank them sincerely.

My cover team deserves special thanks: Tilly, Carl, Ollie, Charlie and Rosie each brought unique talent to bear at a time when nothing was easy. I think you will agree the result is outstanding.

Many thanks also to Mark Connors for his advice, for reading the book and for providing an excellent endorsement.

Others to whom I am grateful for invaluable help and advice are: Nabeela Ahmed, Trevor Alexander, Linda Booth, Michelle Bradley, Jill Lang, Graeme Mason, Susan Tempest and Susan Downs.

THE BEGINNING

1
Mrs Barton

A routine reminder on Edith Gregory's work calendar led Clive, her assistant, to check whether or not Mrs Barton had signed and returned the papers she had been sent two weeks previously. Normally she did so promptly without query and, he suspected, without even reading them. He made further enquiries and found out she had died. Realising the significance, he hurried down the corridor to tell his boss. She made him search the office in case the papers had been sent back and misfiled but there was no trace. She looked worried and pale when she asked him to get the Senior Partner, Mr King, on the phone.

'I'm afraid there could be a problem,' she said when the call was connected.

It might only have been a delay on the transatlantic line but, when she had explained, there was a momentary pause and she thought she heard a sigh of annoyance before he replied.

'This is disappointing. There's a lot at stake, as you well know. I'm relying on you to resolve it quickly, clear away obstacles. Otherwise, there could be consequences.'

Edith swallowed. She knew what he meant but tried to keep her voice steady.

'Of course, I'll get some people onto it.'

***

The church was packed and a blast of cold December air from the back signalled the arrival of the coffin, carried by overcoated undertakers. Jack, sitting a few rows from the front with Dil and Lucy, felt the chill. Everyone expected to see Mrs Barton's family members following. A husband perhaps, children, grandchildren maybe, brothers or sisters but there were none. Only Mrs Grisedale, the current Head Teacher.

There were hymns and prayers led by the vicar, readings by various members of school staff, past and present, and then the eulogy. Mrs Grisedale stood up from a front pew and walked to the lectern. She spoke about how Mrs Barton had given a lifetime of service to the school and, well past retirement age, had continued working until she died unexpectedly, but peacefully, in her sleep; about how she had married over forty years ago but her husband had tragically died less than a year later; and about her having no children or other relatives.

'So,' she went on, 'we are really her family and I see from the numbers of you who have come back here today that it is a big family, a family who loved and respected her and who will miss her greatly.'

Many in the congregation dabbed their eyes and even Jack, who hadn't seen her for years, felt a lump in his throat. He wasn't over-sentimental about her death but he had come to pay his respects because he was grateful to her. He hadn't done well in the first year of the sixth form. He wasn't alone. It was an era of relentless cuts in funding for education and the school was in a deprived catchment area so its resources to prepare pupils for higher education were stretched to the limit. Luckily Mrs Barton and a few other teachers made it their business to nurture those they thought had ability, which included Jack. Under her influence he repeated a year, passed exams and eventually, against the odds, gained entrance to Cambridge University, one of the best in the world. He knew how fortunate he'd been, despite a huge student loan to repay.

The funeral was also an opportunity to catch up with family and friends he didn't often see now that he worked in London.

The service was followed by a buffet lunch across the road at a large hotel. As he, Dil and Lucy walked in, he glimpsed Emily ahead and his mind immediately went back ten years.

She had been near the back of the church with Bina and had smiled to herself when she recognised Jack by his ears. They reminded her of the most extraordinary day of her life.

TEN YEARS AGO

2
Where?

Emily's alarm went off at seven. At least, she thought it had but it sounded like seagulls outside the window.

Clock battery must be low, she thought and reached out to snooze it, but missed. Everything went quiet though, so she didn't need to open her eyes. When it went off again, still sounding the same, she knew she had to get up. It was Friday and she needed to make one final effort for the last exam. She groaned and aimed herself at the bedroom door, eyes still closed, head down. She put out her hand to open it but hit a wall. The door wasn't there.

'Urgh,' she grunted, opening her eyes just a crack.

What she saw made no sense so she shut them again.

Ok, I'm dreaming. Maybe it isn't time to get up after all.

She slid back into bed and hoped. After a minute or so she still felt awake and took another quick peek. Nothing had changed. She knew the room, of course, and what she would see if she looked out of the window. She knew the bed she lay in and also its empty twin separated by a small night stand. She dug a fingernail into her hand to wake herself up, but again nothing changed.

I could have dreamed doing that. How can I tell if I'm awake?

She gazed at the ceiling, listening to seagulls. Finally she thought, *If I'm dreaming it doesn't matter what I do because eventually I'll wake up and if I'm not dreaming I need to know what's happened.*

She got out of bed again and drew back the curtains. There was the cliff, the beach with a few early walkers, high summer sun glinting off the sea. All very familiar.

There was just one problem. She wasn't in the room where she had gone to sleep. Not even the same house. Not even the same town.

***

Jack wasn't fully awake, despite the alarm. He knew it was time to get up but he always took it to the edge.

'Jaaack,' his mother would call up the stairs every few minutes, but his brain and body wouldn't respond. It was only when she'd stormed into the room and flung back the curtains, as she did nearly every school morning, that he could bring himself to move. Even then it was only to swing his feet to the floor and sit on the edge of the bed, head in hand, eyes closed.

He continued to lie there, expecting his mother but she didn't appear. He fell asleep again until a woman who wasn't his mother came into the room and said, 'Come on, Em,' then shrieked and ran out.

He nearly shrieked too when he looked round. Nothing was normal. The window was in the wrong place and so was the bed. He didn't recognise the carpet, the curtains, the cupboards, the desk - wait, the desk! It was littered with little bottles and tubes and brushes and tissues, and there was a big mirror on the wall and a fluffy white cat on a pink chair. No sign of his laptop.

His voice always took a while to get going so instead of a shriek a sort of 'orgh' came out as a man and the same woman rushed into the room and stared at him. Then they looked under the bed and in some cupboards.

'Where's Em?' the man demanded loudly.

'Who?' said Jack hoarsely, wincing at the noise.

'Young man, don't play the innocent with us. You're in Em's bed in her room so you must know where she is. What have you done with her?'

I must be dreaming, thought Jack. *I'll close my eyes until I wake up.*

But he didn't.

'I'm calling the police,' said the woman and walked out of the room.

'If you've hurt Em or anything I'll kill you,' said the man fiercely.

Jack thought he sounded like he meant it.

'What's your name?' the man went on.

'Jack,' said Jack. 'What's yours?'

He thought it a reasonable question to ask someone he'd never met but it seemed to make the man angrier.

'You cheeky little runt,' he shouted. 'Just you wait till the police get here.'

Jack wasn't sure he wanted to. The man turned and stalked towards the door but his phone rang. He took it out of a pocket.

'Police, please,' said the woman, now downstairs on the house phone.

'Em,' said the man, 'you alright? Where are you?'

It sounded like a girl's voice at the other end.

'Scar Bay? Why?'

The man listened for a while.

'Jane, it's ok,' he shouted down the stairs. 'Em's just on the phone. She's at Scar Bay. God knows why but I don't think we need the police.'

Then into his own phone:

'Come on Em, you can't expect me to believe a story like that. If it's a cover for something to do with Jack…'

Words at the other end.

'Jack. He's here. He was asleep in your bed.'

Loud words at the other end.

'I don't know Jack who. Just a minute I'll ask.'

'Wellington,' said Jack, getting out of bed.

The woman came back upstairs.

'I said we didn't need them but they're coming anyway.'

The man put his mobile on speaker.

'Hello, love, are you alright?' the woman went on.

'I'm fine,' said Emily, 'just in the wrong place. I went to bed there and woke up here.'

'Wellington,' said the man.

'Yeurgh, I know who he is. He's at our school and you say he's in my bed? Creepy. Get him out.'

'He is.'

'He must have something to do with my being here.'

'Er, can I say something,' said Jack.

'No, save it for the police,' Emily went on.

'You'd better get dressed, Jack,' said the woman.

'No clothes,' said Jack.

'Even creepier,' said Emily.

'Look,' he said, 'I'm as surprised about this as you are.'

'I bet,' said the man. 'Where do you live?'

'Halsingham Drive.'

'Yes I know it, one of those streets of terrace houses across the main road. Goodness knows what sort of parents you have, letting you run wild in your pyjamas.'

'They don't,' he said, starting to feel angry. 'And I'm not. I have no idea how I got here. For all I know it's your Em that's got me into this. Some girlish trick. How do you know she's at Scar Bay, wherever that is? She could be anywhere. Round the corner with her phone having a good laugh. I'm going home now. Good bye.'

But as he said it he noticed a phone in a pink case on the bedside table.

'Oh yeah,' Emily shouted, 'like I kidnapped you from home and carried you to ours and put you in my bed without waking you up and then caught a magic night bus to Scar Bay?'

Jack was furious now.

'Yeah, just like I carried you to Scar Bay without waking you up and then came back and slept in your bed. Grow up.'

'Don't tell me to grow up, loser. You're the one being childish and sneaking into people's beds in your pyjamas. I bet your only friend's your laptop.'

'Aargh,' Jack shouted in frustration, 'Why aren't the police here yet? I'm going to report you all.'

Emily's parents were stunned to silence. Jack ran out of the bedroom, downstairs and left the house, pausing only to put his feet into a worn and scuffed pair of pink crocs inside the door. They were a bit small but not too painful, better than nothing.

'Where's he gone, Dad?' Emily shouted.

'Downstairs - home, I think.'

'Well stop him. We can't let him get away with it.'

Emily's mother had been thinking.

'Em, dear, I think we should calm down a bit. There could be more to this than meets the eye. It does seem pretty impossible that Jack could have taken you to Scar Bay during the night. Almost as impossible as you kidnapping him.'

Emily's reply was a screech.

'What do you mean 'almost as impossible' - it sounds like you believe what he said. Here I am in a deserted house at Scar Bay with only my pyjamas and no money and I've an exam at two thirty and I don't know how I got here or how I'm going to get back and I'm being accused of abducting a boy I hardly know.'

She began to cry, more from anger than anything. It was all too much.

'No you're not and don't worry, love. Dad'll come for you.'

'Hang on a minute...' he started to say, thinking of work he had lined up for the day.

From suburban Bradford to Scar Bay on the North Yorkshire coast would take more than two hours but his wife gave him a hard stare and he knew he had to change tack, '...if I set off now I can be there about eleven and have you back in good time for the exam.'

The doorbell rang.

'It could be the police,' said Emily's mother and both parents headed downstairs.

'Good morning. Mrs and Mrs Harrison? I'm PC Gemma Audrey.'

She was solidly built with short dark hair and a smart uniform, about a head shorter than Mr Harrison.

'Yes,' said Mr Harrison, 'if it's about the call my wife made, it's alright now. We thought our daughter was missing but she's turned up. At Scar Bay. Bit of a surprise but she says she's ok.'

'Yes, I'm ok,' said Emily from the phone still in her mother's hand.

'Scar Bay? The place on the coast near Whitby?'

'Yes,' said Mrs Harrison, 'my husband's parents live there but they're away at the moment.'

So your daughter's there alone?'

'Yes,' said Emily.

'When did she go there?'

'Hello, I'm here. You can talk to me,' said Emily, irritated.

'What age is she?' PC Audrey asked.

'I'm seventeen,' said Emily, more irritated.

'Nearly,' said Mr Harrison.

'So when did you go to Scar Bay?' PC Audrey asked, getting the message.

'Overnight,' said Emily truthfully.

'Well next time, keep your parents in the loop so as not to cause unnecessary alarm and not to waste police time.'

Emily was incandescent.

'Look,' she started but her mother turned the volume down so PC Audrey couldn't hear.

'I'm sure she will,' said Mr Harrison.

'Strangely enough there's another missing teenager near here this morning,' said PC Audrey. 'Let's hope he turns up too. His parents reported him missing around the time you rang. You might know them. Name of Wellington, live on Halsingham Drive. I'm going over there now. I don't suppose he's at Scar Bay too?'

Even though the volume was down they all heard Emily shouting 'NO'.

3
Abducted

Meanwhile, Jack, feeling conspicuous in blue and white striped pyjamas and pink crocs, was heading for home about a mile away. He'd recognised where he was as soon as he went outside. He'd started to run but fell off the crocs and staggered with flailing arms to keep his balance. Improvising as he went, he found he could make the best speed with a long loping shuffle like cross-country skiing, gripping the crocs with curled up toes. He knew he looked weird and hoped as few people as possible would see him. If word got back to school he'd never live it down. But it was rush hour and the roads and pavements were busy. He had a sinking feeling he wouldn't get away with it and goodness knows what his parents would say. Of course, they wouldn't believe him just like Emily and her parents.

What the hell had happened? Had he sleepwalked? Had he been drugged? Was he still asleep? Was he in a parallel universe? Would he find he had two sisters not one and would his parents call him a different name? Would his home even be there? He had meant what he said about reporting Emily and family to the police but now he realised it wouldn't work. They would deny abducting him and ridicule him, and his parents would almost certainly not back him up so he'd be stuffed. Thoughts of running away started to appear in the back of his mind.

'Cool outfit,' shouted a voice from a passing car.

That was it – he was as good as dead. It was Billy Worth from school. Jack was too big to be physically bullied now but Billy and his gang, who were in the year above, had been merciless to him and his friends when they were smaller, and these days continued abuse by word of mouth and online.

What if he'd taken a photo? It could be on the web already. When he went into Assembly would the entire hall erupt in laughter? And would that awful stupid aggressive Emily and her friends who'd got him into this mess be laughing the loudest? Why had they done it? What had he ever done to them? They were in his year but also a clique of their own that seemed to giggle a lot, mainly at boys, and weren't interested in science or coding or cricket or anything worthwhile. Maybe, like Billy, they just liked humiliating people. Maybe Billy was in on the plot. He turned into Halsingham Drive and was relieved to see his house but there was a police car outside.

Oh shit, he thought. *The only thing I can do now is run away and live rough.*

But he couldn't, dressed as he was. Maybe he could sneak into the house, pack a rucksack, sneak out and never be seen again.

Here goes, he thought as he went down a side alley and climbed over a fence into the garden. He made it through the back door to the bottom of the stairs before his mother saw him.

'Jack!' she shouted. 'Where've you been? We've been worried sick and what do you mean going out in your pyjamas and what are those ridiculous things you've got on your feet? Is this some kind of joke? Your Dad and I are very angry. Explain please.'

His father came out of the sitting room with a policewoman who looked as though she would stand no nonsense.

'Yes,' he said, 'if it's supposed to be a joke it's not funny.'

'And you've wasted a lot of police time, just like the other incident,' said PC Gemma Audrey.

'What other incident?' asked his mother.

'A girl reported missing from Ambleside Grove about the same time you rang us. Turns out she'd bunked off to Scar Bay without telling anyone.'

'So she said,' said Jack, not able to stop himself, at once realising his mistake.

'Oh you know something about it?' said his mother and PC Audrey at the same time.

Jack's mind was racing. How was he going to get out of it? He tried closing his eyes again to see if he would wake up.

'Jack,' said his mother in a strangely quiet, more sympathetic tone, 'have you and this girl got something going between you? Is that what all this is about?

'No,' said Jack, flushing with anger.

'He's blushing,' said PC Audrey. 'I think you might be on the right track.'

'No you're not,' said Jack angrily, reddening even more. 'I hardly know her and I already hate her.'

'Ok,' said his father, turning to PC Audrey, 'I think we can handle it from here. We don't know the details but it's obviously about hormones or crushes or angst or something. We're sorry to have got you here on a wild goose chase. I hope you'll be able to forget the whole thing.'

'Well, a missing minor is serious so you were right to call but no crime's been committed and the other parents said the same so I'll let it go. I'll just file a routine report that they were found and recommend no further action.'

'Thank you, Officer,' said Mrs Wellington.

PC Audrey gave Jack a piercing stare.

'Just think of others before getting up to pranks like this in future,' she said as she left.

Jack stood there, fuming and depressed. He was a victim, yet being blamed for something he hadn't done.

'We'll talk about it this evening,' said his father looking at his watch. 'I've got to go now. And don't you be late for school.'

Wearily Jack went upstairs as his father set off on his daily walk to work.

'I'll make some toast to take with you,' said his mother, 'and it's fine if you want to ask that girl round sometime.'

'I don't,' said Jack through clenched teeth.

***

'Oh and Dad, bring my phone.'

Emily hung up the landline in her grandparents' cottage and groaned with frustration and anger. Jack had made her so mad. As if she would or could somehow spirit him away from his home, someone she hardly knew, and into her bed of all places. The very idea made her feel sick.

She thought she could remember what he looked like, tallish with unkempt brown hair and stick-out ears. He was in a geeky group of boys who weren't quite as dorky as they used to be but were still pretty spotty and smelly.

Anyway, she knew she hadn't arranged it so the explanation had to be that Jack and his friends had abducted her. Wait - abducted! When a teenage girl is abducted people think only one thing - rape. Panic swept over her. Had she been drugged? Suddenly it was much more serious.

She felt hysteria rising. She tried to hold herself together and took stock. With the help of a mirror over the living room fireplace, she examined her arms, legs and bum for pinpricks but found none. And anyway she would remember someone giving her an injection or forcing pills down her throat. She felt normal, apart from exasperation and panic. No injury, bruises, or soreness or sign of interference or worse.

And if someone had broken in and drugged her, surely it would have made enough noise to wake up her mother or father. She remembered that her bedroom window had been shut so they must have found another place to enter the house. But Dad was always careful about locking up at night. Unless – gas. Maybe they'd used anaesthetic gas to knock her and her parents out.

She thought back carefully and had a vague impression from sometime during the night, or maybe as she went to sleep or woke up, of a flash of light and a short rumbling sound. It could be nothing or it could have been a summer thunderstorm or maybe it was gas being released.

Then she thought *OH GOD what will he be saying at school?* Of course, the whole story would be out, already being shared on the web, and here she was without her phone so she couldn't put her side of it. She pictured herself walking into the exam hall to waves of laughter. How would she ever hold her head up again?

She would run away. That was it. She would do it now and stay away until the whole thing had blown over and then when she came back her Mum and Dad would be so pleased that she hadn't been murdered they would welcome her.

Or maybe not. Maybe they would be angry. Hmm, that was more likely based on recent experience when she'd been out too late or forgotten to tell them something she was doing after school. And she had no clothes, just pink flowered pyjamas. Not even a pair of slippers for her feet. No, running away wouldn't work.

The kitchen clock showed a quarter to nine, well past breakfast time. She looked in the fridge but it was pretty bare. She knew Granny and Grandpa would have cleared most things out before they went. They'd been away the whole week visiting Auntie Jane and family in Scotland and were due back on Sunday. Still, there were some eggs and Wensleydale cheese and although there was no bread for toast she found crackers in a cupboard, so she made cheesy scrambled eggs on crackers with a cup of tea.

Afterwards, she showered in the small bathroom at the top of the stairs and washed her dark pixie-cut hair, blow-drying it with an old hair dryer of Granny's she found in their bedroom. She began to feel better, less angry.

4
Exam

Jack threw on yesterday's clothes, still in a heap by the window, picked up his phone and hurried downstairs with his school bag. His mother pushed toast and marmalade into his hand and looked at his hair.

'You might have brushed it,' she said, trying to smooth it down with her hands.

He ducked out of her way, ran out of the house and round the corner, just as a bus was arriving at the stop, later than the one he normally caught. He sat crunching toast in one hand and opened his phone with the other, scared of what he might see. He groaned. Billy had posted a photo and there was a video from someone else who'd seen him crossing the main road. Already, both had attracted dozens of comments, laughs and shares, and he hated to think what people would actually say when they saw him in real life. It was awful but there it was. He'd have to face the music. Added to that he was in danger of being late for Assembly which meant a detention.

He arrived at a run, hoping Dil would be on the lookout. They always sat together. Luckily he was, and dramatically fell over a chair to divert the attention of a teacher on door duty so Jack could sneak through. Dil was an enthusiastic member of the theatre club and his apparently painful ankle was convincing.

'Thanks, Dil,' Jack breathed, helping him up.

'Hey,' Dil whispered, grinning. 'Street jarmies, cool. Pink crocs, not.'

'Shh,' said the teacher as the head strode onto the stage.

But others had noticed Jack, and snorts of laughter could be heard from all over the hall. He closed his eyes and died a thousand deaths. Once again he considered running away but then remembered the geography exam at two thirty. If it wasn't for that he could just go home and pretend to be ill. Well, he could do that anyway, but missing the exam would mean a re-sit and having it hanging over him through the summer holiday. He'd just have to grit his teeth and bear it.

By the end of the morning he was heartily sick of people coming up to him and making remarks like 'Style guru', 'Sleepwalking?' or 'Cool crocs.' Not to mention 'Lost your boots, Wellington?'. Some used half-admiring tones but most just laughed or jeered.

At lunchtime, he found Dil eating a sandwich on his own in his customary summer place, on the steps of the cricket pavilion, over the far side of the playing fields. He knew Dil wouldn't give him stick so he told him the whole story.

Dilkashan Akhtar, to give him his full name, lived a few doors away from Jack. At five years old they'd started school on the same day and been close friends ever since. Their mothers were friends too and often told the story, much to their sons' embarrassment, of how their little boys cried lustily every morning when their mummies first took them there. The teacher had said they sat together every day, howling till mid-morning break, and carried on doing it for weeks, long after other children had stopped. It was only recently that Dil and Jack had worked out that their Mums were secretly proud of it.

Somehow it had developed a bond between Dil and Jack. A shared understanding that they were there for each other in a crisis, had each other's backs like brothers. But they also knew how to wind each other up.

'Weird,' said Dil after listening quietly. 'And why exactly have you made up this fantastic tale? Obviously you secretly love Emily but are afraid of the humiliation of rejection.'

'No,' Jack shouted hotly. 'Just because your shallow mind can't think of anything but girls doesn't mean I'm the same.'

It was true that Dil thought about girls a lot. They both did. But Dil now had a girlfriend, Lucy, whereas Jack hadn't. He felt awkward in the presence of girls, blushed a lot and could never think of anything sensible to say. He always felt they were laughing at him or at something that everyone knew about except him. Dil, on the other hand, seemed more confident and had a silver tongue.

Dil was laughing. 'Calm down bruv, I know.'

'Well, concentrate on the problem. Number one how did it happen? Number two what do I do now?'

'Ok, we know it happened but not why. Did the wicked Emily and her ghoulish girl witches do it for some evil purpose of their own or was it an alien abduction?

'Be serious.'

'I am. Of the two an alien abduction seems more likely. I don't see why or how those girls would do it. They hardly know you and getting you from home to Emily's house without your knowing in a few minutes sounds impossible. Your alarm went off in your own room and the next thing you knew you were sharing her bed.'

Jack shuddered. 'I wasn't sharing her bed. I had it to myself.'

'Whatever, but you must have been the victim of teleporting or something.'

Jack had to admit Dil had a point. The transit time from one bed to the other couldn't have been more than a few minutes. Emily had got him so mad he'd overlooked the obvious. And if she was in Scar Bay she had an alibi because she couldn't have moved Jack and got there in the time.

'Ok, so not Em but maybe her friends?'

'Nah. No-one could have done it. Broad daylight. Streets full of people. Your Mum and Dad up and about.'

'Well what about the storm? Just after the alarm. That could have covered something up.'

'What storm? There wasn't one at our house. Now, let me see where d'you live? Oh I remember – about thirty metres from us. We had no storm.'

'There was a flash and sort of rumble like weak thunder.'

'A well-known sign of teleporting.'

'Oh yeah fine but there's no such thing except in *Star Trek*.'

'Look at the evidence, Sherlock,' Dil grinned. 'Maybe you're the first.'

Jack rolled his eyes and stood up.

'Got to go. Geography exam. This is just between us ok? It's important.'

'Yeah, man. Promise.'

Jack knew a promise from Dil was solid. They fist bumped.

5
Escape

Traffic to the coast was building up so it was nearly noon by the time Mr Harrison arrived at Scar Bay. Emily quickly changed into school clothes her mother had sent and they set off back. It was lucky he'd brought a spare key his parents had given him 'just in case' because all the doors and windows were locked, which raised questions about how Emily was inside.

'Ok, so what really happened?' said Dad once they were on the way. 'Mum and I just want to know, not to judge you, and we're worried in case someone's, you know, done something to you against your will. If you like that boy it's not a problem...'

Emily felt anger flaring. 'I TOLD you what happened and I DON'T like that boy,' she shouted. 'I hardly know him. Why does everyone assume I'm in love with him? He looks pretty awful if you ask me and as for breaking into our house and getting into my bed' – she began to feel sick again – 'I hope he's been arrested by now and charged with abduction. Stranding me at Scar Bay like this.'

Her father felt he'd been hit by a hurricane.

'And, OBVIOUSLY,' she went on, 'I've been worried that someone did something to me while I was asleep but there's no sign of it. The only thing I can remember that's the least bit unusual is a flash and a sort of rumbling sound, not very loud. Probably Jack and his friends letting off anaesthetic gas to drug us all so they could take me away without you hearing.'

'Gas? What do you mean?'

'Well, think about it. How could they get into the house without you or Mum or me hearing unless we were all out cold?'

He had to admit she was right. 'Ok, but gas – a bit far-fetched isn't it?'

'How else?'

They were both silent for a moment until Dad asked: 'You're convinced Jack's behind it?'

'What other explanation is there?'

'I don't know but he did seem pretty clear it wasn't him.'

'Well it wasn't me so it must have been.'

If she was honest with herself, though, she was beginning to feel less certain.

Reunited with her phone she braced herself for what she would see online but there was nothing about her. Billy and another had posted a photo and a video of Jack on the main road in his pyjamas and pink crocs. There were dozens of ridiculing comments, gifs and emojis.

'Those are Mum's gardening crocs,' she sniggered. 'He looks a total idiot. Serves him right.'

But a nagging doubt remained.

***

Jack was early for the exam and sat outside the hall. Others began arriving and he kept his head down to avoid eye contact, not that it stopped people making remarks or sniggering but he ignored them and pretended to be lost in a textbook.

'Nice pyjamas,' said a girl as she sat down next to him.

He looked sideways. She was grinning. At least she hadn't mentioned the crocs.

'Hi Lucy,' he said, his face reddening, 'Don't remind me.'

She was in the same study group. She had blue eyes and straight fair hair to her shoulders with a fringe. In a poetic moment Dil had told him it was finer than gossamer.

'Some girls are saying running in pyjamas looks cool and they might try it themselves.'

Jack saw a chink of light at the end of the dark tunnel he had been in all day.

'But most aren't and we think the crocs were a mistake.'

The light went out.

'Yeah, well, I didn't have much choice,' he mumbled.

'More people should take fitness seriously like you, instead of hunching over laptops with pizza and fizzy drinks. Dil tells me you go to the gym and swimming and stuff. I tell him he should too but he reckons he gets enough exercise at theatre club.'

Jack had never thought of himself as taking fitness seriously but he enjoyed running and swimming and working out in the gym. It helped his alertness for cricket and somehow cleared his mind, helping him think through problems - endorphins or something. He liked Lucy's positive attitude, too. It made him feel a bit better.

'He loves that club, eh?'

'Yes and he's good at it too. Oh here we go.'

Mrs Barton, the Deputy Head, was opening the doors of the exam hall. Tall, slim and neatly dressed in a grey skirt and cream blouse, she had short grey hair and had been at the school so long that she had been a teacher to the parents of some of Jack's contemporaries.

'You can go in now,' she announced.

'Hey, Lucy,' said a small, smiley girl with purple plaits.

'Hey, Bina.'

'Don't mention crocs,' said Jack.

Jack knew her but the school had nearly a thousand pupils and although she was doing the same exam she wasn't in the same study group as Lucy and him, so he had rarely spoken to her. Just as he had hardly spoken to Emily until that morning.

Bina laughed. 'Ok but you're a celeb, now. It's in the balance whether you'd be voted out of the house, though.'

'I know,' said Jack miserably, getting up to go into the exam.

'Em not here yet?' he heard Bina say as he walked away.

The simple question hit him with such force that his feet got tangled and he tripped, only just recovering his balance with big clomping strides that made everyone turn to look.

'Steady, pyjama boy,' he heard someone say to suppressed laughter.

Emily coming to the exam! He wasn't ready for it. He didn't want to meet her. He'd had enough of the whole thing.

Oh fuck, he thought.

Emily would tell Lucy and Bina what happened and further humiliation would be round the school like wildfire.

When Emily rushed in looking flustered, Mrs Barton was just shutting the doors of the exam hall and gave her a withering stare. Traffic had been dreadful and Emily was strung out from the tension of whether or not they would make it. All the other candidates were in their seats at individual tables laid out in rows with place names, question papers face down. She, Lucy and Bina were several rows behind Jack. He didn't dare turn round to look.

'You may turn the papers over now. The exam has started. No talking,' Mrs Barton announced as Emily sat down.

'Tell you later,' she whispered to questioning glances from Bina and Lucy.

She recognised Jack from behind by his ears and unruly brown hair that looked the same as when she had last seen him. He'd had the sense not to turn up to the exam in his pyjamas but obviously hadn't thought to brush his hair.

Emily forced herself to concentrate on the question paper but her mind was still buzzing from what had happened, to which was now added the extra problem of how to avoid Jack at the end of the exam. If he saw her, goodness knows what he might say or shout and whatever he said, even if it was a grovelling apology, which was unlikely, it would make the whole thing public and be extremely embarrassing. Her best chance was somehow to sneak out before him and get right away before he noticed her.

***

Jack had hardly been able to focus on the exam for worrying about how to avoid Emily at the end. He decided the best solution would be to run out as soon as the doors opened. Part of him felt ashamed because he'd done nothing wrong and he wasn't someone who normally ran away from a challenge.

'Stop writing,' said Mrs Barton at the end. 'I will now collect your papers. Stay in your seat until the doors at the back are opened.'

Jack waited, tense and listening. When he heard them he was up and sprinting for the exit. As he got there he noticed to his surprise that they were closed and everyone else was still sitting down. Mrs Barton, still collecting papers, was looking at him, mouth open, about to shout.

Can't stop now, he thought and let himself out.

Phew, he thought, as he left the building, *I think I've made it.*

Then he stopped. About fifty metres ahead, a girl was running in the same direction, towards the school gates. Emily. It must have been her he heard opening the doors. There was a large black SUV parked at the side of the drive near the gate, a no parking zone. She was running towards it.

Maybe her parents come to collect her, he thought, which would suit him nicely.

As she reached the vehicle, two men in green shirts and slim-fitting green trousers jumped out and tried to grab her. She swerved round them but one deliberately tripped her and she fell to the ground. He heard her yell.

Jack reacted instinctively. Something wasn't right. He raced towards the SUV, reaching it just as the two men had picked Emily up and were trying to bundle her into the back of the vehicle. There was blood on her knees. She was struggling violently and screaming but they were too strong for her. Jack ran straight at the one who had her feet, and simultaneously head-butted his face and kneed him in the groin. He groaned, doubled up, let go and staggered backwards.

The other man was backing into the SUV, arms under her armpits from behind, trying to drag her onto the seat. Emily bit his hand hard and he screeched in pain, letting go on one side. Jack lunged towards him, fist outstretched and hit him a glancing blow on the nose. He grunted and the grip of his other hand on Emily loosened enough for her to wriggle free. Meanwhile the first man was recovering and ran at them but Jack blocked his path to Emily.

'Run,' he shouted, as the attacker grabbed him in a bear hug from behind.

Emily did run, dodging out of reach of the man she had bitten, but not away from the vehicle. She felt she couldn't leave Jack but she needed something to use as a weapon. The driver's door was open and there on the floor was a wooden something, like a mini baseball bat, a cosh maybe. She snatched it and hit the man holding Jack as hard as she could on the ear. Jack felt the grip relax, drove backwards with his elbows and was free. His attacker swore and stumbled sideways against the SUV. The other man lunged towards Emily but she threw the weapon at him, delaying him for a microsecond during which Jack grabbed her hand and pulled her away so strongly that she almost lost her balance, but she recovered quickly and they ran back towards the school buildings as fast as they could.

Jack risked a glance over his shoulder and saw that the men weren't following. They climbed into the SUV and its tyres squealed as it headed at high speed towards the gates. In a moment it turned onto the main road and was gone.

THE PRESENT

6
Funeral

A buzz of conversation over the buffet lunch started low but quickly became deafening as former pupils of several generations were reunited. Despite the funeral being a sad occasion there was a lot of laughter as people who hadn't seen each other for years reminisced and re-lived escapades. Emily and Bina were soon drawn in, talking to old friends and eating at the same time.

'This is good,' said Emily in an aside, taking a bite from a vegetable samosa.

'It's Dad's,' Bina replied, nodding.

Her father owned a big catering business.

Neither Emily nor Bina had achieved the 'A' level exam grades they wanted. If they were honest with themselves they would admit they didn't work hard enough. So after leaving school they had spent a year at Bradford College for re-sits and it paid off because they both got to Leeds University, their first choice. Bina had studied Law and Emily Physics and they were able to keep in close touch with each other and with Lucy, who was living in Bradford.

After graduation it hadn't been so easy. Bina had gone to law school, then moved to London on a training contract with a firm of solicitors, where she had stayed after qualifying. Emily had taken a year out travelling, during which she was accepted for the following two years on an exchange scheme at Massachusetts Institute of Technology. As that drew to a close she had, by hard work and determination, been accepted on a PhD course in particle physics at Cambridge University. She had been back in the UK since September, more easily able to see family and friends.

Jack, Dil and Lucy spotted them across the large room but progress through the crowd was slow because of so many other familiar faces. Lucy nudged the other two, pointing discreetly at Billy Worth a few metres away.

They instinctively steered away from him. He had continued his nasty behaviour until they left school, by which time most people wanted nothing to do with him, and certainly he wasn't surrounded by a group of laughing friends today. He was talking to an older man with a beard that none of them knew.

'Surprised to see him here,' said Lucy. 'He was always rude to Mrs Barton.'

The five friends finally circulated round to each other and suddenly the years dropped away as they found themselves talking like they were back at school. After the bed mystery, as Jack and Emily had come to call it, and the abduction incident, the two of them had gradually got to know each other, not only because they were thrown together by the events of the day, but also because Dil and Lucy were an item and Jack and Dil were as inseparable as Emily, Lucy and Bina. Every now and then Jack and Emily had talked about what had happened, when no-one was listening, but could make no sense of it.

When they had run back to the school buildings on that day, quite a crowd had already come outside and seen what happened. Some were pointing phones and there was a hubbub of comments.

'Whoa, pyjama boy, cool.'

'He chased Em. Must be love.'

'Holding hands.'

Jack realised he still was and quickly let go.

'Who knew they're together?'

There was more interest in Jack and Emily's relationship than the attack. He raised an eyebrow. 'You ok?'

'Bit shaky now.'

Bina and Lucy forced their way to the front of the crowd and grab-hugged Emily.

'I told Mrs Barton she should call the police,' said Bina.

She had, and was now pushing through too. A police siren was approaching.

'Stand back everyone,' Mrs Barton shouted.

The police car raced up the drive and stopped. Two policemen jumped out.

'Injuries?' one asked.

'Just grazed knees and bruises,' said Emily.

'I'm ok,' said Jack.

'We called an ambulance just in case. It'll be here soon.'

'Attempted abduction? Any video?' said the other policemen.

About ten phones were thrust at him. He took one and played it. It was only three seconds and blurred.

'Anyone get the whole thing?'

'Pretty much,' said a boy.

It started just after Emily was tripped by the first man. Emily, Jack, Mrs Barton, both policemen and as many others who could crane their necks watched. There were cheers and wows as they saw Jack and Emily fighting off the two men. The SUV's number was clearly visible and the second policemen radioed an alert for it.

'You make a good team,' said the first policeman.

'Great blow on his ear, Em,' said Jack admiringly.

'Lucky your boyfriend was there, though,' said the second policeman.

A snigger rippled through the crowd.

'He's not my boyfriend.'

She sounded fierce and Jack blushed, mumbling agreement, but she regretted it straight away. She was really grateful to him.

'Oh well, whatever, it's a good thing he helped.'

'Yes,' she said, trying to redeem herself, 'it is. Thank you, Jack.'

On impulse she leaned forward as though to kiss him on the cheek but stopped before making contact.

I'd probably regret it, she thought, but the crowd noticed and a long 'woo' went through it.

Later they had had a short chat when they were left alone for a few minutes in Mrs Barton's office after police interviews. The door was slightly ajar and Mrs Barton was outside, quietly briefing the Head. Jack heard whispered words like 'narrow escape', 'security measures', 'full report to the Governors'.

'Er, Em,' he said in a low voice, blushing bright red, 'we don't know each other well but I want to say I definitely didn't have anything to do with you going to Scar Bay and I'm sorry if I was rude to your parents. I certainly didn't intend it but I've absolutely no idea how I came to be in your house' – he couldn't bring himself to say 'bed' – 'and you probably have no idea how you got to Scar Bay. Something weird happened but I think it's best if we don't talk about it. Our parents will never believe it or let it go.'

'So you weren't running after me to confess you did it?'

He felt anger rising.

'No. If you must know I was trying to get away without seeing you,' he said, nearly too loud.

She smiled. 'Shh, I'm winding you up, pyjama boy. I totally agree and I was running away to avoid you. I don't think you did it and I know I didn't and I agree we need to let it drop and calm down and be forgotten. Life's complicated enough without it becoming a major problem which it would be with our parents, and everyone at school thinking we're together. Thank goodness that policewoman didn't want to make a thing of it. Oh and I'm sorry I shouted at you and called you a loser. You're not.'

She grinned sheepishly in a way that made Jack smile. Later, they made up a story to tell their parents that it had been a practical joke by their classmates that had gone wrong, that Emily and Jack were innocent victims and had received an apology. Then the holidays came and other priorities arose.

They didn't let Lucy and Bina into the secret but Jack told Emily that Dil knew and that his promise to keep it secret was dependable. Although it was years in the past now, it had remained the most remarkable thing that had ever happened to either of them and they both felt it was unfinished business hanging over them. They had each thought about it at some point every day since.

As to the attempted abduction, the SUV's number plates had turned out to be false and the vehicle had disappeared without trace. It remained an open police file and for some time after there had been chat among parents on social media blaming the school, the police, the Government, the local authority, organised crime, news media, violent TV shows, the EU, Brexit, the Church, and so on until Emily's and Jack's involvement seemed to become irrelevant. Emily had felt unsafe for some time after but by the end of the holidays that, too, had become less. At the beginning of the autumn term there were new security measures at school, CCTV cameras and so on, but everyone accepted them and moved on.

'Don't you think so, Jack?' Bina asked.

'Wh-what?' He realised he'd been tuning out of the conversation.

'Come back from wherever you are,' said Dil in a faraway voice, 'she was saying we must all never lose touch and must meet as often as possible.'

'Definitely. It's too long already – Dil and Lucy's wedding when we were last together – and that's over a year ago.'

'Is that all?' said Dil. 'Seems a lot longer.'

Lucy screeched and swiped his head as he ducked, laughing.

Dil hadn't done well at school. When he was twelve his father had died of cancer and Jack remembered how badly it had affected him, although spending too much time at theatre club and a local drama group may also have diverted him from school work. He never made it to the sixth form but talked himself onto an arts foundation course at Bradford College. After encouragement from a tutor and some cramming, he had scraped into a Leeds stage school from which he emerged three years later with a drama degree and a large amount of debt.

Lucy's parents had split up when she was at primary school. She wanted to live with her Dad because she didn't get on with her Mum, who was volatile, drank too much and kept losing her job, but he went overseas so she left school at seventeen to earn money to get her own place.

She found a job in a florist's shop, learned the trade well and was now manager at a corporate and contract flowers company in Bradford. She and Dil had been inseparable since they were fifteen.

The talk and banter continued until late afternoon and it was dark by the time they all left to go their respective ways. Dil and Lucy lived locally and headed for a bus stop near the school gates. Jack, Emily and Bina hugged them goodbye and walked to the rail station together.

7
Letter

A month later Jack was, as usual, at the last minute leaving for work on Monday morning and ran down the stairs from his second floor flat. He flung open the door to wheel his bike out of the lobby and noticed mail on the floor. He picked it up and slapped it on the table but one envelope was addressed to him so he stashed it in an inside pocket of his waterproof jacket and hurried out into sleet. It was barely light and he gritted his teeth for the freezing thirty-five-minute journey to Canary Wharf.

He was getting used to being soaked on his way to and from work. Commuting had been short and easy from where he and Claire had lived but now they were no longer together or sharing the rent he had moved to a less costly area to economise and the new place was further away. Cycling was good exercise but it wasn't pleasant on mornings like this and he preferred more challenging ways to maintain fitness like the gym, or bouldering, a recent interest.

He could have used buses or the DLR but there was still a walk at each end and it took longer, not to mention the cost. London rents didn't leave much spare after food and other necessities. He was glad to have his job, software development at a government agency, but it was boring, not well paid and not in his chosen field of Artificial Intelligence. Still, it gave him an income until the right opening came along and many of his contemporaries had fared worse.

Dil, Lucy, Em and Bina were managing, like him, and it had been great to see them at the funeral. They all knew each other so well they could pick up where they left off no matter how long it was. Bina had been right, they must never lose touch. It wasn't the same with new friends, although he'd never had difficulty making them. Deeper relationships were proving more of a problem, though. Something had seemed to be missing with the two he'd had and he was beginning to realise it could be his fault, that the bed mystery was such a big secret it prevented his opening himself up. It was only last October when he and Claire had parted, after eighteen months. She got a job in Bristol, which wouldn't have been an insurmountable problem, but she said he was too reserved and she often felt his mind was elsewhere. He knew she was right.

***

Emily didn't want to get out of bed. From where she lay, she had peeped through the curtains and seen sleet turning to snow in dim morning light. She shivered, not just at the thought of going outside but because it was also freezing inside. Her tiny room had no heating, indeed there was none in the whole building, a tall terrace house on Chesterton Road. Apparently, the boiler had broken down last summer and when she moved in she was assured by the agent it would be repaired but she and the other five occupants were still waiting.

She checked the time and steeled herself to get up. Hurriedly putting on her dressing gown she made a dash to the bathroom, still warm from the previous user's shower. After breakfast of cornflakes followed by banana on toast, she muffled up in her mid-grey winter coat, long yellow scarf and green woolly hat for the daily thirty minute walk to the Mott building where she and other physicists worked. As she left the house, she picked up a couple of letters addressed to her and put them in her pocket but didn't look at them until lunchtime. One was just advertising but the other was more interesting. As she read, her eyes widened with surprise and interest.

***

On Sunday it was raining for Jack's regular walk to the launderette. As he sat waiting inside, he felt the letter in the pocket of his waterproof jacket. He read it and then read it again.

'Dear Mr Wellington,
Re: Mrs Enid Barton Dec'd
We are the executors of the will of the late Mrs Barton and have to inform you that certain provisions of it are to your advantage. So that we can fully explain the position we should be grateful if you would attend our offices on Sunday, January 26th at 4pm. Please bring your passport, together with a utility bill or some similar item to prove your identity. If you are unable to attend please call the number above.
Yours sincerely
Clarence & Thirkill
Solicitors'

Hmm, he thought, interested. *This is the sort of letter you get when someone leaves you something in a will. But why?*

He couldn't help feeling touched if it was, but presumably he must be one of lots of others from school who'd be getting similar letters. There was no reason he knew for him to be singled out and he really didn't deserve anything from her. Still, he might as well go. It might be like a school reunion, transposed two hundred miles to the South. He took out his phone to add the appointment to his calendar when it dawned on him it was today. He looked at his watch. It was nearly quarter to four.

'Aargh,' he shouted, grabbing his clothes, and raced back to the flat for his bike.

8
Meeting

Jack knew he would need about twenty minutes to reach the address on the letter but at least the roads would be quieter than a weekday. He arrived five minutes late at a tall modern block in the financial district of the City. The street was deserted and the large glass doors were locked but inside he could see a caretaker sitting at reception. Jack peered through and knocked. The caretaker pointedly looked at his watch before strolling over to open the door a crack.

'Yes?' he said without much welcome.

'I've come to see Clarence & somebody,' he panted, dripping wet, out of breath and fumbling for the letter.

'Name?'

'Jack Wellington.'

'You're late.'

'Sorry.'

Jack's apology was automatic, and probably unnecessary when he thought about it. The caretaker opened the door, looked disapprovingly at the battered bicycle and let him in.

'Twentieth floor. Leave your bike against the wall over there,' he said, nodding his head towards the desk, as he relocked the door.

'Thanks,' said Jack.

One of three lifts opened as he approached and when he pressed the button it shot up quickly, the twentieth being the top floor. The doors opened again to reveal a stylish reception area, all grey slate, thick Mexican rugs and stainless steel. Behind the desk was a young man in a dark suit, white shirt and red tie.

'Ah Mr Wellington,' he said getting up. 'You've made it. We'd almost given up hope.'

Jack wasn't sure who 'we' was and whether it was a polite greeting or a reproach.

'Sorry. I was a bit late reading the letter. Busy. You know how it is.'

'Of course.' The man's tone was patronising.

He took Jack's wet jacket, hung it in a closet and led him silently along a corridor with a thick grey carpet. At the end he knocked gently on double doors, opened one and poked his head in.

'Mr Wellington has arrived,' he said.

'Oh good, ask him to come in please.'

The man beckoned Jack forward into a spacious conference room with huge corner windows giving a spectacular view over central London and beyond. It was the backdrop to two women sitting opposite each other at a large oval table that Jack thought was oak. One of them was slim with shoulder length dark hair, in a navy blue suit, who Jack guessed to be about forty. The other was Emily.

'Hey, Jack,' she said, smiling. 'You turn up in some unexpected places.'

Jack gaped, his voice temporarily out of action. Why was she the only one here? What about all the others who must have received letters? Was she as surprised as him or did she know something he didn't? He began to get that feeling he got when talking to girls as a teenager, made worse by feeling dishevelled after his bike ride.

Emily was as surprised as Jack. She had expected more people to be there but she didn't mind that he was the only one. She smiled to herself as she noted he still wasn't good at brushing his hair. He looked flustered.

'Clive,' said the lady to the reception man, 'may we have some tea, please?'

He nodded and left, shutting the door behind him. The woman stood up and held out her hand to Jack.

'Er, hello,' he finally managed to say, shaking it.

'A pleasure to meet you, Mr Wellington. So glad you could make it. Do come and sit down. I'm Edith Gregory – call me Edith – head of the private client department here at Clarence & Thirkill.'

She gestured towards the table. As she turned back to her seat, Jack directed a discreet quizzical eyebrow at Emily. She gave him an imperceptible 'don't know' shrug.

'I was just telling Miss Harrison here it's not often I come in on a Sunday but Mrs Barton was quite explicit in the instructions she left that we shouldn't ask you to come here on a weekday, as it might interfere with your work.'

'Very considerate,' said Emily.

Since she had received the letter she had been puzzling over why she'd been contacted and until she arrived at the office had assumed there'd be others, possibly many of them, out of hundreds, thousands even, of Mrs Barton's former pupils.

And there was that mention of something being to her advantage. She knew it was a hint she might receive a gift from Mrs Barton's will. If so she felt mixed guilt and excitement. Guilt because she'd never given Mrs Barton much thought, even though she respected her as a teacher, and excitement because maybe it would be a small sum of money, something of which she had never been so short. She made ends meet with casual work such as cleaning or waitressing that made her permanently tired.

'Wow,' Bina had said when Emily mentioned the letter to her yesterday, 'that's one of the biggest and most prestigious firms in the country and they don't usually work on wills and stuff on Sundays. Other departments, corporate, international and such usually work twenty four seven of course, but that address is just the private client department so they'll have to open up specially. Sounds expensive.'

'What d'you mean?'

'Well, they'll have to open the building, get someone senior to come in, more than one person probably when you think of backup staff and security and so on. Could easily cost hundreds.'

'I won't have to pay will I?' Emily had asked, panicking.

'No course not, the cost'll come out of what Mrs Barton left but she was a school teacher, not exactly a highly paid occupation. Big bills from firms like that could soon swallow everything.'

The whole situation had really tickled her curiosity, though. Bina's too. They had arranged to meet for a coffee afterwards. She realised Jack was talking.

'Yes it's kind of her to make it convenient for us,' he was saying, 'but I'm wondering why she wanted us here and I'm sure Emily must be too. We knew her as a school teacher but not sort of personally. We're only two of thousands she must have taught.'

'Of course,' said Edith, 'I can understand how you feel and I hope we'll be able to explain everything to your satisfaction. We being me, as one of the joint executors of her will and the other being our senior partner, James King. He's in New York on business at the moment but now that you're here we'll have a conference call. It's around eleven in the morning there.'

Clive knocked and came in without waiting. He put a tray with tea and biscuits on the table and handed them round. Edith thanked him and, as he left, dialled a number on a conference phone in the middle of the table. After a few durrs of US ringtone, a man answered.

'Good morning, Jim,' she said, 'I'm here with Emily Harrison and Jack Wellington.'

'Hello, both of you. Glad you could make it. Sorry I can't be with you in person.'

Emily and Jack said hello. He sounded older than Edith, well-spoken but husky, and Jack thought he detected a residual Yorkshire accent.

'Edith, I suggest you explain the situation and I'll chip in if I have anything to add.'

'Right. I've told Emily and Jack that you and I are the executors of Mrs Barton's will. She made it about seven years ago and I don't know what you know about her but she has no family at all.'

'I don't think anyone at school, us included, knew much about her private life,' said Emily, 'but we were at her funeral and the Head said the same.'

'Sad,' said Edith. 'She lost her husband very early in the marriage and I don't think she ever really got over it. Having no relatives gave her the problem of what to put in her will. It's good that she made one, though, because if she hadn't everything would go to the Crown.'

'What, the Queen?' Emily asked. 'Hasn't she got enough already?'

'A bit of legalese,' said Edith. 'It just means the Government.'

'Well, same difference,' said Emily, wishing Edith would get to the point.

'You must be wondering what was in the will.'

Jack thought Emily discreetly rolled her eyes. It made him want to laugh.

'Mm,' said Jack with what he hoped was a hint of irony.

'Well, it's to your advantage but it's not straightforward.'

'Perhaps I could comment here,' said Jim. 'It's an unusual situation but perfectly legal. The will was drawn up in this firm by a partner who sadly has since died but the file notes and the will itself make clear what Mrs Barton wanted. By the way, he and I were to be the executors and Edith has kindly stepped in to replace him. That's all legal too of course because the will requires at least two executors. Now, the first thing to say is that, in accordance with Mrs Barton's wishes, just for turning up here today you will each receive a hundred pounds.'

'Wow,' said Jack unable to stop himself.

He knew Dil would have told him it wasn't cool but it would make quite a difference to his budget for the month. Emily managed not to say anything but was just as pleased.

'Yes, generous isn't it?' said Edith. 'I'll need to check your identity material before you leave but assuming it's ok and you're willing to sign a receipt I can hand each of you an envelope containing the money in cash.'

Oh no, Jack thought.

He'd been too rushed to remember.

'Er, sorry, I forgot my passport and stuff.'

Emily snorted with laughter. It was just like him. He was bright but sometimes had his head in the clouds.

'No problem,' said Edith. 'Call in with it anytime but I can't hand the envelopes over until we've checked it.'

'Envelopes?' Emily asked, puzzled. 'I've brought mine. Will I have to wait too?'

'No, there's two envelopes for each of you. One has the cash in it.'

'So what's in the other?'

'I don't know. Let me explain.'

Jack could see Emily was irritated. She'd always had a short fuse and Edith saying 'Let me explain' sounded patronising even though she probably didn't intend it. He felt irked, too, but with himself.

'Along with the hundred pounds, we're instructed to give you each another envelope. The will says that we are to do nothing more with her estate until we hear from you in response to whatever's in the envelope, a letter I assume. What we then do with her assets will depend on what you say. But you both have to sign an agreement that you'll never disclose what the letter says, except to each other if you choose to do so.'

'So we'll be the only ones who know what's in those envelopes?' said Emily, intrigued.

'Yes,' said Jim. 'Notes on the file say Mrs Barton gave the letters to my partner already sealed, with instructions they were only to be opened by you as set out in the will and then only if you qualified for the hundred pounds. If you didn't qualify for the hundred pounds the will says they are to be incinerated without being opened, in the presence of two independent witnesses who must then swear affidavits that it has been done.'

'Affidavits?' Jack asked, checking the jargon.

'Sworn statements,' said Edith. 'Like when people give evidence in court they have to swear to tell the truth.'

'So,' said Emily, 'when we've read the letters we've to get back in touch with you?'

'Yes, except you don't need to do it together and the will says that if neither of you get back in touch within fourteen days from receipt of the letter we are to deal with the assets as though you had never qualified for the hundred pounds.'

Emily thought it might have been good to read their letters together but now it wouldn't be possible because Jack wouldn't receive his until tomorrow at the earliest. It was disappointing but there it was.

***

They left Clarence & Thirkill's office together, Emily with her envelopes, having signed the secrecy agreement Jim King had mentioned. Jack signed it too and would return late on Monday afternoon with his passport and photo key card from work. Edith had said she wouldn't be there but would leave the envelopes at reception and they would be handed over provided he showed the identity items.

As the caretaker let them out onto the deserted street, the rain had stopped, the sky had cleared and a cold winter sunset was imminent.

'Well, that was weird,' said Jack.

'Yeah. Pity you forgot your passport and stuff. Otherwise we could have read our letters now.'

'It was lucky I came at all,' he grinned and told her about leaving the letter in his jacket pocket.

Emily smiled but wondered how he could get a letter like that and not be bothered to read it. It's not as if it looked like a bill or anything. It was expensive notepaper and a normal person would have found it intriguing like she had. It was funny but a little annoying too. What had he been thinking about during the week he had it? His mind must have been full of something – or somebody! Yes, maybe that was it. Bina told her some time ago that he'd broken up with Claire but maybe he'd met someone new, although it hadn't been mentioned at the funeral. She could ask Lucy because Dil would be sure to know.

Anyway, what did she care? She'd not been in a relationship since Justin at M.I.T. There had been times when she thought he was the one, but it ended when she won the PhD place and he expected her to turn it down and move to Seattle with him, where he came from. They'd had a blazing row when they both said hurtful things but the one that really struck home to her was when he said there was always a part of her he couldn't reach, and she knew he was right.

That bloody bed mystery has a lot to answer for, she thought.

Despite her smile, Jack sensed disapproval at his forgetfulness. He couldn't really blame her and would probably have felt the same in her position.

'How's Cambridge?' he said to change the subject.

'Cold. And expensive. This hundred quid's a godsend.'

'Yeah, isn't it just?. Fancy a coffee or something?'

Emily felt a pang of guilt about meeting Bina. She looked at her watch.

'I'd better go for my train.'

'Ok. Good to see you.' He smiled. 'A bit strange we're in this together and no-one else but glad it's you and not someone I don't know. I'll call you when I've got the letter.'

Emily warmed to him. He had a genuine smile with a touch of vulnerability. They hugged when they parted as they and the rest of the gang always did but with Emily, Jack had always felt a slight reserve.

He cycled away through quiet city streets, thinking over what had happened. He was annoyed with himself for forgetting his identity material and consumed with curiosity about the letter, but he felt there was something about it all that didn't add up. Mrs Barton's salary as a teacher wouldn't have been enough to justify her being represented by what looked like an expensive firm of solicitors who would normally have large corporations or wealthy individuals as clients and who thought nothing of picking up a phone for a conference call to New York. There had to be more to it. Had she won a lottery perhaps? Or more likely was there family money somewhere in the background? And yet she apparently had no family.

It was dark by the time he reached home. He wheeled his bike into the lobby and went up to his flat. It was unlocked which was odd, because normally he was careful about such things, but perhaps in his hurry to get to the meeting earlier it had slipped his mind. He hung his jacket on the back of the door, walked into the living room, closed the curtains and switched on a lamp. It took him a moment to register the man sitting on his sofa.

9
Request

In the train on the way back to Cambridge, Emily wondered whether she should open the envelope or wait until she was somewhere private. She had the hundred pounds safely in her bag and it gave her a warm feeling as she thought over the unusual meeting and what to do now. There were no strings attached to the money. She could keep it even if she tore up the envelope and threw it away now but she was dying to find out what it said. It was the second most extraordinary thing that had happened in her life.

She had met Bina at a coffee shop near King's Cross Station and told her everything that had happened. She had even wondered about opening the letter there and then.

'No you mustn't,' Bina had said. 'I'm desperate to know what's in it too but remember you've signed an NDA.'

'A what?'

'Sorry – non-disclosure agreement.'-

'You're as bad as Edith,' Emily had smiled. 'Are all lawyers indoctrinated with gobbledygook?'

Bina was proud of being one and grinned. 'A lot of NDAs are unenforceable because they're too broad. They make it sound like you're breaking it if you just tell someone if it's raining. But that's not allowed and I bet Clarence & Thirkill's will be watertight so you'd better keep the letter to yourself. I don't want you opening it now and accidentally letting on what it's about. You don't want to be hauled into court or have an injunction slapped on you.'

'There you go again.'

Emily did have a vague idea what an injunction was, however, because Edith and Jim had explained before she and Jack signed. If the firm heard they had told someone what was in the letter they would get a court order against her and whoever she had told, and she would at least have to pay all the legal costs and probably compensation too. It made the whole thing sound very serious.

Bina ignored her comment. 'The important thing is to open the envelope in private.'

'Ok, but what d'you think it's about?'

'My guess is something to do with the school. Maybe she wants to set up a prize or give a seat to the cricket pavilion or something and wants you to arrange it all.'

'Why me? Or Jack? We didn't know her any better than you and anyway wouldn't Mrs Grisedale be a better candidate?'

They couldn't answer those questions.

'D'you think Jack's letter will be the same as yours?' Bina asked.

The question took Emily by surprise. 'I'd assumed so but now you mention it I don't know for certain.'

'So if you want to know you'll have to ask Jack.'

'Yes, but he said he'd be in touch when he got his so that's when I'll find out.'

She decided not to open the envelope until she was back in her room but she felt it was shouting 'Open Me' all the way to Cambridge. By the time she arrived she was hungry and because she had the money she succumbed to an enchanting smell from a pizzeria she passed. She ordered her favourite to take out – a thin eleven inch 'Veggie' with tomato sauce, mozzarella, spinach, peppers, sweetcorn, red onions and extra mushrooms.

It was noisy and warm inside and as she sat waiting she began to feel drowsy, only becoming aware of her phone ringing in her bag when the person next to her gave her a nudge. She fumbled for it as quickly as she could but it stopped before she had it in her hand. It was Jack who'd phoned but she decided not to call him back there and then, remembering what Bina had said about the NDA. There was too much risk of others in the pizza place hearing if he tried to talk about it and anyway it couldn't be urgent, as he hadn't got his letter yet.

Once back in her room, keeping her coat on against the cold, she put the pizza box on her desk, opened it along with a bottle of beer left over from Christmas, and sat down with the envelope. It was DL size, white and ordinary-looking, thin enough to contain only one or two sheets of paper. Her name was printed on it and when she opened it she saw the letter was printed too. The address at the top was in Bingley where Mrs Barton had lived. She started to read, munching pizza at the same time.

'Dear Emily,
    We did not know each other well at school but I always thought of you as one of the more level-headed and independent girls in your year, even if you were inclined to be a little volatile, and I have no doubt you will be able to make your way in the world.'

Emily smiled. Mrs Barton had always been outspoken, and her ability to assess her pupils' characters was legendary, finely honed by generations of them passing through her hands.

'However,' the letter continued, 'that is not why I am writing to you. You may not know that I was once married and we loved each other very much but my husband John disappeared less than a year after our wedding. I know that he disappeared because I was lying next to him in bed, fully awake, when it happened.'

'Whoa,' Emily spluttered into her beer bottle but read on quickly.

'As you can probably imagine it was such an inexplicable and shocking event that at first I was disorientated and did not believe it. Things like that simply don't happen. Yet I was awake and of sound mind. We had gone to bed and put out the light but continued talking. We were lying in each other's arms just talking, not making love, because that evening he had returned from a business trip to the USA and was exhausted. Suddenly, he paused in mid-sentence and I couldn't feel him anymore. He was gone. I desperately searched the house, hoping he was hiding as some kind of joke but of course he was not.

'Looking back, I realise it was a mistake to report him missing to the police but I was near-hysterical with shock and grief and had no-one else to turn to. Of course the police did not take me seriously and questioned whether I had merely dreamed that he returned from his trip, let alone dematerialised beside me.

'He worked for an international insurance company, assessing property damage after fires, which was why he travelled a lot – to see burned-out buildings all over the world. I informed his boss because I thought he might know something relevant. He was polite and supportive but explained that the job could not be held open indefinitely. He probably did not believe me. Eventually, I received a letter saying my husband was dismissed.

'For years I hoped in vain that he would return and his disappearance would be explained but as time went by I gave up. After seven years the law allows a missing person to be declared dead so I followed the proper procedure and obtained the necessary order from the High Court. It helped with practical details like our bank account, taxes and so on and I hoped it might give me some sort of closure. Neither of us had family so I put the story around our small circle of friends that his remains had unexpectedly been washed up on a Long Island beach and it was therefore assumed that he had accidentally drowned while swimming.

'After the declaration of his death I was contacted by Clarence & Thirkill who informed me that my husband had been immensely rich and, as his only living relative, I was now a wealthy woman. I was astounded because he had never said anything that even hinted at his having money. We lived modestly and both worked hard at our jobs.

'Clarence & Thirkill told me that his immediate family – parents and two sisters – were killed when a German bomb, one of the last of the London Blitz of World War 2, landed on their house in 1944. John was less than one year old but miraculously survived in their basement air-raid shelter because he was asleep in a cot under a grand piano with a substantial iron frame. It is thought that it was kept there for his mother to play to distract from the sound of the bombs.

'John's grandfather had founded the insurance company he worked for, which had built up a large property portfolio as well as the insurance business and on his death it had passed to John's father. After the bomb the shares were held in trust for John.

'I understand the trustees received a favourable offer for the company a few years after John's disappearance and sold the shares for many millions of pounds. The money has been invested and grown considerably but I had my job at the school and everything I wanted except John, so it has continued to accumulate. Clarence & Thirkill look after it all for which I am grateful. My only involvement is to sign papers from time to time.

'Now, to business. You will no doubt remember the day at school when you were sixteen or so and some men tried to abduct you. After the police interviews you and Jack Wellington were in my office and I was talking to the Head outside the door. When she left, I could not help hearing you and Jack through the open door having a quiet conversation and it led me to think that you and he may have experienced something similar to what happened to John.

'If I am wrong please ignore this letter, keep the hundred pounds and do not bother to get in touch with Clarence & Thirkill again.

'If I am right, I should like you to consider a proposition. That you investigate what happened to John, and try to find out why and how it did. If you are successful you will each receive a legacy from my will of at least a million pounds.'

Emily so astonished she nearly choked on pizza. Dazzling thoughts about uses for a million pounds cascaded through her mind. A house, a holiday, help Mum and Dad, donate to good causes… Wait, it was only if she was successful. She read on.

'In my opinion it could take some time to get to the bottom of it and you are probably working hard and having trouble making ends meet so if you accept the challenge, Clarence & Thirkill will arrange for you to receive a monthly income for one year equal to twice your current monthly income. This is to enable you to devote the necessary time to the problem.

'Of course, you are free not to accept this offer, and I appreciate you may prefer to pursue your chosen path without delay, in which case do not contact Clarence & Thirkill again. I have written a similar letter to Jack and like you he is free to accept the offer or not.

'If you are reading this it means I have passed away so you may ask yourself why I should care about what happened. There are two reasons. First, John's disappearance has defined my life and I should like to die with the hope that a reason for it may be found and that the story has not yet ended. You can have no idea what a thrill it was for me to overhear your conversation with Jack. Secondly, the phenomenon is so extraordinary that the human race should know about it, perhaps even harness it for the benefit of humankind.

'Good health and good luck in everything you do.'

The letter was signed 'Enid Barton' in handwriting that Emily knew well from school reports and notice boards.

She was dumbfounded. How could one letter contain so many surprises? Her world had been turned upside down in a few minutes. She was bursting with curiosity and excitement and badly wanted to talk about it to someone but because of the NDA she couldn't, except to Jack. Jack! She remembered he had called her.

She took out her phone and saw that he had sent a text. *Bolt your door.*

10
Intruder

'Who the hell are you?' Jack asked loudly. 'Get out.'

He picked up the nearest thing he could find to use as a weapon and advanced menacingly towards the man brandishing a red tea mug.

'Er, steady on,' said the man and stood up.

He was white, about forty five Jack thought, with black hair and a ducktail beard. He was lean, but spindly, probably not very fit. He wore a dark blue overcoat. There was something familiar about him.

'Well?' Jack went on loudly, mug raised.

'Er, sorry, the door was unlocked. Thought you wouldn't mind if I came in. Just wanted a quick private word.'

There was a military briskness in the way he spoke.

'Of course I mind. You can't just go round walking into people's flats. There are laws against it. So I ask you again, who the hell are you? Answer quickly before I call the police.'

'Jason Hubbler.'

Jack put the mug down, pulled his phone from his pocket and took a photo.

'Ok Jason Hubbler. Get out and if I see you within a mile of here again I'll call the police.'

'It wouldn't do any good,' said Jason Hubbler confidently, alarming Jack by putting his hand into an inside pocket.

'Stop,' Jack shouted.

'It's ok, I just want to show you this.'

He pulled his hand out holding a small leather wallet and flipped it open.

An ID card said: 'Jason Hubbler, Security Analyst, Secret Intelligence Service.'

Jack had heard of the Secret Intelligence Service but didn't know what it did. It must have shown on his face.

'Can't go into what it is but it's secret and government. The police won't interfere. I'm here to give you a tap on the shoulder.'

'Tap on the…' Jack's voice tailed off, mystified.

'Shoulder. Old fashioned phrase. Originally used in the sixties to recruit agents from Oxbridge and now being used again. There are spotters among university teaching staff and details of likely candidates are passed on to us. Then we contrive an apparently accidental meeting to sound them out.'

'So…'

'So I'm asking if you're interested. If so, come and see us when you're ready. If not forget we ever met.'

He gave Jack a card from his wallet and turned to leave. Jack followed him to the door, feeling upstaged.

'Oh and by the way,' Hubbler added, smiling, as he started down the stairs, 'you didn't leave the door unlocked.'

Jack heard him open and close the lobby door but, just to make sure he really had gone, checked from his window. Hubbler was outside, looking up at the building, saw him and waved, then turned and walked off down the street. Jack checked the door lock. It didn't look broken and his key turned normally so either Hubbler was lying about its being locked or had somehow unlocked it. As a precaution he closed a bolt he didn't often use. He sat down on the sofa, feeling shaky. It had been a shock to find the man in his living room and his reaction had been adrenaline-fuelled but now it was wearing off.

Secret Intelligence Service, tap on the shoulder – it was like a spy novel and yet Jack had understood Hubbler to be asking if he wanted to do that sort of work. He had to admit it was intriguing and he certainly had no wish to keep his current job any longer than necessary but it was all a bit strange. If he was thought to be a 'likely candidate', why wait till long after he'd left university and why approach him today of all days which had already been one of the strangest in his life?

Wait, was there a connection between Hubbler and the meeting at Clarence & Thirkill? He didn't see how there could be but the events of the day seemed to be telling him to take nothing for granted. Maybe he'd know more when he'd read the letter.

Jack looked at the card Hubbler had given him.

International Enterprises AG,
Laurence Counting Lane,
London EC4S 0DB
+44 207 0909 9009

He realised it was in the financial district of the City not far from where he had been that afternoon but he noticed there was no email address and more importantly no mention of the Secret Intelligence Service. Then he remembered James Bond always said he worked for Universal Exports. If you were a secret organisation you might have a cover name.

He shook his head. In a few seconds he'd thought himself into a fantasy world of espionage.

Get a grip, he thought.

By any standard Hubbler had behaved suspiciously, so it would be unwise to trust him. He could well be a conman or crook.

Then he thought of Emily. What if there was some connection between the meeting they had both attended and Hubbler? What if someone was waiting for her in her darkened room when she arrived home? What if they didn't leave as easily as Hubbler, who could probably see he'd get nowhere in a fight with Jack, but it could be different with Emily. She might even be abducted. It had been tried before.

Slow down, he said to himself, *your imagination's running away with you.*

Still, he'd better warn her. It would be awful if he didn't and something happened. He picked up his phone and dialled her number but the call wasn't answered, so he sent a text.

***

Bolt my door? Emily thought, puzzled. *What's he on about?*

She always did, of course, but why was he suddenly telling her to? She knew enough about how his mind worked not to dismiss it but what on earth had prompted it? Presumably concern for her safety.

Touching, she thought, smiling, *but I don't think I'm in danger.*

Yet there was a sense of urgency about the message. She'd seen in the past that when he felt strongly or angry or frustrated he had a tendency to become inarticulate or shout 'Aargh' or similar. Had something happened to upset him, something that related to her too? Maybe arising out of the meeting that afternoon? It had certainly been surreal, as had the letter. She would call him to find out and was about to tap her phone when she hesitated.

What if he asked about her letter? He hadn't received his yet. She wanted very much to discuss it with someone and he was the only possible person but the talk with Bina had not only raised the possibility that his letter might be different but also that she'd be breaking the NDA if she told him what was in hers before he'd read his.

Oh, this legal stuff's frustrating, she thought.

It got in the way of normal conversation but maybe it was best to avoid the issue and not speak to him until after tomorrow evening, when no doubt he'd be in touch. She texted back 'Done' with a smiley and a thumbs up.

***

Jack was eating pasta with tinned tomatoes when Emily's text arrived.

Sounds like she's ok, he thought.

He realised she would probably have read her letter by now and part of him wanted to speak to her to see if he could glean any information but Mrs Barton obviously intended that they shouldn't compare notes until each of them had read their letters, and then only if they chose.

Maybe there's something in her letter that'll make her want to keep it to herself, he thought, *and I don't want to put her under pressure. Equally, when I've seen mine I might feel the same.*

He kicked himself again for not taking his identity material but tomorrow would soon come and then all would become clear. But, he suddenly realised, it depended on his passport and keycard still being where he kept them and Hubbler had been alone in his flat.

He jumped up from the table to check. Phew! His keycard was hanging on the back of the door where he'd left it. He pulled open a desk drawer and saw that his passport was there too, along with a few other important papers. He tried to remember the positions they'd been in and as far as he could tell nothing had been disturbed. He briefly checked the other two drawers but noticed nothing different about them either What about his laptop, though? It was there on the desk and didn't look as though it had been moved but he opened it from sleep and typed in his password. Again everything looked normal but he quickly checked the system to see if anything had been copied or changed or sent anywhere and it hadn't. Relieved, he finished his meal.

11
Fire

On Monday Jack left work on time to cycle to Clarence & Thirkill. Earlier he'd noticed a news headline on his phone about a fire in the City of London. He thought no more about it but when he was a few streets away he saw a pall of dark smoke overhead and there was a smell of burning in the air, becoming stronger as he approached. He had to stop at an emergency barrier across the road and realised the fire was in Clarence & Thirkill's building. There were fire engines, ambulances, police cars and a chaotic scene of hoses, ladders, firemen, paramedics and water. It seemed the fire was nearly out but the top three floors were blackened and burned. There were dark gaps where the conference room windows had been yesterday.

He cursed his previous failure to take his ID stuff because he could see that no-one was being allowed into the building now and for obvious reasons it wouldn't be business as usual there. He wouldn't be able to pick up his envelopes and he realised with a sinking feeling that they could have gone up in smoke. He contemplated trying to get into the building round the back or through the underground car park but what would he do then? Walk up the staircase to reception on the burned-out twentieth floor and ask a fireman if a letter had been left for him?

Then he spotted Clive who had greeted him and brought tea on Sunday. He was sitting in his shirtsleeves on the steps of an ambulance holding an oxygen mask to his face, looking dishevelled and shocked. A policeman beside him was just standing up, folding a notebook. There was a crowd of onlookers at the barrier and Jack forced his way to the front, making himself unpopular with his bike, to see how near he could get to Clive. He made it to about five metres away, intending to have a word but the closer he got the worse the poor man looked. He must have had a bad experience in the fire so at the last moment Jack decided not to try. He would contact Edith and she could tell him what to do. Disappointed he turned away to cycle home when he heard a hoarse voice shouting, 'That's him.'

It was Clive, oxygen mask dropped, pointing towards Jack with one hand and waving at the retreating policeman with the other. The policeman turned, looked at Clive, then ran towards Jack. Jack didn't know what to do so stood his ground.

'Would you mind coming along with me, sir,' said the policeman.

'Er, no, er, why?'

Jack was flustered. It felt like Clive was accusing him of something. The crowd parted as though they expected trouble they didn't want to be near.

'If you'll just come with me, sir,' said the policeman more forcefully, putting a hand on Jack's shoulder.

Jack didn't know what to do and had a strong feeling that something was wrong but he had nothing to hide and if he went along with the policeman maybe he could talk to Clive or someone else from the firm who could tell him what to do about the envelopes. He even started to feel a little hopeful.

'Fine,' he said as another policeman appeared who moved the barrier aside to let Jack and his bike through but then that policeman took his bike and wheeled it away.

'Hey, where are you taking that?' he shouted.

'If you'll just come along with me, sir,' said the first policemen yet again, taking a firm grip on Jack's arm.

'But I want to know what's happening to my bike.'

'All in good time sir. It'll be quite safe with my colleague.'

Jack gave in. He couldn't turn and run now, not without his bike, and anyway he had no reason to run. He would just have to ride out whatever was happening. The policeman took him to a large police van with a door at the back which he opened and showed Jack in. There were two chairs and a table, fixed to the floor.

'Sit down please, sir,' said the policeman.

Jack sat down and was about to ask what was going on when the policemen turned and left the van, closing the door behind him. Jack heard it being locked. He jumped up and tried the door but it wouldn't open. There was a small slit-like horizontal window at head height but the glass was opaque, with laminated wire netting. He was a prisoner.

***

Emily spent Monday and Tuesday unable to concentrate on work and in a tormented state of excitement alternating with anxiety, all because of a two page letter. She read and re-read it, realising that for too long she had suppressed her desire to solve the mystery of what happened that day when she and Jack woke up where they hadn't fallen asleep. Fear of ridicule, fear of a big fuss, fear of peer pressure, fear even of admitting that something as scary as that had happened, not to mention the attempted abduction, had all conspired to push it into the background. Now, however, Mrs Barton was forcing her to confront it and a small voice somewhere inside was saying it was right. The only trouble was it could scarcely be less convenient.

As she ate her lunch in the canteen on Tuesday, she took stock of the situation. Here she was, settled in Cambridge for at least the next six months, lucky to have been accepted to pursue a prestigious doctorate, and Mrs Barton was asking her to give it up for what might prove to be a fruitless task. Well, perhaps not entirely fruitless. There was the hundred pounds and the monthly payments for a year, which was more than she could expect if she didn't accept the offer, even if she didn't qualify for the million pounds. But if she abandoned her PhD she might never have another opportunity, which could adversely affect her career for the rest of her life. She was hooked on particle physics and wanted to specialise in it more than anything in the world. There would be no chance without the PhD.

Unless...what if she spoke to her Director of Studies and asked to postpone for a year? Hmm, she would have to give an excuse though. The NDA meant she couldn't tell the truth and anyway it was too fantastic to be believed. She would have to make something up and lie. But what? And even then there was no certainty she'd be allowed to. The competition to be accepted on the course was tremendous. She felt certain such a request would attract strong disapproval from the university authorities.

So the safe thing to do was not to accept Mrs Barton's offer, much as she would like to. And yet the bed mystery deserved to be investigated. Jack might be able to do it, though, and they could keep in touch. He'd said his job wasn't what he was aiming for so probably he could leave without consequences except loss of income and if his letter was the same as hers there wouldn't even be that. He was steady and sensible and bright but she felt he sometimes didn't see the obvious and there would be more chance of success if they did it together.

She finished her lunch and went back to the lab in the same state of confusion as she had left it. Except she made one decision. She wouldn't make up her mind what to do until Jack had read his letter and they had compared notes. With any luck, if he picked up his letters as arranged, it could be this evening or tomorrow.

***

At the best of times, Jack couldn't stay sitting down for long and liked to pace while he was thinking, but trapped in the police van, feeling agitated, he was even less inclined to sit than usual. He wasn't really aware that he was walking in small circles around the table but it matched the state of his mind. What was happening? Why was he locked in? How long would he be here?

After ten minutes, he began to feel angry. He had done nothing to deserve this, the police had no right to hold him. What was it he had learned at school? Habeas corpus or something. No detention without trial. He decided it was time to do something so he crossed the few steps to the door and raised his arm to bang on it, ready to shout too, but it rattled and opened. A feeble 'aargh' escaped from his mouth.

A stocky white woman in police uniform stood in the doorway and Jack froze, his arm still in the air. He recognised her.

'If you're going to hit me, get on with it,' she said, 'but I recommend against it. Assaulting police officers doesn't go down well in court.'

'Er, sorry,' said Jack, caught off balance. 'I was about to hammer on the door. Getting a bit frustrated. I thought you weren't supposed to lock people up without some reason.'

'That's right, not unless they're arrested but in your case you've kindly agreed to help us in our enquiries and if the door was inadvertently locked I can only apologise.'

She smiled archly and Jack was speechless with frustration.

'So let's get started. Shall we sit down?'

Still dumbstruck, Jack did as she asked. A policeman had followed her in and now stood with his back to the closed door.

'I should like to ask you some questions about a fire that has taken place in the offices of Clarence & Thirkill.

'Why?'

'I suspect that you may have been involved in causing it.'

Jack's mouth opened but his brain couldn't process anything to say.

'You do not have to say anything but it may harm your defence if you do not mention when questioned something which you later rely on in court. Anything you do say may be given in evidence.'

'Court? What do you mean?'

'Do you understand what I've just said?'

'Not the bit about court obviously.'

She sighed. 'I'm talking about possible criminal proceedings. Obviously.'

Jack noted her tone. He guessed it might be unwise to irritate her, although she was irritating him.

'I see.'

'So you've no objection to my recording our talk?'

Jack sighed this time.

'I suppose not.'

'Do you want your solicitor present?'

'I haven't got one and I can't afford one so no.'

The woman switched on a recorder.

'I'm Detective Inspector Gemma Audrey of the City of London police here with – your full name and address, please?'

Jack told her. 'I know you,' he added. You came to our house in Bradford ten years ago.'

He held out his hand to shake DI Audrey's and could see she was taken by surprise.

'Mr Wellington is holding out his hand for me to shake. For the record I have never met this gentleman before.'

'Yes you have. You've probably forgotten. I was a teenager and my parents thought I'd gone missing.'

DI Audrey didn't look happy and clicked off the recorder.

'I don't know what you're playing at but it'll do you no good.'

'I'm not playing at anything. We met when you came round after my parents called the police first thing one morning. You had another call that morning too about a missing girl called Emily Harrison. We can call her and ask if you like. She was at the same school as me.'

A light seemed to go on somewhere behind the Inspector's eyes. Jack felt he'd scored a point but there was an awkward silence during which she studied his face, as though not sure if he was genuine. After a few seconds she pressed the record button.

'Mr Wellington has reminded me that we did in fact meet about ten years ago when he was at school and I was a Police Constable. I had responded to a call from his parents about his possibly being missing but he turned up. A youthful prank had misled them. Initially I did not recognise Mr Wellington as he has changed somewhat in the past ten years.'

'Now,' she went on, 'back to today. Please tell me your movements since first thing this morning.'

Jack thought about asking if it was really necessary but decided to co-operate and told her, including what time he had left work and what time he had arrived here.

She asked him why he had come and Jack explained the arrangement with Edith Gregory to pick up two envelopes. She asked what was in them and he said he understood there would be a hundred pounds in one and a letter in the other.

'Why did she want you to have these envelopes?'

'It's to do with the will of a teacher at my old school.'

'How long have you known Mrs Gregory?'

'Since Sunday.'

'Have you a passport?'

'Yes, it's in my pocket as it happens.'

He took it out and DI Audrey held out her hand for it.

'Mr Wellington is handing me his passport.'

She opened it and looked at the page with his photograph and other details.

'Who gave this back to you this afternoon?'

'What?'

'Have you been given this passport by someone this afternoon?'

'No of course not.'

'When did you receive it?'

'When it was issued about six years ago. I can't remember the date. It's inside.'

'Have you ever given this passport to someone else?'

'No.'

'Think carefully, Mr Wellington.'

'Definitely not.'

'Then how did a man claiming to be your representative produce it at the reception desk of Clarence & Thirkill this afternoon?'

Jack's brain was racing.

'I have no idea. Who says they did?'

'Clive Walls, the receptionist.'

'It's been in my pocket all day.'

Jack was becoming annoyed. Why would Clive say such a thing when it couldn't be true.

'Have you a keycard from work?' the Inspector asked.

'Yes it's here round my neck.'

He held it out.

'Who gave this back to you this afternoon?'

'No-one. I suppose the man produced that as well.'

'Yes. When did you give it to him?'

'I didn't,' said Jack loudly.

'May I see it please?'

Jack took it from his neck and handed it to her.

'Do you have a phone, Mr Wellington?'

'Yes.'

'May I take a look at it?'

'Can I have my passport and key card back, please?'

'In due course. We need to examine them properly.'

She put each one in an evidence bag.

'So you're going to confiscate my phone too?'

'Not confiscate, examine. It will be returned to you…'

'In due course,' said Jack, frustrated.

It wasn't as if he had anything to hide but it would be very inconvenient without it.

'Please let me have it back quickly.'

The Inspector took it and said nothing.

'I have a picture from CCTV of the man who showed your passport and keycard. Have you ever seen him before.'

She showed him a photo on her own phone. It was Hubbler.

'Yes I know him. He forced his way into my flat on Sunday evening claiming to be from the Secret Intelligence Service and asked if I wanted to work for them. In fact, I took a photo of him before I threw him out.'

She asked for his phone unlock code and looked for the photo.

'Ah, found it. Yes the timestamp corroborates your story. '

Jack bridled inside at 'your story', as though he was making it up.

'You could contact him. Here's his card.'

Jack took it from his pocket.

'Not the Secret Intelligence Service then,' she said drily, looking at it. 'I'll look into this but I don't expect it'll lead anywhere. And by your own admission you've met him and could have planned the whole thing.'

'What, the fire?'

Jack felt he was being pushed into a prickly corner.

'Yes. He was there on your behalf, wasn't he?'

Jack shouted his reply. 'No he wasn't.'

'After Mr Walls refused to hand over the envelopes, Mr Hubbler went to the eighteenth floor where a fire broke out almost immediately and it's strongly suspected he started it. Unfortunately CCTV only shows the lobby and lift areas on that floor and according to the fire brigade the seat of the fire was in a storeroom on the other side of the building. We assume he escaped down the stairs, also not on CCTV. Luckily the fire alarm went off so everyone got out. Half a dozen or so were taken to hospital though.'

'If you don't know for sure that he started it, you surely can't think I had anything to do with it?'

'I think you may have, Mr Wellington, because Mr Hubbler had your passport and keycard and you have been unable to explain how or why. I am therefore arresting you on suspicion of aiding and abetting an offence of arson.'

12
Deal

Emily felt her life was on hold waiting for Jack to get in touch. Tuesday went by, then Wednesday.

Surely he must have collected his envelopes by now, she thought on Thursday morning. *Oh wait, he'll probably keep them in his pocket for a week before opening them.*

By Friday morning, she didn't know whether she should be angry or worried or what. Had he received his letter, walked out of his job and begun already to investigate the bed mystery on his own? Except he'd definitely said he'd get in touch when he'd got his letter but come to think about it he'd not said 'as soon as', so maybe he would eventually but when would that be? Surely he'd be desperate to talk about it like she was. Unless he was talking about it, contrary to the NDA, with the girlfriend she reckoned he must have, and that made her angry.

Then again, maybe he was ill or had been in an accident, knocked off his bike or something. She remembered the text about bolting her door. Maybe that was when something had happened and she had a pang of guilt that she had held back from speaking to him when maybe he had been in trouble. It was worrying. Usually she could decide quickly what to do about anything but the combination of Jack and the letter seemed to be upsetting her equilibrium.

In the afternoon, instead of the usual full and satisfied feeling that came over her after a good subsidised lunch, she was short and irritable in the lab. Even her Director of Studies noticed and asked if something was wrong but he was a man not known for empathy and it came over more as a warning than genuine concern.

Emily gritted her teeth and kept to herself as much as she could until it was time to leave. As she was walking home her phone rang. She looked at it. Jack! She felt relief and annoyance at the same time.

'About time,' she said, answering without the usual pleasantries.

'Hello. You've probably been expecting me to call.'

'No, if you picked up your letters on Monday and, let's see, it's only Friday now. You probably put the letters in your pocket and forgot about them or didn't take your passport again.'

Jack could tell she was annoyed and smiled.

'I thought that's what you'd think.'

'It's a miracle you remember your own name and where you live.'

'I was arrested.'

'First you send me a weird message then total silence for…'

She was in full flight but her voice tailed off as she realised what he had said.

'Arrested? Why?'

'I was in gaol for a night and a morning and the police confiscated my phone and my passport, oh and my bike. I've only just got them back. I haven't got the letters because Clarence & Thirkill's office has been burned out in a big fire. I badly wanted to get in touch but I'm sorry I couldn't and it wasn't my fault. It think something funny's going on.'

Emily didn't know what to say so she said 'Oh.'

'I don't know if what's happened is connected with Mrs Barton and the letters but I need to tell you about it in case it is and in case something funny happens in your life.'

'Like what?'

'I don't know. Getting arrested or a strange man breaking into your room or something.'

'What? Someone breaking in?'

'Em, it's too complicated to explain on the phone. Could we meet? Maybe tomorrow or Sunday?'

'Where? You're welcome to come here.'

'Er, I'm a bit short of cash until payday next Thursday but we could meet halfway, maybe. How do you feel about a trip to Stevenage?'

He chuckled and in spite of herself Emily laughed too, her mood changing.

'It's not often a girl gets an offer like that. But look I tell you what, I've got this hundred quid. I'll lend you the train fare to Cambridge until you get yours. Deal?'

'Deal.'

***

'The fire should have been bigger,' said the man on the phone.

'Yes it should,' said the woman. 'I'll take that as an apology if the object in question wasn't destroyed.'

'Unfortunately it wasn't. Over-zealous precautions. However, as hoped it's landed one of the parties in trouble and also given our technical people an opportunity, as a result of which we know that both parties are due to meet shortly, so we'll be able to redeem the situation.'

***

Jack had called Edith before he spoke to Emily.

'Ah, Mr Wellington,' she had said, 'I'm pleased to hear from you. I gather you've been in a spot of bother.'

'You could say that but I believe you and the firm have had a spot of bother too.'

'Yes it's been awful but at least people's injuries were minor as it turned out and everyone's back at work now. We've had to set up a temporary office in another building but luckily not much was lost in the way of papers or data. We use very little paper these days and important documents and files are kept in fireproof strongrooms elsewhere. The only things that were lost were what happened to be left on people's desks as the building was evacuated and anything unsaved on a workstation.'

She paused.

'I had a couple of conversations with Inspector Audrey, yesterday and the day before. At first she seemed to think you were in league with the man they suspect of starting the fire.'

'I know. He somehow had my passport or a duplicate because I had the original all the time. And a key card that was round my neck all the time.'

'Luckily Clive was alert and had instructions to hand over the envelopes only to you.'

'Is he ok? He didn't look well on Tuesday.'

'Yes he inhaled a lot of smoke but the effects have worn off now.'

'Good. So, about the envelopes.'

Edith paused again. Jack noticed and prepared himself for bad news.

'I'm sorry to say the fire took them. They were in a drawer at the reception desk. Completely burned.'

'So that's the end of the story?'

He felt worse than he sounded.

'Not quite. I'm afraid the hundred pounds is a goner but, according to notes on the file, Mrs Barton told my partner that the two letters were pretty much identical mutatis mutandis.'

'Mute what?'

'Sorry – I mean you could read Emily's letter substituting your name for hers and that's what yours would be like.'

'So if she lets me see hers I'll know what mine would have said.'

'Yes I think so.'

***

'Wow,' was Jack's first comment when he had read Emily's letter.

He had caught an early train to Cambridge and by mid Saturday morning they were at Folds, a popular coffee shop in the town centre, about half way between the station and Emily's room.

'My treat,' said Emily as they entered.

She was feeling guilty about her negative thoughts when Jack hadn't been in touch. She ordered a cappuccino, Jack a double espresso and they shared a chocolate caramel slice in a quiet corner, enjoying the stylish retro decorations and comfortable old furniture. First he told her about finding Hubbler in his room on Sunday and explained the text about bolting her door.

'You could have been more explicit,' she said, smiling.

Then he moved on to the fire, Clive and the arrest. Emily remembered Inspector Audrey too and boggled at the coincidence that she was involved.

'A bit scary being cautioned and charged, though,' she said.

'You can say that again and I felt angry too but I think it helped that the Inspector and I had met before, even though she'd given me a telling off for wasting police time which of course I hadn't.'

Emily sniggered.

'So after that I was put in a cage in a smaller police van, like a criminal, and driven to a police station. I didn't know where at the time but it turned out to be Bishopsgate. They emptied my pockets, took away my belt and shoe laces and locked me in a cell with two bunks and another guy who'd been arrested for burglary. This was about seven o'clock in the evening. They brought a meal round not long after. Not bad – aubergine curry with chapatis – and I asked the PC who brought it how long I was likely to be there but he said he'd no idea.

'The other guy, Kevin something, said all night probably because the day shift knocks off at eight o'clock and never gives a thought to people in the cells. It turned out he'd had a lot of experience of the system but he said this time they'd got it wrong and he had a clean alibi. He said he was going straight now because he got married six months ago and his wife was expecting. We chatted until late.

'They woke us at six with breakfast and about ten I was taken to an interview room to see Inspector Audrey. She was more friendly than before and said she'd been checking my story, as she called it, and now accepted it. She'd been in touch where I work and spoken to Edith, and everything was as I'd said and it was against my interests to burn the office down before I'd collected my envelopes so I wasn't going to be charged and I was free to go but she might want to question me again as she didn't know how Hubbler had a duplicate of my passport.

I asked for mine back and my phone and bike and key card but she said they were still being examined and I'd get them back in due course, which turned out to be yesterday.'

'Quite a story,' said Emily, 'not to mention the inconvenience. What about the letters?'

'Lost in the fire. I spoke to Edith, though.'

He told her what she had said.

'So I can show you my letter?'

'Edith said you could check with her if you're not sure.'

'I'm desperate for you to see it and to be able to talk about it but all this legal stuff's got me spooked.'

She texted Edith and to her relief got the all clear within a few minutes.

'Tell Jack,' the text added, 'I've spoken to Jim and we've decided to give him a hundred pounds from the firm as the envelopes were lost on our premises.

'That's good,' he said. 'At first it sounded like it was gone and that was that.'

Emily enjoyed watching Jack's reactions as he read the letter, his double-take and astonished glance at her when he got to the bit about John Barton disappearing and his involuntary expletive about the million pounds. When he reached the end and said 'Wow,' he was speechless with incredulity. He sat back shaking his head and smiling and something about the letter and the tension of the past week made him start to laugh. Emily found herself joining in and in a few seconds they were both in hysterics. They didn't really know why – it was just a rare and spontaneous moment and they understood each other perfectly without words. When they were able to speak again they discussed what to do about the letter's offer. Emily explained her doubts about accepting. Jack had none.

'I've no long term commitment to my job and the more I think of the bed mystery and Mrs Barton, the more intriguing it becomes. The letter's sort of re-adjusted my priorities. It was only because we were young and had all sorts of other pressures that we didn't follow it up at the time. We've suppressed it for ten years and now it feels right to give it the importance it deserves.'

'Just what I think but I also think my PhD's a once in a lifetime opportunity.'

'I can understand that but I'd enjoy investigating with you,' said Jack, meaning it. 'And there's the money too, of course, but that's not why I'd be doing it and I think you'd feel the same.'

'Yes, the money'd be a great bonus but I have to weigh it against the rest of my career and the rest of my life.'

'I get it but I'm definitely going to accept. I'll contact Edith on Monday. I've absolutely no idea how to start but I'll think of something. At worst it'll be an entertaining year and in my spare time I can keep a lookout for the sort of job I want. You've still got a week to think about it but if you decide against, I can at least talk to you about what I'm doing. In fact you're the only person I can talk to because of the NDA and I'd appreciate any help you can give. Sometimes someone less involved in a problem can see the obvious more easily.'

She thought so too and her heart told her to throw everything up and go with the investigation but her head told her otherwise. It was frustrating. Two great opportunities at the same time, mutually exclusive. But there it was, she'd have to live with it. She wondered what Bina and Lucy would say if they knew her dilemma but of course she couldn't tell them. She was pretty sure Bina would opt for career. Not so sure about Lucy but she had a job she wanted and seemed serious about progressing. Then again, no-one had offered either of them a million pound gamble.

'What would you do if you were me?'

'Honestly? I don't know. But thinking about Dil and Lucy and Bina, they're all focussed on careers just as I would be if I had an interesting job with prospects. I'm just lucky that I'm in a position to accept the offer.'

Emily knew he was talking sense and made up her mind.

'Ok, I've decided. I'm going to stick with the PhD. The prospect of the million is dazzling but in reality highly uncertain. I'll help if I can, though.'

Jack grinned. 'Yay, a decision, and a good one. Also, if you're helping and we're successful we can share my million pounds. I'm going to enjoy being Sherlock to your Watson.'

'What? It's the other way round, oaf. I'm not the bumbling pedestrian in this relationship.'

They laughed.

'And that's a kind thought about sharing,' she added, 'but let's see how things work out and whether I make a contribution that's worth anything.'

13
Cracks

Later Jack showed Emily around his old college, founded in the sixteenth century, and where his room had been. Then they strolled along The Backs, wide open areas of grass and garden beside the river, behind some of the colleges. There were few people about because it was still cold but remaining snow had melted and there was low winter sun. Emily wore her coat, scarf and green woolly hat, Jack his waterproof jacket. It had a thick lining.

'Lunch?' said Jack, pulling a paper package out of a rucksack. 'Here's some I made earlier.'

They sat on a seat overlooking the river with ancient college buildings on the other side, sharing sandwiches and talking about how Jack would start the investigation.

'You remember those men in green that tried to abduct you?' said Jack. 'There was a logo on the uniforms. Can you remember what it was like? I could follow it up in case it's connected to the bed mystery.'

'I think there was a 'Y' in it. You could try searching the web, and you could check on Hubbler. Did you say you had a photo of him?'

Jack brought it up on his phone and showed her. Emily's reaction was immediate.

'He was at the funeral.'

'I thought there was something familiar about him but I couldn't place it. He was talking to Billy wasn't he.'

'Yes but surely Billy wouldn't have a connection with the Secret Intelligence Service?'

'No, and we don't know that Hubbler has either. He's definitely a suspicious character. If it's not raining or snowing on Monday on the way to work, I'll cycle past the address he gave me. It's a long way round but worth taking a look. I don't feel like calling in though. Not if it's a firebomb factory.'

'And all that money of Mrs Barton's. There could be people who know about it and want to get their hands on it. Edith may know something if she and her partners have been looking after it for a long time.'

'Yes, I'll talk to her.'

'Ok that's a few lines of enquiry. At this rate you'll have it solved in a couple of weeks.'

'Yeah but we've somehow got to explain how we were transported. We can rule out road or air or anything like that. It must have been more or less instantaneous. It's like 'Enterprise, two to transport,' except we weren't together and there's no such thing.'

Emily was thoughtful. 'Physics is all about particles these days and there's this thing called quantum entanglement. It's what Einstein called 'spooky action at a distance'. Not exactly teleporting but it's like two particles in different places are connected so whatever happens to one also happens to the other. Think of yourself as a particle in one place and then being in another.'

'Yes but we weren't in two places at once.'

'I know but we may have been for a microsecond and then consolidated in one of the places.'

'Wow, you think it could happen?'

'I've not heard of anyone trying it with anything bigger than a single particle and obviously there's a big difference between that and a whole human being, although...' she gave an impish smile, '...perhaps not in every case.'

Jack laughed, ignoring the jibe. 'You could ask around couldn't you? After all, where you work's at the cutting edge. If someone doesn't know about it there, it's probably not happening.'

There was a cracking sound behind them. Emily groaned and her head fell onto his shoulder, staying there.

'Er, what…'

But he didn't finish the sentence. Her eyes were closed and blood was running down her forehead from under her woolly hat. Shocked and horrified, he didn't hesitate. He took out his phone and called 999. The crack sound had taken him back to an outdoor survival course he and Dil went on with Explorers when they were fourteen. They had been shown how to fire .22 rifles on a range.

The call was answered immediately. 'I think my friend's just been shot in the head,' he said. 'Please hurry.'

There was a second crack and his phone shattered, fragments flying everywhere. He looked at blood on his hand in disbelief. He threw himself to the ground, pulling Emily with him, as he heard a third crack and felt a sharp pain on his ear.

Time seemed to stand still as he lay on the ground on his front, partially over Emily. As quickly as he could he pushed and dragged her under the seat. It wasn't much cover but it was all there was. He remembered first aid training at Explorers that said don't move people who've been injured, but being under fire left him no choice. He hoped it wouldn't make Emily worse. She was unconscious.

The cracks had come from across the river and although his hand and ear were starting to hurt badly he forced himself to look. The buildings opposite were rustic red brick four stories high and rose out of the river. There was no grass or footpath on that side so the shots must be coming from a window.

As if to confirm his conclusion there was a flash and a crack from a small open window on the top floor. Simultaneously he felt as though someone had punched his left side above the waist and he knew he'd been hit.

Surely it ought to hurt, he thought, feeling strangely detached.

Time continued to pass in slow motion as he dragged himself and Emily further under the seat and out behind it. He reckoned the wooden slatted back would give better protection because of the angle of fire from above. Another two shots. One bullet hit turf where he and Emily had been a moment ago and the second hit wood above them. Splinters flew and he heard a whine.

That must be what a ricochet sounds like, he thought, still disconnected.

The whine merged into sirens from emergency services, distant at first but becoming stronger as they turned off the main road half a kilometre behind and raced towards Jack and Emily along straight gravel paths between neat lawns. He raised his head and peeped between slats on the seat back. The window with the gun was closing. His head started to swim and there was a stab of unbearable pain from his side that made him cry out. He heard running feet as darkness descended.

14
Hospital

Dil and Lucy learned of the shooting on the Saturday evening TV news. Emily and Jack were said to be in a critical condition. They called Bina at once and, after flinging a few clothes into Dil's rucksack, went for the night bus to London. It was slow but cheap and got them into the capital, crumpled and yawning, by half past five in the morning. They had slept fitfully and continued to doze in a café at King's Cross station whilst waiting for Bina who they had arranged to meet for the half past seven train to Cambridge. Their conversation was unusually subdued as they scanned the web for further information about their friends but there was nothing new. They reached the hospital by nine and weren't allowed to see either Emily or Jack as they were still critical.

'So still alive, at least,' said Dil.

They decided to wait and as they left the reception desk a sandy-haired muscular man wearing jeans and a sweatshirt approached them.

'Could we have a word, please?' he said, showing a police badge that said he was Detective Inspector Duncan Kennedy.

His Scottish accent was undiminished by fifteen years in England and now in his late forties, he was leading the investigation into the shooting. He quizzed them about why they had come, how they knew Emily and Jack and whether they might have enemies. He quickly realised they knew nothing that would help him and that it was simply concern for their friends that had brought them there.

'I hope you haven't had a wasted journey. It'll be up to the doctors whether or not you can see them,' he said, 'and of course the parents will have visiting priority when they arrive because they tell me neither have partners at present. Is that right as far as you know?'

They confirmed and headed for the café but Bina excused herself, mentioning the loo, and went back to find the Inspector. He was about to use his phone but saw her heading his way and raised a questioning eyebrow.

'It may be nothing but last Sunday Emily had an appointment with a firm of solicitors and they gave her hundred pounds and a letter, something to do with the will of an old school teacher of ours. She also signed a non-disclosure agreement.'

'And you know this how?'

'She told me about the appointment and we met for a coffee after. I've no idea what was in the letter and I told her not to open it until she was alone in a safe place.'

'Safe? Why safe? Did she expect danger.'

'Oh no, nothing like that. It was the NDA, the non-disclosure agreement. I know a bit about them and warned her to make sure to stick to its terms. She might be sued or something if it was proved she hadn't. I recommended her to read the letter when she was on her own and not to speak to anyone about what it said, even me. If she told me things she shouldn't I might be sued too.'

'These NDA's are usually to hush up something shady, aren't they?'

'Sometimes but not always and what Emily said didn't make me think it was. Hardly likely in the case of an elderly schoolteacher's will.'

'Hmm. Well thanks for telling me.'

***

Edith Gregory heard about the Cambridge shooting on the Saturday evening news too. After a hurried telephone discussion with James King she made arrangements to travel to Cambridge the next day. She reached Addenbrookes Hospital by ten o'clock in the morning, enquired at reception and was asked to wait. DI Kennedy appeared and invited her to join him in a borrowed office nearby.

'So who are you?' he asked.

She handed over a business card.

'I saw about the shooting on the TV and I recently met Emily and Jack as the executor of a substantial estate from which they may benefit.'

'They're from wealthy families, eh?'

'No, quite the opposite.'

'Do you know the parents?'

'No.'

'They're on the way. I spoke to them on the phone last night. Three friends arrived earlier too. Why are you here?'

'Well, apart from natural concern for people I know, how we deal with the estate I mentioned depends on Jack and Emily so I need to assess whether or not they'll be able to make the necessary decisions. I could just wait and see what happens but because of the terms of the will, my co-executor and I feel an obligation to keep in close touch. Especially after what happened last week which may be connected.'

She explained about the fire.

'Hmm, this estate is big you say?'

'Yes, very.'

'So there could be other people with hopes who'd like to see these two not benefiting?'

'Theoretically, yes.'

'Did you have thoughts like that when your office was burned?'

'We did but it doesn't alter the fact that we don't know of anyone with a claim to the estate of the deceased. There's a man the City of London police would like to interview in connection with the fire but as far as I know they haven't run him to earth yet.'

She gave him DI Audrey's details.

'Ok, I'll follow up with her. I'm going to work on the assumption there's a possible financial motive for these crimes.'

'How are Emily and Jack?'

'Not good. Doctors hope they'll pull through but they're still not sure.'

'I'll keep my fingers crossed. Sounds horrific. What on earth happened?'

'I can't say but we're treating it as a case of attempted murder, not to mention wounding and the rest. Doctors don't know if or when they'll be fit enough to talk. In the meantime they're under guard.'

There was a knock at the door and a nurse popped her head round.'

'The parents are here.'

'Right,' said the Inspector, standing up, 'I must see them right away if you'll excuse me Ms Gregory?'

'Mrs.'

'Thank you. I might need to speak to you again.'

'Anything I can do to help. I'm staying in Cambridge for a couple of days. By the way, I don't think the parents know about the estate of the deceased because Emily and

Jack signed a non-disclosure agreement, one of the conditions of the will. I'd be grateful if you don't mention it to them.'

DI Kennedy gave her a long look. 'We might need to talk about that.'

Edith didn't respond and left the room. In the reception area she saw four people she presumed were the parents. Two mothers looking worn from lack of sleep and worry and two fathers with grim expressions standing awkwardly together as though not sure what to do or say. It was easy to identify Jack's father. Slim, clean shaven, the same unruly brown hair, now greying, and determined jaw. She guessed the slight, auburn-haired woman was the mother, something about her upper lip and nose. The other woman had darker hair and complexion with similar oval face and build to Emily. The second man, Emily's father Edith assumed, was the tallest of the four but overweight, thinning dark hair and red face. He looked angry.

'I'm not waiting around any longer,' she heard him say, volume increasing as he spoke. 'I want to see Em right now.'

He strode over to the reception desk and spoke loudly.

'I demand to see my daughter.'

The young man at the reception desk was polite.

'I'm sorry but as I've said the police need to see you first and the surgeon also needs to speak to you before you see her. Rest assured she's in good hands.'

'I'll be the judge of that. Tell me where she is or do I have to search the hospital?'

Emily's mother joined her husband at the desk.

'Paul, dear, wait a moment. This young man's doing his best. I'm sure the police will be with us any minute.'

As Edith left the building she didn't envy Inspector Kennedy having to deal with worried parents. Over her shoulder she saw him approaching them.

'I'm so sorry to have kept you waiting,' he said disarmingly, 'you must be desperate to see your children.'

'Yes,' said Mr Harrison brusquely, 'and who are you?'

'Detective Inspector Kennedy. We spoke last night.'

'At last, someone who might know something! Why can't we see our children? What's going on?'

'You can see them,' said DI Kennedy, 'in just a few minutes but I need to talk to you briefly beforehand, bring you up to date. I've just told the doctors you're here and they'll be along in a moment.'

He led them to the office.

'Let me tell you what I know,' he said when they were sitting down.

Mr Harrison was redder in the face and looked likely to explode. Mrs Harrison gave him a stern look.

'The first thing to say to you all is I'm sorry I couldn't give you more information yesterday evening when I phoned but as I said we weren't sure what we were dealing with, apart from the fact that Jack and Emily had been shot and taken to hospital. We had to secure the crime scene and we didn't know if there were other victims or if the shooter might strike somewhere else. And of course news media are very quick to pick up on such events so naturally I wanted to speak to you right away so you didn't learn about it from the TV or some other source.'

'Thank you, Inspector. We understand,' said Jack's mother, echoed by his father and Mrs Harrison but Mr Harrison scowled.

'Now we know there are no other victims and our investigation's in full swing. Not that there's a lot to report yet but I tell you what I know. So, yesterday afternoon we received a 999 call…'

'Tell us something we don't know,' Mr Harrison muttered but his wife glared at him and DI Kennedy ignored it.

'The bare facts are these. There were no eyewitnesses but someone looked out of a window before the shooting and saw Jack and Emily sitting on a seat with sandwiches. Responders to the 999 call arrived within three minutes and found them both unconscious behind and partially under a wooden seat on The Backs beside the river. Emily was bleeding from a head wound and Jack had three injuries, to his right ear and hand and his upper body just above the waist on the left side. It's likely he took at least one of those bullets as a result of shielding Emily. The paramedics found him lying over her. They were at Addenbrookes within ten minutes and in operating theatres five minutes later. We've recovered a number of bullets and they came from a .22 rifle probably fired from an upper window in the college buildings on the other side of the river. We've searched all the rooms but found nothing suspicious.'

'Good grief,' said Mr Wellington. 'Shots fired straight at them. It was deliberate then?'

'We think so.'

'Any idea who?'

'I'm afraid we've no leads so far and are hoping Emily and Jack can give us something to go on if or when we can speak to them. In the meantime, do you perhaps know anything that might help us or of anyone who might wish them harm? Were they involved in anything that could give rise to violence of this sort. Perhaps connected with work or some outside business or activity.'

'Not as far as we know,' said Mr Wellington. 'Jack has a job in a government department in London, something to do with software or computers.'

'We know of nothing,' said Mrs Harrison. 'Em's half way through a PhD in particle physics, whatever that is.'

Mr Harrison had been silent as they listened to the Inspector's description of the shooting but now sniffed loudly. The others turned and saw he was in tears.

'I'm sorry,' he said hoarsely, taking out his handkerchief, 'I know I've been an arse and I apologise. We were just so worried and now to hear that Jack was protecting Em, it tipped me over the edge. What a hero.'

He blew his nose loudly.

The two wives stroked his shoulders and Mr Wellington's eyes watered.

'I understand,' said the Inspector. 'Believe me your reactions are quite normal and I'll not keep you any longer. I'll just say we're treating it as attempted murder and we'll do whatever it takes to get to the bottom of what happened and bring whoever's behind it to justice. Ah, here are the doctors.'

A man and a woman, both in scrubs, came in. The woman, Mrs Wittingdale, spoke first, introducing herself as a neurosurgeon.

'Mr and Mrs Harrison, your daughter was hit in the head by a bullet. It shattered part of her skull and came to rest in the meninges, that's the soft covering of the brain inside the cranium, so I operated to remove it along with bone fragments and repaired the damage with a small titanium plate. Nothing penetrated beyond the meninges, so the likelihood of brain damage is small but of course there's swelling and pressure in the area of the injury that we'll be monitoring carefully. We're keeping her unconscious for now as it helps the healing process and if the signs are right we may bring her round late this afternoon or early evening. In her favour she's young and in good physical shape but I won't deny that she's still critical and things could still go wrong. I'm optimistic, though. I've seen a lot of brain injuries and many patients far worse than Emily make a full recovery.'

'Thank you,' said Mr Harrison, still tearful and unable to say more.

'Can we see her,' asked Mrs Harrison, only just holding it together.

'Of course but I suggest my colleague Mr Ahmed briefs Mr and Mrs Wellington first.'

'I'm a general surgeon,' said Mr Ahmed, 'and Jack was referred to me from A & E a few minutes after he was brought in. He has three injuries, two not so serious and one more so. The more serious one was a bullet in his left side just above the waist. It had nicked his left kidney and come to rest a couple of millimetres from his stomach. I removed it with minimal damage to surrounding tissue and a scan of the kidney shows no damage to nephrons, its internal working parts, although sometimes such damage is difficult to see. My best guess, though, is that there'll be short term discomfort but no lasting problem.

'The not so serious injuries are first to his ear. A small part of the top of his right ear was removed by what we assume was a bullet. The missing piece is about one centimetre long and three millimetres wide. The paramedics didn't find it at the scene so I've had to repair the damage with stitches as far as possible and it will heal completely in time but will look slightly different from the left ear. If it worries him plastic surgery may be possible in due course. The second injury was a large laceration to the palm of his right hand. I've no idea how it was caused and there's muscle damage that I repaired as best I could but it will take some time for proper movements to return, especially the finer ones, but in my view there'll be no lasting effects.'

'We're so thankful to you Doctor,' said Mrs Wellington quietly.

15
Patients

Jack knew it was time to get up because he heard Claire talking. She was brighter in the mornings than he was. Wait, it wasn't Claire, it sounded like his mother, right here in the bedroom. Now he remembered, Claire had left. Gone to Bristol. So what was his mother doing here? He tried to open his eyes but they wouldn't and his mind was telling him he needed more sleep. Then he felt a hand on his arm so he tried again, this time getting them open a crack. It was brighter than he expected and he didn't recognise the room.

Oh no, he thought, *it's happened again.*

He tried to turn his head but it hurt and so did his hand, triggering memories. A seat, the river, shots from a window, blood on Emily's head. Pain.

'Em,' he shouted, trying to sit up but he couldn't and only a croak came out.

'You're in hospital, love. You've had an operation but you're going to be fine.'

He understood but what about Em? Was she in hospital too? Was she ok? He tried to grip his mother's arm, intending to ask, but his hands and eyelids wouldn't respond and darkness rose. He didn't see his mother's tears as Mr Wellington hugged her. The policeman sitting close by averted his gaze, feeling like an intruder.

'That was normal and encouraging,' said Mr Ahmed. 'In an hour or so he'll probably come round again, ready for the official, yet compulsory, cup of tea.'

Mrs Wellington laughed tearfully.

'After that he'll be high for a while until the anaesthetic gets out of his system and sore in various places for the next couple of days but we'll get him up and about and if that goes well he could be ready to go home by the end of the week.'

***

Mr Harrison was silent as he and his wife stood beside Emily's bed in a side ward at the other end of the ICU. She lay on her back, eyes closed, pale face barely visible under a thick head bandage and tubes to her nose and mouth. Wires connected her to beeping screens.

Mrs Harrison began to cry quietly at the sight of her daughter, helpless and unconscious. Mr Harrison swallowed several times.

'If I get my hands on whoever did this...,' he growled, unable to finish the sentence.

Mrs Wittingdale, looking at a chart, sounded upbeat. 'She's doing ok. Her brain waves are still disturbed but I don't think there's any cause for tears. She's still critical, pressure around the wound is high but it's no worse than it was an hour ago and we're hoping to see more positive signs during the afternoon. You're welcome to stay here as long as you like, but we won't wake her up until we know she's over the worst so I suggest you don't settle in for the day. Go out, have a walk in fresh air, maybe some lunch. It'll help to relieve stress. Then come back about five and we'll review her condition. She'll be monitored the whole time.'

'That sounds like a good idea,' said Mr Harrison. 'We need to find a hotel too but we'll stay for a little while.'

Mrs Harrison agreed.

'Dad and I are here, Em,' she said softly, taking Emily's hand and stroking it. 'Don't worry about anything. You're safe and in hospital. You've had an operation but you're going to be fine. And we love you.'

She went on saying similar things while Mr Harrison stood quietly by, studying what he could see of his daughter's face, hoping for a sign, any slight movement, that would indicate an improvement. He knew it was unreasonable to expect it but his protective instinct was too strong. Tears welled up and he had to wipe them away with a handkerchief. Partially they were tears of relief that Em was no worse and might soon turn a corner but partially they came from fear of the horrifying possibility that still remained of her nor surviving. He and Em had always been close, shared the same independent streak, and he didn't know what he'd do if she didn't come through this. He couldn't face the prospect of her not being there. And even if she did come through, what emotional or physical scars might be left by such a dreadful experience?

***

At Mr Ahmed's suggestion Mr and Mrs Wellington left Jack for a while and went to the café for a cup of coffee where they were surprised to see Dil, Lucy and Bina.

'We just had to come,' said Lucy. 'We were so worried. You must have been beside yourselves too. Have you seen Jack? How is he and what about Em? Any news?'

Mrs Wellington told them everything they knew. When they went back to the ICU an hour later they found that Jack had been moved and were directed to a room off a long surgical ward in a different part of the building. This time the policeman sat outside the door. He opened it for them with a smile. Inside, Mr Ahmed was standing by the bed and Jack was propped up, awake. They were talking. He grinned as his mother and father entered. He still had a drip into his hand but the wires and monitoring equipment there earlier were gone.

'Hello,' he said, smiling. 'Sorry about all this.'

Mrs Wellington rushed over to hug him and Mr Wellington smiled from ear to ear,

'Don't be ridiculous,' she said, 'this isn't your fault.'

'Ouch, careful. I'm a bit sore.'

'Oh dear, I should have realised. Now it's my turn to say sorry,' she said, recoiling, 'but so glad you're awake. How do you feel?'

'Like I've been kicked all over but sort of good at the same time. It's weird, it's not really hurting unless someone touches the wounds like you did then, just achy. Mr Ahmed says it'll probably hurt more tomorrow.'

'Well, we'll manage the pain carefully and keep you comfortable,' he said. 'You'll feel more normal in twenty four hours and I was telling your parents we could well turf you out of here by the end of the week.'

'What day is it?'

'Sunday.'

'Ok, I've sort of lost track. Anyway look I think I'm going to be ok so the important thing is Em. Mr Ahmed was just telling me they've taken a bullet out of her head and are keeping her unconscious for now but might wake her up this evening. Can you keep in touch with her Mum and Dad and tell me how she's getting on?'

There was a knock at the door and DI Kennedy poked his head round.

'Ah, heard you were awake,' he said looking at Jack. 'Is this a good time?'

'Jack, this is Detective Inspector Kennedy,' said Mr

Wellington. 'I think he wants to talk to you.'

'Ok,' said Jack.

'Thank you,' said the Inspector, coming in. 'I'd like to hear from Jack what happened, preferably in private.'

'I'm just going anyway,' said Mr Ahmed, heading for the door. 'Due in theatre shortly.'

Mr Wellington was about to protest that he and his wife also wanted to hear Jack's account but Mrs Wellington forestalled him.

'We'd like to hear it too, Inspector, but we can talk to him anytime and you should take priority so you can find whoever did this. We'll wait outside.'

Jack nodded.

'Let's pop out for some lunch,' said Mr Wellington. 'We'll come back in an hour or so.'

'I've just had a conversation with Inspector Gemma Audrey,' said DI Kennedy when he and Jack were alone. 'She filled me in about a fire at Clarence & Thirkill that I think you know about. I'm assuming there could be a connection between that and the shooting.'

'I bet you're right. There've been too many strange coincidences recently but I've no idea what it's all about.'

'Just talk me through what happened yesterday.'

Jack told him about speaking to Emily on Friday, coming to Cambridge on the early train yesterday to meet her, having coffee, visiting his old college, walking along The Backs, eating sandwiches then being shot at from the window.'

'You're sure the shots came from a window?'

'Definitely. I saw a gun barrel being pulled back inside as I started to hear an ambulance siren, just before I passed out.'

'Can you say which window?'

He was pleased that Jack could tell him exactly.

'We've searched the rooms overlooking the seat and found nothing but they're all locked up and sealed now, so we'll have a more thorough go at that one. Now, moving on, Mrs Gregory says you might come into some money.'

'Oh you've spoken to her?'

'She's here in Cambridge. Came hot foot from London this morning.'

'I'd have thought she had more important things to do. I know I'm due to get a hundred pounds but I can't really talk about it because I signed a non-disclosure agreement.'

'So I understand but I do know from Mrs Gregory that Mrs Barton's estate was large so the motivation for the fire and the attack on you could well be about money. Perhaps someone who thinks they have a claim on it. Any ideas?'

'Not a clue. Unless Mr Hubbler's involved?'

'Ah, the mysterious Mr Hubbler. Allegedly SIS but neither I nor DI Audrey can find any record of him, or trace of his whereabouts. She put that photo you took through facial recognition and there was no match.'

'He probably gave me a false name.'

'Yes but he's never been photographed for a passport or a driving licence or a keycard or anything like that which is suspicious because he must have been, which suggests his photos have been erased and that's not easy. It actually does suggest SIS or someone with access to protected databases. Also the address he gave you was right for SIS. They have an office there and DI Audrey got in touch but drew a blank. Of course security services are always cagey with police so you can't assume anything from it.'

Jack wasn't surprised. It was always how it was

portrayed in TV thrillers.

'Was my phone destroyed? I think it took a direct hit but it may have protected my hand a bit.'

'Yes there was debris around the seat and we've recovered most of it, including the sim card, but we can't let you have it back I'm afraid. It'll be needed for evidence if we find the shooter.'

'It's ok. I'll get a duplicate. My photos and other stuff are backed up. The phone's insured under my contract so I can order a new one.'

'Do you know of anyone or any organisation that might want you or Emily dead?'

It was surreal to be asked such a question and of course the answer was no but Jack couldn't help feeling that the bed mystery and Mrs Barton's will had enmeshed them in something they didn't understand. Then, again, it could all be coincidence and perhaps the anaesthetic was making his mind run riot with unfounded conspiracy theories.

'No idea,' he said, 'and it's very scary to think about.'

'Ok. We'll leave it at that for now but I'll need to talk to you again and to Emily when she's fit enough. You take care and concentrate on getting better. You're both under guard and safe here and when you leave we'll review if you need protection, depending on how our enquiries are going.'

'Protection?' Jack's eyes widened.

It hadn't occurred to him that he and Emily might still be in danger but now he realised it was obvious if the attack was intentional rather than random.

'So you think whoever it was will try again?'

'I'm working on that assumption.'

The inspector's phone pinged.

'Hmm,' he said, frowning as he read a message.

'Cambridge is becoming a popular spot. DI Audrey's coming to see you tomorrow.'

'Why's that?'

'The fire enquiry's taken an unexpected turn. They've found a body.'

16
Emily

After the Inspector left, Jack felt tired. The aching from his wounds was worse and his mood lower. He was worried about Emily, and DI Audrey's visit too. If someone was killed in the fire, was he to become a murder suspect? Would his life whirl yet further out of control?

'You need something to eat,' was his mother's diagnosis when she and his father came back and saw him looking exhausted.

He had to admit he was feeling peckish, not having eaten since sandwiches the previous day. The hospital evening meal wasn't due until later so Mrs Wellington brought a mug of tea with toast and jam from the café. He wolfed it while telling his parents the story of the shooting. They were horrified.

'How come you were in Cambridge?' his father asked later.

Jack knew he couldn't talk about Mrs Barton's estate or her letter.

'Well Em and I keep in touch and now she's here I thought it might be a nice day out, revisit old haunts and so on. It's been a bit of a grind at work recently, cold commuting, dark evenings. Turned out to be a bad decision.'

He grinned ruefully. His father accepted the story and moved on. Around four o'clock they heard voices in the corridor.

'Hey Jack,' said Dil, his head appearing round the door.

'Hey, Dil,' said Jack, smiling. 'Mum and Dad said they'd seen you downstairs.'

'Shh,' he said coming in with a finger to his lips, looking theatrically furtive. 'We're not supposed to be here. We had to sneak up the stairs past security.'

'What about Lucy and Bina?'

'They're here too, charming the policeman outside.'

As he spoke, Lucy appeared at the door, grinning and waving.

'Now just a minute,' said a man's voice beyond the door. 'I only said one of you could poke your head in.'

'It's alright, officer,' Mr Wellington called. 'We can vouch for them.'

'What – all three?' came the policeman's doubtful voice.

Mr Wellington reassured him so Lucy and Bina came in all smiles. and hurried to either side of the bed, saying hello to Jack's parents and talking over each other. Mr and Mrs Wellington watched amused as Jack tried to find a gap to answer their questions about how he was feeling.

'I'm ok,' he managed to say eventually, 'but everything's starting to hurt a bit now. Anaesthetic wearing off, but they say I might be out by the end of the week.'

'What happened?' asked Dil. 'First-hand account, please. The full monty.'

Jack explained yet again.

'Horrible,' said Bina, shuddering.

'Terrifying,' said Lucy.

***

Emily was watching cricket with her Dad. He had always been keen and, right from her being small, had taken her with him to watch at his local club, explaining the rules, what was happening, making it interesting. So she grew up understanding the game well and enjoyed the time alone with her father but in her teenage years she had begun to lose interest, even though she had been in the under fourteens team.

The afternoon was hot and sultry and she was feeling bored. Everything was happening too slowly, runs coming in ones and twos and no wickets. She began to feel drowsy and her eyelids drooped but she heard the crack of a ball against a bat and her eyes jerked open to see a cricket ball coming straight at her head. She froze and wham! it hit her. Everything went dark.

The afternoon was hot and sultry and she was feeling bored. Everything was happening too slowly,…

'I think she's starting to surface,' said Mrs Wittingdale, studying the encephalograph. 'Dreaming, maybe.'

It was half past five and Mr and Mrs Harrison were standing anxiously at Emily's bedside, her mother holding her hand. The tubes to her nose and mouth had gone.

…runs were coming in ones and twos and no wickets. She began to feel drowsy and her eyelids drooped but she heard the crack of a ball against a bat…

'Yes, there's the pattern again. And look, there's rapid eye movement under her lids. This is very promising.'

…and her eyes jerked open to see a cricket ball coming straight at her head. She froze and wham!…

Emily's whole body jerked and she opened her eyes wide, trying to yell through her dry throat but nothing came out.

'Well done, Emily,' said Mrs Wittingdale.

Emily heard but didn't recognise the voice and her vision was blurred so she couldn't make out the face of the person standing over her. She knew she was lying down, in a bed probably, but there were unfamiliar sounds in the background and other people near her bed.

'Hello Em, dear.'

Her mother!

'You're in hospital.'

Her father!

The ball must have knocked me out or something, she thought.

Her head was swimming and she felt dizzy.

'Did we win?' she tried to ask her father, lips moving but still no sound.

'Don't try to talk yet,' said the unfamiliar voice. 'There's been a tube down your throat and it'll take an hour or so for your mouth and voice to get back to normal.'

Her mother stroked her hand. 'You were quite badly injured, dear, and we've all been worried about you but Mrs Wittingdale here, she's the surgeon, says you're going to be fine. You've had an operation on your head.'

The ball must have done more than just knock me out.

But now there was a niggling question at the back of her mind. Why had she gone to a cricket match? She hadn't done that for years and how could there have been one anyway because it was winter. She tried to think back. She'd met Jack for coffee and then they'd walked on The Backs. Then they'd had sandwiches he'd brought. What a good friend he was, and they'd been discussing something important about her PhD course and his work that she couldn't quite remember... but there was definitely no cricket match.

'I'd like to test your reflexes,' said Mrs Wittingdale.

She spent a few minutes tapping and stroking her hands, feet and knees as well as her jaw and forehead.

'All fine,' she said, smiling.

'You're quite safe now,' said her father, 'there's a policeman on guard here and this morning we met Inspector Kennedy, who's investigating who shot you.'

'Shot?' Emily tried to say, heart pounding.

'Steady, Mr Harrison' said Mrs Wittingdale, 'that shocked you didn't it Emily? Your pulse spiked and I can see a lot of brain activity. It's encouraging but we need to take things more gently until Emily gets her bearings.'

'Oh dear, sorry. I didn't think.'

Emily looked towards her father. Everything was still blurred and she kept blinking to clear her vision and trying to focus.

'It's ok,' she tried to say but all that came out was a croaky 'ok'.

'Your hearing's obviously alright but how's your vision?' Mrs Wittingdale asked.

Emily rocked her free hand in a so-so gesture.

'Yes I'm not surprised. Is it blurring or is there anything else such as dark or blank spots? Hold up your index finger if it's just blurring, or two fingers if there's more.'

Emily held up her index finger.

'Splendid. That should clear quickly. I'm very pleased with you. So for now just lie back and relax. You'll be feeling much more normal soon.'

Emily smiled. *As if I could do anything else.*

Mrs Wittingdale chuckled. 'I know you've not much alternative but I'm going to ask your parents to leave you for an hour or so and I will too, then we'll come back and have another short talk, take things a step at a time.'

Mrs Harrison kissed Emily's cheek and Emily smiled again. If her vision had been clearer she would have noticed tears in her mother's eyes.

***

Jack's parents were still with him when the policeman knocked gently and asked if Mr and Mrs Harrison could come in.

'How's Em?' Jack asked as soon as he saw them.

Her mother and father told him everything that had happened when she woke up.

'We'll go back later and hope we can talk,' said Mrs Harrison. 'She must be mystified about everything.'

'Give her our love,' said Mrs Wellington.

'And tell her I'll be along to see her as soon as they'll let me,' said Jack.

'We will,' said Mr Harrison. 'And Jack, you saved Em from much more serious injury by quick thinking and protecting her. We can't thank you enough.'

Jack was embarrassed and didn't know what to say.

***

Left alone, Emily closed her eyes and re-ran what she knew. She been shot – in the head, she assumed because of the bandages, and the wires going to a monitor. There were no dressings anywhere else but she still had a drip into the back of her hand and wires to her chest.

The last thing she remembered was being on a seat by the river with Jack. Wait! Jack! Where was he? The doctor and her parents hadn't mentioned him. Had he been shot too? Was he ok? Were they keeping bad news from her? Her heart began to pound again. She opened her eyes. They were starting to clear. She saw she was in an open ward with screens on either side of her bed but none at the foot. There were two beds across the aisle, one of them occupied, and a lot of monitors attached to the person in it. A policeman in uniform sat with his back to her near the end of the bed. Maybe he knew about Jack.

'Hello,' she tried to say but 'o' came out.

The policeman turned and came towards her.

'Can I help?' he asked.

'Jack?' she tried to say but 'Jaa' came out.

'I'll get a nurse.'

He strode off and a few seconds later a well-built middle aged man in a white coat and surgical mask appeared, a stethoscope round his neck

'Just need to check your drip,' he said.

He came to the bedside and turned off a tap at the top of the pipe that fed into the back of her hand. Then he unhooked the bag of clear liquid from the stand and replaced it with another from the pocket of his white coat. He was wearing surgical gloves.

'Jaa,' said Emily but he was connecting the tube and appeared not to hear.

As she spoke her right eye, now clearer than the left, saw the card on his lanyard. It said 'Mrs A. Wittingdale', with a photograph of a woman. There were footsteps from beyond the screen and the policeman reappeared.

'Someone's just coming,' he said. 'Oh, I see someone's here already.'

Emily wanted to know about Jack but couldn't get the words out so she tried to shake her head on her pillow but could hardly move it and the policeman and the doctor didn't notice. Then the doctor turned on the tap at the top of the pipe and left. The policeman nodded to him and sat down in his previous position, back to Emily.

That's funny, she thought. *The doctor had the wrong lanyard. And he's replaced a nearly full bag of drip with another nearly full bag. From his pocket.*

It was odd but she presumed he knew what he was doing. Or did he? Or was it something he shouldn't have done? She realised he'd appeared as soon as the policeman went out of sight. What if...? No, surely she was having delusions of conspiracy.

Out of sight down the ward she heard a commotion like someone banging on a door, followed by running feet and someone shouted Mrs Wittingdale's name. She started to feel dizzy as though she was going to faint. What was going on? Mrs Wittingdale had said she'd soon be feeling more normal. She had been feeling better but now she was going the other way. The drip. What if the doctor had attached the wrong one? Was someone coming to check? But they would see nothing wrong because it looked the same as the old one.

She felt hot and sweaty. Dizziness gave way to buzzing in her ears. She wanted to shout but she couldn't and felt she could pass out any moment. She decided to take no chances. With her right hand she took hold of the cannula on the back of her left, gritted her teeth and pulled. She knew it would hurt. It did but it didn't move. She tried again with as much force as she could muster, only just aware of what she was doing. She felt a sharp pain on the back of her hand and in a detached kind of way heard a sound from her own throat that was more like a gurgle than a cry, and the cannula came free with such force that she yanked the tube. The stand with the bag of liquid crashed to the floor as she lost consciousness.

17
Vodka

'Let's see if we can sneak back to Jack's room,' said Lucy. 'We've sat in this bloody café all day and it's nearly six o'clock and they've only let us have ten minutes with him, and still no more news about Em.'

'Yeah,' said Dil, 'and we'll have to decide whether to go home tonight or wait till tomorrow.'

'Tomorrow,' said Lucy. 'We can't possibly leave without seeing Em or at least knowing she's going to be alright.'

Bina agreed.

'I bet hotels are extortionate here,' Lucy went on.

'I'll have a word with Dad,' said Bina. 'I think he has a cousin in Cambridge. He's got a lot of cousins. My nan, his mum, was one of eleven.'

'Yes, my cousin Nabeela,' Bina's father said on the phone. 'She's a Professor of Economics and her husband Hamid Choudhry's a fellow of one of the colleges. Can't remember what he's a Professor of.'

A quick call established that the Choudhrys would be happy to welcome them for the night if they didn't mind 'the chaos'. Bina arranged that the three of them would turn up at the house about half past seven. It wasn't far out of town.

'She sounded nice and there was a lot of noise in the background, like children.'

'That's great,' said Lucy, Dil echoing. 'Now, back to Jack.'

She headed for the lifts a little ahead of the others. As she passed a door to the stairwell, it flew open and a heavyset man in a dark suit ran out, straight into her. She was knocked flying and the man cursed as he tripped and fell. Dil ran to Lucy while Bina, nearest to the man, went to help him. She noticed he was wearing surgical gloves.

'Get away from me,' he snarled as she bent to ask if he was alright.

He jumped to his feet and set off towards the main entrance, half limping, half running. A second later DI Kennedy ran from the stairwell.

'That way,' said Bina, pointing, and the Inspector raced out of the building, pulling a radio from his pocket.

Dil helped Lucy up.

'Think I'll have a bruised knee but otherwise no damage,' she said.

A couple of minutes later DI Kennedy rushed back through the doors.

'Gone,' he panted. 'Did you get a good look at him? Would you recognise him again?'

Dil and Lucy thought not.

'Yes, definitely,' said Bina. 'What's he done?

'Tried to murder your friend Emily, I think.'

'Whaa..?' from all three.

'Is she ok?' Lucy asked.

'I'm just going back up to find out.'

'Can we come?'

'It'll be up to the ICU people but come in the lift with me. I want to keep an eye on Bina.'

'Why?'

'If he's a murderer, potentially anyone who can identify him's at risk. Also, I want your details Bina so I can get you to look at some photos.'

'Oh my god, Bina' said Dil dramatically, 'You're an endangered witness.'

As they came out of the lift at ICU they saw Mr and Mrs Harrison hurrying towards the far end of the ward. The Inspector followed, Bina, Dil and Lucy behind. At Emily's bedside a dishevelled Mrs Wittingdale was giving her an injection. Emily was awake.

'What's this, a delegation?' she croaked.

'Oh love, thank God you're alright,' said her mother. 'And your voice is coming back.'

'I think she'll be Ok,' said Mrs Wittingdale, 'thanks to her own quick thinking. If she hadn't pulled that cannula out of her hand she could have been killed. The bag of saline was switched for alcohol, vodka possibly, but fortunately very little of it got into her system.'

'Vodka?' said Dil, Lucy and Bina in unison.

'Yes, in Emily's condition with anaesthetic and other drugs still in her it would have killed her quite quickly. In fact, anyone would have been killed if enough had gone in. She passed out for a minute or so but it was more through shock than anything and I've just given her an injection to counteract remaining alcohol.'

'I knew something was wrong when I saw the doctor had Mrs Wittingdale's lanyard,' Emily grated, 'except he probably wasn't a doctor.'

'Who knows,' said Mrs Wittingdale, 'but he certainly knew what he was doing. He just breezed into the locker room like any doctor, snatched my lanyard and pushed me over, then ran out and locked the door. You can't get into the main part of ICU without a card like mine. Luckily, I wasn't knocked out, just dazed, but it took me a minute or two to gather my wits and raise the alarm. A good thing you turned up at that point, Inspector.'

'Yes, but where were you, constable?' said the Inspector, looking at the policeman now standing beside his seat, looking uncomfortable. 'You're supposed to be guarding the patient.'

'Blame me for that,' said Emily, her voice improving to a hoarse whisper. 'I tried to ask him about Jack but it came out wrong and he thought I wanted a nurse so he went to find one and the man came.'

'Ok but from now on, no-one has access to Emily unless Mrs Wittingdale approves and has told the constable here.'

'Speaking of which,' said Mrs Wittingdale, nodding agreement, 'we've got too many people here and a patient who's vulnerable to excitement, so everyone please leave except for Emily's parents and I'm afraid I must ask them to go shortly too. We'll move Emily out of ICU into a private room and then she needs peace and quiet until tomorrow.'

'But I need to know about Jack please,' said Emily.

They reassured her that Jack was doing well and after some tearful hugging and repartee, Bina, Lucy and Dil went back downstairs. DI Kennedy asked them to wait in the lobby while he made some more enquiries in ICU. As they left they saw him giving the guard what looked like a quiet but thorough dressing down.

'Some police guard,' Mr Harrison muttered darkly when they were alone.

'No, Dad, don't go there. It wasn't his fault.'

He started to protest but Mrs Harrison held up her hand.

'She's right, Paul. Luckily no harm was done and we've learned something, that it definitely wasn't a random shooting.'

***

Downstairs DI Kennedy spoke seriously to the three friends.

'Bina, you're the only one who can identify the man who ran out. He was wearing a surgical mask in ICU. We found it and his white coat discarded in the stairs. We're looking for fingerprints but I'm not hopeful because he was wearing gloves. So I want you to come to the police station first thing tomorrow morning. Shall we say nine o'clock? Where will you be until then?'

She explained about her father's cousin.

'Good, I'll get a car to take you there and someone to keep an eye on the place.'

Bina, Dil and Lucy were shocked at how serious he sounded, and a little afraid, but it also felt exciting to be involved in such events. Nabeela was shocked too when a police car turned into the drive and pulled up outside the door. There was a neat lawn behind tall shrubs that hid the big, rambling house and its garden from the road.

'Oh my goodness,' she said on the doorstep, 'what on earth have you been up to? Come inside at once, you're just in time to eat and there's plenty for everyone.'

She was a bustling, smiley woman wearing a brown and beige patterned *shalwar kameez* and matching *hijab*. She hugged Bina, Lucy and Dil as though they were long lost children. Bina introduced her as Auntie Nabeela.

'Please call me Nabeela,' she said. 'Auntie makes me feel old and I'm your Dad's youngest cousin.'

She shooed them into a large dining room. Glass doors looked into a conservatory full of exotic plants.

'Tell us about the police later,' she hissed, pointing behind her hand to two young children already seated at the dining table.

An enticing smell of curry spices came from an open kitchen door on the other side of the entrance hall. The house was not a little untidy but in a comfortable, lived-in way. The furniture and decorations weren't modern but were good quality, slightly shabby, and the floors were polished wood with threadbare Persian rugs. The friends felt immediately at home.

'Hamid,' she said, giggling, to a big man with a full black beard who came out of the kitchen carrying a tray, 'this is Bina and her friends Dil and Lucy. They came here by police car. I think they may be master criminals.'

'Then they are welcome,' he replied, laughing. 'This house is a sanctuary for criminals and non-criminals alike and if they're criminals they look like respectable ones.'

'*Baba*, are they really criminals?' asked a little girl beside him, in awe.

'Yes,' said Bina, joining in the joke, 'we're planning to steal the crown jewels but please don't tell anyone.'

The little girl's eyes widened and she looked round the table for confirmation.

'Of course they're not criminals, Meshi,' said a small boy, her older brother, 'otherwise the police wouldn't have let them go. And I bet she's joking about the crown jewels.'

'Quite right,' said Nabeela, smiling. 'Now move up everyone and let Bina and her friends sit down.'

It was a chatty, sociable and delicious meal with pakora, bhajis and samosas to start, then large bowls of spicy curries with home-made chapatis. Afterwards the three friends cleared away while Nabeela and Hamid put the children to bed.

Later they all sat round the fire drinking tea, and Bina told them the real reason she and the others were in

Cambridge and of the dramatic events at the hospital. Nabeela and Hamid were shocked.

'We guessed there was more to it,' said Hamid, 'so thanks for not mentioning it to the children over supper, but little did we think it was to do with that dreadful shooting. And now a further murder attempt you say, with you becoming a possible target, Bina. I'd better make sure we've locked the doors.'

He stood up with a worried glance towards his wife.

'Oh,' said Bina hurriedly, 'I'm sorry, I didn't mean to alarm you. The Inspector said he'd have someone keep an eye on us here overnight, so I'm sure we'll all be safe.'

Nabeela went to the window and parted the curtains.

'There's a policeman standing at the gate,' she said. 'Poor fellow must be freezing. I'll pop out with something.'

Hamid relaxed and sat down again while Nabeela headed for the kitchen.

'That's reassuring,' he said. 'Sounds like your Inspector's doing a good job. I understand he's already been to our College, St Peters, which is where your friends were shot from. It's a horrible thought that a colleague could have been responsible and I'm hoping it's unlikely because those rooms overlooking the river are for undergraduates and there's always a lot of coming and going at weekends.'

'Two nice young officers at the front,' said Nabeela when she came back ten minutes later. 'A man and a woman. And another man round the back. I've taken them some samosas. The woman's in the car at the moment. They're taking turns and swap places every hour. They say they'll be here all night.'

18
Chase

By seven o'clock on Monday morning, hospital nursing staff were on their rounds checking patients, noting charts and administering medication prior to the arrival of breakfast trolleys. Jack's separate room was in a short corridor between the ward entrance and the open part of the ward but the sound of it all woke him and he was already wide awake when his turn came. He felt more alert than yesterday but his three wounds were hurting. While he ate, a newscaster on his wall-mounted TV mentioned 'Saturday's dramatic shooting in Cambridge.'

'Police enquiries continue,' she said. 'The two victims Emily Harrison and Jack Wellington remain in hospital in a serious condition under police guard. Detective Inspector Duncan Kennedy is in charge of the investigation.'

The picture changed to show the Inspector standing on The Backs in low dawn light beside the seat where Jack and Emily had been sitting.

'We're treating this as a case of attempted murder and have no reason to believe it's terror-related. Late yesterday doctors and family allowed me a brief conversation with Jack and we're following a number of lines of enquiry. I'm hoping Emily will be well enough to speak to me today. It's early days but Doctors are optimistic that both of them will eventually make a full recovery. So far no witnesses to the shooting have come forward but I urge anyone who thinks they may have seen something or may know anything about what happened to get in touch with our confidential phone line.'

The picture changed back to the studio as a number appeared on the bottom of the screen. Jack turned it off. He wanted to find out who was behind the shooting and why, but the TV wouldn't tell him. He also wanted to see Emily for himself to make sure she was recovering as he had been told. He was about to try getting out of bed when Mr Ahmed arrived.

'And how are we today?' he asked.

'Better for a night's sleep, but sore. When can I get out of bed?

'Now if you like. The physiotherapist will be here any minute.'

Right on cue, a young man in a white coat came in.

'This is Nigel,' said Mr Ahmed. 'He'll have you up and about in no time. I'll just examine you first.'

He checked Jack over, listened to his heart and lungs, examined the temperature chart.

'You're doing well. I'll pop in again late afternoon. Oh and I'll prescribe something to take the edge off the pain. Over to you, Nigel.'

Nigel showed Jack how to swing his legs over the edge of the bed without putting excessive strain on the wound near his waist.

'You'll feel the most pain when you stretch your stomach muscles and that's when you're putting strain on the site of the operation,' said Nigel. 'So treat the pain as a warning signal.'

It wasn't long before Jack was standing up and walking round the room with small steps. When he felt confident, Nigel showed him the way to the bathroom a few doors away. On the way back, Jack noticed another policeman sitting outside another door a little further along the corridor, presumably where Emily was.

Once back in the room Nigel went off to another patient and a nurse brought some pills. When Jack had taken them he went out into the corridor again.

'Going visiting,' he said to the policeman, pointing to where his colleague was sitting.

The policeman at Emily's door stood up as Jack approached.

'I think she's awake,' he said, reading Jack's intention, and knocked gently.

'Yes?'

'A visitor. Is that ok?'

'Depends.'

Jack poked his head round the door. She was sitting up in bed connected to a beeping monitor from an index finger. There was a tube into her hand too.

'Oh Jack, thank goodness,' said Emily. 'They said you were ok but I had a nagging doubt that they might just be protecting me.'

'Same here. I had to see you as soon as possible. How're you feeling? Cool hairstyle.'

There was a bandage around her head and some hair had obviously been shaved off but what remained was sticking up out of the middle of the bandage.

She laughed. 'Don't be cheeky. My stylist's late. And d'you know that's the first time I've laughed since Saturday. It feels good.'

To Jack's surprise she started to cry. He didn't know what say. He went over to her bed and took her hand.

'What's happening,' she sobbed quietly. 'People shooting at us. The will. The bed mystery. Everything's out of control.'

'I know. I feel exactly the same. It's like life has a life of its own.'

There was a pause and they both laughed as he realised what he'd said but tears still to rolled down Emily's face.

'Oh this is doing me so much good,' she said and let go of his hand to blow her nose on a tissue, 'but Mrs Wittingdale, she's the surgeon, says I'm going to have to take it easy for probably two to three months so I don't know if I'll be able to carry on with the PhD. My life's wrecked.'

'Well maybe not wrecked altogether,' said Jack, beginning to feel emotional himself but not sure why.

'Yes it is. I had it all planned and now it's gone down the drain.'

The policeman knocked and said 'Your mother and father are here.'

'Oh crikey,' said Emily as they walked in. 'Hello Mum and Dad. Jack's really helping. He made me laugh and that made me cry.'

She laughed and cried at the same time.

'It's probably a natural reaction,' said Mrs Harrison, sitting down on the bed and taking her hand. 'Release of tension, relief it's all over. Heaven knows what two murder attempts in twenty four hours do to your mind but you're safe now.'

'Two?' said Jack.

'Oh, of course, how would you know, yes someone pretending to be a doctor tried to kill me last night.'

She recounted the story, to Jack's horror.

'I know I'm safe – we're safe, for now,' she continued, 'but my life's in ruins and what if the police don't find who's trying to kill us and we have to have guards for the rest of our lives or worse still no guards at all?'

Tears ran down her cheeks again.

'Your life isn't in ruins,' said Mrs Harrison. 'You're recovering well and by the time you're back to normal I'm sure all this will have blown over and they'll know who's behind it. Probably some maniac who picked you at random.'

Jack wanted to agree but didn't really think so. He exchanged glances with Emily and saw similar thoughts reflected in her eyes.

'Look,' he said. 'Take things a step at a time, Em. First you need to talk to Inspector Kennedy and tell him everything you can remember and then you need to follow your surgeon's advice and concentrate on recovering. I'll be around for the next few days so we can talk too.'

'But what about my PhD?,' she said, choking a sob. 'If I've to take two or three months off like Mrs Wittingdale said, they won't want me back.'

'Listen to Jack's advice,' said Mr Harrison. 'A step at a time. When you're up to it you can talk to your Professor and the University authorities. They won't have had time to react yet and you earned that place so they'd be in the wrong if they suddenly took it away from you. For now, just concentrate on recovery and helping the police.'

'Yes, I suppose you're right,' said Emily quietly, sniffing and wiping her eyes, but sounded sceptical.

Jack walked back to his room and sat down heavily in the bedside chair. He looked at his watch. It was a quarter to nine in the morning and already he felt worn out. Nigel had said building up stamina would take time.

That must be medicalspeak for feeling tired quickly, he thought.

***

At about the same time Bina, Dil and Lucy, having phoned in sick to work, got into the police car outside the Choudhry's house. Strictly speaking only Bina was needed to look at mugshots but the three had agreed to stick together. They thanked Nabeela and Hamid warmly for their hospitality.

'You're welcome to stay tonight too,' Nabeela had said over breakfast but they had explained they would need to be back at their jobs tomorrow.

The policewoman told them her name was Donna and she drove, leaving her two colleagues at the house to wait for another car that would pick them up. Bina sat in the front.

As they turned right onto a main road at the end of the Choudhry's street, a large black SUV with darkened windows pulled out in front of them from the other side of the road. At the same time a similar vehicle came up behind so that the police car was sandwiched between them.

They travelled a short distance like that, then Donna realised the vehicle behind was coming closer and the one in front slowing down. She couldn't see round or over it but when she'd turned onto the main road she'd not noticed any obstruction or traffic jam ahead that would account for it. It looked like the police car was in a trap.

'Not happy about this,' Donna said. 'Hold on.'

She pulled out to the right, changed down and gunned the engine to overtake. The SUV in front also swung to the right to block her, past the middle of the road, so she swerved back to the left and undertook, not a moment too soon as the offside front of the SUV hit an oncoming van and they both spun away with a mighty crash and screeching tyres. The SUV behind accelerated to keep on

Donna's tail but she put her foot down, starting the siren and blue light. Traffic ahead parted to let them through.

'See if you can photo the number plates of the one behind,' she shouted.

She knew her dashcam would have captured the one in front. The three passengers had been paralysed with surprise but now Dil and Lucy turned their phones to the back window and took shots of the pursuing vehicle, as well as the traffic chaos in their wake. Donna thumbed the radio switch on her steering wheel.

'Charlie four nine. This is alpha golf. Urgent. Being pursued by hostile SUV. Similar vehicle in RTA behind us. Send RTU and ambulance there. We're coming in hot. Alpha golf, over.'

'Alpha golf, charlie four nine,' was the laconic answer.

After a three second pause the radio spoke again.

'Alpha golf, charlie four nine. We see you. Unit dispatched to RTA. Two units heading for you. Keep going Donna. Gate open. Over.'

As the message ended, Bina, Dil and Lucy began to hear police sirens ahead. 'We'll be at base in less than three minutes,' said Donna. 'Help's coming but keep low in case they have guns, and hang on. It might get bumpy.'

Mention of guns scared them and they did as she asked. A lot could happen in three minutes. As Donna wove her way through traffic the SUV behind was at times close enough to touch and at others further back but they were unable to shake it off. Sirens were approaching quickly on the other side of the road as two police cars raced towards them. They arrived in seconds. One veered across the road at speed and passed between them and the SUV, forcing it to brake to avoid a collision, while the other skid-turned to fall in behind it. The braking had been momentary, though, and the SUV soon caught up, dangerously close. The car suddenly lurched and slowed, pulling to the left.

'Fuck,' Donna shouted, 'a back tyre's gone. Maybe shot.'

A loud grinding sound came from the back nearside wheel. The car bucked and slewed but she kept the accelerator floored, trying to right it as they shaved past a van that pulled in to the side in response to the blue light.

'We're heading for that grey two storey building to the right of the next roundabout.'

Bina raised her head to look. She heard a 'phut, phut, phut' and felt a breath of wind near her left ear. Three small holes appeared in the windscreen in front of her. She and the others knew exactly what they were.

'Charlie four nine, alpha golf. Under fire. Over.'

'Alpha golf, charlie four nine.'

More 'phuts' and the offside wing mirror shattered. In the back Dil put a protective arm around Lucy as they crouched lower. Bina curled as far into the front footwell as she could. They had never been so afraid. The SUV was almost touching. Donna knew the back wheel could cause them to whirl off the road or somersault if it gave way or jammed but she judged stopping was a greater risk. It was four hundred metres to the roundabout, about 15 seconds away, and she saw that another police car had stopped traffic on the other side of the road beyond it. The two pursuing police cars were edging forward on either side of the SUV. The sound from the back wheel changed and became worse as the remains of the tyre fell away.

'I'm taking a short cut,' Donna yelled as they reached the roundabout and swerved round it the wrong way.

The SUV didn't follow Donna's sudden turn but four more bullets shattered the back window behind Dil, and exited through the nearside front window above Bina. The SUV continued straight, mounting the roundabout, bouncing into the air but driving over it across grass, through flower beds and straight ahead on the road beyond.

A hundred metres after the turn and still at speed, Donna swerved into the police compound with three protesting tyres, drove straight to the entrance of the building and stopped. Two policemen with automatic rifles and bullet-proof jackets emerged, flung open the car doors and pulled all four occupants into the building

'Everyone ok?' Donna asked, once inside.

Dil could only nod and roll his eyes, stunned. Lucy's mouth opened and shut a few times but nothing came out.

'That was some ride, Donna,' said Bina. 'You're incredible.'

'Isn't she though?' said one of the armed men. 'I'm scared of her.'

'This is Pete,' said Donna, shaken but smiling.

They hugged as Lucy found her voice. 'Good thing you turned when you did or we'd have been toast.'

'Definitely,' said Bina. 'The bullets missed us by a hairsbreadth.'

19
CCTV

Jack's parents arrived about ten o'clock in the morning. He was still feeling tired.

'We've been thinking,' said his mother. 'When they let you out of here, it'd be sensible for you to come home until you're fit enough to go back to work.'

Jack had mixed feelings. He would welcome home cooking and a comfortable place to live but having left home years ago, could he stand going back? He and they might well get on each other's nerves. Dil and Lucy would be near but would be working most of the time. And anyway he'd decided to pursue Mrs Barton's offer which he couldn't tell his parents about because of the NDA. He opted to play for time rather than offend them by refusing.

'Thanks, Mum, good idea,' he said, 'but let's wait until they're ready to discharge me and tell me how long it'll be before I get back to normal. I'll need to talk to them at work too, about being off and sick pay and stuff.'

'Ok, you let us know as soon as you can, because I'm sorry but we'll have to go back home today. I've got to be at school tomorrow and your Dad's delivery job is zero hours but they let you go if you have more than one weekday off a month.'

'That's terrible,' said Jack. 'Surely it's not allowed?

'It isn't,' said Mr Wellington, 'but that's how it is if you want to work.'

For the first time since he came round Jack noticed how tired his father looked and how strained his mother seemed. He knew they found it difficult to make ends meet now and the shooting could only have added to their troubles. His father used to have a steady job as a machinist at a local engineering company but it had gone bust a few years ago. His mother's job was low paid as a part-time teaching assistant. He wished he could help them and felt guilty for not wanting to convalesce at home. They left after Mr Ahmed had been on his rounds.

***

Mr and Mrs Harrison stayed with Emily until mid-morning when Mrs Wittingdale came in.

'How d'you feel this morning,' she asked.

'Fine,' said Emily, once more starting to cry, then laughing at the same time.

The surgeon laughed.

'Conflicting feelings. I've seen it before. Sometimes in military people wounded in action. Partly relief, partly fear, partly just emotional overload. It'll pass, and the most significant thing is that it's a good sign. Your brain obviously hasn't lost any of its complexity or what Jane Austen might have called delicacy of feeling.'

Emily continued to cry quietly, all smiles, while her mother held her hand.

'Jack visited earlier and made me laugh and it felt so good I couldn't stop crying,' she grinned.

'That'll have confused him,' said Mrs Wittingdale and laughed again.

Her parents waited outside while she examined Emily and went through a number of tests.

'No trace of alcohol in your blood, head wound healing. I think we'll try and get you walking today. I'll send Nigel the physio to see you.'

***

Jack's parents hadn't been gone long when the policeman outside announced the arrival of DI Audrey.

'Hello,' he said. 'Inspector Kennedy said you were coming.'

'I'm glad to see you're out of bed despite the wounds. Alright if I ask some questions?'

'Yes, fine.'

'Did he mention we've unfortunately found someone was killed in the fire at Clarence & Thirkill?'

'Yes he did. Who was it?'

'I need to ask you some more about your passport.'

'Why?'

She ignored both questions.

'When was the last time you used your passport before the day of the fire.'

Jack was irritated but decided to go along with her. After all, a death made the fire much more serious.

'Over a year ago. I went on a stag weekend to Amsterdam with my friend Dil and some others. October, I think it was.'

'Amsterdam. Why Amsterdam?'

'We got a cheap deal on Eurostar by booking months in advance. None of us had much money.'

'Was it your idea to go to Amsterdam?'

'Not really.'

'What does that mean?'

Jack bridled a little but kept his cool. He was becoming used to her way of asking questions. Impolite verging on aggressive. He supposed she was trained to do it.

'What I say. Dil and I planned it together. We must have looked at half a dozen trips to various destinations but we thought this was the best value.'

'Did one of you find it and put it to the other?'

'Does it matter? It's not easy to remember. Dil was in Bradford, I was in London. We messaged and spoke over a couple of weeks. I found some trips and he found others.'

'It could matter and I'd like to know who first suggested Amsterdam.'

'I think it was Dil but I'll ask him. I think he and some other friends might call in later.'

'Don't. If I need to I'll do it myself. I want to keep this tight until we know what we're dealing with.'

'So what *are* we dealing with? Is the person killed from the Netherlands or something?'

Again she ignored his question.

'Did you show your passport on the way there?'

'Yes at St Pancras International.'

'When you were in Amsterdam where did you keep your passport?'

'In a leg pocket of my shorts.'

'Why?'

'So I knew where it was, obviously.' Jack was only just containing his annoyance. 'It has a zip under the flap so anything in it can't fall out and also I can feel whatever's in there against my leg as I walk.'

'Did it ever leave your pocket while you were in Amsterdam?'

'No."

'Did you take your shorts off while you were in Amsterdam?'

Jack laughed. This was becoming ridiculous.

'Surprisingly enough I did. For showers, bed and so on.'

'Did you sleep alone?'

'Yes apart from the five women I had an orgy with every night.'

'Who were they?' DI Audrey asked, humourless.

'That was a joke,' said Jack.

'So who did you sleep with?'

'Dil and I shared a twin room in a hotel. Wait… I think we showed our passports when we checked in."

'Which hotel?'

'It was on a boat actually. I'd have to look it up to remember the name.'

'I thought you said it was a hotel.'

'It was. There are quite a few hotels on boats in Amsterdam. They've got a lot of water there.'

'Can you look it up for me then?'

'My phone was shot to pieces. I could let you know when the replacement arrives.'

'When you came back from Amsterdam what happened to your passport?'

'Nothing happened to it. I keep it in a drawer of my desk at my flat. The next time I took it out was after Hubbler's visit.'

'So anyone could have had access to it?'

'No. You may be surprised to know I lock my door when I go out and only the landlord has a key.'

'Name and address?'

'I'll let you know when my new phone comes. It's a company in Greenwich, I think, but if you're asking about access to my passport, as I told you before, Hubbler was alone in my room for a while before I got back from Clarence & Thirkill but it didn't look as though the drawer had been disturbed because I checked later. I remember that my keycard was hanging on the back of the door, though.'

Jack waited for the next question, but none came.

'You asked who was killed in the fire. All we know is that it was a man because the body was so badly burned it was unrecognisable and although we have DNA, the person isn't on record. There's no match to dental records either which is strange. It means he's never been to a dentist in the UK or the EU, or if he has, the records have been deleted. But we have one clue. Charred remains of a passport that exactly matches yours. We were able to recover information from the chip.'

Jack forgot she had been annoying him.

'Wow. So is it Hubbler?'

'We don't think so because street CCTV shows him outside the building shortly after the fire alarms went off so he must have met someone on the eighteenth floor after failing to get your letters at reception on the twentieth.'

'And he must have given that person the copy of my passport.'

'Exactly. And the relevance of Amsterdam is that we've analysed the passport remains and it has characteristics similar to fake passports we know were made there by creative criminals in an enterprise shut down by police last year. So I'm trying to establish if the burned one was one of those or someone was trying to make it look like it was. If it's the latter, we're dealing with pretty sophisticated counterfeiters.'

Jack didn't know what to make of it.

'I'll be in touch if I want more about where you stayed and your landlord and so on,' said the Inspector, 'but it sounds like you kept your passport pretty tight and the criminal enterprise wasn't connected with floating hotels. Also Hubbler had clear access to it and SIS use passport fakers. So thanks for answering my questions There's just one more thing, though. I'd like you to take a look at CCTV from the eighteenth floor lobby around the time of the fire, to see if there's anyone you recognise apart from Hubbler. It'll take about five minutes.'

They sat side by side on the bed looking at her phone. It was speeded-up footage showing the lift doors. There was no sound but the lift came and went a few times with a handful of people using it, as well as Hubbler arriving and walking out of the picture, then a lot of people started pouring past, presumably towards the fire escape stairs, and smoke could be seen. He watched carefully but saw no-one else familiar and the flow of people quickly diminished to a trickle. As the smoke became thicker, almost obscuring the view, he assumed it was the end and began to look away when he half-saw something.

'Wait, stop, go back slowly.'

A few seconds later he saw it again. Someone he knew coming out of the lift.

Billy Worth.

20
Insane?

Dil, Lucy and Bina turned up at the hospital just after DI Audrey left Jack. Bina had tried without success to identify the bogus doctor from mugshots and DI Kennedy had debriefed them about the car chase.

Jack went with them to Emily's room. They found her out of bed, sitting in a chair, no tubes or wires. Her parents were with her.

'Yay, you're up,' said Lucy. 'How're you feeling?'

'Not too bad. Pretty tired and a bit dizzy when I tried to stand but the physio showed me how to do it by stages and now I'm ok. I've walked to the end of the corridor and back. What have you been up to?'

Lucy and Bina poured out the story of their staying with the Choudhrys and the hair-raising car chase to the police station, with added colour from Dil. Emily and her parents were horrified.

'God! That's so sinister and scary,' said Emily. 'I thought things like that only happened in thriller movies. Thank goodness you're ok.'

'It's no thrill,' said Mr Harrison, 'and it's not a movie. It's real life and frightening. Inspector Kennedy was right when he said Bina might be at risk. Has he found out who it was?'

'Not so far. The SUVs had darkened windows and false number plates,' said Bina. 'One was damaged but still running and Inspector Kennedy said they both drove out of town at high speed in opposite directions, somehow managing to evade pursuers, and apparently there are fewer traffic cams outside the central part of the town.'

'Thank heavens you're all safe,' said Mrs Harrison. 'You must have been very shaken.'

'We were,' said Lucy, 'but it didn't hit me till afterwards. I felt quite trembly while we made statements.'

'Same here,' said Bina, 'but Donna, the policewoman, was awesome. She seemed to take it all in her stride. Cool driver. We'd have been in trouble without her. She's in uniform but she told me she's training to be a Detective Constable.'

There was a lot more conversation and after a while Emily felt a headache coming on. She was tired, too. Mrs Harrison read the signs and suggested a rest.

'And Em, love, I think Dad and I'll go back to Bradford this afternoon. Work and so on. You're doing fine and we'll come and get you when they're ready to discharge you.'

'What? Go home?'

'Yes, dear. We can't possibly leave you on your own after what's happened. You need time to recover. Look – you're already tired after an hour's chat. It's going to be a while before you get back to normal.'

'Thanks, Mum, it'd be lovely and you have heating,' – she giggled – 'but let's see how I am when they let me out of here. I'll need to speak to my Director of Studies and what I really, really don't want to do is give up the PhD.'

So it wasn't decided either way. Lucy and Dil had to go back to Bradford too and Mr and Mrs Harrison offered them a lift. Bina couldn't stay off work any longer and needed to go back to London. She had mentioned it to DI Kennedy earlier who had contacted DI Audrey before she saw Jack. DI Audrey agreed to accompany her back to

London and arrange protection there. By early afternoon, everyone had gone, and Jack left Emily to rest her headache away. Later she walked round to his room.

'Excitement over for now,' she said.

'Let's hope so. Good to see everyone though. Your parents look to be coping ok now.'

'They were relaxing a bit by the time they left but it's easy to forget how worried they must have been.'

'Same with mine. Now they want me to go home to convalesce like yours which is attractive in a way but what I really want is to investigate the bed mystery. I must talk to Edith as soon as I can. And I've something to tell you about the fire at Clarence & Thirkill.'

He was interrupted by voices outside the door, first a conversation but quickly becoming an argument.

'I must be able to see them. I've waited nearly two days. I spoke to Inspector Kennedy yesterday morning and I've tried to contact him today but they tell me he's too busy.'

'Right on cue,' said Emily. 'Sounds like Edith.'

'I'm sorry, Madam. My orders are only certain medical staff, family and three other people who were here earlier.'

'It's alright officer. I know this lady,' said Jack, opening the door. 'Both of us would like to see her.'

The policeman was still stinging from being carpeted the previous day.

'Righto, but for security can you tell me her name?'

'Edith Gregory. She's from a law firm called Clarence & Thirkill.'

'Ok, that tallies with what she said. I'll have to call it in though, just for the record.'

'No problem.'

'Thank you so much,' said Edith, coming in. 'How are you both? I'm so pleased to see you up and about. What a terrible ordeal you've had. Jim and I and the other partners thought I ought to come in case we could help. Anything to do with the Barton estate is very important to the firm.'

'We were just talking about you,' said Jack, 'and thanks for the concern. We're starting to come round. Em's been worse than me but they're telling us we could both be fit enough to leave here around the end of the week.'

'That sounds promising, but listen, it's near the end of the day and I believe you've had family and friends here so I could understand if you want to rest for now. All I want to say is that I'd like to have a chat about the letter when you feel up to it. I can come back tomorrow.'

Jack raised an eyebrow at Emily.

'I'd rather talk now,' she said.

'Me too,' he said. 'We both read Emily's letter and discussed it before the shooting. I'm happy to leave my job and take up the offer but Em wants to continue her PhD instead.'

'Er, you must excuse me. I haven't seen the letter, nor have any of us at the firm, so I don't know what the offer is or how to reply. All we were told was that we have to respect your decision about whatever the letter says and deal with the rest of the estate accordingly.'

'Whoa,' said Emily. 'We never thought of that. Does the NDA mean we can't tell you what we've read?'

'No. The NDA is between you and the executors and if you read the small print it says we all have the same secrecy obligations. So if we disclose anything about the letters you could get court orders or damages against us, just as we could against you.'

'Oh, thank goodness,' said Emily. 'So should I show you the letter?'

'We'll never get anywhere if you don't,' said Jack.

'Yes I think it would be appropriate,' said Edith.

'It's in my bag in my bedside cupboard.'

The three of them walked across the corridor to her room. She took out the envelope and gave it to Edith. They all sat down, Jack and Emily in the two chairs and Edith on the bed. Edith read quickly.

'Well,' she said, 'Surely her husband died? I'm afraid what she says raises questions about her sanity which could have implications for the entire will. How could her husband just dematerialise as she puts it. I'll have to consult Jim about this.'

Jack and Emily looked at each other in surprise.

'What d'you mean, implications for the entire will?' Jack asked.

'If someone makes a will when they don't know what they're doing or are obviously incapable of understanding it, the will is invalid.'

'So then the assets would go to the Crown?'

'They might, but we'd have to make an application to the High Court and ask a judge to decide if the will was valid and if not who the assets should go to.'

'So if a judge thought she was mad, no-one could benefit according to the will?' Emily asked.

'The Judge could decide the whole will was void, in other words to be ignored, or perhaps just parts of it. It would depend on what evidence was put forward.'

'We could put forward evidence,' said Emily.

'What do you mean?' There was an edge in Edith's voice.

'We know of something similar that happened.'

There was a short silence as Edith looked first at one and then the other. Jack noticed something in her eyes but couldn't work out what.

'Look, you've both had serious injuries and I don't want to overtire you. Let's leave it there for today. I'll call in tomorrow morning about ten and we'll talk again. In the meantime, don't worry about anything. Concentrate on recovering. Alright if I copy the letter?'

She took a phone out of her handbag. Jack looked at Emily and tried to shake his head without Edith seeing but Emily was ahead of him.

'Not for now,' she said evenly. 'Let's leave that until tomorrow too. Jack and I need to rest.'

A momentary look of annoyance passed over Edith's face.

'Of course,' she said, recovering herself. 'Forgive me, you're right. I'll see you in the morning.'

Emily and Jack looked at each other when she left.

'What just happened?' Jack asked

'Edith's friendly helpful front nearly cracked. There's something not right about what she said. She never asked what Mrs Barton overheard us saying which I think any normal person would have and then she immediately launched into saying Mrs Barton could have been insane, which she clearly wasn't.'

'Yes, it almost sounds like she'd like the will to be declared invalid.'

'Exactly and someone else might then stand to benefit.'

'And her firm would be able to charge, no doubt handsomely, for the application to the court.'

'And she never asked about the shooting either, which is a bit odd.'

Jack was thoughtful. 'That could just have been being considerate but she didn't like not being allowed to copy the letter did she? I loved the way you told her not to. Polite but firm, showing a bit of steel.'

He grinned and she laughed.

'Steel? I'm not usually like that. Maybe it's the titanium?'

'No it's not new. Remember when you were sixteen? There was steel that famous day.'

'It's because you were so annoying.'

'Oh so it's my fault?'

They smiled, comfortable with the memory.

'Speaking of copies,' Jack continued, 'd'you think we should make one or even two. If yours was lost or stolen we'd have no means of proving what it said.'

'Yes.'

Emily took out her phone, scanned the letter into a file and sent a copy to Jack on an encrypted messaging app.

'You won't see it till you get another phone but at least we've got two copies now as well as the original.'

'That reminds me, could I borrow yours to order a new sim and phone?'

***

'It's as we thought,' said the man on the phone. 'The obstacles need to be cleared away but your people have been incompetent and messy. You need to get a grip on them. Tell them if they can handle the witness we'll consider continuing to use them. No loose ends this time, please.'

'I know. I'm sorry. In the meantime we'll go along with the subjects.'

'Yes. We need to know where they are and what they're doing.'

'I understand. I know what's at stake.'

21
Clarity

That night Jack and Emily were exhausted but sleep eluded them. Jack's wounds were sore and his mind was in a whirl. There seemed to be so much to worry about. The shooting, the attack on Em, the car chase that put Bina, Dil and Lucy at risk, what to do about his parents, the letter, his job, whether or not he and Em could trust Edith. And Billy! Was he killed in the fire? He had intended to tell Em about the video but the strange talk with Edith had driven it out of his mind. He drifted off a few times, only to be jerked awake by a new anxiety or sounds out in the ward, some like trolleys being wheeled.

Emily's head ached and similar worries kept her mind in a spin. Later, just when she was too exhausted to stay awake, she was disturbed by sounds like marbles rolling round on the floor. Something about them was familiar but she couldn't place it. Later, she must have dropped off but awoke at seven, still tired. At least the headache had gone and she was able to distract herself by watching TV news. There was an item about her and Jack.

'The Cambridge shooting,' said the newscaster. 'A spokesperson for Addenbrookes hospital says that the two people injured on Saturday are out of danger and making good progress. They have had visits from close family and friends and were able to answer police questions. Detective Inspector Kennedy of Cambridge police said they have obtained valuable information but have so far made no arrests.'

After breakfast and Mrs Wittingdale's round, Emily was given permission to have a bath provided she kept her head dry. She longed to wash her hair but was told it would be out of the question for at least a few days. She did the best she could by tying it back.

I look awful, she said to herself, peering in the mirror at the shaved patch on her head, a plaster covering most of it, *but I suppose I'm lucky it wasn't worse.*

Back in her room, feeling more positive after a good soak, she settled down to read a trashy novel she picked up from the library trolley. She had read only a few pages when the policeman outside knocked and said a Professor Hinkles was here to see her and was that ok?

Oh no, she thought, conscious of her appearance, and instinctively smoothing her hair as she stood up.

'Ask him to come in. He's my Director of Studies.'

He was a lanky two metres in height with unkempt clothes, hair and greying beard, almost a caricature of an eccentric Professor.

'Good morning, Ms Harrison.'

'Hello, thanks for coming. Do sit down. I was planning to come and see you when they let me out of here.'

She returned to her chair and he sat on the bed.

'Well the Faculty thought it better if I come to you.'

She smiled to herself, noting it was the Faculty that had thought it, not him. He was intellectually brilliant but notoriously bad at social niceties.

'It's kind of them, and you.'

'Well you've had a nasty injury and obviously won't be back to us for a while, so we've been having a think.'

Emily realised this was the closest to sympathy and concern she was likely to hear from him but she wondered what was coming next. Was she about to be chucked off the PhD course? Was her worst fear about to be realised? She couldn't think of anything to say so she waited.

'You see we have to keep standards up and having someone on the course who for whatever reason isn't up to scratch could affect our research grants.'

He closed his eyes and opened them. It was something he did when he felt he'd made an important or difficult point and didn't want to be challenged. She'd seen it before in socially awkward people. So she was going to be chucked off. She could feel tears close by.

'So we think on the whole it's better if you pull out this year and start afresh next year.'

'What?' said Emily, not sure she had heard right.

'Skip this year and start again in October. That'll give you time to recover properly. It'll leave us a body down in theory but as it happens there's a candidate from China who could come in to take your place at short notice. He's been working on the same kind of stuff in Beijing and has highly placed connections there, so it gives the Faculty an opportunity to do them a favour at no cost which they think could stand them in good stead in the future. I don't go in for all this political stuff. I leave it to them. If you agree you'll need to pop in and sign some papers when you're fit enough. You're under no obligation to agree but the Faculty very much hopes that you will and might even be able to find a bursary for you.'

Emily couldn't believe her luck. It was the answer to her dilemma about the letter. She could accept Mrs Barton's offer along with Jack without losing the PhD. She wouldn't be able to spend a full year trying to solve the bed mystery but nine months or so until October might be enough and a bursary meant money towards her living expenses.

She stood up and hugged the Professor. He didn't quite know what to do and looked embarrassed.

'Thank you, Professor. I've been worrying about the course and not being able to pull my weight. It's a perfect solution. Please thank the Faculty too.'

Emily hurried to tell Jack as soon as the Professor left.

'That's fantastic,' he said. 'Now we can do the job together. Provided Edith doesn't stop the whole thing of course. I still can't get over how weird she was yesterday.'

'I wonder what she'll say this morning. Probably have us declared insane if we tell her about the bed mystery.'

'Em, before she arrives, I must tell you something. I was going to yesterday but there was too much happening. You know the fire at Clarence & Thirkill that I was arrested for?'

She nodded.

'Well, Inspector Audrey gave me another grilling yesterday. They've discovered a body, well, charred remains really, someone killed in the fire but holding a copy of my passport. She showed me CCTV of people coming out of the lift on the eighteenth floor where they found it. Guess who I saw?'

'The guy who tried to get the letters? Hubbler wasn't it?'

'No, well yes he did go to that floor after the twentieth but also I saw Billy Worth.'

'What?' Emily was incredulous. 'What was he doing there?

'No idea, but it's interesting that he was talking to Hubbler at the funeral.'

'So is he the body?'

'They haven't been able to identify it – no match to DNA or dental records – and it could be entirely coincidental that Billy was there, and have nothing to do with the fire or Hubbler and he could have got out of the building like everyone else. Anyway I told Inspector Audrey who Billy is and what I knew about him and where he lived. It was Ilkley wasn't it? One of those posh houses on the north side. I think his parents were pretty well off.'

'Yes, I once went to a party there. There was a swimming pool in the garden and of course everyone ended up jumping in. Alcohol galore, everyone wasted. His parents must have been away.'

'My Mum and Dad never went away but if they had, a party would have been impossible. Mum would have known, however well we cleared up.'

'Same with my Mum,' Emily chuckled.

'Anyway, much as I didn't like Billy, I hope the body doesn't turn out to be him. She said she'd probably be in touch so maybe I'll get to know. But the passport thing is peculiar. Only the chip was identifiable and they reckon it was somehow made in Amsterdam, probably on Dil's stag weekend.'

Edith turned up as arranged.

'Look, I owe you an apology for yesterday,' she said as soon as she arrived. 'I'm sorry if I worried you. We lawyers are taught to look for the snags in things and on reflection I think my concerns were a bit out of proportion. After all, you say you've heard of something similar to what Mrs Barton says happened to her husband, plus Mrs Barton continued teaching until she died, so her colleagues would have known if she was losing her mind. In any case the will was made and the letters written seven years before that. I've looked at our file and as always when we draw up a will there's a note to say we checked that she appeared perfectly rational and understood what she was doing.

Also the firm had dealings with her for years and our partners or staff would have noticed if she was behaving strangely. I'm told by those who knew her that she was always down-to-earth and straightforward.'

Emily and Jack were relieved and said so.

'Everything seems to be coming right this morning,' said Emily and explained about the Professor's visit and postponing her PhD.

'So that means I'd like to take up the offer too,' she added.

'Good,' said Edith. 'We've got a clear position and we all know where we stand. Your decisions mean we as executors put the estate on hold and give you a year to solve the mystery. I'll set up the monthly payments for you. After the year, or earlier if you're successful, we'll deal with the estate as set out in the will.'

Emily emailed Edith a copy of Mrs Barton's letter before she left and Edith agreed with them the amounts of the monthly payments they would receive. It was easy to work out Jack's as he had a regular monthly salary but Emily's income varied a lot depending on what work she could get and what she had time for. In a week where Emily worked a lot of hours she could earn the same as Jack so in the end Edith suggested they assume her income would be the same as his.

'After all,' she said, 'the important thing to Mrs Barton would be that you don't have to worry too much about money while you're working on her behalf.'

'That's wonderful,' said Emily. 'It'll be so nice not to be permanently tired and broke.'

Edith said she'd try to arrange the first payments for the following Monday. Emily and Jack wouldn't be under any obligation to keep her informed about what they were doing but if they solved the mystery either within the year or earlier they would be expected to show her and Jim their findings.

They were both excited and for the time being pushed to the back of their minds the black cloud on the horizon: someone was trying to kill them.

22

Removal

Emily and Jack slept soundly and woke on Wednesday morning feeling much better. Over the next two days, with their parents and friends gone, they spent time with each other talking, reading or watching TV. DI Kennedy visited each morning to keep them informed about the investigation into the shooting, the vodka incident and the car chase but so far no credible leads had emerged. On Thursday evening Bina called Emily.

'Hamid phoned. He's a Fellow at St Peters where the shots came from. He says all the College senior members and staff were horrified about the shooting and how it had damaged the College's reputation so there was a big kerfuffle on the College Council about how to put it right and about security. And it's not only them who are upset. Apparently there's people in high places in Government both here and in other parts of the world who either were students at the College or have other connections and they're all putting pressure on the Master to do something. So the first thing to happen is an outside security firm's been appointed but there's also some big news coming about particle physics.'

'Wow, my field, what sort of news?'

'Well, it seems an American billionaire who studied at the College in his youth has been in talks with the University about making a big gift for research and they've persuaded him to have a press conference to announce it. Not sure where or when but sometime soon. They think it'll help to improve the College's image to have some positive news like that.'

'Yes I bet they're right. News media have a short attention span. Inspector Kennedy says he got dozens of calls from reporters on Monday and Tuesday but it's dwindled to a handful now and apparently the press corps that was outside the hospital has more or less gone.'

'There's one more thing he said for what it's worth. He's not on the College Council but he picked up from the Head Porter, who knows everything that's going on, that bids were invited from outside security firms at least a month ago and that Saturday was a kind of open day for the bidders to have a final look around before submitting their proposals. There were ten security experts in the College at the time of the shooting.'

'So... a security expert could have been the shooter?'

'Just what I asked Hamid and he said he wasn't suggesting anything but he wanted to be sure the police knew. Oh, and the firm chosen yesterday wasn't the lowest bidder.'

Emily walked along the corridor at once to tell Jack.

'Interesting,' he said. 'Let's add Hamid and Nabeela to the list of people to talk to when we get out of here.'

'It's all getting a bit strange, though. You remember just before the shooting we talked about quantum entanglement while we were wondering how the bed mystery happened?'

Jack nodded.

'So suddenly particle physics pops up in the same place we were shot. Coincidence or is there a connection?'

'I see what you mean, but you said yourself probably no-one's applied it to whole human beings or even objects. On the principle that the simplest explanation is the most likely, it's probably a coincidence, but let's check it out when we can.'

'I'll try to find out what Professor Hinkles knows about entanglement research when I see him to sign the papers he mentioned.'

On Friday morning Mrs Wittingdale and Mr Ahmed said the two of them could leave the hospital on Saturday provided they came back for checkups on Wednesdays for the next three weeks. Jack's new phone arrived and he called work for the first time since the shooting. His boss had, of course, heard about it and wasn't surprised when Jack said he wanted to hand in his notice.

'I need time to recover and take stock,' he added.

He would receive sick pay until the end of the month and papers would be sent on by post. Feeling pleased he'd finally done something instead of just hanging around in hospital, he discussed the next move with Emily.

'I don't think I'll go back to London,' he said. 'I've nothing much to take me there now I don't have a job and I thought I might stay here in Cambridge for a bit. I wonder what you think about the two of us sharing a house or a flat. I think we could afford it and we could look out for each other. Inspector Kennedy's nearby too.'

'Oh so you want to keep tabs on me in case I solve the bed mystery first or try to have you shot?'

'No...' he started to protest until he saw her grin and laughed.

'It's a great idea,' she continued. 'I feel a lot safer when I'm not alone and neither of us wants to go back to our parents because it'd be too difficult to explain what we have to do. They may want to know how we can afford it, though.'

When DI Kennedy called in he had an answer.

'We have a police safe house near the rail station and I'd like to suggest you go there for now. It'd be easier for us to keep an eye on you than if you rented somewhere. Just until we've got to the bottom of this mess.'

It was an ideal solution. Reassuring and easy to explain to their parents. Emily also told the Inspector what Hamid had told Bina about security experts being in the College on Saturday.

'Well, well,' he said, 'I've interviewed a lot of senior academic and College staff, including the Master, but no-one's mentioned it. I'll have another go. Thank you for telling me.'

The Inspector said he was having Saturday off but would send someone to pick them up. As expected, their parents liked the safe house idea and didn't try to persuade them to go home. By late morning on Saturday, discharge letters had been issued, pills provided by the pharmacy, and Jack and Emily found themselves standing at the entrance ready to leave. The weather was bright but cold. After a short wait a police car drove up and a policewoman got out.

'You must be Emily and Jack,' she said, holding out her hand. 'I'm Donna. I met your friends a few days ago.'

She was roughly the same height as Emily, but stockier, with short cropped auburn hair.

'Really pleased to meet you, Donna,' said Emily, Jack echoing. 'Your reputation precedes you. Dil, Lucy and Bina were singing your praises, how you got them out of trouble.'

Donna blushed a little and smiled. 'Just doing my job. Hope we have a less eventful trip today.'

They were about to get into the car when a young black woman in a yellow puffer jacket and blue beanie ran up holding out a microphone, pursued by a man with a camera on his shoulder.

'Emily and Jack, Indigo Charles, BBC East, how are you feeling after your dreadful ordeal?'

'Oh, ok,' they said in unison, caught off guard.

'Are you satisfied with how the police are handling the case? Some people are saying they should have made an arrest by now.'

Jack was surprised at the question and saw that Donna was irritated.

'Inspector Kennedy and his team have been great,' he said.

'What leads do they have?'

'Hi Indigo, you'll have to ask him about that,' said Donna.

'Oh, hi Donna. We saw Inspector Kennedy chasing a man from the hospital on Sunday. Is it true an intruder tried to get past the police guard?'

'Don't know where that came from,' said Emily instinctively before Donna could speak. 'but if you'll excuse us this is the first time we've been outside for a week and it's chilly here.'

She stepped into the car and Jack got in after.

'Yes of course, sorry. Thank you,' said Indigo as they closed the door.

'Well done, Emily,' said Donna. 'I know Indigo from school and she's ok, doing well with the BBC, but she's driven to being pushy because of pressure to get a story. Nothing she'd like better than a *Victims Criticise Police* or *Intruder Threatens Victim* piece on the evening news.'

Their first stop was Chesterton Road to pick up Emily's clothes and other belongings. They stopped outside the house on double yellow lines.

'One of the perks of the job,' Donna chuckled.

With Jack and Donna to help it didn't take Emily long to pack her stuff into a suitcase and a cardboard box and in less than half an hour they were heading back to town. The safe house was a Victorian terrace of pale yellow brick on Tenison Road. Inside it felt solid and dependable with thick walls. Downstairs there was a spacious living room at the front and a dining kitchen at the back with french doors to a small garden. Upstairs were two bedrooms, one at the front with an ensuite bathroom and one at the back. Between were the house bathroom and a smaller room, now an office but presumably once a bedroom.

'Ok, here's the briefing,' said Donna. 'Doors to the outside are specially strengthened, likewise the windows. All bulletproof. There are panic buttons in every room that will bring three police cars with armed police within three minutes. So please don't press one by mistake. And there's an explosion-proof panic room in the cellar, reached through the cupboard under the stairs. There's comms down there too and of course secure wi-fi everywhere inside plus CCTV in every room.'

'Except bathrooms,' she added, grinning, as she saw their expressions.

'Who watches?' asked Emily, thinking it was like Big Brother and not sure she liked it.

'Don't worry. We haven't enough staff to sit watching empty rooms. It's monitored by AI and only flagged if there's something unusual, like an extra person in the house or one of you missing or sudden movements or noise.'

'Oh so there's microphones as well?' Jack asked.

'Yes, but no-one's listening in. Loud sounds or shouting set off a visual warning at HQ.'

Despite Donna's reassurance Jack felt uncomfortable with the surveillance and a glance at Emily told him she felt the same. Still, it was for their protection so he supposed they could tolerate it for now.

'Are we allowed to go out?' Emily asked.

'You can go into the garden – it's not big but there's a reinforced fence round it and CCTV, of course. If you want to go out of the house for shopping or a walk or anything, I'll need to come with you which I'll be happy to do. In plain clothes, of course. It'll make a pleasant change from deskwork or traffic duties. I've been assigned as your minder for now.'

'What if we see a neighbour?' asked Jack.

'They know the house belongs to the police. The story is that it's for police from around the country who come to the University for criminology courses. It's not used much actually. Right, I've to go back to HQ so I'll leave you to it. It'd be good if you stayed put for the rest of the day. Inspector Kennedy might pop in but don't let anyone else in. There's a peep hole in the door. Food in the freezer and fridge but when it's gone it's gone and you'll have to pay for your own. Feel free to order deliveries.'

They exchanged numbers and she left. They both felt tired but also needed lunch so they looked in the fridge and there was plenty of stuff to make sandwiches, plus fresh fruit and vegetables. Also some ready meals in the freezer. After eating they both rested in their rooms because Emily had a headache and Jack's wounds were hurting, reminders that they were still recovering. Jack suggested Emily took the front bedroom with its own bathroom and he took the back.

23
Progress

In the late afternoon, Jack went downstairs to make a cup of tea and Emily joined him a few minutes later.

'So what now?' Emily asked. 'Living here's safe but it's like being in a goldfish bowl prison. We can't even go out on our own.'

'True but for now I'm not sure I'd want to be anywhere else. We'll find our own place as soon as we're fit so we can get on with our job.'

Time there passed pleasantly enough. Every morning they took a long walk with Donna, often ending in a pub lunch, but without alcohol because the doctors had forbidden it. In the afternoons and evenings they read or watched TV. In a way it was boring but also therapeutic and gradually they regained strength.

DI Kennedy called in occasionally to update them on the investigation and after three weeks came for a more thorough summary.

Meticulous searches of the room where the shots had come from had recovered hairs and minute flakes of skin but the DNA related only to recent student occupants, as did fingerprints, and they could all account for their whereabouts at the time of the shooting. There was no CCTV in the College and although representatives of security firms were there on that day they had all either been interviewed, or given a written account, about their movements at the time of the shooting and all appeared to have solid alibis.

'The black SUV's are proving elusive, too. They could have gone anywhere,' said the Inspector. 'We asked to see satellite footage of the day of the shooting and the day your friends were chased but requests take ages to go through channels because the satellites are either EU or American military so we don't have much priority. Anyway they've both replied that their satellites were looking elsewhere at the relevant times.'

'What about SUV suppliers?' Jack asked.

'No luck yet. They're a make and model used widely by governments, security firms, large companies and even well-off individuals, more than a thousand in the UK. We're plodding through contacting the owners of all of them but that and our checks with repairers nationwide have so far drawn a blank. We're checking with motor insurance companies too but no result so far.'

'What about the bogus doctor?' Emily asked.

'Again, no progress. Neither Bina nor anyone can identify him from national police records. We followed him on CCTV until he merged into crowds in the town centre and disappeared. There's all sorts of nooks and alleys without CCTV in a town as old as this. He's probably long gone. How are you two doing?'

'Feeling stronger every day,' said Jack, 'and hoping the doctors will sign us off soon. At which point we'll want to get on with our lives and leave this house, grateful though we are that you've provided it for us.'

'I feared you'd get round to that eventually but do remember that someone out there wanted you both dead and we've no reason to suppose they've changed their mind.'

'We know,' said Emily, stroking her head wound, still covered by a dressing, 'but we don't think we'll find out who by hunkering down here, away from the world. And we've got jobs and careers to get on with.'

The Inspector sighed. 'I understand. Where are you thinking of going?'

'Well, for me probably staying here in Cambridge because of my PhD.'

She told him about the postponement.

'The attack's made me rethink my priorities,' said Jack, 'and I wasn't enjoying my job in London so I've decided not to go back to it and maybe stay here too, look for something I really want to do. In fact Em and I have been talking about sharing a flat or house.'

'Oh, I didn't realise the two of you were...I mean are...' He looked uncomfortable.

'An item?' Emily grinned. 'No we're not but we've been friends for years and we could look out for each other. Also we know where to find you if we need to.'

The following Wednesday at the hospital Mr Ahmed told Jack there was no need for him to come back weekly unless he developed symptoms or pains he was worried about. As it was over four weeks since the operation and both wounds were well healed, the next check-up, probably a final one, would be in a month. He said Jack could start going back to the gym and running or swimming again provided he took it gently at first. Jack was elated. He'd been feeling much stronger in the previous few days with hardly any pain from the wound and was glad his own assessment of himself accorded with the surgeon's.

Emily's wound had healed well and the headaches were less frequent and painful. Her hair was growing back too.

'But,' Mrs Wittingdale said, 'your brain's had a significant trauma and the swelling will take a few more weeks to subside completely so you may continue to have some minor effects for a while. I suggest you come back in a month unless anything crops up before then that you'd like to talk about.'

'That's great,' said Emily. 'This last week or so I've been feeling much stronger but you're obviously right about minor effects because I've been having a recurrent dream in the small hours...well more hearing something really, like marbles rolling round on a hard surface. It's like I'm awake but everything's black and there's just the sound. You didn't leave any marbles in my skull by any chance?'

They laughed as Mrs Wittingdale shook her head. 'Well I've never heard a patient describe an hallucination, because that's what I think it is, quite like that but every brain's different and visions, or rather dreams, and sounds are common after-effects of surgery like you've had. I've heard people report music, monkey chattering, explosions, even voices.'

Donna was waiting outside to take them back to the house but they both felt upbeat after seeing the surgeons and more like celebrating than going back to their domestic incarceration, as they had come to view it. They were still off alcohol and it was mid-afternoon so Donna suggested a posh afternoon tea at the Cambridge House, an upmarket city centre hotel.

'If you can afford it,' she added.

'Let's do it even if we can't,' said Emily, grinning wickedly. 'I feel like a bit of pampering with cream cakes. Great idea, Donna, I hope you'll be our guest.'

She and Jack knew they could afford it.

24
Bina

Emily continued to keep in touch with Lucy and Bina, passing on news of the successful hospital check-ups, adding that now she and Jack felt almost fully recovered they hoped they would soon be able to move out of semi-imprisonment of the police house.

Yay, Lucy messaged. *You tough + have reinforced head now. All good here. Keep us posted. xxx.*

Gr8!!!, Bina had sent. *Careful though. No police progress yet. Feel a bit locked up here too. xxx*

Although not living in a police house Bina understood why Emily and Jack would want to leave it as soon as they could. DI Audrey had arranged police protection for her but not the same kind, as it had to be discreet. She lived in a rented one-bedroom flat on the first floor of a three storey converted Victorian terrace house. Anything as obvious as a minder sitting outside her door would have had the neighbours' grapevine buzzing in minutes and raised all sorts of questions about why. In any case police budgets wouldn't stretch to it so other solutions were found. Her doors and windows were quickly and discreetly strengthened and made bullet proof. A small internal panic room was installed with full communication to the outside world, together with an alarm that would bring, as with Jack and Emily, armed police within three minutes.

Away from the flat at work or elsewhere, and travelling, she wore a tracker watch with a radio alarm that would summon armed police like the one at home. It even worked on the underground. It was reassuring but, as DI Audrey pointed out, she could still be shot at or attacked when outside so it was advisable to stay in the flat as much as possible.

DI Audrey had also advised her to vary her routes to work or other places she visited regularly but there were only a limited number of alternatives that would get her there. The effect of everything was to make Bina feel stifled and somewhat cut off from the world. The Inspector had also advised her to take self-defence classes but Bina was able to reassure her on that score.

'I'm a small woman of Asian heritage – three reasons I'm vulnerable to bullies and bigots – and like many others I've suffered sexist and racist behaviour all my life in this so-called liberal country of ours. So when I was a teenager my Dad encouraged me to keep fit and learn karate, which I did, and I entered local competitions. Eventually I made the Uni karate team and in my final year we won the national championships. Still go to the local karate club.'

The morning after she'd had the optimistic messages from Emily she took the tube to Moorgate on the way to work and, as she often did, called for a cappuccino to take out from a small coffee shop round the corner from her office. There was a short queue but the regular barista, Dan, wasn't there. Instead it was a square-featured middle aged woman with straight dark hair tied back in a bun who she hadn't seen before.

'Cappuccino please,' she said when she got to the counter. 'Dan not well?'

'He's out back.'

Reflected in the chrome of the coffee machine she saw a man behind her closing the shop door from the inside, which was unusual because there were always plenty of customers at that time of day and usually a queue. Now that the person in front of her had left she was alone in the shop with whoever the man was and the woman making her coffee.

Hairs on the back of her neck began to rise as she saw a distorted reflection of the man approaching her and she knew she was under attack. In a split second she turned round, pressed the alarm button on her watch and dropped to a crouch. The man wore jeans and a green hoodie and was unmistakably the man who knocked Lucy over while running from the hospital. He was clearly surprised by her manoeuvre and began to stoop to grab her but she punched his groin with as much force as she could and he paused, gasping in pain. She launched herself towards the door like a sprinter off the blocks and yanked it open as the man gathered himself and pursued. A short, older woman in a dark blue trouser suit who was just about to come in stood aside to let her pass then stuck out a foot so the man tripped and fell.

Before he could get up Bina delved into her bag for a rape alarm she always carried. She had often rehearsed in her mind using it but had never needed to before. It was deafening and passers-by immediately cleared away to avoid it. She now saw that the attacker had a silenced gun in his hand and was nearly standing up again. The other woman unexpectedly launched herself at his knees from behind, flattening him again, face down. Bina ran back to join the attack and put all her weight onto his shoulders with her knees, to cries from the crowd of 'He's got a gun'. Most ran away but two young men in dark grey business suits ran forward and one stood on his gun arm with one foot while stamping repeatedly on his gun hand with the other until he let the weapon go. The second young man stood on the gunman's other arm.

Through the deafening rape alarm Bina could hear police sirens and looked back into the shop. The woman who had been at the counter had disappeared. Then she heard a crack from behind and screams from the crowd. Her attacker's head rolled to one side and he stopped struggling, blood seeping from a bullet wound behind an ear. She ducked and heard another shot that threw up splinters of concrete from the pavement beside her. A police car screeched to a halt, half on the kerb, and two policemen in body armour with guns jumped out, shouting to Bina and her helpers to lie face down on the ground. She glanced behind to see the woman from the counter running off along Moorgate, already almost lost in a throng of rush hour pedestrians.

DI Audrey was in the next police car to arrive, simultaneously with an ambulance.

'Can we turn that alarm off,' she shouted.

Bina complied as she, the two young men and the woman were herded into the coffee shop while paramedics worked on the man lying on the pavement. The Inspector told the four of them to wait while she went outside to secure the scene. She quickly had the whole area taped off as the paramedics continued but within a few minutes they declared the man dead. Scene of crime officers erected a tent over the body.

Bina had been fuelled by adrenalin during the attack but now realised the narrowness of her escape and began to feel dizzy and light-headed. She guessed the bullets were meant for her and she felt a flood of emotions. Horror at what might have happened, gratitude to the woman and two men who helped, disbelief that a man had just been killed, panic that she was on a hit list. She felt it overcoming her and tears began to flow.

'Sit here with me, dear,' said the woman, who looked to be in her fifties. 'Let me give you a hug and you have a good cry. It'll help. I've seen a lot of women who've been attacked but I don't often get the chance to fight back. I didn't want him to be killed, mind you, just taught a lesson, but goodness knows what would have happened if you hadn't got out of the shop.'

It turned out she worked in a women's refuge and from the doorway had seen the man advancing on Bina from behind, gun in hand. She said in her younger days she'd played rugby, which explained the tackle.

'Thank you,' Bina replied tearfully, and, looking up at the two young men added, 'and thank you to you two heroes as well. All three of you deserve a medal. You could have been killed.'

'Nah,' said one of the men, grinning. 'We had him outnumbered.'

DI Audrey came in looking grim.

'We've found the body of a man in the yard at the back. Shot. His wallet says his name's Daniel Charles Wimborne. Mean anything?'

Bina's heart lurched and couldn't speak.

'Steady,' said the woman, hugging her again.

'You know him?' the Inspector asked.

'The barista,' Bina sobbed. 'I see him nearly every morning.'

They made police statements one by one in an incident van outside. Bina insisted that she went last so the others could carry on to work as soon as possible and it gave her time to gather herself. The two attackers had been after her and it was bad enough that one of them had been killed but now she felt responsible for Dan's death. It bore down on her like a tonne weight. By the time it came to her turn to give a statement reporters with cameras were on the scene and DI Audrey told them that a man had been murdered on the street but the attacker, a woman, had got away. The police were now searching for her and anyone with information should get in touch.

Giving her account in the van, Bina was still in shock and horrified at the deaths.

'Listen,' said the Inspector 'It's dreadful that two men have lost their lives but you're not the one who killed them. The killer nearly got away with murdering Emily. He and his accomplice were out to murder you and the bullet he took was intended for you. Shed no tears for him. It's hard to accept, I know. The tragic fact that the barista was killed shows how far they were willing to go to get at you.'

'But,' said Bina, crying, 'I could have stopped going to the coffee shop when I knew I might be a target.'

'In which case they'd have found another way to reach you, putting other people at risk. I'll put you in touch with a counsellor. And by the way I'm impressed at your presence of mind at the beginning of the attack. Your karate training came in handy.'

'Well, a punch in the nuts isn't exactly karate,' she said.

25
Edith

'A catalogue of incompetence,' said the man on the phone.

'I know. I'm sorry. They were experienced operatives with a successful record. I don't understand what happened.'

'You told me you would handle it and you didn't. Our Principal is unhappy and is making other arrangements. There will be consequences.'

***

The shooting was mentioned on the national lunchtime news but Bina's name wasn't, so Emily and Jack were shocked when she phoned in the afternoon. They and Donna had just arrived back from a pub lunch and Emily put her on speaker to tell the whole story. By the time she had finished she was in tears again. They were all horrified.

'Oh my god, Bina,' said Donna. 'That's dreadful. You must be feeling awful.'

'Yes, awful, scared, angry, shaken, all over the place. Two people are dead because of me. Poor Dan, the barista, and then the killer, shot while I was sitting on him. It makes me feel both are my fault.'

'No they're not. Absolutely not. The guy you sat on tried to kill Emily and was out to kill you. He or the woman with him shot Dan. You're a victim here.'

'I suppose, but I still feel guilty.'

'Don't,' said Emily. 'Donna's right and for all we know he could be the one who shot at me and Jack.'

'Anyway,' Bina went on, 'I told my boss what

happened, and Dad, in case anything came on the news. He said I should go home for a bit but honestly I couldn't face it. He and Mum would make such a thing of it.'

'What did your boss say?'

'She was really nice, somewhat to my surprise. She's quite formidable on work issues but she said I should take some time off because there could be a delayed reaction and I'd need time to get over it. She didn't want me there unless I could give a hundred percent. Obviously I didn't tell her or Dad that someone was trying to kill me so they just think I was randomly caught up in something. Anyway, the outcome is I've got a month off that I don't know what to do with. DI Audrey suggested counselling.'

'Come here,' said Donna. 'You can help me look after these two and I can give you some counselling. I did a PTSD course last year. You'd be safer than in London or at home and you could tell your parents you're helping Emily and Jack. I'll have to clear it with the boss though.'

'Brilliant idea,' said Jack. 'You could give us a hand looking for a flat too.'

Bina didn't need much persuasion and DI Kennedy had no objection. In the meantime Jack had been in touch with his landlord in London and given notice to end his tenancy. Donna suggested she went with him by train to pack up his stuff and bring it to Cambridge and they could call for Bina on the way back. By Friday evening Bina had moved into the police house, sharing Emily's room.

Before Donna left for the night they sent out for a Chinese and sat comfortably round the kitchen table. Emily and Jack had been given a green light to have alcohol, in moderation, so they opened a bottle of wine.

'Just like normal people,' Bina said.

'We're all normal people,' Donna replied. 'It's just that

we've got caught up in some things without intending to. I see a lot of it in my line of work. Criminals and victims are ordinary folk on the whole, and I'd like to propose a toast to three of the nicest victims I've met.'

She held up her glass as the others laughed and clinked against it.

'And I'd like to propose a toast to the nicest plod and craziest driver I've ever met,' said Bina.

'Plod?' Donna shouted in mock anger but her cheeks coloured with a smile she couldn't hold back as they all laughed and clinked glasses again.

***

On Saturday morning Donna arrived with mail for Emily picked up from her old place on Chesterton Road. It was mainly spam but Emily found a handwritten envelope that was stiff, as though it contained a greetings card. It was an invitation.

St Peter's College, Cambridge
The Master and Fellows
Invite
Ms Emily Harrison
To dine in the Senior Combination Room
on Tuesday, 4th March
at 7pm
Dress Formal   RSVP

There was also a letter from The Master on his personal headed notepaper:

'Dear Ms Harrison,

The College Council and I are keenly aware of your unfortunate experience on The Backs last month and we are doing everything we can to help the police with their enquiries. Needless to say we are delighted to hear that your recovery is going well and we should very much like to meet you to assure you of our commitment to bringing those involved to justice. We therefore hope that you will feel able to accept the enclosed invitation. The Dinner will follow a press conference to announce a significant donation to the University by an alumnus of the College to fund research into particle physics, a field in which I am told you are interested. You are also welcome to attend this event, at 6pm in the College Hall.

Please feel free to bring a partner or friend with you. An indication in advance of whether or not you accept these invitations would be welcome. You can reach my office on the number above.

Yours sincerely
Sir Hector Blatchford
Master'

'Wow,' said Jack. 'You're moving in high circles.'

He, too, was looking a mail, retrieved from London.

'Jealous, eh?' Emily sniggered.

'What, have dinner with a bunch of fossilised academics?' Jack laughed. 'I'll be having an evening in with pizza and a movie. Now who's jealous?'

'Will you go?' Bina asked, looking over Emily's shoulder at the letter.

'Might be interesting. Nothing to wear though.'

'What about that dress you wore at the M.I.T. Ball last year? It looked great from the photos. The long lemony one.'

'Mm, yes it would just about do. I'll try it on. But I'll need a bodyguard.'

She looked at Donna and Bina but they shook their heads. Neither had anything suitable to wear.

'I bet Hamid will be there, though,' said Bina. 'I could ask him to keep an eye on you.'

But Donna had another idea. She nodded towards Jack and looked meaningfully at Emily and Bina. He noticed and ostentatiously ignored them, pretending to be concentrating hard on his own letters.

'Jack…' Emily started to say but he interrupted.

'Oh-oh, I've got one too.'

His invitation was the same as Emily's and the covering letter similar but omitting the part about being interested in particle physics.

'And it's next Tuesday,' he went on. 'Short notice.'

'Hmm, yes...but look, the letters are dated a couple of weeks ago. They've been waiting at our old places since then.'

Bina's phone rang.

'Ever heard of Mitzli?' DI Audrey asked. She spelt it out.

'No. Is it a clothes shop?'

'It's a Swiss security company, been operating in this country for twenty years or so. Big in corporate protection and private intelligence. Highly conservative and respectable. Very expensive. Only has top grade clients. The guy who was shot worked for them as a minder. I've spoken to his boss but apparently he'd been off sick for a couple of months with depression. Just wondered if by any chance you'd had any contact with the firm through work or something.'

'No, never. Are you saying his attacking Emily and me was caused by mental illness?'

'Not sure, could be.'

'Sounds a bit unlikely. Just a minute, I'll ask the others.'

But they hadn't heard of Mitzli either. She put the phone on speaker.

'It was a longshot but thought I'd better check. His gun was unregistered and untraceable. Typical hitman.'

Emily shuddered. 'And mental illness doesn't explain his female colleague.'

'We haven't been able to trace her. We didn't get a good enough shot from CCTV but we're appealing for witnesses who may have photos or video. There's a bit of interesting news though. Now we have a photo of the man, Inspector Kennedy ran a CCTV search in Cambridge and guess what? He was near St Peter's College about half an hour before the shooting.'

'So you think he did it?' said Jack.

'Almost certainly and that's not all. Guess which security firm won the St Peter's contract? Inspector Kennedy's just told me.'

They all guessed and Donna said it.

'Mitzli?'

'Right first time! I think we may be getting somewhere. I've borrowed some people from our cyber-crimes unit and they're delving at Mitzli's online profile and connections as a matter of urgency.'

'I wonder if Mitzli have a place near Cambridge those SUVs could have come from?' said Jack when she'd ended the call. 'If they're providing security to St Peter's, maybe they have a base here, or could be setting one up.'

'Nothing's coming up,' said Emily, already on her laptop.

Later in the morning Bina and Donna went out for a walk and, not long after, Jack's phone rang.

'Jack Wellington?' The voice of the man at the other end was slightly husky.

'Yes.'

'This is Jim King.'

The name and voice were familiar but for the moment he couldn't place it.

'Clarence & Thirkill.'

'Oh, yes. You were in New York.'

'That's right. Are you alone?'

'No Emily's here with me.'

They were in the sitting room with coffee. Emily had guessed who it was because of the mention of New York.

'I've some rather important news for the two of you.'

'Ok, I'll put you on speaker.'

'I'm afraid the news is bad as well as important,' Jim said. 'Edith's had an accident.'

'Oh dear, is she ok?' Emily asked.

'No.' Pause. 'I'm afraid she didn't survive.'

Jack and Emily were horrified.

Jim went on to say it was a freak hit and run while she was walking home from the station yesterday evening.

'A car went by too near the kerb and the police think one of its doors must either have been open or flew open as it passed. She was knocked over, had severe head injuries and died at the scene. They're still investigating of course but there was only one witness. He was about 50 metres away on the other side of the road, and thinks the car didn't stop but he heard a door slam. He was the one who found her and called the ambulance.'

'Did he get the car's number?' Emily asked.

'Apparently not and it was a residential street with no CCTV. They've got the make and model of the car but there's thousands like it.'

'What an awful thing to happen,' said Jack. 'Did she have a family?'

'Yes, a husband and teenage children, I think.'

'Tragic for them,' said Emily.

'Yes. I've had a quick look at the file but I need to check how she left things with you.'

Emily and Jack explained that they hadn't really begun the investigation arising from Mrs Barton's letter.

'We told her we'd be in touch when we had something to report but it could be a few months.'

'Right, as I'm the other executor I'll leave it with you to let me know when you have something. In the meantime can I just remind you about the NDA? There could be serious consequences if you told anyone else about what you're doing.'

'Yes we know that.'

'By the way, where's the original letter?'

Emily and Jack looked at each other. Something in Jim's tone or what he had said had raised an alarm bell in their minds. Emily still had the original in her bag.

'In a safe place,' she said.

Jim paused. 'Fine.'

'Why did I feel slightly threatened by that call?' Emily asked when it had ended.

'Mm, reminding us about the NDA and wanting to know where the original letter was. Also, if a close work colleague of mine had been killed last night I think I might feel more cut up about it than he sounded and when you mentioned the family he didn't sound at all sympathetic.'

'No he didn't. I'm building up a picture of a rather cold, controlling character. And d'you remember when we met Edith at her office Jim said the partner who'd drawn up Mrs Barton's will had since died? Partners in that firm seem to have a high mortality rate.'

'Meaning their deaths may not have been accidental?'

'It's a bit far-fetched...but a few weeks ago I'd have said it was far-fetched that someone would try to murder us.'

They talked until the others came back and agreed they felt well enough to start the investigation. The first step was to move out of the police house and away from surveillance as soon as possible.

26
Entanglement

On Monday morning, after Emily and Jack had phoned their acceptance to the dinner and press reception, Emily decided to visit Professor Hinkles to pick up her work stuff from the Mott building and sign the papers he had mentioned. Jack knew she'd quietly pump him about quantum entanglement research.

'I'll ask Donna to come with me as minder,' she said. 'You could have a look online for a place for us to live.'

'Actually I've looked at a few already,' said Bina.

'Oo, show me,' said Emily as Bina opened her laptop on the kitchen table.

'I found two houses and two flats that might do.'

They spent some time looking at the details and narrowed it down to a flat and a house. Jack and Bina would try to view both.

'Wow, look at the rents, though,' said Donna. 'Huge.'

'Yes, but let's look anyway. They might be willing to negotiate,' said Jack, not wanting to say that he and Emily could easily afford it on their respective double salaries.

***

It was cold and the sky looked heavy but Emily and Donna wrapped up well and walked to the Mott building. Emily had phoned ahead to check that Professor Hinkles was available to see her.

'I'll wait here outside the door,' said Donna when they reached his office.

'Hello,' said the Professor when Emily walked in. He

was sitting at an untidy desk. 'Here are the papers.'

He took them from a drawer and held them out with his characteristic long blink. Emily smiled inwardly at the lack of pleasantries. No 'come in and sit down'. No 'how do you feel and how are you recovering'. She moved a pile of papers from a chair and sat down anyway.

'Thank you,' she said.

'Sign in three places, marked with post-its.'

He looked down and continued his work in silence. Emily quickly read the four pages. They said exactly what he had led her to expect. She willingly signed and handed them back to him. She had discreetly to clear her throat to alert him to her holding them out for him.

'Oh, give them to my assistant. He'll make copies for you to take away. See you next October.'

He picked up a pen and looked down at his work again.

Obviously, the meeting's over, Emily thought, chuckling inwardly, but she didn't get up to go.

'Professor, where's work on quantum entanglement going on in this country?'

The Professor looked up at her and stared.

'Well, here, of course.'

'Really? That's exciting! In this building?'

'It's Professor Lambert and her team. Matter of fact I'm helping with the mathematics. Fascinating. Whole new way of looking at the universe and reality. I think they've actually entangled photons between here and London. It has tremendous implications for computing and a whole host of other things. But of course, you know that.'

He paused and stared out of the window in silence with a half-smile as though watching for photons flying past.

'When you come back, I'll see if you could help them.'

'Oh thank you, Professor. Are they leading the field.'

'I think so, but we keep hearing rumours of a private organisation, perhaps American, doing similar work. And there's an announcement about to be made at St Peter's College about an endowment for particle research. We've been wondering if the two are connected.'

'D'you think we'll ever get to the stage of moving objects or even humans?'

'Who knows? Could be. In fact, some of the rumours I mention are of people disappearing in one place and reappearing in another but they seem to be confined to wacky websites of the type that say the Americans faked the moon landing and aliens landed in Area 51. In reality I think we're decades away from teleporting, if ever.'

'I see. Well, thanks for seeing me Professor and I'm really grateful to you and the Faculty for allowing me to postpone the PhD. I'll look forward to October.'

But the Professor was already writing and not listening. Emily was intrigued by what he had said and wanted to share it with Jack as soon as she could speak to him alone but when she and Donna arrived back at the house he and Bina were excited after viewing the house and the flat.

'They're both great,' said Bina, 'but we think the flat has it by a small margin. It's in a new block near the old Addenbrooke's site, on the second floor so it's more secure than ground level. Open plan living area with two bedrooms and two bathrooms, fully furnished. Oh, and there's a small balcony and another room they call a study/snug that has a sofa bed.'

'What about the rent, though?' Donna asked.

'Yes, it's high,' said Jack, 'but I offered lower and he said he'd ask the owners and get back to me.'

'I don't think the boss'll be pleased,' said Donna.

She called him and he dropped in an hour later.

'I'm not keen because you're still in danger. I think DI Audrey's told you that the guy who was killed in London was the one who tried to kill Emily in hospital and almost certainly the one who shot her and Jack but we don't know if it was his idea or if he was hired to do it and if so by whom or why, or who his female accomplice is. So there could be further attempts on your lives. Having said that, I can't force you to stay here but anywhere else wouldn't be as safe. If you decide to move out I might have to ask you to sign a form that it's against police advice.

'What do you think?' Emily asked Jack and Bina.

'No-one knows how long it'll be before the risk of attack goes away, if it ever does,' said Jack. 'I can't spend the rest of my life in hiding and anyway we still don't know why someone wants you and I dead.'

'I can't stay in Cambridge because my job's in London,' said Bina. 'I'm only here for a month I feel much the same. If we haven't got to the bottom of things by the time I go back, I'll just have to carry on as best I can.'

'I agree, Inspector,' said Emily, 'but I'd feel a lot better if Donna could stay with us.'

'No problem for now but a lot depends on how investigations go here and in London. She can't babysit you indefinitely. Let's hope we can wrap the case up soon. After all, we've got two police forces on it now.'

'What's Inspector Audrey saying about Mrs Gregory?' Jack asked.

'Nothing. What should she be saying?'

'Well, about her being killed.'

The Inspector's jaw dropped and there was a moment's silence. Bina and Donna looked shocked too.

'Where did you hear that?' he asked.

'James King, a partner of hers, phoned Em and me on Saturday.'

'And you didn't think to tell me?' He sounded angry.

'No I, er, didn't. I suppose I thought Inspector Audrey would know and tell you. I'm sorry.'

'I need to know the details. I'll speak to her.'

'King said it was a freak hit and run,' said Emily.

The Inspector looked sceptical and gave a wry smile. He took his phone from his pocket and went outside to call DI Audrey.

'Amazingly,' he said when he rejoined them, 'DI Audrey's only just heard. It was reported Friday evening to the local police where Mrs Gregory lives, not City of London police, and the information was only picked up by chance in DI Audrey's team. It sounds like a tragic accident but we both agree that her connection to Jack and Emily reinforces the idea that the murder attempts on them are connected with the teacher's will.'

27
VIPs

Later that afternoon Jack heard from the flat's letting agent that the owner would accept his rent offer. He, Emily, Bina and Donna went round to the office straight away, paid two months' rent in advance and picked up the keys. By six o'clock they had moved out of the police house and into the flat, having signed the form that DI Kennedy had referred to.

Donna checked on security. The pedestrian entrance to the building required a key code and there was an intercom system for visitors. The basement parking garage, accessed down a ramp, required a key code too. There were five floors above ground with two flats on each floor, reached by a lift or a staircase to a small lobby. The doors of the flats faced each other across it, with peepholes and integral key-operated locks.

'It's not bad,' she told the others, 'but obviously don't let anyone in you don't recognise. The door's solid hardwood, so it should stop most bullets.'

The others looked shocked, visualising machine gun fire coming through the door, movie-style.

'It could happen,' said Donna, realising what they were thinking.

Despite that, Emily, Jack and Bina felt a sense of liberation at the absence of cameras and their mood was lighter as they and Donna went out shopping for food.

'I'll sleep on the sofa bed,' said Bina.

'No take a bedroom,' said Jack. 'I'll have the sofa bed.'

'Aw, thank you,' she said and stood on tiptoe to kiss him on the cheek. It made him blush.

***

In the evening when Donna had gone home and Bina to bed, Jack and Emily talked on their own. She told him about her meeting with Professor Hinkles. Jack was disappointed that he had said teleporting was decades away, if ever.

'He should know,' said Jack, 'but ten years ago we were moved somehow or other and I can't think of another explanation. At least he did say there were wacky rumours of more.'

'Yes and there's John Barton too, even before we were born. If it really is teleporting, someone's been sitting on a big secret for a very long time.'

***

The next morning Bina had a message from Hamid to ask if she'd like to go to the reception as his 'plus one'.

She phoned him. 'Surely Nabeela will be yours?'

'She could be but she's got an invitation in her own right, so she'll be there anyway and you're welcome to come with us. I believe your friend Donna may be invited as Nabeela's plus one, even though it may start College tongues wagging.'

He laughed loudly down the phone.

'Do them good,' he went on. 'Small-minded lot, some of them. Anyway, between us we should be able to protect your friends. And you. I hear you've had a nasty experience too.'

A few minutes later Donna had confirmation from DI Kennedy that Nabeela had requested her attendance and he had agreed.

'But I've never been to anything formal like this so I've no clothes that would be remotely suitable,' she said, looking worried.

Bina had, but back at her flat in London. Emily and Donna were similar sizes but on looking through what Emily had, could find nothing acceptable except the lemon dress Emily planned to wear herself.

Jack overheard. 'Students here usually hire or upcycle so there are good places in the town. Em and I can help with the cost because, after all, you're acting as our bodyguards.'

But they didn't need to because Bina had a word with her Dad who liked that she'd been invited to a formal dinner at a college and assumed it was through Nabeela so came up with money for her to buy a dress. It was quite enough for her and Donna to put outfits together by hiring and buying vintage. They spent a happy couple of hours in the town with Emily.

'I wish I had a Dad like that,' said Donna.

'He's actually quite restrictive,' said Bina, 'but I know which buttons to press.'

'You're evil,' Donna giggled.

Just before six o'clock, Nabeela and Hamid arrived in a large taxi to pick them up. They felt well dressed and hoped they looked cool, as though they went out like that most evenings. Even Jack wore a tuxedo and Emily made him brush his hair. It was only a few minutes' drive to the College main gate, from which Hamid led them to a cloakroom beside the College hall where they left their coats. There were security people checking arrivals with the guest list, wearing green uniforms with the name 'Mitzli' sewn on the lapel and a logo looking like two 'Y's side by side, one upside down.

'That green colour and the logo,' Emily whispered to Jack. 'Remind you of anything?'

Jack had noticed too. The attempted abduction after the bed mystery.

'No photography except press,' said a burly Mitzli man standing behind a table. 'Please leave cameras and phones here. I recommend you turn them off.'

He gave each of them a named bag. They were all surprised and Donna protested.

'I need to keep this with me,' she said, showing her police badge.

'Sorry Madam, those are our orders,' he said.

'I don't care. I'm not doing it. I'll call my Inspector.'

She started to dial and the man looked doubtful. 'Wait, I'll ask the boss.'

He referred to another green uniformed man behind, who then came forward.

'Are you on duty,' he asked.

'None of your business, but yes, I am. I'm minding these two who were shot in the College grounds.'

She indicated Jack and Emily. The man hesitated for a moment, then said. 'Ok, but they must leave their phones.'

Jack glanced at Emily, worried, but she gave a what-can-we-do shrug as they all, apart from Donna, put their phones in bags and left them on the table.

'Now I know why Pete's scared of you,' Bina giggled to Donna. 'I take it he doesn't mind you going out on your own like this?'

'Why should he?'

'Oh I thought you two...I mean aren't you...'

'Seeing him?' Donna giggled. 'Definitely not. He's a great guy and I love him to bits but he's not for me.'

'Ok,' said Bina with a smile.

Emily noticed an expression on Bina's face that she hadn't seen before.

Normally the hall was used for dining at long tables but they had been removed, apart from two across a platform at the far end. Rows of chairs faced it and the first few were obviously for press and TV, occupied by people with notebooks, recorders and cameras. Several photographers squatted on the floor in front of the platform and there were cameras on tripods wherever they could fit down the sides. Two people with TV cameras on their shoulders walked around, hovering here and there. The rows behind the news media were labelled for VIPs, which was where seats had been reserved for the Choudhry's party. A lot of other VIPs were already there and Jack guessed they were high-ups from other colleges and senior members of the academic community.

Despite living in Cambridge all her life, Donna hadn't been inside a college before and was awestruck by the sixteenth century hall's lofty style, ancient beams and panelling, the black and gold roof and the stained glass windows.

'Wow,' she said, 'This is fabulous, like Westminster Abbey and Hogwarts rolled into one.'

Bina had seen pictures and also been inside Inns of Court in London which were of similar vintage and style, but she was also impressed.

'It's pretty magnificent,' she said.

'Nearly all the colleges have grand halls where the fellows and undergraduates eat,' said Jack quietly, 'but I don't think they often have press conferences and when they do I don't think they normally choose the hall for it. Looks like St Peter's is pulling out a few stops, trying to impress.'

'Yes,' said Nabeela. 'This is very big for the Master and College Council. They want to squeeze every possible ounce of kudos and publicity from it.'

Nabeela and Hamid waved and chatted to colleagues and acquaintances as the seats gradually filled up. Emily, Bina and Donna realised they were the youngest women among the VIPs and needn't have worried about what to wear because the older ones, mainly academics not known for chic, wore a wide selection of outdated clothes, many that even in their day had lacked style, so they enjoyed clocking it all and giggling.

As six o'clock rang out from the College clock tower the Master and five other people walked in a line onto the platform from the Fellows' entrance at one side. They took their seats behind the table, each place laid out with a notepad, water and large name card. Feet shuffled and audience conversation died down. Cameras clicked and whirred. Jack and Emily noticed for the first time the name card of a man near the middle of the table. It read:

'James King,
Senior Partner
Clarence & Thirkill.'

28
Dil and Lucy

Lucy was as pleased as Dil about the audition when he got the email. It was for a part in a much-heralded new play to be staged at the West Yorkshire Playhouse in the spring. It wasn't a lead but it was a good speaking part. It would be his biggest break to date if he got it and a definite step up from one-liners in TV productions.

One of the many things she loved about him was his passion for the theatre. Actors were sometimes portrayed as delicate, over-emotional and selfish but Dil was nothing of the kind. He had a strong conviction that acting was the only thing he wanted to do. It was all he thought about, which often meant he forgot practical details of life, but delicate he was not. It needed hard work to put yourself out there seeking work, auditions, networking, ear to the ground, keeping going and being ready to be at your best at a moment's notice. There were hundreds of actors looking for jobs, all competent, energetic and well-trained. It needed strength of character to withstand not being chosen at auditions, seeing others do well. Rejection could bruise him internally, but after a setback he always got up and fought on. That's what she called grit.

'I'm only one audition away from the big time,' he would say, which could even be true.

In the meantime they were just happy to be together and making their way in the world. She enjoyed her work and it paid reasonably well. Between jobs he worked at a call centre and his supervisor seemed to have a soft spot for him – Lucy knew he was a charmer – so didn't mind when he took time off for auditions. Lucy gave him a big good luck kiss as they set off for work on Tuesday morning.

'Text or call me afterwards,' she said.

The auditions, in Leeds, started at four o'clock in the afternoon and Dil was very excited. He thought he had a good chance of getting the part and his strategy was to try to be the last or near to the last so his performance had more chance of being remembered. It went reasonably well, he thought, and he was back out on the street not long after six. His first thought was to call Lucy but it went to message. Probably her phone was muffled in her bag. She would call him back when she noticed. Talking to her was his way of validating everything he did. She always had a sensible comment or good advice. Just what he needed. He couldn't imagine life without her.

***

It was dusk when Lucy left her office on a small industrial estate in South Bradford, heading for a bus stop a short distance away. She went at a good pace because it was cold and, despite street lighting, she always felt vulnerable after dark. Halfway there she heard footsteps behind and a man walked abreast of her.

'Hi, Lucy,' he said.

She stopped and looked at him, momentarily alarmed, but recognised him at once.

'Billy?'

'The same. How are you?'

'Good, and you? Saw you at Mrs Barton's funeral.'

She had never liked him but felt she should be polite. He wasn't as tall as Dil and carried more weight. His fair hair was a little unkempt and she had always found his eyes unreadable. She knew Emily and Bina thought he was a creep. It was unusual to see him alone. At school he had always been with loutish friends.

'There's something I need to speak to you about,' he said. 'Could you spare me a few minutes – maybe have a coffee across the road?'

Lucy was surprised how polite he was and a little intrigued. She had never thought there could be anything of mutual interest between them but she had time, so why not? She would miss the five to six bus but they were every half hour and Dil wouldn't be back till later than usual.

'Ok.'

The Factory Café was on the ground floor of an old mill building nearby and was mainly a lunch venue, quiet at this time of day. They sat at the back, past the counter, and sipped cappuccinos. Billy didn't seem keen to start the conversation so Lucy made small talk, where he was living, the funeral and such. He still lived in Ilkley, he said, worked from home and was unmarried.

'So?' said Lucy after silence fell again.

He looked uncomfortable.

'It's about Emily and Jack. They're in danger.'

'Tell me something I don't know,' said Lucy. 'Someone tried to shoot them.'

'I know but it's not going to stop there. They've had the bad luck to become involved in something big that started about ten years ago, none of it their fault.'

'Why don't you talk to them?'

'I will, or a colleague will, but I also want to warn you. Any friend of theirs is at risk because these people are ruthless. Bina already knows that. They'll do anything to get Jack and Emily to do what they want.'

'How do you know this? Who do you work for?'

'SIS,' he said quietly, glancing round, as though for eavesdroppers.

Lucy had heard of it because Dil and she kept up with the latest spy thrillers, but she was sceptical.

'Oh really?' she said, giving him a look.

'You probably think I'm lying or a fantasist but please, be extra careful about your safety and Dil's and if you speak to Jack and Emily, tell them the same. I know I was rotten to all of you when we were at school and one day I'll explain but the truth is I've always admired how you, Dil, Emily, Jack and Bina have stuck together. The thing that happened ten years ago threatens all that and more.'

His phone buzzed and when he looked at it he said he had to go, so they got up and went outside. Lucy didn't know what to say so she just said, 'Thanks for the coffee,' and left him at the door. She headed for the bus stop, looking back once but couldn't see him in the gloom. She checked her phone at the stop and noticed Dil had called while she was in the café so she called him back.

'Hey, lover, how d'you get on?'

'Ok, I think but it's hard to judge really. I knew one of the director's assistants so that may help. I'll hear in about a week they say. Just on the way to the station.'

They chatted until he reached it and looked at the departure board so he could tell her when he'd be home.

'Oh and by the way,' she added just before they ended the call, 'you'll never guess who I met on the way to the bus stop – Billy Worth.'

'Billy? What was he doing there? I hope you gave him the kneegroining he deserves?'

'Actually no. He was quite civilised for once. He was worried about Emily and Jack. Something about something that happened ten years ago. Said we were all in danger. I'll tell you all about it when you get home.'

During the half-hour bus journey, she wondered whether or not to believe that Billy worked for SIS and why he was concerned for the safety of Emily and Jack, not to mention herself, Dil and Bina. And even more intriguing – what was it that had happened ten years ago?

Wait, she thought, *it must have been about ten years ago when Em was almost abducted from school after an exam and Jack saved her.*

As far as she knew the police had never found out who'd done it or why, but she smiled at the memory. Everyone had thought Emily and Jack must be together because of it but she and Bina were close to Em and knew they weren't. Although it had changed Em's attitude to him. She had barely acknowledged his existence before but afterwards seemed to look at him with new respect and, Lucy thought, perhaps something more.

When she got off the bus, she had a five minute walk to home, a Yorkshire stone Victorian terrace house on a quiet street. It was a good location with a nearby cluster of shops and cafés. Across the road, behind a low wall, was a park that gave the house a nice outlook in daylight. About a hundred metres from her gate she noticed two men standing near it but they didn't look threatening. One was on the phone and kept breaking off to speak to the other, pass a message maybe. As she reached the gate the call ended and they walked towards her.

'Excuse me,' said one.

He was clean shaven with a dark overcoat and grey beanie.

'Yes.'

'Do you live here?'

'Yes, why?'

'Are you Mrs Akhtar, then?

'Yes.'

'We'd like a word with you,' said the other man.

He wore jeans and a navy car coat and had ginger hair and beard. Something in the way he spoke sent a shiver down Lucy's spine and she decided she definitely didn't want a word with them. She turned into her gate and tried to shut it after her, fumbling for her key and intending to make a dash for the door, but Ginger was too quick for her. He grabbed her from behind and as she took in a breath to scream he put a hand over her mouth and nose so she couldn't. A black SUV screeched to a halt at the kerb. Ginger lifted her off the ground, Overcoat took her feet and they bundled her, kicking and bucking, into the back.

29
Dinner

The Master opened the press conference in conventional style by welcoming everyone, thanking them for coming and introducing those on the platform. The President and Vice President of the College Council, both elderly men, were at either end of the table, in full academic regalia like the Master. On the Master's right was Robert C. Anderson, who he described as an entrepreneur, Chairman of The Anderson Foundation and alumnus of the College. Applause rippled round the audience but Jack, Emily and the others hadn't heard of him. A woman with greying hair in a well cut dark grey suit on the master's left was introduced as Mrs Rhona Latimer, Minister of State for Universities, Science, Research and Innovation.

'What a mouthful,' Donna chortled quietly. 'I've seen her on TV.'

The final person the Master introduced was James King, 'whose wise counsel has guided the College and the Foundation in discussions leading to this important day.'

'Now,' he went on, 'to business. It is my very great pleasure to announce that those discussions have come to fruition and Mr Anderson will now outline his magnificently generous plans that have, I need hardly add, been unanimously accepted by the College Council. Mr Anderson.'

The Master sat down and Mr Anderson stood up to applause. He was a tall, tanned elderly man with grey hair, who Emily guessed to be in his seventies, but well preserved for his age, wearing a tuxedo and red bow tie. He spoke with a refined American accent, probably from the Boston area. She had tuned in to American accents during her time at M.I.T. It made Jack think of a recording he had heard of John F. Kennedy, the famous US President assassinated in the sixties.

Mr Anderson spoke for some time, first recalling his time at the College over fifty years ago, paid for by a scholarship, recounting amusing incidents and about his passion for advanced physics. Then how jobs in that field were so poorly paid in both the UK and the USA after he graduated that they wouldn't even cover rent, let alone food. So he took a lowly job at an insurance company in Boston, progressed, and later created a successful reinsurance business in New York. He explained that reinsurance was used by insurance companies who wished to share risks they had taken on.

'Life was kind to me,' he went on. 'I worked hard and made a lot of money but I'm not from a wealthy background. My parents were farm workers in rural New England and lived a hand-to-mouth existence, especially during the harsh winters, often going without so that my sister and I could eat. They couldn't afford to send us to the village school but luckily the owners of the farm where they worked had no children and kindly arranged for us to attend, in return for extra work from my father on Sundays. So I know what poverty is and that education can lift people up, which is why I have resolved to make an endowment to Cambridge University, to be administered by the Council of this College. The main object of the endowment is to advance understanding of particle physics and to provide research opportunities for scientists from humble backgrounds. The initial endowment will be one hundred million pounds.'

Gasps went round the hall and reporters stood up shouting questions. A hum of comments and surprise buzzed through the audience. Cameramen reacted like mosquitos heading in a swarm towards Mr Anderson but the Master stood up and raised both arms for quiet.

'Please, please,' he said, eventually making himself heard. 'please...I know it's a huge endowment. We'll answer all the questions but please be patient.'

Gradually the hall quietened and Mr Anderson remained standing.

'Before I answer questions,' he said, 'I too would like to pay tribute to James King for his guidance and advice. You might think it would be easy to give money away but that's far from the truth.' He chuckled. 'Believe me it's a legal and political minefield, and Jim has expertly guided us through it. I should also like to express my gratitude to Mrs Latimer for opening government doors and supporting our plans.'

Mrs Latimer swelled and beamed to a round of applause as Mr Anderson sat down.

'Wow, a lot of money,' said Jack into Emily's ear. 'And Jim King heavily involved.'

Emily's suspicious expression said it all. Jim King made a short but gracious speech saying what a privilege it had been to be a midwife in the birth of such an ambitious plan. Listening to his residual accent again, Jack was more convinced than ever that it was Yorkshire, possibly even his own home town, Bradford.

There were no more surprise announcements. Mrs Latimer, obviously a consummate politician, made a speech of platitudes, hinting, without actually saying so, that the endowment was more or less her idea and that she alone was responsible for it. Some of the audience of independent-minded academics groaned quietly and even Mr Anderson and the Master looked surprised. She clearly had no insight into how her speech was being received – or didn't care because her photo in the news was assured.

Questions from news media followed but added little to the announcement except that the College would be making land near Queens Road available for the building of a large new research facility to be called the Anderson Particle Centre.

When the press conference was over and the Master and the platform party withdrew, Hamid led Emily, Jack and the others through the Fellows' entrance beside the platform and up a wide, and obviously ancient, oak staircase. After a further security check at the top they were allowed into the Senior Combination Room.

It was like stepping back in time. A long, low oak panelled room with leaded windows and an elaborate moulded plaster ceiling. Down the centre of the room, almost as far as the eye could see, was a table laid for a formal dinner with silverware, sparkling glasses and crisp white napkins folded in the shape of a swan. Perhaps the most remarkable aspect was the lighting, entirely candles, in dual holders on the walls and crystal candlesticks along the table. Jack, Emily, Bina and Donna stopped inside the doorway, awestruck. It was a picture of opulence but the low lighting made it intimate and cosy.

'Lovely, isn't it?' said Hamid. 'The room was created in the mid-sixteen-hundreds and hasn't changed much since. There's not even any electrical wiring. It's over forty metres long and the table can comfortably seat upwards of fifty people.'

They found themselves in a queue of people being greeted by the Master and those who had been on the platform at the press conference. Hamid shook hands with the Master who of course he knew well and introduced Bina. Nabeela, who also knew the master went next with Donna. The Master responded with welcoming words to them all and passed them to the next person in line. Then it was Emily and Jack's turn. They introduced themselves and shook hands.

'So glad you could come,' he said, 'and so pleased to see you looking well. I can't tell you how upset I and the whole College have been at the dreadful happening. How're the police getting on with the investigation?'

'They're putting a lot of work into it,' said Jack, 'but no arrests yet.'

'I believe you're living in Cambridge at present.'

'Yes,' said Emily. 'I was living here already, before the shooting, doing a PhD, and the powers-that-be have very kindly suggested I postpone to next year, so rather than move somewhere else until October I'm staying.'

'I was working in London but the shooting's made me re-assess my life,' said Jack, 'so I'm thinking I'll stay here and decide what to do next. I know the place well.'

'Ah yes, of course you're a graduate of the University, aren't you.'

He looked over their shoulders and saw people backing up behind them.

'Well, we'd better not cause a blockage here. I hope you have a nice evening. I know Mr Anderson is keen to speak to you both.'

They moved on to meet the President and Vice President of the Council who simply shook hands and said welcome.

'And who are you?' Mrs Latimer asked imperiously, next in line.

'Oh the shooting. Dreadful, dreadful,' she said when they told her. 'Can't think what the police spend their time on these days.'

Her eyes were already moving to the person following them.

Mr Anderson was next. He gripped their hands one after the other and shook them for a long time, looking them in the eye and nodding with what they took to be sincerity.

'I can't tell you what a great pleasure it is to meet you both. Such an awful incident. I hope they get whoever was responsible.'

Jack felt 'incident' didn't quite do justice to what happened. Emily felt there was something hollow about his effusive manner.

'So do we,' she said, boldly returning his gaze for a little longer than would be normal.

He paused for less than a second. 'I believe you have an interest in particle physics. Maybe we could talk later. There could be opportunities coming up.'

'Fine,' said Emily.

There was no-one else to shake hands with and as they re-joined their friends, standing close by, a waiter offered glasses of champagne from a silver tray.

'Mr Anderson seems sincere,' said Nabeela, 'Knows what it is to be poor and learned from it but I'd like to know more about him. Billionaires sometimes have strange motivations. Not keen on Mrs Latimer, though. I've met her a couple of times before but she never remembers me.' She chuckled. 'I think she only remembers people who can advance her career.'

Emily and Jack had reservations about both of them. Donna and Bina wandered off to look round the room and the Choudhrys greeted colleagues, so Jack and Emily were left alone.

'Something about Anderson I didn't like,' said Jack.

'Same here. Hard to put your finger on but…'

'Jim King,' said a man thrusting a hand towards them. 'Pleased to meet you at last.'

He was tall and slim, dark hair greying at the temples, probably in his fifties. His voice was low and husky adding to an air of authority. Instead of a tuxedo he wore a dark suit, white shirt and red silk tie.

'I recognise you from your photos in the paper.'

'Hello,' said Jack, surprised but taking his hand. 'We saw you on the platform. What a terrible thing about Edith and yet another problem for the firm.'

'Another?' he said sharply. 'What do you mean?'

'The fire.'

'Oh yes I see. You're right, Edith is a great loss.'

'Yes,' said Emily. 'How are her family coping?'

'I haven't met them myself,' he said, sounding vague, 'but I know we're doing everything we can to help them.'

'Do you know when the funeral will be, and where?'

'Not yet, early days. I'll get my secretary to keep you informed.'

'Thank you, we'd like to pay our respects.'

'Mr Anderson would like a chat and has asked me to set something up. Could the four of us have a quick word right now? There's a private room near the top of the stairs.'

He led Emily and Jack back past the greeting line, where the last few guests were shaking hands, to a small room across a landing from the Senior Combination

Room. There was a table with chairs around it. Shadows danced from candlelight flickering in draughts from the door. Mr Anderson appeared almost at once.

'I'll be brief,' he said as they sat down, 'because the Master will be calling us to table in a moment. You're just the sort of people I'd like to have working at the new Research Centre and I'd like to hire you right away. Emily, your chosen field is exactly in line with the Centre's ambitions and Jack, artificial intelligence is going to be at the heart of every scientific and social development of the twenty-first century. Now here's the thing. I understand from Jim here that you two have something on that's connected with a deceased client of Jim's firm. Obviously he can't tell me about it but I'd rather you weren't involved in that because I want your full attention from now on. So this is what I suggest. Stop what you're doing and come work for the Anderson Foundation, which is the body making the investment in Cambridge. I'll pay you what you're receiving now plus a hello payment of a hundred thousand pounds each. Naturally you'll have the standard benefits of Foundation employees, pension plan, health insurance, car allowance and so on. You can carry on living right here in Cambridge but we may want you to travel to the USA and other countries. What do you say?'

Jack and Emily didn't know what to say. They were speechless, but also suspicious.

'Well,' said Emily, 'I don't know about Jack but you've rather taken my breath away. Thank you for a most generous and unexpected offer.'

Mr Anderson looked pleased as she paused and looked at Jack, trying to read him. She hoped he would agree with what she was about to say. The look in his eyes and the hang of his shoulders made her think he might.

'But,' she went on, 'as you say we've committed ourselves to something with Jim's firm and I for one would like to see it through before moving on. I think we owe it to the person who was the client of Jim's firm. She was a schoolteacher of ours and put her trust in us so I think we should respect it.'

'Yes,' said Jack. 'I feel the same. You've made us a dream offer and if it had come two months ago, I'd have jumped at it, but a lot has happened since then and like Em I'd like to stick to what we've agreed. Could we maybe talk again in a year or so, perhaps even sooner?'

Emily guessed Anderson was a man who was used to getting his own way and thought she saw annoyance pass across his face.

'That's commendable loyalty,' he said with a smile that lacked warmth. 'Jim, how do they stand legally? Are they committed to carry on with whatever it is?'

'No, as sole executor of the will in question I can say with complete authority that there will be no consequences for them if they stop what they said they would do. There was no compulsion on them under the will. They're free to accept your offer.'

'So what do you say Emily and Jack?' Mr Anderson asked. 'I can't guarantee the terms will be so generous if we postpone.'

Emily glanced at Jack again, looking for clues as to what he was thinking. His head was imperceptibly tilted backwards so he was slightly looking down his nose at Anderson. It was clear he wasn't going to change his mind.

'Well, that's good to know,' she said, 'but I'm not thinking about legal obligations, so much as moral commitment. I think maybe the shooting has refocused our priorities.'

Jack agreed.

'I can understand that,' said Mr Anderson, 'and if that's your decision, I accept it, but think it over and you might change your mind in the next forty-eight hours. If so, let Jim know. He'll know where to find me. After that it'll be too late.'

He stood up.

'Nice meeting you and good luck,' he said.

Jack and Emily politely thanked him and Jim, shook hands and left the room. As they crossed the landing they thought they heard a burst of laughter through the closed door. They looked at each other in surprise and re-entered the Senior Combination Room as the Master tapped on a glass with a spoon to call everyone to the table.

***

Dil felt good after his talk with Lucy and was intrigued about her encounter with Billy Worth. It gave him something to think about as he waited for the train. Not long after it set off his phone rang. Lucy again. He didn't want to take the call in his seat – too many people listening – so he quickly stood up and walked to the end of the coach to be a little more private.

'Hey, Luce. Wassup?'

There was silence.

'Luce?'

'Dil, listen,' she sobbed, sounding frightened, desperate even. 'You have to do what they say...'

A man's voice came on the line.

'Mr Akhtar, tell your friends Jack and Emily to accept the offer or none of you will see your wife again. Same result if you involve the police.'

The line went dead.

30
Knife

Ginger produced a knife in the back seat of the SUV, his hand still over Lucy's nose and mouth. Overcoat had tied her wrists and ankles, despite her kicking and wriggling. Then he'd rummaged in her bag for her phone. The vehicle hadn't moved. It was surreal to see her own front door through the darkened windows. Like looking into another universe. Overcoat found the phone.

'Lock code?' he said.

She shook her head. Ginger tightened his grip on her face and held the knife where she could see it.

'I don't know how much it hurts poking an eye out, but most people I've done it to scream a lot.'

The point headed towards her left eye and instinctively she pushed back against the seat, trying to shout.

'Lock code?' Overcoat repeated but she stayed silent.

'Knife not sharp enough for you?' said Ginger. 'I'll just check.'

She felt a sting on the back of her ring finger and saw blood. She panicked and started struggling violently again. Ginger slapped her face hard with the hand that had covered her mouth and for a moment she was disorientated. Then she yelled. It wasn't a word or anything coherent. Just an expression of cold fear. These men were prepared to injure, maybe even kill and were obviously without human empathy. In the front seat the driver turned his short fat neck and bald head to look, leering.

'Shut up stupid bitch,' said Ginger and hit her again.

Part of her wanted to stand up to him, not react to what he did but she was hurting and couldn't stop tears.

'Lock code,' Overcoat said again, louder.

She knew if she did what they wanted there was no guarantee they wouldn't kill her because she'd seen their faces and would recognise them again. But it might buy some time for Dil to find her.

'80342.'

He entered it, looked at the screen and tapped to go to recent calls. Dil was top of the list.

'Tell him to do what I say or you'll be in trouble,' said Overcoat, as he called Dil and held the phone to her ear.

When Dil answered she couldn't speak. There was too big a gap between the reality happening now and the previous reality, just minutes ago. Ginger grabbed her hair with one hand and raised the other to hit her again. She found her voice.

When Overcoat ended the call she felt a sharp pain in the arm nearest Ginger and turned to see him injecting her through her coat. She tried to yell but nothing came out. The SUV engine started and the sound formed dark clouds in her mind. As they engulfed her, she wondered, in a detached way, if she'd been killed.

***

Dil stood, frantic, at the end of the carriage as the train rattled its way to Bradford. What was going on? Was it a practical joke? He desperately hoped it was and if so, that Lucy was in on it and acting well because she sounded very frightened. But she had never been a good actor. He could always read her face and voice. The alternative, that she had been kidnapped, was too awful to think about. Where was she? Ah, he remembered they shared their locations with each other on their phones. He quickly looked. She was at home! Maybe it *was* all a hoax, but it certainly hadn't sounded like it. The man had mentioned Jack and Emily. He dialled Jack. It rang several times and went to message.

'Jack, please call me as soon as you get this. Something's happened to Lucy.'

He called Emily and Bina. They didn't answer either and he left similar messages. His next instinct, apart from wailing with fright or shouting in frustration, was to call the police. But the man had said he wouldn't see Lucy again if he did. So what now?

He was shaking and in a sweat. The horror Lucy must be going through made him feel sick, and he retched, almost threw up. A passenger standing nearby looked at him, alarmed, and took a step back but Dil didn't notice. He looked at his phone again. There must be something he could do, someone he could call, but who? His mind was blank with fear and he stood staring out of the window with unseeing eyes. He must go home. That was the only thing to do. There remained a whisker of hope that he'd arrive to find Lucy laughing at the joke that wasn't a joke but he knew it wasn't going to happen.

He went back to his seat and looked at Lucy's location on his phone again. It was still home, but when he zoomed in, it seemed like it was just outside the house. He tapped 'refresh' but her location didn't update. It just said she was there six minutes ago, the time of the phone call. No doubt the kidnappers would have turned it off so she couldn't be traced but he would have to find her. She would be depending on him.

On top of the horror, he began to feel angry. At the kidnappers, at Jack and Emily, and at Billy who had warned that she was in danger. Was he in on it? Dil wouldn't be surprised. He felt an urge to lash out, even kill, for revenge.

The passengers around him were mainly people like himself, on the way home from work. He became aware of a lot of chatter and he had an insane desire to join in, announce his wife had been kidnapped, ask for help, share the anger and hurt. He was sure plenty of people would sympathise and respond. As the journey went on, however, rational thought began to return. The first thing to do was talk to Jack. He tried him and the others again but again the calls went to message. He texted all of them to phone him urgently, that Lucy was in danger.

***

As Emily and Jack headed towards the long table they noticed that each setting had a name card and although there was a table plan near the door there was chaos for a while as everyone tried to find their seats. The Master sat at one end of the table and the President of the Council at the other. Emily and Jack worked out that the closer you were to one of them, the higher in the pecking order you came. Somewhat to their dismay they found themselves quite near the Master and opposite Mrs Latimer. They would rather have been with Donna and Bina who were almost exactly in the middle. The Choudhrys were only a few places down from the other end of the table.

'And you are?' Mrs Latimer asked Jack as a starter was served – scallop and caviar in a dill and cucumber sauce, according to the menu – along with a vintage white wine.

'Er, Jack Wellington.'

'Oh, of course, the dreadful shooting. Can't think what the police spend their time on these days.'

Emily snorted with laughter at the repetition. 'And you are?' she said, a malicious twinkle in her eye.

Mrs Latimer gave her a frosty glance.

'Latimer.'

'Oh, of course. Didn't recognise you in the candlelight. A minister of something.'

Jack sniggered into his wine and dug her in the ribs with his elbow, loving it.

'I'm right behind this new project and I think you should be too,' said Mrs Latimer icily. 'It could be good for you and bad if you're not involved.'

Something in such a strange remark sent a chill down Jack's spine. Was it a threat? Was more going on here than they realised?

The rest of the dinner passed pleasantly. Mrs Latimer turned her attention up towards the bigwigs near the Master, while Jack and Emily had good conversations with senior academics nearby. They were older, and something about the age gap, the excellent food and the wines seemed to remove inhibitions. Perhaps it was also the absence of rivalry, through Jack and Emily's being outside the academic hierarchy, or perhaps Emily's insult to Mrs Latimer had been overheard and admired. Everyone they spoke to was horrified and sympathetic about their awful experience and injuries.

'Some really nice people here,' said Jack quietly to Emily at the end of the meal just as the Master again tapped a glass for silence and thanked everyone for coming, whereupon Mr Anderson stood up and thanked the Master on behalf of the guests.

As they were getting up from their seats, Donna and Bina appeared behind them looking happy and excited and saying what a wonderful time they were having. Then

Nabeela and Hamid came over and joined the conversation so Jack and Emily still weren't able to talk about their meeting with Mr Anderson. Gradually the Combination Room began to empty, signalling the end of the event, and Hamid led them back down the stairs to retrieve their phones and coats.

'Whoa,' said Jack when he switched on his phone. 'There's eight messages from Dil.'

***

When Dil reached home he realised, with a cold feeling in his chest, that Lucy wasn't there, his last hope dashed. He kept leaving messages and texting Jack and the others but it wasn't until after ten o'clock that Jack called.

'Thank god,' said Dil, answering. 'They've kidnapped Lucy and you're in danger. Where the hell have you all been? I've been going out of my mind.'

'Wait, slow down, you're not making sense. Is Lucy ok?'

'NO. They've taken her. I don't know where she is and I can't call the police and I don't know what to do.'

Jack heard a deep breath at the other end that sounded suspiciously like a sob.

'Who's taken her?'

'How the hell would I know? Surprisingly enough they didn't give their names.'

'Look, Dil,...'

'It's you and Em got Lucy and me into this,' he interrupted

Jack was taken aback.

'What? What are you talking about?'

'I don't know what I'm talking about. You must know better than me. Whatever you're mixed up in, put it right.'

'Hey, Dil, this is me, your friend Jack. Whatever it is or whatever we've done of course we'll put it right but first we've got to know exactly what's happened and what we're supposed to have done. We've been without our phones all evening so I'm sorry you couldn't get me but we'll be back home in about fifteen minutes. Can we call you then?'

There was a silence and a sniff.

'Ok,' said Dil in a low voice.

'Hang in there,' said Jack as they ended the call.

He hurried to catch up with the Choudhrys, Emily and the others, crossing the courtyard towards the gate and a waiting taxi.

'We've got a big problem. We need to get back to the flat and call Dil.'

'I was just going to call him,' said Emily. 'He's left several messages.'

'Me too,' said Bina.

Mrs Latimer and two minders walked up behind them.

'Did I hear you say there's a problem?' she asked.

'Nothing we can't handle,' said Emily quickly.

'Good. You'll probably know what to do.'

Was that a smirk, Emily wondered as Mrs Latimer overtook and reached the gate ahead of them.

'That woman,' said Donna, 'gets my goat.'

'Can Hamid and I help?' Nabeela said in the taxi.

'Honestly, I don't know,' said Jack. 'Dil says Lucy's in trouble but we need to know what and he says it's connected with Em and me but we'll talk to him and find out what's going on.'

'We're here if you need us,' said Nabeela. 'We've both got a lot of contacts. By the way, how did the meeting with Mr Anderson go?'

'He offered Jack and me jobs,' said Emily, sounding as relaxed as she could even though she didn't feel it. 'Bit of a surprise really but we said no.'

'Good,' said Nabeela. 'Best not to rush into anything after what you've been through. I have my doubts about Mr Anderson and I'm not the only one.'

31
Glitch

The four friends called Dil on Jack's phone as soon as the Choudhrys dropped them off at the flat. He answered immediately and poured out the story as they sat, stunned, round the kitchen table.

'So who's offered you what and can you please accept?' Dil finished.

Jack told them the details of the offer and that they'd said no because Emily wanted to pursue her PhD and he wasn't yet ready to commit to anything long term following the shooting. He couldn't mention the bed mystery investigation because of the NDA.

'Wow – a hundred thousand pounds hello payment! And the rest. That's some offer,' said Bina, 'but who so badly wants you to take it that they kidnap Lucy?'

'The same people who want Jack and me dead,' said Emily. 'If they're prepared to murder, they won't give a second thought to kidnapping.'

They heard a sobbing sigh from Dil, then a sound like him hanging up. Jack looked at his phone.

'It's turned itself off. Battery must be down.'

Emily's phone rang. It was Dil. The conversation continued.

'Does it matter who it is?' said Dil desperately. 'It's really simple. Jack and Em accept the job, money showers on them and Lucy's released. End of.'

Emily looked at Jack. 'Dil's right. Let's not overthink. One step at a time. If we don't like the job we can leave.'

'The job offers are so good they're fishy,' said Donna. 'And I have doubts about this Mr King now Mrs Gregory's dead and he's all buddy-buddy with Anderson. And then there's the Mitzli connection and the teacher's will.'

'Oh god, who's dead and the what connection and who's will?' Dil asked, exasperated.

'It's complicated,' said Jack.

'And smelly,' said Bina.

Dil sighed. 'Meanwhile Lucy's in hell and so am I.'

'Look, Dil,' said Emily, 'we'll accept the Anderson offer first thing tomorrow.'

'Why not now?' said Jack. 'We know how to reach Jim King.'

Emily nodded. 'Jack, give me Jim King's number. We'll call you back in a minute, Dil.'

She disconnected and Jack looked at his phone. The battery wasn't flat after all.

'So why did the call end on your phone if the battery wasn't flat?' said Donna.

'Maybe Dil hit a wrong key or something.'

'Or maybe someone was listening and hit a wrong key. They could have bugged our phones this evening.'

'Oh come on,' said Bina, 'that's a bit far-fetched.'

But at the same time she mimed a lipzip and showed them a note she had quickly written on a scrap of paper: *bugged at college.*

'Yes it is,' said Emily loudly. 'Probably just a network glitch.'

Emily dialled Jim King's number with the speaker on so they could all hear. It rang several times before it was answered.

'Hello,' said Jim King.

Just before he said it they caught the echo of voices near him, as though he had been talking to someone with him. Maybe more than one person.

'Hello Mr King, Emily Harrison. Sorry to ring you so late. Jack and I just wanted to say we've thought over Mr Anderson's offer and we'd like to accept it after all.'

'That's good,' said Jim, 'I'll tell him. There'll be some papers to sign. I'll get back to you tomorrow to make arrangements.'

'There's a condition,' Emily went on, and Jack, Bina and Donna pricked up their ears.

'Yes?'

'We finalise it and sign the papers in Bradford, because beforehand we have to see our friend Lucy Akhtar who also lives there.'

There was a pause. 'I'll see what I can do,' he said.

'Ok, bye.'

Then she called Dil.

'It's done. We'll be in touch. Keep us posted.'

'So what did he say?'

'That he'd pass it on and be in touch tomorrow. Hang in there. That's all I can say for now. We'll phone as soon as we have news. Try not to worry.'

She hoped Dil would pick up that she wanted to end the call and wouldn't think she was being insensitive.

'Ok. Bye,' he sounded disappointed.

He rang off. They all wanted to talk at once but Emily shook her head, walked to the fridge.

'I'm worn out,' she said loudly. 'I'm off to bed.'

Then she put her phone in the fridge.

'Me too,' said Jack. 'Night everyone.'

He did the same. Bina followed suit. Donna knew her phone would be alright but headed for the door.

'Bye folks, see you tomorrow,' she said as she opened it, then firmly shut it from the inside.

Emily led them to her bedroom.

'That was inspired, Em,' said Jack when they were shut in. 'Signing the papers in Bradford and so on.'

'He didn't react, did he?' said Donna. 'Strong evidence against him and Anderson.'

'Yes,' said Bina. 'If he knew nothing about it he'd have asked why and what Lucy had to do with it.'

'I'm going to give Dil a video call on his laptop,' said Emily. 'I'm not leaving him to stew with that stilted phone conversation. Poor lad, he's beside himself. And poor Lucy. I can't even begin to imagine what she's going through.'

First she used an encrypted messaging app on her laptop to ask Dil to put his phone in the fridge because it might be bugged.

'Done,' came back almost at once.

Then she started a video call. Dil looked pale and worn. He was sitting on the bathroom floor.

'I thought something funny was going on by the way you were talking just now,' he said. 'I'm in the bathroom. Less likely to have bugs.'

He had a radio on too. Jack explained Emily's quick thinking about finalising the job offer in Bradford.

'Come and stay here,' he said. 'It'll be a bit cramped but we can all just about fit in. That is, if you're all coming.'

They all said they were and they talked a bit more. Whenever Dil said Lucy's name they heard a catch in his voice and could tell from his face and the way he swallowed and paused that he wasn't far from weeping.

'What we don't know,' said Donna, 'is why it's so important to them that Em and Jack take this job but if you put big money and politics into the mixture there could be all sorts of dark and dirty stuff going on.'

'Politics?' asked Bina, 'what d'you mean?'

'Anderson said as much.' said Donna. 'About it being difficult to give money away and Mrs Latimer being there. You know how slippery some politicians can be.'

'She was awful,' said Jack. 'Em got a dig in, though.'

He told them about their conversation at the table. It made them smile.

Jack and Emily hadn't discussed it but they both knew the job offer was almost certainly about stopping them investigating the bed mystery.

'Em and I have an idea what it might all be about but we can't tell you,' said Jack.

'Oh,' said Bina, 'you mean Mrs Barton's will and the NDA.'

'The what?' said Dil.

'Mrs Barton left Em and I a letter but we're not allowed to talk about it because of a non-disclosure agreement with the executors.'

'I don't care,' said Dil. 'I just want Lucy back.'

'I know they said what would happen if we involve the police,' said Donna, 'but I'm police, already involved, and I think I ought to tell the boss. I'm sure he could help.'

'Oh no,' Dil shouted. 'They'll know, I'm sure they will and then they'll kill her. Please…'

His voice tailed off and they could see his tears.

'I can see why you say that, Donna,' said Bina, 'because if anything goes wrong you'll get a bollocking for not telling him but, honestly, I think it'd be a mistake. I'm glad you're with us because we're all friends now and you've saved my life and Dil's and Lucy's and supported me after my attack and it's not like you're police, even though you are, but rule books aren't made for situations like this and the more people that are involved the more risk there is of something going wrong.'

Donna was silent.

'Yes,' said Emily, 'and because we're all friends we'll be on your side if anyone criticises you.'

'They're right,' said Jack, 'but I know it's not an easy decision for you. Following your training's usually the right thing to do because it's based on years of experience of thousands of people but you have to use your own judgement too. And think how you'd feel if you told Inspector Kennedy and then something awful happened because of it.'

Donna was in a dilemma, *but,* she thought, looking at Dil on the screen, *I'm learning that life's not always cut and dried and I trust these people.*

'Alright,' she said, 'I'll keep it among ourselves for now. It won't be the first time I've gone against regulations. But if things get ugly I reserve the right to change my mind.'

A weak but heartfelt 'thank you' came from Dil.

'Thank you from us all,' said Bina, giving her a hug.

Jack noticed Emily was looking pale and tired. His own wounds were aching too.

'Dil, let's leave things till morning now. Em looks exhausted and I think we should all try to sleep.'

Emily admitted she had a headache.

'Sorry,' said Bina, 'you two are doing so well we keep forgetting you're still recovering from being shot.'

'Ok,' said Dil. 'I won't sleep, of course.'

He sighed, more of a groan, and wiped his eyes with a tissue as he disconnected.

'I think we're all whacked,' said Donna as they left Emily's bedroom.

She headed for her coat on a hook near the door.

'Why not stay tonight?' said Bina. 'You haven't got the car and it's quite a walk to your place isn't it?'

Jack and Emily nodded.

'Well I could get a taxi but it'd be great just to flop here,' she said, sounding relieved. 'I could sleep on the couch. And I could keep an eye on you all.'

'I'd offer to take the couch so you could have the sofabed,' said Jack, 'except my kidney's aching and I need to lie out flat. The couch isn't long enough.'

'Chivalry's not dead, eh?' said Bina, 'but no worries, take the other bed in my room, Donna.'

'Aw, thanks Bina,' said Donna, beaming.

'Night, Em,' said Jack, hovering by her door as they left. 'Hope you sleep well.'

'I'll either drop unconscious or not sleep a wink. See you in the morning.'

32
Balls

Emily slept until three a.m. but woke to the sound of marbles and found it hard to go back to sleep. She got up and tiptoed in her dressing gown to the kitchen area for cornflakes. As she was sprinkling them into a dish, Jack emerged from the office/snug with wild hair and blue and white striped pyjamas. She giggled.

'You look just like that video of you running home after the bed mystery,' she whispered.

Jack smiled and winked. 'I'm saving up for pink crocs.'

'And a hairbrush?'

'Don't be cheeky.'

He, too, helped himself to cornflakes and they sat together on the couch.

'Couldn't sleep?' Jack asked.

'I went to sleep ok but then the marbles woke me.'

Jack almost spilled his cornflakes. 'Marbles?'

'Yes, since the shooting I've sometimes woken up to a sound like marbles rolling round on a hard floor. Mrs Wittingdale said it'll probably wear off.'

'That's weird. I have noises like that. They're like snooker balls on wood. They've just woken me up.

'But you've not had a head injury.'

He grinned. 'Not unless you count a bit of missing ear but they started in hospital. I put it down to trolley wheels or something. To be honest I haven't paid too much attention to them. Your brain plays funny tricks when you're half asleep.'

Emily's mind was racing.

'When the bed mystery happened, did you see or hear anything unusual.'

'Yes, waking up in your bed.'

He coloured slightly.

'No, I mean before it happened, or as it happened.'

'Actually yes. There was lightning and a rumble. I thought it was a thunderstorm but Dil said there wasn't one'

'Whoa, I saw a blue flash and heard a rumble.'

They looked at each other.

'I can't believe we've never discussed this,' said Jack. 'Marbles aren't so different from snooker balls and rumbles. They have to be connected with the bed mystery, or teleporting if that's what it is?

Emily's eyes were shining.

'Yes, and you don't hear other people say they've been woken up by marbles. Maybe there's something about our minds that makes us susceptible to it.'

'There's nothing special about us, we're just normal people, but maybe it's a sign that whoever or whatever caused us and John Barton to disappear is still out there.'

'What, trying to move us again?'

'Perhaps. Or experimenting. Who knows. It's what we need to find out.'

'Jack, if Anderson and King are behind kidnapping Lucy and if it's connected with Mrs Barton's will and the bed mystery, it'd be much better if we could tell the others about her letter and stuff. I feel bad that we're holding out on them. In fact, I hate it. What d'you think would happen if we ignored the NDA and told them everything.'

'It's risky. If King found out, he could tie us up in court orders and things.'

'Yes but there's a lot at stake. Lucy's life for one thing. Let's ask Bina. She knows the legal side.'

The more Jack thought about it the more he thought she was right. He'd feel better telling their friends the whole story rather than just part of it.

'Ok, but let's concentrate on getting Lucy back first. That's the highest priority and we don't want anything to interfere with it.

'I keep trying to reassure myself by thinking that if they want us to work for Anderson, Lucy's no use to them dead.'

Donna emerged from the bedroom.

'Sorry,' she said, looking embarrassed. 'I was awake and heard you talking but I don't want to be a gooseberry.'

Emily looked at Jack and grinned. He found her expression hard to read but noticed how pale and vulnerable she looked. He grinned back.

'No,' he said, 'we're just worrying about what to do next. Neither of us could sleep. It's cornflakes time.'

Donna helped herself and sat down.

'I've been thinking,' she said. 'I could look for CCTV footage around Dil and Lucy's house, and at mobile phone location records. Might give us some clues and I can do it secretly and unofficially from my desk so it's not involving the police, or at least not any more than me being here.'

Emily and Jack thought it was a great idea.

'Also,' Donna went on, 'if it's Anderson and King behind Lucy being nabbed, she's only useful to them if she's alive because I presume you won't sign up with Anderson unless you get her back.'

'You bet we won't,' said Emily. 'I just hope we can pull it off. If they're willing to kill and kidnap there could be no limit to what else they're prepared to do. I was starting to get my confidence back after the shooting but this has taken it away again.'

Jack had an impulse to give her a reassuring hug.

33
Flicker

The next morning Donna was up and off before seven. As her phone wasn't bugged she left it with Bina who would give her an update call at her desk when King had been in touch. Emily installed a call recorder app on her phone for when the call came through. She thought it might be useful if they needed to involve Inspector Kennedy.

So as not to raise suspicions of anyone listening to the bugs, they took their phones out of the fridge but were careful not to say anything important among themselves.

Dil rang at eight o'clock.

'I couldn't leave it any longer. I've been sitting here with my phone in my hand since five. I don't think I've slept at all.'

'Nah, we didn't sleep much either,' said Jack. 'Hang in there mate. I'm sure we'll hear something this morning and I'll call you the minute we do.'

Dil phoned every half hour after that until Jim King called Emily mid-morning.

'Hello Emily. I've spoken to Mr Anderson and he agrees to the papers being signed in Bradford, but he won't be there himself. He's asked me to be there instead. And it's got to be tomorrow.'

'Tomorrow's fine but if Mr Anderson isn't going to be there how do we know he agrees?'

'Your employment contracts will be with his Foundation and I'll be authorised to sign on its behalf.'

'Lucy needs to be there too.'

'Fine by me.'

'Is that a promise? You'll see she's there?'

'I didn't say that. '

'Ok, we'll call the police.'

'It would be unwise.'

'Why?'

'It might make it difficult for her to attend.'

The quiet way he said it was chilling. Emily shuddered.

'Where do you suggest?'

'There's an art gallery called Cartwright Hall. The café, eleven o'clock tomorrow morning.'

'I'll call you back in a few minutes.'

Jack and Bina had been listening beside her but she played it back to them, then put the phone on the table.

'We need to discuss this,' she said, a finger to her lips, and led the way to her bedroom.

'At first the weaselly snake was trying to make it sound like he had nothing to do with Lucy,' said Bina when the door was closed, 'as though it was us who were going to arrange for her to be there but when you mentioned the police he had to change tack.'

'And I liked the way you said you'd call back and then hung up on him,' said Jack.

'I just felt we needed to think over what he suggested.'

'Yes you're right. At least we know Cartwright Hall. Remember the school visits? And it's in the park near where Dil and Lucy live. Could mean she's still somewhere around there.'

'On the plus side,' said Jack, 'it's a public enough place so it'd be difficult for them to kill anyone without being noticed. On the negative side we'll have to sign up to something we don't know all the implications of.'

'If I was your lawyer,' said Bina, 'I'd advise you to see the papers beforehand, not sign them blind.'

'Good idea,' said Emily. 'I'll agree to the meeting on condition he ensures Lucy's there and emails the papers to us today.'

They left the bedroom and she called him back. He agreed to everything so Jack called Dil to give him the bare facts. He ended the call by saying 'See you soon. Get the bathroom ready.'

Dil twigged and Emily briefed him in a video call from her bedroom after Jack had put the phones back in the fridge. Dil looked even worse than the night before and was still tearful.

'But least I have some hope now,' he said.

'We'll be with you this evening.'

'Ok,' said Jack. 'Let's hire a car and pick Donna up. We're going to Bradford.'

Once outside the building, Bina called Donna to update her.

***

'It's set up,' said the man on the phone. 'Your technical people confirm no outside parties involved. They've been very helpful.'

'No hitches this time, please. We need to stabilise the position.'

'My people understand that. They know there will be consequences for failure. The girl is secure.'

The man made another call.

'Have you been testing?'

'Yes but I have no subjects.'

'I'll be able to help with that soon.'

***

DI Kennedy wasn't happy about the trip when Donna told him just after he arrived for work. By that time she'd been home, packed a small bag and been at her desk for an hour.

'Here in Cambridge there's at least some chance of our helping Emily and Jack if there's another murder attempt,' he said, 'but up north – I hate to think what could happen.'

'It's just that their families want to see them, and vice versa of course, and it interferes less with their jobs if it happens up there. I'll make sure to be with them all the time if it's ok for me to go too. I could liaise with the local force and maybe a message from you would help.'

'I can spare you as long as it's only a few days and you call me every evening so I know where you are and what you're up to and you promise to bring them back immediately if I say. I'll need you back here if anything goes south with the shooting enquiry, although frankly there's not a lot happening at the moment. DI Audrey hasn't found the shooter's female accomplice yet and her web people haven't found any dirt on Mitzli, which comes out as a top drawer outfit, even does a lot of work for governments including in the UK. Their story about the dead guy being off work checks out on social security and hospital records.

***

Jack, Emily and Bina called for Donna late morning in a hired Fiesta. They'd bought three cheap phones with pay-as-you-go sim cards. They brought the three smartphones from the fridge too, turned off, and put them in the car boot.

'Good work, people,' said Donna as they shared the new numbers.

Jack had also dropped in on a friend from his university days who was now in line for a Professorship. He was an expert on high frequency radio and Jack wanted some advice.

The journey under dull skies and drizzly stretches took around three hours. Donna and Bina shared the driving. Emily didn't feel confident enough. As they travelled, Donna told them about her research that morning.

'First, I followed Lucy's phone when she left work. She didn't go straight home. She stopped at a café near work for about twenty minutes. Is that normal d'you think?'

'Don't know,' said Bina. 'We'll ask Dil later.'

'Ok. Then her phone went home but stopped outside the house and hasn't moved since. Presumably turned off or smashed. I picked her up on CCTV when she left the café. She got on a bus and got off at a stop on a main road called Manningham Lane. She turned into a road called Oak Lane, then onto the road where they live but there's no CCTV there so she went off camera. I looked at CCTV at the other end of the road but nothing went out or in until hours later. No vehicles no pedestrians. It was the same at the end where I last saw Lucy.'

'Nothing coming in or out of either end for hours? That's unlikely isn't it?' Emily asked.

'Yes, so I had a look at slow speed and just after Lucy went off camera there was a flicker in the feed at both ends. Then flickers again about four in the morning.'

'So the feed's been tampered with?' Jack asked.

'Exactly, so then I looked at other cameras in the area around the time Lucy got off the bus, and I saw a black SUV on Oak Lane a few minutes after Lucy went off camera. It was slowing down and indicating to make a turn into her road. I looked up its number and it was false.'

'Good sleuthing,' said Bina. 'It's got to be involved somehow. Lucy must have been taken away in it. Could you trace the SUV any further?'

'It needs a number recognition search that I couldn't do from my desk but I met a Detective Constable from Bradford called Arun at a conference last year and I've asked him to do it. I may not hear anything till tomorrow, though.'

"Someone's done some clever manipulation,' said Jack. 'Would the system keep a record and give a clue who's done it?'

'I think so, but I don't know how. Pete would be able to, but I can't ask him for obvious reasons.'

They had arranged not to talk to Dil on the way and when they arrived at his house around dusk they parked a couple of streets away as a precaution.

'God, it's good to see you all,' said Dil, hugging each of them. 'I've been going spare on my own. Can't think of anything apart from what Lucy's going through.'

'We're the same,' said Emily, handing him a note.

Dil looked at it in surprise.

We need to check for bugs, it said.

Jack produced something from his pocket that looked like a phone. His Cambridge friend had lent him it and he proceeded to walk round the house watching its screen. Being a substantial terrace house the rooms were bigger and higher than in a modern house so it took some time. He checked the hallway and staircase first with no result so until he'd swept the rest of the house the others stayed there chatting, with internal doors shut.

Jack got three reactions from the device. One in the kitchen, one in the sitting room and one in Dil and Lucy's bedroom. It took them a while to find the bugs but eventually Dil noticed a small irregularity in the kitchen wall and found a carpet-tack-sized camera and, presumably, microphone embedded in the plaster. It had a neutral colour that made it almost invisible but it was easy then to locate the other two, similarly installed. They quietly dug them out and put them in a dish of water.

'All clear folks,' Jack shouted.

'They must have come in using Lucy's key after they snatched her,' said Donna. 'Presumably the bugs are to make sure you did as they asked.'

'So what will they do when they go quiet?' Dil asked.

'They'll be suspicious but as we've got the meeting tomorrow, fingers crossed they'll just wait.'

Emily ordered curry from Dil's favourite takeaway nearby. Bina shared with him the new phone numbers for herself, Emily and Jack.

Emily checked her emails and found one from James King with attachments. It was headed 'Documents' and the message said 'Herewith.' She used Dil's printer and gave them to Bina.

34
Dome

Lucy could tell it was morning, even without opening her eyes, because the room was bright and she sensed light on her face but she wasn't a morning person. She usually took getting up slowly and didn't open her eyes until she absolutely had to. She stirred to turn over and snuggle up to Dil but she couldn't. Something was gripping her wrist. And there was no duvet. And she was fully dressed. Memory hit her like a missile and her eyes shot open.

Ginger, Overcoat, the knife, the phone call, the needle. The sudden realisation of it was too much. She felt her mind was about to burst and she wanted to scream and shout and break free and run away. It was like her heart had stopped and she had forgotten how to breathe. After a long moment some basic reflex forced her to take in a breath and her heart changed to racing. Gradually it passed and she began to get herself under control, to take stock.

She was alive, alone and handcuffed by a wrist to a metal bedstead, on a bare mattress with an old black-and-white-striped pillow. She could lie on her back or turn to her right side but not to her left. She was cold, even though she was wearing a winter coat. The room looked like a small attic room with a skylight window above the bed. The walls and sloping ceiling were featureless and grubby white. There was a fusty, disused smell. She pictured herself at the top of an old house. She held her breath and listened. There was no sound from inside and none from outside. She strained her ears for traffic noise or something that would give a clue to where she was but there was nothing. She saw dark clouds through the window.

The bed was in the middle of the room, the only item of furniture. There was no covering on the floorboards which were wide and old fashioned. The door, painted white, was smooth and featureless, possibly metal-covered. She tested the handcuff and could almost fold her hand enough to pull it free but not quite. She grimaced as she tried which caused pain on the side of her face, where Ginger had hit her. She felt it gently with her free hand and found her cheek to be tender and her ear hot and swollen. There would be bruising but there didn't seem to be a cut, unlike the back of her ring finger where Ginger had slashed it. There was dried blood around it and smears on the front of her skirt. She couldn't see her bag but she still had her watch which also gave her the date. It was quarter past eight the morning after.

'Good morning,' said a voice behind her she recognised as Overcoat.

She jerked her head round and saw no-one but there was a small security camera, presumably with a loudspeaker, mounted high up in a corner.

'I need the bathroom,' she said.

There was a click from the speaker but otherwise no response. She lay back on the bed and pondered. Dil would have been in touch with Em and Jack by now and something would surely be happening. Either Em and Jack would do whatever-it-was or Dil would somehow get help and find her. Of the two she hoped it would be the latter because once Em and Jack had done whatever-it-was she would have no value to whoever-it-was.

There was a sound outside the door. Someone was unlocking it and drawing back bolts. The door opened and Overcoat came in without his overcoat, in a grey two piece suit, Ginger behind in jeans and brown sweater. They didn't speak. Ginger came over and unlocked her wrist from the handcuffs, indicating for her to stand up. She felt dizzy for a moment when she was upright. He grabbed her and pushed her towards the door.

The fat driver was standing outside barring her way to a corridor straight ahead but he pointed to an open door on the left. It was a small bathroom. She went in and slammed the door but there was no lock on the inside and nothing she could use to wedge it shut.

'Don't be long,' Overcoat shouted and there were sounds like him walking away and down some stairs.

Ginger and Driver exchanged some words she couldn't hear, then one of them, Driver she thought, also left. There was a walk-in shower, a washbasin with a mirror, and a loo that she thankfully used before bracing herself to look in the mirror. Her hair was tangled and the left side of her face, as she had suspected, was blue with bruising. There was nothing she could do about it but there was soap in a disposable dispenser, and a comb. A few minutes' work made her feel better, more presentable. There was a small first aid cabinet and she found antiseptic cream and plaster for her finger. She hoped to find scissors or something sharp but there was nothing. There was a window behind the loo, though. Frosted glass but a small transom at the top. What if she could open it? She heard footsteps approaching. The door opened and Ginger poked his head in.

'Get out,' she yelled and kicked the door hard.

It hit his nose.

'Bitch,' he shouted and pushed it open again, coming towards her.

She dodged into the shower and grabbed the shower head to use as a weapon.

'Don't you dare,' she screamed.

'Ryan?' came a voice from outside.

Overcoat appeared in the doorway and she glimpsed Driver's back going into her room.

'Ryan, back off. Remember our orders.'

Ryan looked annoyed and pointed a finger at her.

'Later,' he said menacingly under his breath.

Lucy shivered.

'Get out both of you,' she shouted as she slammed the door on them. 'I'll tell you when I'm ready to come out.'

She turned on a tap as cover and crossed to stand on the loo seat. The transom catch worked and she managed to open the window but there were screws in the frame on the outside to stop it opening more than a few centimetres. Squinting through the gap she could see tangled vegetation on the ground, an overgrown garden maybe, and, beyond, a couple of mature oak trees. She stepped onto the floor again and turned off the tap, tapped her ring on the basin a couple of times to sound like she was still busy there, then hopped quietly onto her perch again. This time she craned and stretched to see if there was anything else to see through the slits at the sides of the window. At the extreme right she saw something that looked like the domed roof of a tower, lead covered. It had a spike and was vaguely familiar, but she couldn't place it. Not wanting to risk another confrontation she gently closed the window and quickly returned to the washbasin.

'Ready?' shouted Ginger from outside.

She opened the door by way of answer and allowed herself to be pushed back into the room with the bed. This time Ginger didn't handcuff her to it but locked the door as he left. There was a tray on the bed with cornflakes, buttered toast and a cup of tea but she had no appetite. She sipped tea and noted there was a plastic spoon but no knife or fork. She thought over the last few minutes. Driver must have brought the tray. Obviously he was the gopher and Ginger was the muscle. Overcoat must be the boss.

She took stock of what she'd learned from visiting the bathroom. She racked her brains trying to remember where she'd seen a dome like that. And there was something else, a question mark about what she had seen, but she couldn't resolve it into a coherent thought. She re-ran it in her mind. She had looked at the undergrowth below the window. Wait, that was it! The ground below the window. It wasn't as far down as she had expected. Not as far down as it would be from an attic, nor even from upstairs in her own house. She was above ground level, though, like on a mezzanine. A distance it would be fairly safe to jump. Not that it did her much good. The window wouldn't open far enough and even if it did it was too small to crawl through.

Now, the dome. She thought hard. Obviously a tall building. Ah, it came to her! It reminded her of one on the roof of Cartwright Hall, an art gallery in the park opposite their house. It was opened in 1904 and named after Edmund Cartwright who invented the wool combing machine that contributed so much to the prosperity of Victorian Bradford. She felt a rush of excitement. Could it be Cartwright Hall? The more she thought about it the more she thought it could. If it was, it meant she was close to home. Dil could walk past at any minute. All she needed to do was run out of this house and she'd probably recognise where she was. Except she was locked in with no way to get out. Unless…

She looked at the skylight but not for long because she was aware of the camera in the corner. She didn't know when or even if they watched but she'd better work on the assumption that it was all the time. She lay down on her back on the bed to study the window. Its fastening, though old-fashioned, looked to be in reasonably good condition with no special lock but it would be difficult to reach. She measured with her eye how high it was. She reckoned if she stood up and stretched her hand above her head she would be about half a metre below the lower end of the sloping glass. She needed something to stand on. The bed was the only thing there was and it would have to do. But how could she do it with the camera and microphones in operation? She had nothing to smash them with and anyway the minute they stopped working one of the men would come in to investigate.

Then it dawned on her that she couldn't see a light fitting on the ceiling or the wall. And she'd been handcuffed to the bed overnight. When it got dark they might not be able to see her. Could that be an opportunity? It was a long shot but gave her something to focus on. If she could get through the skylight onto the roof she could slide down it, hang off the edge and let go, hoping for a soft landing. It was on the same side as the bathroom window so there was a chance she wouldn't be injured. She was scared about that part but she knew it was better than waiting to be killed.

35
History

Bina settled down in the sitting room with the papers from James King, leaving the others in the kitchen with the remains of the curry. Donna phoned DI Kennedy, in accordance with her instructions, but he didn't answer. She left a message that they were all alright, not mentioning Lucy. Dil looked worn and worried, so as they drank tea the others tried to distract him. They had talked for a while, dissecting some of their school acquaintances and exchanging other gossip, when Donna said:

'Lucy's phone showed she called at a café near work on the way home yesterday. Is that normal?'

'No, at least I don't think so. Oh wait, something to do with Billy maybe.'

Jack sat bolt upright and Emily did a double take. They had serious doubts about whether or not he was still alive.

'What to do with Billy?' Emily asked.

'When they talked.'

Everyone looked blank.

'What, yesterday? What about?, said Jack.

'And who is he anyway?' Donna asked.

Dil theatrically clapped his hand to his head.

'Oh God, my mind's been so screwed I forgot to tell you. When she called me, the last time before she was taken, when I was coming back from Leeds…'

Tears leaked from his eyes. Emily stroked his arm as Bina rejoined them, providing a helpful distraction until he could speak again.

He told them what Lucy had said about Billy's warning of danger and how it stemmed from something that happened ten years ago.

Emily and Jack looked at each other. Jack raised an eyebrow. She responded with a nod. This had to be the right moment.

'Look,' said Jack. 'Em and I were talking last night and we need to tell you all a few things. You may already know some of it.'

He told them how he and Emily had met Edith Gregory at Clarence & Thirkill's office, with King on the phone; about Mrs Barton's will; the letters she had left but the contents were subject to NDAs; Hubbler's visit to Jack; the fire; the body; and the CCTV that DI Audrey showed Jack of Billy Worth coming out of the lift.

Dil was open-mouthed.

'Wow,' said Donna. 'I knew about Hubbler from Inspector Kennedy but I didn't know that about the CCTV and Billy.

'Nor me,' said Bina.

'There's more,' said Emily. 'The NDAs Jack and I signed are getting in the way of our levelling with you about everything but now King seems to be implicated in Lucy's kidnapping we wonder if we'd be justified in breaking them. What do you think, Bina?'

'Without reading them I can't say for sure, but if they're designed to protect interests that aren't legitimate and proper, I think you could well have a case. Also it would probably be difficult for the executors to prove that your telling us about Mrs Barton's letter causes loss to her estate, and even if they did manage it, any such loss would be difficult to quantify. Also I'm guessing that you two, like the rest of us, haven't much in the way of money or assets to pay damages or costs. Worst case, you could be made bankrupt but then the estate would lose out.'

Jack looked at Emily. 'That's good enough for me.'

'Me too,' she replied.

She thumbed her phone, retrieved a copy of the letter and read it out to a silent and stunned audience.

'What a story,' Dil exclaimed.

'So,' said Donna, 'what's that bit about what she overheard you talking about.'

'I think I can tell you, if Jack and Em agree?' said Dil.

They nodded and Dil related the bed mystery, with added drama as only Dil could, and how he'd told Jack it must be teleporting, without really believing it. Bina and Donna were increasingly astonished as they listened.

'What – you literally fell asleep in one place and woke up in another?' Donna asked, although she knew that's what Dil had just said. 'Could it have been drugs or someone pranking?'

'No, we thought through all that at the time,' said Emily, 'and pretty much every day since. It's just as Dil said and the only credible explanation is teleporting, which of course doesn't exist. Or almost doesn't.'

She went on to tell them about quantum entanglement and her talk with Professor Hinkles.

'Well, I'm gobsmacked,' said Bina, 'but probably not as gobsmacked as Mrs Barton must have been when she overheard you, or as you were when you read her letter. I always thought there was something funny about that day. You didn't say much about it, Em, but your attitude to Jack changed then.'

Emily looked embarrassed and Jack blushed.

'I think she'd hardly noticed me till then,' he said to cover his confusion, 'but after I turned up in her bed and she accused me of abduction and shouted a lot she couldn't really ignore me.'

They all laughed.

'Also, he saved me from abduction by men in green uniforms and a black SUV.'

'We think they could have been from Mitzli,' said Jack. 'That double Y logo, but we never found out how we were transported. We called it the bed mystery and it sort of got buried with holidays and exams and everything else going on. That's how things would have stayed if it hadn't been for Mrs Barton's letter.'

'It explains something I've read in the employment agreements King sent,' said Bina, 'which I must say are very generous. There's an exclusivity clause which says you can't do any work for anyone else. Hang on, I'll look it up...' she leafed through it, '...ah here it is "including without limitation any work, paid or unpaid, or any activity, research or investigation in connection with the late Mrs Enid Barton or her estate." They want to tie you up so you let all that drop.'

'Yes, Em and I turned down Anderson's offer at first, so we could honour Mrs Barton's wishes but it turns out he doesn't want us to.'

'So now,' said Donna, 'they suddenly change from murder to kidnapping and throwing money at you.'

'It's getting complicated, too, if SIS may be involved,' said Bina. 'By the way, these agreements require Jack and Em to drop everything immediately they've signed and go to New York for six months induction training. Like tomorrow.'

'We can't do that,' said Emily. 'We need to know more about what it involves, have time to pack a case and get organised.'

'Too right,' said Donna. 'And whether you'll be quietly killed when you get there. It could just be an elaborate murder plot rather than a change of tack.'

'But we've said we'll do it,' said Jack. 'And we have to, to get Lucy.'

'Ok,' said Emily, 'we get Lucy back tomorrow at the meeting, sign up, then go to ground somewhere, call in the cavalry – Inspectors Kennedy and Audrey – and leave it all to them.'

'Except we might not get the chance to go to ground,' said Jack.

'True,' said Bina, shuffling the papers. 'It's quite explicit. You have to be ready to leave the minute you've signed.'

Emily looked at Jack. 'Then we will. And trust that you guys will come up with some way to find us.'

Jack saw defiance in Emily's face. She was formidable when she felt strongly about something and he liked that about her. He could tell she was ready to take him on if he disagreed, but he didn't. They had to get Lucy back and it was the only way they could.

'Fine,' he said. 'I promised Dil we'd do whatever it takes to get Lucy back and we will.'

Dil was quietly weeping.

'I don't know what to say,' he whispered between sobs. 'No-one ever had friends like you guys.'

***

DI Kennedy was driving home when DI Audrey called.

'My cyber people have found a faint trail from Mitzli to a security company near Cambridge called BML Partners Ltd,' she said. 'It's at Cottenham, owned by two offshore companies and Mitzli has a small shareholding in one of them. May be nothing but worth checking.'

'Many thanks. I guess my people will have been there or at least spoken to them about SUVs but I'm just on my way home so I'll swing by and take a look.'

He called Pete to ask if someone had already checked the company but it went to message. It had just turned seven o'clock in the evening so he wasn't surprised. He ended the call without leaving a message.

It didn't take long to find BML. It was on an industrial estate and enclosed by a high metal fence with anti-climb spikes and razor wire. The closed gates were equally fortified and unwelcoming. He got out of the car and presented his badge to a uniformed security guard behind them, who told him everyone had gone home and anyway a special Government permit was needed to come in, even by appointment. Beyond the guard he could see lights inside the two storey building and a couple of executive cars parked outside. There was also an open warehouse door revealing tall storage racks and, at the back, what looked like a black vehicle with a tarpaulin over it, about the size and shape of an SUV.

He drove away and didn't argue with the guard. No doubt it was what he'd been told to say to visitors but Kennedy didn't believe a word of it. He wanted a better look at the vehicle in the warehouse and wasn't going to wait for a permit. The map on his dashboard told him he could reach the back of the compound across a field from a narrow lane that forked off the main road a few hundred metres away. He knew he had bolt cutters in his boot.

36
Plan

It was boring just lying on the bed. Lucy had nothing to read and, despite feeling she needed to stay alert, had dozed. Driver brought lunch around noon, lukewarm pasta and mushrooms still in its microwavable container. There was also an apple, a banana and water in a plastic cup. She'd been cold beforehand despite a watery sun coming through the skylight but ate some of the ready meal and the apple and felt better for it. Otherwise she was left alone. She had a plan though.

Mid-afternoon she asked to go to the bathroom again and they followed the same procedure as before, except that, to her relief, Ginger wasn't there. It was just Overcoat and Driver. While inside she tested whether or not the soap dispenser would fit into her coat pocket and it comfortably did. At half past five, by which time it was dusk, Driver appeared with two sandwiches, one cheese, one chicken salad, and a bottle of water. He brought a battery lantern too.

'It's pretty cold in here,' she said. 'Can I have a blanket or a rug or something?'

'I'll ask.'

At half past six she heard footsteps. Ginger came in and tossed a blanket onto the bed.

'Beddy-byes,' he leered. 'If you want to use the bathroom go now.'

He stepped back to stand where Driver had stood that morning, to block her access to the corridor, but she would have to pass close to him as she turned into the bathroom. She gritted her teeth and walked quickly but, as she reached the bathroom door, he stepped forward and grabbed her, pulling her to him.

She could smell stale breath as he pressed his face close to hers and she felt a hand groping her bottom. She didn't hesitate. She kneed his groin and screamed at the same time. He grunted loudly, let go and she darted into the bathroom, closing the door behind her. She heard footsteps along the corridor and Overcoat's voice.

'What's going on?'

'Bit of fun,' said Ginger, forcing his voice to sound natural while still in pain.

She'd fought him off for now but she was afraid of what could happen later. She quickly used the loo and washed, then shoved the soap dispenser into her pocket. She emerged from the bathroom to find Overcoat outside blocking the way into the corridor. She turned into her room and saw Ginger leering by the bed.

'Come to daddy,' he said, with a chilling smile.

He held a hypodermic needle and the handcuffs. First he attached her left wrist to the bed then injected her right arm.

'I'll be in later for some fun,' he whispered, 'and you won't know a thing about it.'

She looked at him, then Overcoat, opened her mouth to speak and collapsed onto the bed. Overcoat threw the blanket over her and they left, taking the lantern. She lay motionless, eyes closed, for at least twenty minutes after their footsteps had died away. When she opened them it was fully dark. She put her free hand up the sleeve of her jumper under her coat to retrieve the chicken, cheese and banana she had discreetly wedged there to absorb the injection. She wondered if Dil would have approved of how she dropped unconscious.

She pulled the soap dispenser from her pocket and smeared soap liberally from wrist to knuckle on the hand in the handcuff, to act as a lubricant. Then she folded her hand into as narrow a diameter as possible and pushed, pulled and struggled, little by little to manoeuvre the cuff towards her fingers. The compression on her hand bones became extremely painful but she knew she had to persist and bear it silently. After what seemed like an age there was a sudden 'slop' sound and she was free.

She lay recovering and quiet for half an hour until her next move. Her eyes were acclimatising to the darkness and she could see a faint outline of the window. There was no moonlight. She stood up, stepped out of her shoes, wiped her soapy hand on the blanket and tiptoed with it towards the corner where the camera was mounted. Even if the watchers couldn't see in the darkness, any sudden noise might alert them. She folded the blanket into a strip about a metre wide and peered up at the camera. It was white but she could only vaguely make it out. Holding both ends of the blanket she tried to swing it over the camera but she misjudged the height and it fell short. She stepped nearer and tried again. This time the blanket looped over the camera and stayed put. As far as she could tell it was drooping over the lens and she hoped it would also deaden the microphone.

She went back and lay on the bed to wait for any reaction to what she had done but all seemed quiet and after another half hour she stood up again for phase two of her plan. She gently moved the bed so that the head was right underneath the skylight. She did it slowly so as not to make a sound that could be heard below or through the microphone. She waited another half hour or so for a reaction but there was none. Now was the time to go for it. She put her shoes into her coat pockets and climbed onto the bed head, balancing precariously in bare feet.

Yess, she thought, *I can reach the catch.*

It was an old fashioned one with a serrated arm on the window and a lug on the frame for it to hook onto. It wasn't locked, but it was heavy, held shut by its own weight. She pushed and it moved upwards with a grating sound. She paused, holding her breath to listen but all was silence. She pushed a little more and it opened further, more quietly this time, but she knew she couldn't hold the weight for long. She pushed again and at the full extent of her arms the lowest serration engaged with the lug. The window was now open to the fullest extent of the catch, but the gap wasn't wide enough for her body.

I'll just have to push my way through, she thought, not sure if she could. She reached up, grasped the edges of the window frame and half sprang, half pulled herself up to get first one elbow and then a second through, one on either side. Her head was touching the glass. As she hung by her elbows, feet in mid-air, she was glad of her coat sleeves acting as padding. When she pushed up with her shoulders and head, to her joy the window opened further, the arm of the catch coming free, but now her elbows and shoulders carried the entire weight of the window as well as her own body. She was testing them to breaking point and the load was overpowering. For a moment she thought she would fall but with mixed desperation and willpower she leaned alternately towards one elbow and the other, at the same time pushing herself up and trying to straighten her arms so she could grasp the frame first with one hand and then the other, pulling and pushing herself forward. There was a moment when her muscles were protesting so much she thought they would give way but one last-ditch effort thrust her far enough to wriggle through the opening to her waist.

She paused to rest, half out of the window. Shortly after she dragged herself all the way through and gently closed it behind her. She lay spread-eagled on the tiled roof, elated but panting, and aching everywhere. Now all she had to do was get safely to the ground and run home. It might only be round the corner.

Wait, there was a sound. Footsteps below her inside, and lantern light. She froze. She wanted to look or move down the roof away from the window but any movement might be heard. Ginger was swearing and walking round the room, then there was a sound like him clambering onto the bedhead. The window rose and his head poked up, only half a metre from her own, but he was looking the other way and struggling to lift the lantern through. If he turned, he would see her. She had to do something. As he got the lantern onto the roof she pulled a shoe from her pocket and hit it with the heel as hard as she could. Ginger was taken by surprise. It flew out of his hand down the roof, off the edge and out of sight to the ground. Lucy's second blow hit his cheek somewhere near his right eye and her third, a second later, his knuckle holding on to the window frame.

'Fuck,' he shouted, making a vain attempt to grab her but he unbalanced himself and fell. The window crashed shut on his other hand and she heard a yell of pain as his own weight tore it free.

Lucy didn't wait. She slid down the roof, legs first, away from the window, much faster than was safe. Her feet reached the edge and connected with a gutter, momentarily slowing her, but it gave way under the force of her slide and she fell. In the next instant she landed in bushes with prickles that she felt through her clothes but nothing was broken and she hardly noticed the pain as she desperately pulled herself free and rammed her shoes on.

Inside, Ginger was cursing loudly and Overcoat was shouting. An outside light came on. She was in an overgrown herbaceous border around an equally overgrown square lawn, overlooked by a large Victorian house on one side and on two further sides by outbuildings, perhaps former stables, from which she had just escaped. She ran for the gap, onto a drive, towards gates, a road beyond. She heard running feet behind but was well ahead, then saw the gates were shut, perhaps locked, so veered off the drive onto another lawn then into a shrubbery. She reached a stone wall with street lighting on the other side but its top was above her head. She ran along it away from the gates, ducking and dodging to avoid bushes and small trees, looking for something, anything, that would help her over the wall.

She knew she was making noise as she ran and part of her wanted to stop to listen for pursuit but she knew Ginger and the others would be after her and she needed to keep as far ahead as possible. Suddenly she tripped and fell sprawling, grazing her shins, knees and hands on something hard and rough. Adrenaline suppressed her cry at the intense pain, and had her on her feet again in seconds. She couldn't stop the tears, though, and now heard two pursuers, one behind and one over to her left beyond the bushes.

About to run on, she saw in light from the street that she had fallen over a block of stone and there was a pile of them against the wall. Deliverance! She stumbled up it, only a metre high but it made the difference. The top of the wall was now shoulder height and with strength she didn't know she had, ignoring painful arms and legs, she hoisted herself onto it and dropped down the other side into the street.

There was no-one about and opposite she saw another street at a right angle going downhill, so she limped across the road and forced herself to run. Hurting everywhere, she pushed it to the back of her mind. Her only thought was finding home and Dil. If she was right about her location, it would be nearby. She heard a sound behind and looked over her shoulder. Ginger was over the wall and gaining on her. She speeded up. The street was lined with what had been substantial terraced houses, now offices, and at the bottom was a well-lit major road with cars starting and stopping at traffic lights and a few pedestrians. A shiver of doubt sneaked into her mind. The hill she was running down, the traffic lights, didn't feel like home territory. She needed to get her bearings, see something familiar, but above all she needed sanctuary because she was near the end of her strength. If home was round the corner she could make it. If not...

She reached the main road, turned left in front of an old high building and stopped, shocked. Its corner took the form of a round stone tower with a lead-covered dome, just like on Cartwright Hall. Her heart lurched with fear and dashed hopes. She knew now where she was. Ten miles from home.

37

Bouncers

Donna's phone buzzed an alert from her office desk.

'Can I use your laptop, Dil?' she asked.

He nodded and it turned out to be a message from Arun. He'd sent a video link.

This it? the covering message asked. *Sorry reg no. false.*

'It's got to be the one,' said Bina as they all gathered round the screen.

The timestamp was yesterday at 19:38.

'Looks like Manningham Lane,' said Dil, 'heading out of the city. They could easily be at that point from here in about ten minutes.'

They followed it for about ten miles to Keighley, the next big town along the Aire valley.

'Pronounced Keethly,' said Bina for Donna's benefit.

At traffic lights in the town centre, it turned up a steep side street and CCTV ran out.

In two minutes, they were out of the house and into the car.

***

Lucy cowered in a shadowy shop doorway, panting heavily, hurting all over. Tears still ran down her cheeks. There were few passers-by and those that there were either didn't notice her or assumed she was just another homeless person, and walked on. Part of her wanted to rush out and ask for help but she knew Ginger was close, and speaking to someone would only advertise her presence. He was likely to be violent.

She sat in a heap. It was the first doorway she had come to on rounding the corner. She realised she was not hidden but she was exhausted and could go no further, overcome with misery and disappointment that she was so far from home. She expected Ginger to appear any second and he would be bound to see her. There was intermittent traffic on the road and a muted buzz of conversation with music from a pub next door. Suddenly the pub noise became louder, then softer again as someone came out. A pub! Why didn't she think of it before? She could 'Ask for Angela'. A last reserve of strength enabled her to stand up and peep out at the street. Her heart stopped. Ginger was about twenty metres away, walking in her direction, his head swivelling as he scanned the area. She ducked back, realising he would be there in seconds. It was now or never. She darted out of the doorway and a few metres to the left into the pub. She heard Ginger's 'Fuck,' as he spotted her.

Once inside she ran to the bar but the three staff were serving other customers. Ginger came up behind her.

'Hello darling,' he said with a creepy smile, 'wondered where you'd got to. Shall we go?'

He took her hand and twisted her arm up her back.

'No,' she shouted at the top of her voice.

Everyone including the bar staff turned to look.

'Sorry, she's had too much again,' said Ginger.

'Angela,' she shrieked at the top of her voice, the other drinkers still watching.

'Just a minute,' said a middle-aged dark haired woman from behind the bar. 'She looks like she's hurt herself. I'll get the first aid kit. Come into the back, love.'

Lucy glimpsed herself in a mirror behind the bar. Her face was streaked with blood from her hands, bruises were still prominent and her hair was at crazy angles. She looked a wreck.

'No need,' said Ginger, pulling Lucy towards the door. 'I can take care of her.'

'She insists,' said a thickset man with a shaved head loudly, standing up from a table close to Ginger.

'Yes she does,' said his equally thickset friend with a crewcut, also standing up.

Ginger hesitated.

'Alright, lads,' he said. 'No problem. I'll wait outside.'

He knew when he was out-manoeuvred. The buzz of conversation in the pub started again.

'We'll wait with you,' said Shaved Head.

'No need,' said Ginger.

'We insist.'

Once in the back room, Lucy collapsed onto a chair.

'Is he giving you a hard time, love?' said the woman. 'My name's Paula. It's my pub.'

'He kidnapped me,' she said, starting to sob. 'Can I use your phone to call my husband? Then maybe the police.'

'No problem, love, and I think my two bouncers will be having a word with him.'

'Bouncers?' she said as she dialled Dil.

'Well not official. It's a good-natured crowd in here usually but every now and then someone has too much or something kicks off so I need support. They're lovely lads, call in most nights, just in case. They get beer on the house.'

Dil answered. Lucy began to sob as soon as she heard him.

'Dil...' was all she could say.

'Lucy? Where are you? Are you ok? We're in the car looking for you. Are you still with those people?'

His voice was choked too and she couldn't speak. She handed the phone to Paula.

'She's ok,' said Paula. 'Battered, I think, but she's obviously got guts. She ran in here a few minutes ago asking for Angela. Dog and Fox, North Street.'

She paused. 'Yes, Keighley.' Pause. 'Five minutes? Ok. She'll be fine here. The guy who came in after her is outside giving my bouncers a good listening-to. I haven't called the police. I will if you really want but it all gets recorded and counted and reported when my licence comes up for renewal.'

Pause.

'Ok, we'll talk about it when you get here. See you in a few minutes. I'm Paula.'

***

When Dil took Lucy's call they were already on the edge of Keighley. With Donna driving they got to the pub three minutes later. Dil, Jack, Emily and Bina rushed inside while Donna parked.

Outside the pub door a ginger bearded man was sitting on the pavement with his back against the wall and two solid young men were standing over him. The sitting man had a cut on his cheek and his eyes were half closed. Donna deduced it was the guy Paula had referred to. She took a couple of photos.

'What would you like us to do with him?' asked one of the men. He had a shaved head.

'Could you just keep him here for a minute until I've seen Lucy?'

'No problem, love.'

Donna went inside and Paula beckoned her to join the others in the back room, where Dil and Lucy were having an emotional reunion in each other's arms.

'What are we going to do with the guy outside?' she asked.

'I can tell you what I'd like to do,' said Dil from Lucy's neck.

'Me too,' said Bina.

Paula giggled. 'I think my lads may have gone some way towards it. They have strong principles when it comes to women being harmed.'

'Yes he looks like he's had an argument with a wall,' said Donna, 'but we need to call the police. Kidnapping, assault, goodness knows what else and he can't have been alone. There'll be others involved too.'

'Yes there were at least two others,' said Lucy.

'Can't we just go home,' said Dil. 'It'll take all night to explain to them about Em and Jack and how it all arose, make statements, find the place where Luce was held and everything.'

'That's true,' said Donna, 'and they'll probably want to check everything with my boss and DI Audrey too, and neither of them know about Lucy being taken yet, so we'd have to explain. Then they'd need a search warrant. It could all take well into tomorrow or longer but we ought to do it because these people are dangerous and the trail could lead to King or Anderson and the murder attempts.'

'Hmm,' said Jack, 'it'd great if it did but I bet they're good at covering their tracks. And I doubt if the kidnappers would admit to receiving orders from them even if that's where they came from. More likely the orders would have come from someone else in a chain.'

'We've got the phone recording,' said Emily, 'which implicates him in kidnapping.'

'True,' said Bina. 'but there could be a problem about the recording being admissible evidence in court, because it was made without his knowing.'

'What we really want to know,' Emily replied, 'is why King and Anderson want Jack and me. We certainly ought to call in the police about Lucy but it won't necessarily tell us that.'

Paula was still listening. 'It sounds complicated,' she said, 'and none of my business but if you want to think things over you could get sonny-Jim's details outside and reel him in another time. He'll be on my CCTV and you can rely on me to give evidence whenever you need it.'

'That sounds like an idea,' said Dil, Lucy echoing. 'The guy's already had tlc from Paula's bouncers, which does my heart good, and now I just want to curl up with her and help her recover.'

Quiet tears began to roll down Lucy's cheeks.

'Yes, let's just sleep on what we do next,' she said. 'I can easily identify where I was held and although the other two kidnappers might disappear for now, I'd recognise them anywhere. I just couldn't face an all-nighter giving police statements.'

'Nor me,' said Emily. 'Let's get Lucy home.'

'Yes,' said Jack. 'She's been through too much already.'

'It goes against the grain, Donna,' said Bina, 'because it might mean the kidnappers get away, but I have to agree with them.'

'Ok,' said Donna. 'It's against my training again too but we can have another think tomorrow. After all, we know the kidnappers' SUV so Arun would be able to find it via traffic cams and CCTV.'

'Paula, you saved my life,' said Lucy, hugging her though tears. 'I can't thank you and the bouncers enough.'

'No problem, dear. We girls have to stand up for each other.'

'We can't fit six in the Fiesta,' said Emily, 'so could you take Lucy and Dil home, Donna. Bina could ride shotgun. Jack and I'll get a taxi.'

Paula called one. On the way to the car Lucy hugged the two bouncers, somewhat to their embarrassment, but kept well away from Ginger. With the bouncers' help, Donna searched Ginger's pockets and found a wallet with his photo driving licence and an address in Bradford. He also had an ID card from a security company called BML Partners Ltd but there was no address for it. Donna photographed them both. He had no phone.

'You may not have heard the last of this,' said Donna.

Shaved Head nodded approvingly. 'We let him go for now?'

'Yes, and thank you very much.'

'No problem, love. Happy to help. By the way you'd better take this. He had a go at us before you arrived.'

He held out a folding knife.'

'No thanks,' she said. 'You keep it. Or throw it away. Up to you.'

He nodded and they fist-bumped. As she headed for the car she heard him say: 'Off you go, sunshine,' and there was a thud as of boot connecting with flesh-covered bone.

38
Billy

Emily and Jack sat in the back of the taxi behind the Fiesta. Bhangra came faintly through the partition from the front.

'So what do we do about meeting King tomorrow?' said Emily.

'The only reason I'd want to see him is to punch him.'

'Me too and obviously we're not going to sign up with Anderson.'

'Too risky to meet him, Em. A phone call's enough.'

'So now our priority is to find out what Anderson and King are up to and solve the bed mystery.'

'Nothing to it,' Jack smiled, looking straight at her, 'but not tonight. I think you've done enough today. You're looking peaky.'

Emily nodded and was silent for a while.

'It's good we think the same way. You know what you said earlier about me not being able to ignore you after the bed mystery?'

Jack laughed a yes.

'Well, you're right. We were pretty young then, feelings out of control, raging hormones and stuff and I still feel embarrassed about the things I said to you on the phone that day…'

'Don't be…'

'No, hear me out. Up to then I'd just seen you as a spotty boy like all the rest. But after those guys tried to abduct me I realised you were more than that and had actual thoughts in your brain and were really quite sensible and empathetic…'

'Praise indeed,' Jack chuckled.

'Yes I probably didn't say that right but you know what I mean. And you still are…'

'Quite sensible?' he grinned from ear to ear.

'Shut up, I'm trying to say something important. You're more than that. You saved me from the shooting as well and I find myself agreeing with you about a lot of things, and then seeing Lucy parted from Dil and how they felt about it made me realise I value having you as a friend and I should tell you so you know.'

'Ok,' said Jack.

There was a short pause.

'Ok? Is that all you can say? I've been opening up my innermost thoughts and saying I value our friendship and all you can say is ok?'

Jack turned to her and grinned. 'I love it when you get stroppy.'

She giggled. 'I take it all back. I hate you.'

Jack felt something important had just happened.

***

Dil and Lucy were still wrapped around each other when they arrived home.

'Bath and bed,' said Bina to Lucy. 'You look like you're in a daze. Come on, we need to do something about those bruises and cuts. And your hair.'

In the car Dil, Bina and Donna had listened in horror to Lucy's account of her ordeal and were full of admiration for her resourcefulness and courage. In return they explained about Anderson, King, Mrs Barton's will and the bed mystery.

'You'll need Em and Jack to fill in all the details,' said Donna, 'but before you escaped they were planning to meet King tomorrow at Cartwright Hall and sign up to work for Anderson. Which meant going off wherever he wanted the minute they'd signed. If you ask me they'd be signing their own death warrants. Anderson's people failed to kill them so they were trying to make sure by sweet-talking them into going somewhere nice and quiet and they'd never be heard of again.'

'Wow,' Lucy had said. 'They were prepared to do that for me?'

'Well it's not as if we'd just have waved goodbye and asked them to send us a postcard. We'd have had a plan of some sort. We were going to work something out.'

When Jack and Emily arrived a couple of minutes behind their friends, Dil was about to follow Lucy and Bina upstairs.

'We've got two bedrooms apart from ours, and a long sofa down here. Can you sort yourselves out?'

Jack suggested Emily might like a room of her own. She looked drawn and pale. Donna said she'd share with Bina, so Jack took the sofa.

***

What a day, Jack thought as he settled down to sleep. Out of control didn't come near it but at least it had ended with Lucy escaping and all of them ok. They made a good team. Especially him and Emily, and he realised with a stab of self-reproach that what she had said in the taxi about their friendship had moved him but he hadn't replied as he should have done. He couldn't always think of the right thing to say at the right time about that sort of thing. He remembered how it had been when he was young and girls somehow made him feel slow and stupid but Emily was different. She was sensible and straight and, as she put it, a good friend, but at the same time was her own person, independent and thoughtful. He wouldn't want to be caught up in all this stuff with anyone else. He'd made a joke of what she said and he shouldn't have. He would tell her when the moment was right

Later he woke up with a start. It felt like a bright light had just been switched off and he had heard the snooker balls. He tried to sit up but he couldn't move. It was like a dream where you need to run away but you're paralysed.

'I'm not awake,' he told himself, and closed his eyes again.

Then another sound, bare feet running down the stairs and into the room. Emily jogged his shoulder.

'Jack,' she whispered loudly, 'I had the marbles and this time there was a blue flash before it.'

He sat up, awake after all, and able to move.

'Yes, I had the snooker balls and I didn't actually see a flash but I felt as though there'd been a bright light just before I opened my eyes.'

Emily sat on the edge of the sofa.

'It's like someone's transmitting something that we tune in to. But who and where from and why does it only affect us? Why isn't everyone in the house awake and talking about it?'

'Good questions. It's like we're being targeted, as with the shooting. There was something new this time though. I was paralysed. Just before you came down. I'd convinced myself I was still asleep.'

'Maybe the transmission's getting stronger.'

They sat in baffled silence. Then Emily started to shiver. Dil and Lucy's heating went off at night.

'It's chilly. I'm off back to bed. We'll talk in the morning.'

She stood up and headed for the door.

'Em, when we talked in the taxi I didn't reply properly and I'm sorry. What you said was so nice it took me by surprise and I shouldn't have been flippant. I completely agree and I value our friendship very highly.'

'I know,' she said. 'I saw it in your face.'

***

Oh god, Emily thought, *it can't be time to wake up already. I've only just gone to sleep.*

She looked at her watch. It was six o'clock in the morning. Someone was banging on the front door and ringing the bell. She was about to get up when she heard feet on the stairs.

Good, she thought, *none of my business,* and turned over for more sleep.

She heard the door open and Dil's voice sounding surprised.

'What is it, Dil?' Donna shouted from somewhere near. 'Need help?'

'No,' he called, 'but we've got a visitor.'

'Who is it?' said a sleepy sounding Bina.

'Come and see. Luce are you awake?'

An inanimate sound came from their bedroom. No-one could possibly still be asleep. As Emily put on her dressing gown, she heard Jack's voice, also sounding surprised. She left her bedroom as Donna and Bina emerged in dressing gowns. Her eyes were only just open but she noticed they were arm in arm. She went down the stairs and saw Dil standing in the hall with Billy Worth. He looked the same as when they'd seen him at the funeral. He'd filled out since he left school but it didn't seem like flab. He obviously worked out. He wore a smart dark blue suit, white shirt and maroon tie and was just taking off a grey overcoat. His head with its shock of fair hair was hatless. Pretty much a city gent, she thought, though not as tall as Jack and Dil.

They gathered in the sitting room and Dil brewed tea.

'Sorry to wake you at this early hour,' Billy said, 'but it's important. It's really Jack and Emily I want to talk to but Jack says there's no secrets between you.'

They all nodded. He hadn't met Donna before and Jack introduced her.

'Glad you've got the police on your side,' he grinned. 'I take it you and Bina are the minders. I've heard great things about your personal combat skills, Bina.'

'I learned the need for it at school,' she said coolly.

She was one of Billy's worst critics, having been amongst those he and his nasty friends picked on for no reason other than that they were small or vulnerable or had different coloured skin. Jack, Emily and Lucy hadn't been exempt from his cruel humour either, so were not inclined to be friendly.

'You were right when you said we should look out for our personal safety,' said Lucy.

'Yes,' said Billy. 'I wanted to warn you about trouble coming down the track.'

'We found out thank you,' said Dil angrily. 'Now please say what you came for and then go.'

'Ok, ok, I'm just trying to help and to re-establish rapport,' he said, holding up his hands.

'Sounds like there wasn't much rapport to re-establish,' said Donna. 'Bina's told me a few things about her school days.'

Emily half groaned, half yawned. 'It's too early in the morning for an argument. Can we just chill? None of us have slept enough and Lucy and Dil still look awful. So Billy, as Dil said, please say your piece and go.'

'Ok,' said Billy. 'I'm sorry. I know I can't undo the past but I'd really like to make amends and maybe I'll be able to later. I went to Cambridge to speak to you, but someone in DI Kennedy's office told me you'd come here. I didn't mention I was SIS…'

Jack's reaction was immediate. 'If you work for them like Hubbler you can leave right now. Breaking into my flat, cloning my passport, setting fire to Clarence & Thirkill…'

Emily put a restraining hand on his arm. 'Let's just listen for now,' she said, looking at him with raised eyebrows and affirming nods. He opened his mouth to reply, then thought better of it.

'I'll come to Hubbler,' Billy went on, 'but first I need to tell you that SIS is interested in Robert Anderson and James King. Anderson's amassed great wealth and King, a close associate, although not as wealthy in his own right, controls similar amounts through his firm. Governments always keep an eye on individuals like that for two conflicting reasons. First, because politicians like to be friendly with them in the hope of political donations and second, because they don't want them to get too powerful.

'The interest in Anderson goes right back to the late seventies or early eighties. SIS, often known to the public as MI6, picked up stray intelligence that Anderson was involved in scientific research of some kind that he kept very secret. I don't know what it was, but it was thought to be so special that it got referred right up to Cabinet level. The Home Secretary approved surveillance and phone tapping, some if it outside the UK, but we don't know the result because in 1994 SIS moved into its current building at Vauxhall Bridge – you'll know it from James Bond films – and the file was lost in the removal.'

Donna shifted restlessly, looking at the clock.

'Bear with me, I'm getting there. Or at least lost is what was thought until someone recently spotted that it was reviewed in the early nineties by a young lawyer from the Legal Department called James King who left SIS at the time of the move, to join a legal firm called Clarence & Thirkill.'

Jack and Emily were interested now and Donna was intrigued. Bina was trying to maintain an aloof expression but even she was listening carefully.

'However, despite enquiries in the UK and the USA since then, no evidence has ever been found that King stole the file and no dark secrets have been uncovered about his firm. Quite the contrary. It's now one of the top city firms, respectable as the Queen herself. The only caveat is that Mr Clarence and Ms Thirkill died in a tragic helicopter crash about seven years ago, leaving him as senior partner. The enquiry afterwards put it down to pilot error so no blame was attached to anyone else, but I have my doubts.'

'Another partner's just died,' said Jack. 'Edith Gregory who Em and I met. We're thinking the partners are accident-prone.'

Billy looked surprised. 'I didn't know. What happened?'

Jack told him what they knew.

'We don't believe King's whiter than white,' Jack continued, 'especially after what's happened in the last few days.'

'Which is what?'

'We can tell you but first you tell us what you wanted to warn us about.'

'Ok. SIS heard about the shooting in Cambridge, of course, the fire at Clarence & Thirkill and the attack on Bina. I've read all the files, which refer to Jack and Emily having business with the firm. Something to do with Mrs Barton's will. Anyway, somehow or other the Home Secretary's got the idea that you're standing in the way of an important step forward in research by Anderson and the boffins at Cambridge University.'

'What?' said Jack and Emily at the same time, incredulous.

'That's rubbish,' said Lucy. 'Em and Jack are definitely not standing in anyone's way.'

'Nevertheless,' said Billy, 'that's what she's heard.'

'Surely she can't believe it?' Bina asked.

'She doesn't know what to think. She's sceptical about Anderson's motives for the big endowment but there's no hard evidence and there are voices in Government that say it's a great act of philanthropy and you're stopping it happening.'

Bina was thoughtful. 'This wouldn't have anything to do with Mrs Latimer?'

'It most certainly would,' said Billy. 'Why do you ask?'

Jack, Emily and Donna opened their mouths to speak but Bina silenced them.

'Billy,' she said. 'Could you give us a moment? I want to have a private word with Em and Jack?'

'Ok,' he said.

He got up, went into the kitchen and closed the door.

'Look,' said Bina quietly, 'it sounds like Mrs Latimer is up to something with Anderson and King and your investigating John Barton's disappearance is obviously something they don't want to happen, which tells me there's a secret they want to bury.'

Jack and Emily agreed.

'We have to decide whether or not we can trust Billy,' Bina went on. 'If he's on the level it gives us a powerful ally in SIS but if he isn't or if he's on a fishing expedition for some other purpose or on behalf of Latimer or Anderson or whoever, it'd be better to say nothing more and send him on his way. If we decide to trust him we should tell him about Mrs Barton's letter and Lucy being kidnapped and the job offer and everything.'

'Which means,' said Donna, 'it'll probably be passed upwards because he'll report it to his boss and it could go right to the top of SIS and beyond so that'll be the end of keeping it confidential.'

'True,' said Lucy, 'but it doesn't sound like he knows about those things, which he would if he was in with Anderson and King.'

'Yes,' said Dil, 'but he doesn't exactly have a good track record, does he? He could be lying and trying to manoeuvre us into trusting him.'

'We haven't seen him for years, apart from a glimpse at the funeral,' said Jack, 'and in fairness to him he did say he'd like to make amends.'

'If we tell him everything it could hardly make our position worse,' said Emily. 'We're going to cancel this morning's meeting with King but we haven't exactly got a clear strategy beyond that.'

'So shall we vote?' Dil asked.

'It's for Jack and Emily to decide,' said Bina. 'I just wanted a pause to give them time to think about it. I'll support them whatever.'

'Me too,' said Lucy.

Dil agreed and Donna said, 'Bina's right.'

'Jack?' Emily asked, her eyes meeting his.

He nodded.

39
Hubbler

It didn't take long for Emily and Jack to tell Billy about the bed mystery, Mrs Barton's letter and everything that had happened.

'God, this is amazing,' he said, 'and terrifying, not only for you all, which it especially is, but also for the country. If Mrs Latimer knows and approves what's been going on, it's extremely serious. She's an elected Member of Parliament and Government Minister who should behave with integrity. The problem is there are people in SIS that support her, such as Hubbler. They think they'll benefit if she rises.'

'So he's not one of the good guys?' Jack asked. 'We saw you hanging out with him at the funeral.'

'No, he's not and I was surprised to see him there. He had no connection with the school or Mrs Barton and when I asked him he said he happened to be in the area and was there on behalf of a friend who couldn't make it.'

'Sounds a bit thin.'

'Yes and what you've told me makes me think he or whoever sent him knew Jack and Emily were in the will and he was sizing you up.'

'That's a bit scary,' said Emily, 'and at that time the only people who could have told him...'

'...were at Clarence & Thirkill.' said Jack. 'Jim King, Edith Gregory or someone in their offices.'

'And they shouldn't have,' said Bina. 'It's a gross breach of the rules.'

'D'you think they knew what Mrs Barton's letters said, too?' Lucy asked.

'Edith Gregory said the letters were already sealed when she handed them over at the time she made the will,' said Emily, 'so unless they'd been steamed open or something, no-one else would know the contents.'

'But they'd be keen to find out,' said Jack, 'so maybe that's what Hubbler was after when he came to my room.'

'Yes,' said Billy, 'Probably his original intention was somehow to get a look at your letter or even take it off you but someone must have warned him that you hadn't got it so his mission changed to cloning your passport. After that he made it look like one made in Amsterdam and tried to use it to get your letter.'

'If that's so, Jack,' said Bina, 'someone from Clarence & Thirkill must have told him pretty quickly, like while you were on the way back from the meeting, that you hadn't taken your passport with you and would need to produce it with your keycard to get your copy of the letter.'

'That could mean it was Edith Gregory,' said Jack. 'Em and I were a bit puzzled by some of the things she said when we were in hospital. At one point we got the impression she didn't want us involved or would have liked the will to be declared invalid, although in fairness she changed her mind the next day.'

'I bet she and Jim King didn't like things to do with the will being on hold until we responded to the letter,' said Emily. 'Up to then the firm probably had a free hand in what they did with Mrs Barton's money and earned lots of fees from looking after it. Perhaps they saw Jack and I as some kind of threat to its continuing.'

'Maybe more than that,' said Billy. 'King could already be doing things he shouldn't with Mrs Barton's money.

Maybe lost some of it or given some to Anderson or spent some on himself when he shouldn't have.'

'Hmm,' said Bina, 'a criminal court would call that embezzlement.'

'And,' said Dil, 'there's got to be a connection between the new particle centre and teleporting. Anderson and King cooking up something dark under cover of a great act of philanthropy'

'Could well be,' said Jack. 'There's another thing puzzling me too. Who's the body in the Clarence & Thirkill fire.'

'After he funeral I tried to keep tabs on Hubbler. I was in London – often am – on the day of the fire,' said Billy, 'so I followed him when he went to Clarence & Thirkill. I saw the smoke and went up in the lift to find out what was going on but he wasn't there. The fire alarms were going off and everyone was racing to get out of the building and instead of Hubbler I found a man's body in a broom cupboard. He'd been strangled. I photographed him and found out later it was an informant of Hubbler's who may have owed him a favour or maybe Hubbler even paid him. To start the fire, that is. And then Hubbler killed him so no-one would know.'

'Why start a fire, though?' Jack asked.

'I can think of several reasons. For example, to destroy your copy of the letter if he couldn't have it and to implicate you in the fire to stop you doing whatever the letter asked if you got it.'

'But that would still leave me with a letter,' said Emily.

'Edith and King were keen to know where the original was though, weren't they?' Jack replied.

'It probably accounts for the murder attempts, too,' said Billy. 'You were both obstacles.'

'My God,' said Lucy. 'If you're right they're absolutely ruthless.'

'Wait a minute, though,' said Bina. 'If Hubbler's on the side of King, Anderson and Latimer, surely King wouldn't want him to burn down his offices?'

'Well,' said Billy, 'if King's firm's a victim it points the finger of suspicion away from him and maybe he even wanted the will destroyed so he could cook up an alternative method of dealing with the assets.'

'Yes, it would be the same as if the will was declared invalid. As Edith told Jack and Emily, the High Court would decide how the assets should be distributed based on available evidence, which would be mainly King's memory.'

'And no doubt it wouldn't include anything about the letters or Jack and Emily.'

'The bastard,' said Dil.

'Well, it's just speculation,' said Jack, 'but I don't trust King. We're planning to cancel our meeting with him this morning. D'you think we're right?

'Don't go near him,' said Billy. 'It's almost certainly a trap.'

'Right we'll phone and tell him we've changed our minds again and don't want to work for Anderson.'

'Then what?' said Emily.

'Back to bed,' said Lucy, looking worn and bruised.

Dil put his arm around her and kissed her cheek. It was still only seven o'clock.

'Ok,' said Jack, 'Let's all get some more sleep and I'll phone King later. What about you Billy?'

'I'll update my boss. She may have some suggestions.'

40
Mill

The mill was like many others in West Yorkshire. Five stories, flat-roofed, built of locally quarried stone, the heart of a community in its nineteenth century heyday but, now that the wool trade was largely gone, turned over to other uses. Its massive construction made it ideal for many manufacturing enterprises and other types of business. The directory at the entrance from the well-kept car park listed a company on the third floor called Innovative Transportation Ltd, Est 1970. Its website said it provided Logistical Solutions.

Its offices, two rooms on the third floor, were shabby and unexceptional and the middle-aged lady sitting at a desk in the outer office had very little to do other than make coffee or sandwiches for the boss, Mr Twining. Every week she emailed two invoices for 'Service Charge', one to each of the shareholders, who were companies registered in Liechtenstein, and checked that last week's had been paid. There were other minor admin jobs, ordering equipment, paying bills, keeping income tax and VAT records up to date, paying herself and Mr Twining and so on, but they didn't take long. It suited her because she was writing a novel, a steamy romance that was as far from her own life as it could be. She knew she was lucky to have such a good job so close to home in Wilsden, within a short walking distance of her cottage.

Mr Twining made few demands on her and most days she didn't see him after he went into his office in the morning at nine o'clock sharp, until he came out of it at quarter to six. Apart, that is, from days when he worked late and didn't come in until late the next morning. She understood that he spent most of his time in a workshop attached to his office. She had no idea what he did. Something to do with computers. He had a lot of them. In fact, she had no idea of the extent of the workshop. She often poked her head round the door when she needed to speak to him, and she knew that there was a second door on the opposite side of the workshop but she had never seen behind it.

She knew Mr Twining went through because sometimes he wasn't there when she looked in from his office. He'd told her that if she needed him urgently at such a time she should press the red bell button on the wall and wait. She was curious but it was none of her business. He had said at the outset that he didn't want cleaners coming into the offices or the workshop and that it was part of her job to keep the offices and washroom clean but because there was delicate equipment in the workshop, he would keep it clean himself.

She liked the quiet and regularity of the job but this morning was unusual. When she arrived at half past eight, she found the offices open and Mr Twining was already in the workshop. It wasn't unprecedented but it hadn't happened for a few years.

Visitors were rare apart from the occasional cold-calling sales rep, to whom she gave short shrift, so, when the intercom from the ground floor entrance buzzed at about quarter to nine, she took her time to answer and was initially brusque.

'Yes?'

'James King for Mr Twining.'

She blushed with confusion. She had never met him but knew he was important. The nearest thing Mr Twining had to a boss.

'Oh yes of course, hello Mr King. Mr Twining must have forgotten to tell me he was expecting you. Please come up.'

She pushed the door-unlock button.

'Thank you. He wasn't expecting me actually.'

Goodness, she thought, *I'd better warn him,* and knocked urgently on Mr Twining's door. There was no reply so she went through to the workshop where she found him in his white coat with his head and right shoulder deep inside a large computer cabinet.

'Mr King's here,' she blurted, flustered.

'Hmm, I thought he might appear soon. Thank you Melanie. I'll see him in my office.'

She ushered Mr King in with due deference and left to make them coffee. She put it on a tray with the cups and saucers Mr Twining liked – he wasn't a mug person – and added shortbread biscuits on a plate but when she took it in a few minutes later Mr King was just leaving.

***

The six friends went back to bed and Jack told the others to sleep as long as they wanted. He would set an alarm and phone King before ten. He'd downloaded the recording app too so they could all listen later. Lying on the couch he felt he had information overload but he was too tired to work out what was important and what wasn't. He needed rest and a fresh look at it later. He turned over and relaxed into sleep.

His alarm woke him at nine thirty. He called King.

'Hello,' he said, his voice husky as usual.

'Hello, just to say we won't be coming to the meeting today and we've decided not to accept Anderson's offer after all.'

'That's unfortunate.'

'Ok, bye.'

'For both of you,' King continued.

'What do you mean?'

'Mr Anderson would far rather have your voluntary participation.'

'Than what?'

'Than the opposite which, as I say, could be unfortunate, especially for Emily but also for you.'

'That sounds like a threat.'

'Oh come, now. Why would I threaten? I'm simply saying Mr Anderson can be very generous but not if you oppose him.'

'I'm not opposing him, just saying I don't want to join his organisation.'

'And that's your final word? Remember you've changed your mind a couple of times.'

'Final word. Good bye.'

Jack hung up. He wasn't surprised by King's tone. He didn't think the others would be either. The house was still quiet now so he turned over for an extra forty winks.

Flash! Snooker balls…

***

Emily was grateful to be cosy back in bed and for the chance to sleep again. With luck no-one else would demand their attention until they felt more rested. There was plenty to think about because plenty had happened but she needed respite. They all did, especially Lucy and Bina who had both had terrifying experiences, but for now she was too tired to think. She turned over and sank into comfortable sleep. Later she half woke but her watch was out of reach and the house was quiet so she didn't open her eyes.

Flash! Marbles…

41
Mist

Lucy and Dil awoke to Bina knocking on their bedroom door.

'Jack and Em,' she shouted. 'They've gone.'

'Come on in,' Lucy called, looking at her watch.

It was half past ten.

Bina said she'd gone downstairs thinking about breakfast and wondering how Jack's call to King had gone but Jack wasn't there. His clothes were but not his pyjamas. Her words came tumbling out.

'My next thought was that Em and Jack had got together at last – about time if you ask me – and I was desperate to know so I thought I'd knock on Em's door all innocent-like and see if she wanted a cup of tea. She didn't reply so I poked my head in and at first I thought she was still asleep because the duvet was pulled up like she was hunkered down under it but when I looked closer I could see she wasn't there. The impression of her head was on the pillow, her clothes were still there but no pyjamas. Bathroom empty too so I thought maybe they'd gone outside and I looked out the back door but there's a biting wind and it's very cold. They can't have gone for a walk in pyjamas and bare feet. Either someone's been in and nabbed them or they've gone completely barmy and really have gone outside or...'

'...they've been teleported again,' said Dil.

'Yes.' Bina sat down heavily on the bed. 'It would fit with the look of her bed. Like she'd just melted away.'

'Oh hell,' said Lucy, tears forming in her eyes. 'Poor Em. And Jack. So because I escaped, King realises he's got no leverage on them so he's resorted to…this, whatever it is… to get his hands on them. God knows how he's done it, but who cares. If we don't do something he'll almost certainly kill them if he hasn't already.'

'Yes we've got to find them,' said Bina, 'and we need help but who do we go to? Billy might be able to do something but I don't fancy trying to explain it to the local police and anyway Em and Jack won't want us spreading it outside SIS.'

'You're right,' said Donna who'd been listening from the doorway, 'but we don't need to go into it. It's enough to say they've gone and we don't know how. I'll have to let my boss know too. In fact I'll call him now. Couldn't get him last night.'

The call went to message as before, so she called Pete.

'Hi Pete, is the boss there?

The answer sounded like no.

'Ok, well I'm in Bradford as you know and he wanted me to report in every day but it went to message when I tried last night and…'

Pete talked some more and Donna listened.

'So where did he go yesterday?'

Pete told her. She too sat down heavily on the bed.

'Pete, he's very likely in danger. No-one knows this so don't say, but the reason we came here was because our friend Lucy was kidnapped, we believe on behalf of James King and Robert Anderson. She escaped and is back with us but at least one of the kidnappers was a thug from BML Partners.'

The call ended and Donna explained, but the others had already guessed most of it, unbelievable though it was.

'Inspector Kennedy's missing. His wife rang Pete this morning to say he hadn't come home yesterday evening. She was pretty upset. He called Pete from his car about seven last night but didn't leave a message. A phone trace shows he was near BML Partners. They've found his car near there too.'

Lucy shivered, thinking of Ginger.

'If they kidnap a Police Inspector they must think they're above the law,' said Bina.

'Pete says they're going to send some people to BML,' said Donna.

'I think we need to tell Billy,' said Dil.

He was on another call when Dil phoned him but put it on hold long enough for Dil to say that Em and Jack had disappeared, literally, and to call him back, which he did a couple of minutes later. Dil told him the details and that DI Kennedy was missing too, probably while investigating BML Partners.'

'Ok,' said Billy. 'I briefed my boss about our talk. That was her on the phone just now. I'll tell her the latest.'

'So where do we look for Em and Jack?' said Lucy when Dil ended the call. 'I think we can rule out where they kept me but think… where else?'

Donna picked up her phone again and called Arun.

'Hey,' they heard her say. 'Thanks for that lead you gave us yesterday. It was very helpful.'

She put him on speaker so the rest could hear.

'No problem. Glad to help.'

'Much appreciated, but now there's something else. Two missing people. A couple of friends. I think they're likely to be with a guy called King who's probably in the area. If I send you his photo any chance you could give us a lead on where he is?'

'Yup. Your DI apparently got in touch yesterday and asked us to help if requested so I told my boss we already had and he said fine, so send me the picture. If you have his mobile number though, I could tell you exactly where he is."

'Good thought,' said Donna. 'We might have. I'll get back to you.'

'Jack and Em's original phones, the ones we think are tapped, are in the Fiesta boot,' said Bina. 'Let's hope we can access them. Em's burner may be upstairs.'

While Donna ran to look in the bedroom, Dil hurried outside for the two phones in the car. They tried Jack's first. It needed a five digit PIN to open it. Donna looked for finger marks on the glass. There were clear ones on five keypad numbers so she tried entering them but the first two goes were wrong. The phone would lock up completely if another wrong sequence was entered. They decided to try Emily's phone before risking another. Hers was set to face unlock.

'We could try a photo of her,' said Lucy, thumbing her phone to find one.

She found several, tried two and they didn't work. It was the same with her burner.

'Jack was going to use his burner to speak to King this morning,' said Dil. 'May even have done it. Is it here?'

They searched the sitting room and found it under a cushion on the sofa, probably the one Jack used as a pillow.

'Five figure lock code again,' said Dil. 'Any guesses?'

'It could be a birthday,' said Donna.

Dil tried Jack's but no go.

'Try Em's,' said Lucy with a sneaky grin at Bina.

'Six figures,' she replied, shaking her head.

'The bed mystery date's five,' said Dil. 'Let's think. We know the year, and the month was July. What day d'you reckon?'

Lucy and Bina consulted calendars on their phones.

'Twenty-first or twenty-second.'

Dil tried the first with no result.

'So it's got to be this,' he said putting in the second before anyone could stop him.

'Yay, open,' he shouted.

He checked the call history.

'Yes he called King this morning like he said he would.'

He tapped the phone a few times.

'And he recorded it!'

They listened.

'Jack's right. It was definitely a threat,' said Dil afterwards. 'He's like someone out of a mafia movie. What a creep.'

Lucy shuddered. 'They're all creeps.'

Donna was calling Arun to give him the number. He said he'd call back in a few minutes.

***

Emily knew what was happening. She was more scared than last time but years ago she'd said to herself that if it ever happened again she would try to be more alert. The flash and the crack came first, then the marbles, then mist gradually enveloped her head, moving along her body towards her feet, something she hadn't been aware of ten years ago. She began to feel weightless, as though she was floating off the bed. She tried to hold on but her hands wouldn't grip, as though they too had become mist. There was no sound and a few seconds later she could see only mist and had completely lost touch with her surroundings.

She felt she was in limbo. The nearest thing her mind could think of was a flotation tank. She could see nothing but it wasn't dark. She had no sensation of movement but she knew she was alone and didn't feel threatened. She wondered if Jack was nearby and having a similar experience.

She lost all sense of time. It could be seconds or minutes or hours, but the longer she was in this place, if it was a place, the more it seemed not right that she was there and the more detached and lonely she felt. She had been wrenched out of the world away from familiar people and things. She missed them all profoundly. She wanted to see her friends and especially Jack. Was he here in the mist? She hoped so. He was the one person who would understand what was happening and in whom she could confide. She had no idea what was coming next. For all she knew she was dying and this was part of the process but she longed to see him again.

Then suddenly it was over and she was sitting, half reclining, on something like an airline seat. She had the weight of her body back, the mist was clearing and her eyes began to see. There was no sign of Jack.

42
Fire

Bina had the route on her phone and knew the area well. Donna drove, with Dil and Lucy in the back. It was still cold and the sky was heavy grey.

'We're not that far from my home,' Bina said, 'but if I told Mum and Dad I was here they'd be all over us, not to mention grandparents and the rest. Not so sure about my brother. He works hard but he's a bit wild.'

'They're all lovely, Donna,' said Lucy, 'you'd like them. Your brother must be qualified by now?'

'Yes he's a G.P. in an inner city practice. Ah, Sandy Lane. Straight ahead at the traffic lights.'

Arun had tracked King's movements. Overnight he'd been at a hotel in Bradford centre and that morning had driven six miles out to Wilsden, stayed fifteen minutes then driven to Keighley where his phone disappeared off the network. They had decided to investigate his Wilsden destination until Arun found him again.

Donna's phone rang. The conversation came over the Fiesta's speakers.

'He's reappeared,' said Arun. 'Too early to say where he's going but he could be heading back to Wilsden. If he's going to where you're going you'll be there well before him. My DI saw I was looking for King and he said be very careful and we'll come out to you. I think he knows him. Don't do anything till we arrive.'

'Next right,' said Bina, 'at the Ling Bob pub. Yes there it is. Onto the village main street. Look for an old mill.'

After a short distance, Bina directed them to turn left into a narrow cobbled lane with a high stone wall one side and a tall stone mill on the other. After fifty metres or so it led into a square yard and the high wall continued to form one side with a single row car park against it. The main entrance to the mill was opposite. Donna reversed into a parking space.

'I'll go and take a look,' said Donna.

'I'll come too,' said Dil.

'You should wait like we were told,' said Lucy, knowing they wouldn't, and Donna grinned.

Through glass doors was a plain stone lobby with a list of half a dozen tenants on the wall.

'I don't think it's Homely Baking Ltd,' said Dil. 'Or the accountancy firm, or Baronial Bathrooms. That leaves Innovative Transportation Ltd and Wilsden Cycles PLC. My money's on Innovative Transportation Ltd.'

'I agree.'

'Ok we'd better wait outside.'

As they turned to go, a middle aged lady came out of a door from the stairwell and walked past them.

'Excuse me,' said Dil, 'do you by any chance know a Mr King. We're supposed to be meeting him here but he doesn't seem to be around.'

'Oh you've missed him, dear. He was with Mr Twining earlier but he's gone now.'

'Oh right, thank you. There's obviously been some confusion. We hoped to see both of them. It's the third floor isn't it?'

'Yes but I don't think Mr Twining'll want to see you. He told me just now he wants absolute quiet so he's sent me home for the rest of the day. I don't mind but it's not as if I'm noisy.'

She smiled and rolled her eyes.

'Oh,' said Dil, enjoying an acting role, and trying to sound as though he was greeting an old friend, 'you must be …' he paused.

'Melanie.'

'Of course, Melanie. You and I haven't met but he's often told me how he relies on you. I'm Dil.'

He held out his hand and she shook it. She coloured slightly.

'Well I never,' she said. 'I've always thought he hardly notices me.'

'Yes, he hasn't what you might call an open manner has he? Did Mr King say where he was going?'

'No, afraid not.'

'No worries. We'll give Mr Twining a call to see if it's ok to go up. Bye for now. '

He took out his phone.

'He might not hear it if he's in the workshop. I could go up and ask if you'd like.'

'Oh no I wouldn't put you to that trouble and if Mr T wants to be alone we might have to come back another day. It's not a matter of life and death.'

Although it could well be, he thought.

'Well, if you're sure, I'll be off. Nice to meet you.'

Melanie headed for the door and turned right to walk home.

'Smoothie,' said Donna, grinning, as they followed her at a discreet distance and headed back towards the car.

'It's what I do.'

Before they reached the Fiesta, a red Hyundai drew into the car park. It was Arun and his boss Detective Inspector Aftab.

'You must be Donna,' said the Inspector.

'Yes, thank you so much for coming. Arun's briefed you I suppose?'

'Yes. Two friends missing. What happened?'

'We're not sure exactly. The rest of us were asleep and when we woke up they were gone but their clothes and stuff were still there. Wherever they went they were in pyjamas and bare feet so we'd be surprised if they just went out for a walk.'

'Ok, what makes you think King knows something about it?'

'He's been talking to them over a couple of days about going to work for an American associate of his called Anderson but they turned him down and we have a recording of a phone conversation between King and our missing friend Jack that could be regarded as threatening.'

'Have you got it here?'

'Yes.'

Dil took Jack's phone from his pocket and played it.

'I see what you mean. Not a direct threat but clear warning overtones.'

Bina got out of the Fiesta and came over.

'What's the delay? If Em and Jack are in the mill we need to get in there quickly.'

'No delay,' said Donna. 'Bina this is Inspector Aftab, We were just playing him the recording.'

'Hi, Inspector. Anything could be happening to them.'

As she spoke a black saloon car came into the yard from the cobbled lane, drove past them and reversed into a parking spot near the end of the row.

'It's King,' said Donna.

'Let's go and speak to him,' said DI Aftab. 'Arun, could you go and stand at the exit road to stop him if he makes a run for it?'

Bina went back to the Fiesta to update Lucy.

'I came across Mr King a long time ago,' DI Aftab continued to Dil and Donna. 'In fact we were at the same school because he comes from around here, well, Ilkley, a posh area, not where I was brought up. He was bright but not nice to Asian people, thought he was a cut above. Wasn't alone of course but he was at the heart of it in our year. Then about twenty years ago, maybe more, there was an allegation of domestic abuse that never went further and I don't know why. His wife died in a car crash shortly after. I've always thought it a bit strange.'

They reached the car, a new BMW hybrid, and could see that King was inside, talking on the phone. There were muffled loudspeaker tones. DI Aftab tapped the driver's window. King looked but didn't show any recognition or indication that he was going to open it. He waved, then held his thumb and little finger between his ear and mouth, turning away. DI Aftab knocked more strongly and held his I.D. to the window. King looked and waved again, then lowered the window.

'Hold on,' they heard him say.

'Yes, officer?'

'Would you mind stepping out of the car, Mr King. I'd like to ask you a few questions.'

'It's not convenient at the moment,' he said. 'I'm having a confidential talk with a client.'

'Ok, finish your conversation. We'll wait.'

King, expressionless, said nothing but raised the window again and carried on talking. DI Aftab, Donna and Dil stood back.

'He's a cool customer,' said Dil. 'He's talking to someone called Bob and I think I saw him say Wellington.'

'Wow,' said Donna, 'you lip read?'

'Only a bit. We did some at acting school, part of body language training.'

'The Bob could be Anderson,' said Donna.

'I think he's finishing off,' said Dil, watching his head move. 'He's just said bye for now.'

They heard a clunk as the carphone call ended.

'He's still talking, though,' said Dil. 'As though the call's continuing, but he's just rubbed his nose, often a sign of deception.'

'He's going to run,' said DI Aftab.

He waved a warning to Arun and leapt aside as King gunned the BMW forward, heading for the exit road. A couple of seconds later Dil heard a car engine start and the Fiesta leapt forward into the BMW's path. Bina was at the wheel, also heading for the exit. King's car was fast and eerily silent, just a few metres behind the noisily revving Fiesta. When he was almost touching it he pulled out to try to overtake before they reached the exit road that wasn't wide enough for both.

Now abreast of the Fiesta, King swerved towards it, smashing against its offside and pushing it into the wall. There was a scraping, grinding sound that went on and on as Bina tried to steer away from it, pushing against the BMW and leaving a trail of metal debris. Now they were only twenty metres from the exit road and the BMW seemed to leap forward again in an effort to get there first but Bina slammed her foot down. In the next instant both vehicles reached the gap and stopped dead with a mighty crash, side by side, wedged across it.

'Lucy, Lucy,' Dil shouted.

He ran towards the wreckage, Donna and DI Aftab close behind. Steam and wisps of smoke were rising from it. Arun was already trying to open the back of the Fiesta but it was jammed. DI Aftab flung open the Hyundai boot as he passed and snatched two police batons, throwing one to Arun as he arrived at the crashed vehicles.

Dil was still shouting and Donna held him away as the two policemen smashed the Fiesta back window and Aftab half crawled in. Bina wasn't moving but Lucy was and shouted, 'I'm fine, get Bina out.'

Arun used his radio to call an ambulance and the fire brigade as the Inspector climbed over the back seat.

'I'll get out on my own,' said Lucy, 'leave you more space.'

She wriggled out of her seat, slid past DI Aftab, and out at the back into Dil's arms. Aftab crawled into the front seat. Bina's head hung forward over the steering wheel and her eyes were closed. There was blood around her nose and upper lip but no other sign of physical injury.

'Bina,' he said quietly. 'Wake up Bina.'

No response.

'Bina,' he said again and put a hand on her shoulder.

She stirred, groaned and her eyes opened, staring ahead, blank for a moment, then she started shouting, struggling to get out.

'Who are you? Where's Lucy? There's smoke. We need to get out before it blows up.'

'It's ok. You're ok. We'll get you out. Just take it easy. I'm Detective Inspector Aftab, remember? We're ok. Yes there's smoke but we're going to get out in a minute.'

He spoke quietly and calmly. Bina stopped struggling but there was a strong smell of burning and petrol. He looked across to the BMW. King was still in the driver's seat, obviously conscious. Both cars were wrecked, everything bent out of shape, shattered window fragments everywhere. Arun was standing at the BMW's driver's door talking to King, or rather King was talking to him, his normal husky voice loud and strident.

'Get me out of here. Call yourselves police? Standing around watching while reckless drivers try to kill me. I wouldn't bank on your being in the force long enough to collect your pension. Your next pay cheque, come to that. I'm a lawyer and I'll tie you and that stupid Asian woman up in litigation until you're both bankrupt.'

Arun stood listening and when King stopped he said, 'Shall we try to get you out of the car, sir?'

It was obvious the door wouldn't open because the car was embedded to the windscreen in the gap between the mill and the Fiesta.

'Arun,' DI Aftab called, 'Fire extinguisher.'

Arun looked at King. 'Pass me yours, Sir?'

He could see one poking out from under the passenger seat.

'I demand you get me out of here first.'

'Sorry, sir, injured people have priority. The lady in the Fiesta for example. If we can't use yours I'll go and look for one. You'll be ok there for a while won't you?'

He turned and walked away. He knew there was one in the Hyundai that he could fetch in ten seconds but he didn't like King's manner.

'Ok, ok,' said King reaching down to the floor. 'Here it is.'

'Thank you, sir. Back in a few moments.'

The smell of burning was much stronger now and as Arun took the extinguisher there was a boof and flames erupted from under the Fiesta's twisted bonnet. Arun took a run at the back of the BMW, scrambled onto its roof, activated the extinguisher and aimed it at the flames. Inside DI Aftab unfastened Bina's seat belt.

'Any pain anywhere?' he asked.

Bina shifted her legs and rolled her shoulders.

'Chest and face hurt but ok elsewhere.'

'Think you can get out the back?'

Bina nodded.

'Right, let's go. You first and I'll give you a push if you get stuck.'

'Come on, Bina,' said Donna from behind. 'I'll pull.'

The flames were less but not out and the extinguisher was empty.

'Ok Arun, get Mr King out quick.'

Arun jumped to the ground. King was trying to climb out of the driver's window.

'It'll be easier face upwards.' said Arun, 'I'll catch you.'

'You'd better,' King growled as a loud bang came from the Fiesta's engine and a new wall of flame shot up from the bonnet.

Bina was part way out and Donna pulled her the rest. King kicked backwards into Arun's arms like a jet projectile. DI Aftab's shoulders were out. Dil grabbed him under the armpits and yanked him clear, shouting 'Run,' to the others. A second later the petrol tank blew and a sheet of flame engulfed the whole car, spreading to the BMW.

'Phew,' said DI Aftab. 'That was close. Everyone ok?'

Donna and Bina were hugging.

'All your fault,' said King loudly, pointing at Bina. 'There'll be consequences.'

DI Aftab moved between them.

'Mr King, you knew we wanted to ask you some questions, yet you tried to leave without speaking to us and dangerously ran down this lady's car. I should say if anyone's going to feel consequences it's you.'

'She deliberately tried to stop me leaving.'

'She was in front of you and you tried to run her into the wall.'

'We'll see what a court thinks about that. I was going to an urgent and important meeting. You people think you can come here and have everything your own way.'

'Meaning what?' Donna asked angrily but King wasn't listening, he was on his phone calling a taxi.

An ambulance and a fire engine arrived and the firefighters set about dousing the flames. The paramedics couldn't get past the cars but found a side door into the mill and a minute later came running out of the main entrance. A young man and a motherly woman. They examined Bina and found that she'd hit her face on the steering wheel causing her nose to bleed but nothing was broken. She would have bruising and swelling on her top lip for a day or two, perhaps bruising on her chest from the seat belt, too. Her blood pressure and heart rate were up but coming down. They cleaned her up and gave her pain killers.

'We can take you to the Infirmary for a check-up if you like, dear,' said the motherly one, but Bina said she'd be ok.

They examined Lucy and King, pronouncing them fine, and went on their way with thanks from everyone. The fire was now out and the crew were awaiting a crane truck to untangle the two cars and take them away. Bina took photographs for insurance.

'Mr King, walk with me and you can answer our questions. It won't take long.'

'Fine,' he said as he ended the call, 'You don't mind if I record our talk?'

'Not at all and DC Arun Ahmed will record it too.'

They walked slowly around the yard, DI Aftab on one side and Arun on the other.

'We're looking for Emily Harrison and Jack Wellington. I understand you spoke to Jack this morning?'

King was quieter, less belligerent now. 'Let me think, I use the phone a lot...Sorry, I don't remember.'

'It was only about two hours ago. Let me remind you.'

The Inspector played the recording.

'So who are those two people speaking?'

'Don't try to pretend, Mr King. That's Jack Wellington and you.'

'No definitely not me.'

'Don't put me to the trouble of an official check on the phone numbers in that call.'

'That's up to you.'

'Why did you drive off knowing we wanted to speak to you?'

'Sorry, I forgot My mind must have been on phone calls.'

'Do you know where Jack Wellington and Emily Harrison are.'

'No idea.' He smiled.

'In that case, I'm arresting you on suspicion of dangerous driving. You do not have to say anything, but it may harm your defence if you do not mention when questioned something which you later rely on in court. Anything you do say may be given in evidence.'

King smiled broadly. 'I'm afraid you can't arrest me. I have diplomatic immunity.'

He produced a dark blue passport from an inner pocket. DI Aftab looked at it. On the front in gold was the United States eagle and the words 'Diplomatic Passport'. It was in King's name and the photograph was of him. It was due to expire in eight months' time. The Inspector said nothing and handed it back.

'You don't remember me do you?

For a moment King looked confused, then smiled and said, 'Refresh my memory.'

'School.'

If King remembered he gave no sign.

'Long time ago. Afraid I don't remember. I don't think I had any friends like you. Oh, here's my taxi. Bye for now. You'll be hearing from me with litigation.'

A crane truck was arriving to clear the approach road. They could see the taxi flashing its lights beyond. King waved and headed for the mill entrance to go out of the side door.

Dil ran over to DI Aftab.

'Why's he going? Why haven't you arrested him?'

'Slimy toad,' he said after hearing the explanation.

43
Karen

Jack read the signs in an instant, half asleep though he was. Somewhere at the back of his mind he'd been expecting it. Ever since it happened ten years ago, he'd wondered and puzzled not only who did it, how and why but whether there was a way of stopping it. With him and Emily and, probably, John Barton, it had happened when they were asleep or almost so, and lying down, which made him wonder if being awake or standing or moving might prevent it.

Maybe the paralysis he'd felt last night was essential for it to work. He forced his eyes open and moved his legs. They worked. So did the rest of him and although he was aware of mist forming around his head he sat up on the edge of the couch. His muscles felt sluggish and it took more effort than normal.

Next he tried standing up. Hard work, mist already down to his chest. With a big effort he took a step forward. Ahead the mist seemed thinner. His feet now felt like they were stuck to the floor and he only just managed a second step. He was almost out of the mist but, thin though it was, at least to the front, it sank past couch level and the room began to fade. He knew that only a couple of seconds had passed but his brain was registering every little change in each microsecond, as though time itself was being stretched.

He raised his arms in front of him. He was unable to see them but he knew they were there and he sensed they were out of the mist. He tried to force his whole body forward but paralysis had come. It wasn't dark but everything had become opaque and he couldn't see anything or move.

He wondered if the same was happening to Em. Part of him hoped it wasn't because she would be scared but part of him hoped it was because he was sure they'd be stronger if they were together, better able to face whatever came next. He might be able to protect her, too. She was quick and bold and funny and he suddenly realised she was the nearest thing he'd ever had to a soul mate and he hoped intensely that wherever he ended up, she would be there too. Then his hands felt something hard, rough and cold. And he could see. He was alone.

***

'If we can't grill King we can at least talk to Mr Twining,' said Donna.

She explained to the others how Dil had interrogated Melanie. They were amused, but impressed too.

'He's such a sweet-talker,' said Lucy, half mocking, half proud.

'Let's go,' said DI Aftab.

In the entrance lobby Dil pressed the intercom for Innovative Transportation Ltd. There was no reply.

'Ok, up to the third floor,' said the Inspector.

The staircase was stone, worn by many generations of feet, and there was a smell of lanolin in the air, absorbed from bales of wool that had been processed in the building for more than a century. There was only one door on the third floor landing but there was no reply to their knocking and it was locked or bolted. The door was old and substantial.

'I think we need a big red key,' said the Inspector. 'I saw one in the boot, Arun.'

'Yes, sir. I'll fetch it.'

They knocked again without result while Arun was gone. He was back in a few minutes with a red police battering ram. He used it on the door just below the handle and it gave way at the third wallop.

DI Aftab and Arun rushed in but the two office rooms were deserted, as was the workshop beyond. There was another door on the far side of it. DI Aftab knocked and shouted but there was no response. It was locked and this time only two strikes of the ram were needed. They paused in awe on the threshold of a 'room' they estimated was forty metres long. The whole length of it, from floor to ceiling across the full width, was taken up with five uniform rows of humming and blinking computer equipment.

'Come on,' said Dil, starting to run, 'let's each go down a different aisle.'

They found no-one and at the end came together at yet another door. DI Aftab repeated his knocking and shouting. This time they heard sounds inside and a small flap opened at head height.

'Yes?' said a man.

He appeared to be late fifties, with a bald head and a black circle beard. Behind him they could see computer terminals, equipment racks and metal lattices, with things like tv aerials and satellite dishes.

DI Aftab showed his badge. 'We'd like to come in and talk to you.'

'Sorry, this is a top secret Government laboratory that has strict quarantine and contamination rules. No unauthorised access I'm afraid.'

He spoke with a cut glass accent.

'Don't put me to the trouble of getting a search warrant, sir.'

'It wouldn't do any good. Only a Government minister can allow access. I'd like to help but my hands are tied.'

He handed an official-looking paper through the flap. DI Aftab read it.

'Thank you, can I keep it?'

'That's the original but I can give you a copy.'

The inspector handed it back and Mr Twining disappeared.

'I don't buy this,' said Dil quietly. 'It's a bit bloody suspicious that he's not allowed to let us in.'

Everyone agreed, including the Inspector. Mr Twining reappeared and handed over the copy.

'I'll check this out,' said DI Aftab. 'We're looking for Emily Harrison and Jack Wellington.'

'I see.'

'Well, do you know where either of them are?'

'Those names mean nothing to me but even if they did I'd not be allowed to say. Now I'm quite busy so if you want to come in, please get the appropriate authorisation.'

'We've just seen Mr King outside. I understand you met him earlier.'

'If I did, I'd need authority before I confirmed or denied it.'

Bina was fuming. 'Can you confirm it's Thursday today?'

Mr Twining looked her in the eye. 'I don't see the relevance of that. Now if you'll excuse me I'll go and do some work. You know your way out.'

He closed the flap.

***

Every weekday morning Karen walked from her home at Hallas Bridge to Wilsden Nursery School where she worked. It was two kilometres along country footpaths. As she climbed a stile over a dry stone wall into a wood, she was surprised to see a man in pyjamas standing beside a tree. He looked dazed and was shivering.

'Good morning,' she said cheerily. 'Bit chilly to be out without a coat.'

'Yes,' he said. 'Can you tell me where I am?'

'Wilsden village that way,' she said, pointing, 'about a kilometre and Hallas Bridge that way, about the same.

'Wilsden,' he repeated, obviously recognising the name.

She thought he looked very cold. 'How long have you been out here?' she asked.

'I don't know. I've been wandering round the wood for a bit and just came across this path. My feet are freezing.'

She noticed they were bare. She wondered why he was there. Perhaps he'd 'escaped' from a psychiatric hospital but the nearest one was miles away and he certainly couldn't have walked the distance on bare feet in pyjamas. He must have come from somewhere nearby, she decided. Perhaps he was confused and didn't know how to get back.

'Where have you come from?'

He gave Dil's address and said he'd like to go back there. Karen was surprised. She knew where it was. About five miles away.

'You can't walk it dressed like that.'

She realised she couldn't leave him either. He would likely die of exposure if he wasn't warmed up soon. She could take him to the village hall and call a taxi or something but the path was rough and stony and she doubted if his feet would stand up to it. She had nothing with her to improvise socks or shoes.

Then she thought of Dyehouse Cottage, on the other side of the field she had just crossed. Geoff and Sue, a retired couple who lived there would be sure to help and the path was soft grass. She suggested it and he agreed. She took off her waterproof and draped it round his shoulders, some protection at least. Halfway across the field he stumbled and fell, unable to get up. He wasn't unconscious but his eyelids fluttered, his eyes rolling up, and he was muttering 'M'. Damp grass soaked his pyjamas, turning his shivering into a violent shudder. She tried lifting him to his feet but he was too heavy.

'Stay there, I'll go for help,' she said.

She ran the remaining distance to the cottage, climbed over the wall and hammered on the front door. Sue answered and quickly understood.

'Geoff,' she shouted, 'go with Karen. I'll call an ambulance.'

***

Dil, Lucy and Bina stood fuming outside Mr Twining's door but before they could open their mouths to sound off, DI Aftab shushed them, pointing to a CCTV camera on the wall.

'Could be a microphone too,' he whispered.

They followed him quietly out to the third floor landing, down the stairs and outside where Dil, Lucy, Bina and Donna exploded.

'I bet he does know Em and Jack,' said Lucy. 'All he said was they don't mean anything to him.'

'How chilling is that?' said Bina. 'Can I have a look at the paper he gave you, Inspector?'

'Let's just break in,' said Dil. 'I bet Em and Jack are in there. That creep struck me as cold and detached, verging on psychopath.'

'Me too,' said Donna, 'but you'd put yourself in the wrong if you did something illegal. We've got to tackle it properly and in fairness we don't know for sure if Emily and Jack are in there.'

'Donna's right,' said DI Aftab. 'First I'll check out his authority, and if it's legitimate I'll have to go through the proper channels to get access.'

'And by the time you've done that,' said Dil, 'they'll be dead or moved. There has to be a better way.'

Bina had been reading the paper. 'It's signed by Mrs Latimer. We ought to tell Billy about this.'

'Who's she and who's Billy?' DI Aftab asked.

Dil explained while Bina scanned the paper with her phone and sent it to Billy, then called him.

'What d'you think?' she said.

'Amazing. I've never heard my boss or anyone in SIS mention this Ministry having top secret stuff. I've always thought the Home Office or the MoD were the only ones. I'll see what the boss thinks. I'll get back to you.'

Donna's phone rang. It was Pete.

'Wow, Donna, all hell's broken loose here. Superintendent Gray's on the case and our team went out to BML at Cottenham but were refused admittance. Something about it being a top secret Government site. They wouldn't say whether DI Kennedy's there or even if he had been. So Gray's referred it to the Commissioner and is raging at everyone to find another solution because he says the Commissioner's useless, which we all could have told him, and it'll probably be a fortnight before anything sensible comes out of that office.'

'Did they give our people any proof of it being top secret?'

'I hear they handed over a paper of some sort.'

'Ok thanks, Pete. We've got something going on here. I may call you back in a few minutes.'

Donna told the others.

'This is obviously very big,' said DI Aftab. 'If SIS and Government ministries are involved, not to mention diplomatic passports, it's well above my pay grade but to my simple mind it all stinks, especially if King's involved. I wouldn't trust him further than I could throw an elephant. Trouble is, the bureaucracy could tie us up for weeks, and in the meantime they could get away with murder, literally. I wouldn't pretend to understand what it's all about but if I wasn't obliged to follow procedure, I'd be very inclined to do what Dil suggested.'

'I think I ought to tell Pete what's happening here.' said Donna. 'Is that ok to you, DI Aftab? He'll pass it on to Superintendent Gray, my boss's boss and it might help them.'

'Yes. Sensible for us to keep in touch.'

Donna gave Pete a quick account of what had gone in the past twenty four hours. He told Donna that DI Audrey had just phoned for DI Kennedy and, when told he was missing, reported she'd called him the previous evening about a Mitzli-BML connection. Superintendent Gray called DI Aftab a few minutes later.

'Thanks for passing on what's happening there,' he said. 'It reinforces my case for a raid on BML where we think DI Kennedy is but I'm being hamstrung by my Commissioner who needs to go through Government channels. I'll keep you posted if you'll do the same. I'll assign someone as a contact.'

It turned out to be Pete. He and DI Aftab exchanged the papers handed over by Mr Twining and BML. They were more or less identical.

'Mrs Latimer again,' said Bina and copied the BML paper to Billy.

44
Back

Jack began to feel better after Geoff got him into the kitchen beside the Aga and wrapped him in a blanket. Then Geoff made a cup of tea and fed him shortbread.

'I don't know how I came to be there,' Jack lied, 'but I'm so grateful to Karen and you and Sue for your help. I sort of woke up hugging a tree. Maybe my memory'll come back as I warm up.'

The ambulance arrived within a few minutes so there was no time for Geoff and Sue to probe further, intrigued though they were.

'Seems a nice young man,' said Sue as it drove off.

'Hmm, something familiar about him,' said Geoff, 'but I can't place it. What did he say his name was?'

'He didn't.'

***

'I'm not leaving here without seeing Twining's laboratory,' said Dil. 'In films people wriggle through aircon tubes or up fire escapes.'

Lucy rolled her eyes but didn't dismiss his comment. Bina and Donna didn't either.

'Well, I can't help you there,' said DI Aftab. 'I have to go through official channels and I'm off back to the office now to start the ball rolling. Coming Arun?'

'Er, I'm owed some time because of that job last month. Would it be ok if I took a half day?'

The Inspector grinned. 'Good idea. Could you run me back to HQ first?'

'No problem.'

The Inspector's phone rang.

'Hmm,' he said after a moment. 'Keep him there. I'm on my way.'

'He turned to the others. 'A man in pyjamas was picked up by ambulance near here about half past ten. He's in Bradford Royal Infirmary. Says he's Jack Wellington.'

'Whoa, good news,' said Dil, a similar chorus from the others. 'Is he ok? Any mention of Em?'

'Suffering from exposure but recovering rapidly and no, no mention of Emily I'm afraid.'

'Can I come with you?' said Dil and Lucy at the same time.

'I thought you weren't leaving here until you've seen inside the laboratory,' said Lucy grinning.

'Well, I wasn't but now we need to talk to Jack.'

'Lucy you go with Bina,' said Donna. 'Dil and I'll stay here to watch who goes in and out.'

'I'll come back with the car after,' said Arun.

'Here's Jack's phone,' said Dil, handing it to Lucy.

***

Arun stopped briefly at Dil and Lucy's house for Lucy to run in and throw Jack's clothes into a bag and they were at A & E within half an hour. Jack was sitting up in a bed in a curtained cubicle.

'Where's Em,' he asked urgently.

'Gone,' said Lucy. 'We thought she might be with you.'

'I knew it,' he said, throwing back the bed covers. 'I need clothes. We've got to find her. She wasn't with me.'

He was going to add 'and I think I know why' when he noticed DI Aftab and Arun. Lucy introduced them and handed him the bag and phone.

'So what can you tell us?' DI Aftab asked. 'The others seem to think you and Emily were abducted.'

'Yes we must have been. I went to sleep on the couch and woke up in a wood near Wilsden.'

'Sounds like you were drugged somehow,' said DI Aftab. 'I already know there were no signs of a break-in, though. Must be someone you and Dil know, Lucy. Can you make a list of people who either have a key to your house or who could have had access to one long enough to take photos or make an impression?'

'Yes, ok,' said Lucy, even though she knew it would be wasted time.

'Oh and can you let me have a recent picture of Emily? I can have it sent out when I get back to the office.'

Lucy dug one out of her phone and he and Arun left. Arun said he'd be back in fifteen minutes.

'Looks like you've been in a fight, Bina,' said Jack.

Her top lip was bruised and swollen from the car crash.

'Yes it's hurting a bit now,' she said, 'but nothing really. I'll tell you about and we've other things to tell you too but not here,' she indicated the curtains.

'Get dressed and come round to the main entrance,' said Lucy. 'We'll wait for Arun there.'

'I bet Em's inside that mill,' he said when Lucy and Bina had briefed him.

'Maybe they were expecting you and Em to be transported together and you weren't,' said Bina.

'Yes. When I twigged what was happening, I tried to walk away from the couch, which may have confused the technology. I can't believe he intended to send me where he did. Then again I don't really know why he wanted me, except he probably wants Em and me dead for some reason.'

They were back at the mill before two o'clock. The cobbled entrance road had been cleared and the two damaged cars taken away.

'As far as we can tell no-one's been in or out.' said Donna. 'We hung around in the entrance hall and no-one went up the stairs. Everyone used the lift and none went to the third floor. We can't rule out someone going to another floor and walking up or down to the third, of course. Certainly Twining didn't come out.'

'So how do we get in?' Jack asked.

'I've been thinking about that,' said Dil. 'There's a fire escape at the far end of the building, the end nearest the room Twining wouldn't let us into. I nipped up it and there's fire doors without handles at every level but you see that hoist at roof level?' – he pointed – 'I reckon it's near Twining. It used to be for lifting wool bales into the mill and there were doors under it on each floor, except they're windows now. We could get onto the roof and you could lower me down to look in.'

Arun looked doubtful. 'Sounds dangerous.'

'Yes, but we have to know if Em's in there and I can't think of another way. We'll need a rope though.'

No-one could think of an alternative. Arun produced a rope from the Hyundai boot.

***

James King switched off his phone in the taxi and took out the sim card.

'Where to?' asked the driver.

'We're picking someone up at Greengates.'

Twenty five minutes later they stopped at a house. Ginger came out and got in. He had a black eye, a swollen top lip and cuts on his face covered with plasters.

'Your chance to make amends,' said King.

Ginger nodded.

'Ok, back to the mill in Wilsden, driver, but don't stop outside. Drop us a hundred metres further on.'

He did as requested and received a handsome tip. King and Ginger waited until the taxi had gone, looking up and down the main street, but there weren't many people about and no-one was taking any notice of them. At the opposite corner of the mill frontage from the cobbled entrance road, they ducked down a narrow alley between the mill and a row of houses. About twenty metres along it King unlocked a metal door in the mill wall, from where an internal stone staircase led to another door opening onto the first floor landing. They walked up to the third floor and past the broken entrance into the offices of Innovative Transportation Ltd. They hurried through the workshop and long computer room and into the final room, to which King had a key.

Twining was seated at a terminal in his white lab coat. The door was solid and metal-lined. King locked it again and Ginger noisily closed two substantial bolts. Then he stood with his back to it, staring aggressively at Twining, who eyed Ginger suspiciously.

'What happened to the other one?' King asked.

'I don't know. He may have gone somewhere else.

'Where?'

'I don't know. I told you it's delicate and unpredictable. Rats sometimes don't survive but more usually they go a few degrees off course, especially if they move. That's always been a problem as you know. Right from Barton's time. The tighter I strap them down beforehand the more likely they are to go where I set, but obviously I can't do that with people at a distance.'

'I promised our principal that the system works.'

'So it does. It just needs more refinement.'

'Well, we can dispose of half the problem now. The other half will have to wait.'

'Dispose? What d'you mean?'

'I should have thought it was obvious.'

'Now look here, I'm not getting involved in murder.'

'Yet you transport people using a system that sometimes kills.'

'That's different.'

'No it isn't. A judge would call it murder, or at the very least manslaughter. How many have there been now? You're looking at a very long spell in prison.'

'But they were all accidents.'

'Deliberate killing, a judge would say. You might get away with the first one as manslaughter but after that...'

'You're just as guilty as me. You set it all up.'

'No idea it was happening,' said King with mock surprise. 'I employed you to research transporting goods. It's all in your contract.'

'Right, I quit. Thank you for the job. You've paid me well but now I'm moving on.'

He headed for the door.

'You're free to go, obviously, but think about it. The girl's going to die and I'll report to the police how I came to see you and found you'd killed her. Oh and probably you'd have a fatal accident a week or two later anyway. On the other hand, if you co-operate we can get rid of her together. Just set the machine wrongly and off she goes. No-one any the wiser and you can continue the work.'

Twining was silent. It was true he had already killed if you counted six failed human transportations in the past ten years, possibly a seventh this morning, the man. Five others had worked, including the woman today, a second one for her. He realised he was in it up to his neck and he knew King was unscrupulous. But if the work succeeded he might receive a Nobel prize or a knighthood, certainly great wealth. He was far ahead of anyone else in the field and the system would revolutionise the world. He didn't like being coerced by King but it had turned out alright so far. And he had a trump card. King needed him. No-one else knew how the equipment worked or how to operate it. He had been careful not to keep his notes and records on the premises or in a cloud where anyone could access them. More than twenty years' work. They were in a safe place.

'Alright,' he said, 'let's get over this hurdle but then I'd like to review our arrangement.'

'I see' said King in a quiet husky voice. 'Yes, perhaps it might be wise. Let me see her.'

Twining went past the equipment to a frosted glass wall at the far end of the room. He flicked a switch and the opaque glass became clear. On the other side were two reclining chairs facing each other. Emily, in pyjamas, was strapped to one of them. The other was empty. She looked at the two men with fear in her eyes.

45
Together

Bina and Lucy opted to stay near the car, ready to call help or in case quick transport was needed, while Jack, Dil, Donna and Arun went up the fire escape as quietly as they could. The top landing was more than three metres below the roof parapet but by standing precariously on the iron handrail Arun was able to scramble up and over, then help the others. The parapet was about a metre high.

'This is the tricky part,' said Dil. 'I'll go down because Jack's just nearly died from exposure and I'll recognise Emily if she's there. Arun won't.'

'No it's my job,' said Jack. 'She and I got you all into this so I'm going down.'

Dil and Donna started to protest.

'I can do it easily,' he went on, 'but you can do your bit by hauling me up when the time comes.'

Dil had seen Jack's look of determination before and knew he wouldn't change his mind. Arun tested the iron brackets attaching the hoist to the roof.

'Victorian engineering at its best,' he said. 'Take a tank to shift those.'

Jack looped the rope round them and then around his waist and between his legs in proper abseil fashion. He climbed onto the stone parapet and leaned outwards to test the rope and the bracket.

'Looks like you've done that before,' said Arun.

'He has,' said Dil. 'We both learned years ago in Explorers and he does bouldering now.'

'Here I go,' said Jack.

He leaned further back with straight legs and began walking down the wall, releasing the rope gradually as he went. On the ground Lucy and Bina had their hearts in their mouths. Slowly and carefully he walked down past windows on the fifth and fourth floors and was soon abreast of the one on the third floor. He leaned out further and took a step towards it to glance in. To his surprise there were King, a man with ginger hair and beard and a man in a white lab coat. They were sideways on to him, each facing in the same direction. He craned to see who or what they were looking at and for a split second his eyes connected with the man in the white coat.

Dammit, he thought, and quickly sidestepped out of sight but he knew he'd been seen. He signalled Arun he was coming up and hastily began walking up the wall, pulling the rope tight as he went. At the same time Arun, Dil and Donna began to haul and he was on the roof again in less than twenty seconds.

'King,' he gasped. 'And two others, one in a white coat. They've seen me.'

'Whoa,' said Donna, 'how did King get in there? Last seen he was going off in a taxi.'

There was a sound from the direction of the fire escape and it began to resound with feet coming up. There was nowhere to hide if whoever it was got to the roof.

'Quick,' Donna whispered. 'Leave the rope. Lie down below the parapet by the fire escape.'

It was their only option. They quickly took up position and held their breath. They heard scrambling and panting as someone tried to climb up like Arun had. Lying on his back with Arun's feet at his head, Jack saw first the muzzle of a handgun with a silencer, then a hand holding it, come over the parapet. It fell back with cursing, then reappeared suddenly as though its owner had jumped, the gun handle wedging on the inside of the parapet. A second hand followed. Jack realised that any moment a head could appear and they might be seen. He braced himself to stand up and grab the gun but there was scuffling behind him as Arun used his staff to send it flying across the roof.

'Fuuuck,' a voice bellowed and whoever it was fell back onto the fire escape with a clang.

Donna ran for the gun, checked the safety catch was off and gingerly leaned over the parapet to see Ginger getting painfully to his feet.

'Stop, armed police,' she said loudly.

Ginger froze.

'Ok if I stand up, love?'.

'Slowly.'

He stood up, bending to rub a knee. Suddenly a knife appeared in his other hand and was flying towards Donna. She jerked away from it and it missed but the gun went off and fell out of her hand to clatter down onto the fire escape. Ginger fell over and rolled around on the landing, howling with pain and clutching an ankle.

Arun, Jack and Dil were all now on their feet and Donna exchanged horrified glances with them. None of them had any idea what to do.

'We'd better call for backup,' said Arun, 'We can use the rope to go down.'

'No,' said Jack, 'we still don't know if Em's inside.'

'She is,' said the familiar voice of King from the fire escape just audible above Ginger's wailing. 'Please be quiet Ryan or I'll shut you up.'

He picked up the gun in a gloved hand and waved it at Ginger whose volume decreased a little.

'Now,' King went on, 'I'd like you to come down here, Jack. The rest of you can stay up there.'

'Jack don't,' said Dil. 'He'll kill you.'

Jack didn't even consider not doing what King said. *If Em's down there,* he thought, *that's where I should be.*

'I've got to,' he said.

Arun walked away from the edge of the roof and spoke quietly into his radio. As Jack began to climb down he walked back and whispered that help was on the way. When Jack reached the fire escape landing, King gestured with the gun down the steps. They reached the third floor landing, went through the open fire door and King slammed it shut behind them. Inside was the room full of equipment they had glimpsed through the door hatch earlier. In one corner was a large glass-walled cubicle and in it, Emily, strapped to one of two reclining chairs, still in her pyjamas. She looked lost and vulnerable.

'Em,' he shouted, running to the glass. 'Are you ok?'

'It's soundproof,' said the man in the white coat.

Twining he presumed. Jack rattled the door but it was locked. Emily struggled at the straps holding her down, looking at Jack, her mouth moving.

'Open it,' he snarled.

'Sorry, old chap, have to wait for orders.'

He looked towards King who was still pointing the gun at Jack.

'Actually, I think it would be ok,' said King smoothly. 'Open the door Mr Twining. Jack can go in.'

Mr Twining let Jack in and locked the door after him.

'Em, thank goodness. Are you alright?'

'No,' she shouted, 'I'm not alright obviously and why aren't you rescuing me instead of giving yourself up at gunpoint and I'm very glad to see you.'

Volcanic sobs erupted and tears rolled down her cheeks. Jack wanted to hug her but couldn't, held down as she was. He tried to undo the straps but a key was needed.

'Me too,' he whispered, and, with confidence he didn't feel, 'we'll get you out of here.'

'Jack and Emily.' King's voice came over a loudspeaker.

Jack straightened up, holding her hand that was right beside his. King was at the glass with a microphone.

'Mr Anderson and I are prepared to give you one more chance to join us. You know now what we're doing. This system will change the planet for ever, bring immeasurable wealth, and you could be in it from the start. In fact you've already been in it from the start.'

'No, John Barton was the start,' said Jack.

'Yes, he was the first human being to experience it but apparently he didn't survive. I can't answer for those early days, of course, but since I became involved we've made great strides and now the Anderson Particle Centre will take it further. We'll start modestly. Demonstrate moving small objects first, then after more research, small animals and finally within a couple of years, humans. We'll make so much money it'll make Microsoft, Google and Amazon look like backyard businesses.'

'Is money all you think about?' Emily asked.

'No, but someone has to benefit so why not us?'

'Well,' said Jack, 'I've had plenty of time to think about this recently and of course I can't speak for Emily but now I know more I can give an emphatic answer. No.'

He shouted the last word.

'He's right,' said Emily. 'You make me sick.'

'That's unfortunate,' said King smoothly. 'Are you ready Mr Twining?'

'Ready for wh… oh I see, just need to make a few adjustments. A couple of minutes at the most.'

'My conscience is clear,' said King into the microphone. 'You've chosen your own path. It could be interesting but it will be terminal.'

His voice clicked off and it looked like King was shouting at Mr Twining. Emily let out a shrill scream and Jack nearly jumped out his skin but neither King nor Twining turned to look.

'Just testing to see if they can hear us,' she said to a shaken Jack, 'but I don't think they can. Look if we or either of us get out of this let's promise each other that we'll do everything we can to stop this invention ending up in private hands.'

'We're going to get out of this,' he said, knowing they probably wouldn't.

'Don't talk rubbish. You know the chances are slim. Answer me. I promise. Do you?'

'Of course and we also need to talk about where we go from here.'

'What d'you mean where? We're probably headed for nothingness or into the path of a train.'

'Not where, you and me.'

She opened her mouth to speak then shut it again, staring at Mr Twining. 'He's firing up the machine. I think he's sending us somewhere.'

'Or nowhere.'

Suddenly they heard a muffled explosion through the glass and the floor shook. Then a woman and Billy were running through the door pointing guns and obviously shouting. Their friends were behind. Jack and Emily looked at each other in astonishment. King was shouting too, at Mr Twining whose back was to them looking at a screen. King dropped the gun and put his hands up. Mr Twining hesitated for a second, nodded, tapped a keyboard and put his hands up too.

There was no doubt this time that the snooker balls and the marbles happened at the same time. As mist appeared, Jack and Emily's eyes met in a look of sadness and longing.

46
Nabeela

As King and Jack went down the fire escape, Ginger pulled himself to a standing position and hobbled painfully after them, leaning heavily on the handrail and still moaning. King closed the third floor fire door long before he got there. Arun, Dil and Donna climbed off the roof and easily caught Ginger up. They helped him to the bottom where Arun cautioned him and arrested him on suspicion of kidnapping, malicious wounding and attempted murder. He handcuffed him to the fire escape and radioed for an ambulance to come with the reinforcements.

'Inspector Aftab and backup two minutes out,' he said as a dark grey Jaguar screeched into the car park and Billy jumped out with a woman, both carrying handguns.

'Nabeela?' Bina shrieked, astonished.

'No time to explain,' she said. 'Up to the third floor.'

Billy was ahead, carrying a small bag and they all ran. When they reached the entrance to the room where King was, Billy set plastic explosive round the door.

'Stand back,' he shouted and tapped his phone.

The door flew off and Nabeela rushed in, Billy close behind. Arun, Donna, Bina, Dil and Lucy followed, ears ringing from the explosion.

'Do it,' King was shouting at Twining.

King dropped the gun and put his hands up. Twining, looking at a screen, nodded, tapped a keyboard and put his hands up too. Beyond was a large glass cubicle with

Emily strapped to a reclining chair, Jack standing beside her. They were looking towards their friends, then at each other, as mist formed over their heads, expanding downwards. When it reached Jack's chest everything went blurred and when the mist cleared four seconds later they were gone.

'Get them back,' Nabeela shouted to Twining.

'Sorry, impossible.'

'Who d'you mean?' asked King smoothly.

'Emily Harrison and Jack Wellington,' said Billy.

'Oh that was just a holographic projection. A bit dramatic, Billy, bursting in here like that. I trust you'll pay for the damage. How are you by the way?'

'Worse for seeing you. Why were you holding that gun?'

'Me? I wasn't. You must be mistaken.'

He ostentatiously took off a glove and put it in his pocket. Mr Twining was open-mouthed.

'Well,' King went on, 'I've got a busy day so I'll leave you to clear up the mess. There'll probably be litigation to follow.'

He smiled an oily smile and headed for where the door had been.

'Just a minute,' said Arun, 'you've some questions to answer.'

'Another time perhaps? I have a pressing engagement.'

Arun looked at Billy. Billy looked at Nabeela.

'We can't keep him here if he won't co-operate,' she said, expressionless.

'Bye,' said King and walked quickly into the long computer room.

'I'll see him off the premises,' said Donna.

Mr Twining was furious.

'What about me?' he yelled.

'Watch out for consequences,' King shouted.

***

Jack desperately wanted more time with Emily but knew he wouldn't get it because they were about to die. He wished he could somehow spare her that, so she could have a happy life and fight to bring King down. He had no doubt she could.

Emily knew they were about to die but wasn't afraid. After all, it happened to everyone sooner or later. At least she wasn't alone and she couldn't think of anyone she'd rather be with. She thought wistfully about how nice it would be to have more time with him. She also wished she could somehow save him so he could have a good life and make King pay for what he had done, but not with money. Jack would be able to do it.

They continued to hold hands in silent solidarity as they looked at each other. Mist began to descend and Jack remembered to try to move but he was already paralysed.

The sadness in Jack's eyes touched Emily's heart and she was glad to feel his hand in hers. She squeezed, hoping it would convey something of what she was feeling, and felt his squeeze in return. But as the mist came down their hands became insubstantial and she could no longer feel his. For the first time she felt fear. Not of death but of their never touching again. As the mist increased she could see and hear and feel nothing. Whatever was next was about to happen. She could still think though. She would carry on as long as…

***

Donna ran back in from the landing with DI Aftab and three of his team. Arun had already taken down some personal details from Mr Twining and left him on a chair near the glass room.

'Good afternoon, Inspector,' said Nabeela and showed him a card.

'Pleased to meet you Ma'am,' he said. 'I'd heard SIS were involved and you arrived in the nick of time.'

'Not quite, I'm afraid. We've lost Jack and Emily but I'm hoping Mr Twining here may be able to help.'

'SIS?' said Bina in astonishment. 'Did I hear that right?'

'Yes I'm afraid so.'

'Wow,' said Bina, 'Dad never mentioned it.'

'I sincerely hope he doesn't know,' Nabeela replied.

'My cousin's daughter,' she added to Billy, the Inspector and Arun who looked surprised.

Nabeela showed Bina her card. Dil, Lucy and Donna looked over her shoulder, open-mouthed. It described her as Chief Operative. They were stunned to silence.

'I owe you all an apology,' said Nabeela. 'It's a remarkable coincidence that Bina made contact when Jack and Emily were in hospital but I felt it wasn't the right moment to tell her of my connection with SIS or to tell Billy of my connection with her. Small world eh?'

'Look,' said Dil loudly, 'let's talk about this another time. We need to concentrate on getting Emily and Jack back.'

'King said it was a holographic projection,' said Arun. 'but I know Jack wasn't. He walked in through the fire door a few minutes before, so I'd be surprised if Emily was.'

He turned to DI Aftab. 'They just disappeared in a cloud of mist, Sir.'

'Hard to believe but I'll take your word for it. I assume you want it kept it confidential, Ma'am.' said DI Aftab.

'Yes, please,' said Nabeela. 'It's in no-one's interests, especially Emily and Jack's, for it to be broadcast. Mr Twining is the only one who can throw light on it. I intend to interview him but not under caution. Is that alright to you Inspector? You're welcome to participate.'

'Fine. I'll caution him later if it appears he may have committed an arrestable offence.'

Nabeela asked the others to return to the yard. She and the Inspector went over to sit with Mr Twining.

'I'd like to have an off-the-record discussion with you,' she said. 'It seems clear to me that you may have been involved in kidnapping or even murder but at this moment I simply want to find Emily and Jack. If you help us it will go strongly in your favour.'

'I want immunity from prosecution,' he said.

'If your help results in them being found unharmed, I'll see what I can do. I can't promise because it's a decision that needs to be made at a higher level.'

'Ask your boss, then.'

'No, I won't unless you can convince me that you know where Emily and Jack are. That's it. If you choose not to co-operate, I'll hand you over to Inspector Aftab here and he'll no doubt question you under caution if it appears you may have committed an offence. Then you may be arrested and taken into custody or charged or both and goodness knows what else he'll discover.'

'If I tell you things, Mr King's people will come after me. You heard what he said as he left.'

'That's a risk you'll have to weigh up but if information you give us about him is valuable enough, we may be able to offer you protection.'

'I've done incredible work here in the past ten years. If people knew about it I'd probably get a knighthood.'

'Not if you're convicted of offences for which you go to prison for many years. Prisons can be dangerous places, too. Quite possibly you wouldn't be safe there.'

His face had become paler as they talked. He knew enough about King to send any normal person to prison but he also knew that King wasn't normal and might somehow avoid being affected while bringing about 'consequences' for everyone else. He also knew that even if he said nothing today and went to prison, King wouldn't risk leaving him alive. He decided.

'Alright, I'll tell you what I know about the two who disappeared. King told me to disparticle them.'

'Disparticle?'

'Separate them into fundamental particles but not pair them. You know of course that everything and everyone is made of tiny particles. Atoms are made of them. This machine sets up a powerful magnetic field that pulls the particles apart and pairs them with similar particles in the distance. The result is transportation, although it's not really, it's just particles copying each other. There's a lot of physics involved. It's called entanglement.'

'I get the idea, Scottie and stuff. So if you disparticle a person without pairing them…'

'They'll be gone, disassembled forever.'

***

As Superintendent Gray expected, the Commissioner dithered about getting in touch with the Home Office but eventually agreed. An hour later he called Gray and said he would have an answer by close of business the next day.

'Less than useless,' Gray muttered to himself. 'Meantime, Kennedy's in danger.'

It was time to use a bit of bluff with an imaginary search warrant. If he got it wrong he'd get a slap on the wrist but the undying support of his whole team. If he was right, he'd save a life and become a hero.

He assembled a small force of firearms officers and Pete drove the van.

47
Connections

DI Kennedy blinked. *I must have nodded off,* he thought, *and missed them being brought in. Strange that Emily's wearing pyjamas though.*

He was lying on a bed, the only recognisable item of furniture in the room. The rest of it was taken up with a lot of peculiar looking equipment. He'd been kept there since they jumped him the previous night as he tried to cut through the perimeter fence. Obviously he'd been right to come to BML. They'd roughed him up a bit but he wasn't worried. His colleagues would find him.

He looked at Jack and Emily again. They were lying on the floor, not moving. They looked unconscious. In fact, he realised with a start, they seemed not to be breathing. He jumped from the bed and rolled each of them onto their backs. He was right – they weren't breathing. They were dead. Still warm but colour quickly draining from the faces. Whatever had happened to them had only just happened.

They needed CPR. He started on Emily and began shouting for help at the same time. Fifteen compressions and two rescue breaths, twice. She didn't start but he transferred to Jack, still shouting. Same two sequences, and as he transferred back to Emily, he heard keys in the door. Two young men with shaved heads, jeans and T-shirts came in, the thugs who had beaten him up.

'If you've killed these two you'll be in trouble,' he shouted. 'We've got to try and revive them,'

The thugs were rooted to where they stood. They'd been told the police guy was for the chop but they'd no idea where the other two had come from so maybe they could just leave them to die. On the other hand, they'd had no orders about them.

'What do we do, Darren?' said one.

'I'll help, you tell the boss.'

'I've done it before,' he added to the Inspector, and knelt down beside Jack.

'Fifteen to two,' said DI Kennedy breathlessly as he worked furiously on Emily.

The other thug was about to leave to report to the boss when they heard a loudspeaker outside.

'This is Superintendent Gray of the Cambridgeshire Police. I believe there is imminent danger to life on the premises of BML Partners Ltd and I have been refused admittance. Whoever's in charge has one minute to open the gates so we can execute a search warrant I hold in my hand, failing which armed police officers will force entry.'

DI Kennedy didn't ease up on the CPR and urged Darren to continue on Jack.

'Call an ambulance,' he shouted. 'It'll go in your favour.'

'Do it, Chris,' said Darren. 'We're in trouble here.'

Chris took out his phone and dialled 999.

'Right,' said the loudspeaker, 'we're coming in.'

There was crashing and running feet, then silence. Except DI Kennedy thought he heard a sound. From Emily. A barely audible intake of air. Then a gulp and a huge sighing breath and she opened her eyes.

'Jack,' she shouted, sitting up.

'Steady Emily,' said the Inspector. 'You've been unconscious. Just take it easy for a minute. Jack's here.'

She ignored him and scrambled onto her knees beside Jack while Darren continued chest compressions.

'Jack,' she shouted, taking his hand and squeezing it hard. 'Wake up. Don't bloody die. Remember, we've got stuff to do. You're so annoying. Just when we're getting somewhere together you cop out. I need you to listen to me. Wake UP.'

There was no response. Tears rolled down her cheeks and she began to feel dizzy. Darkness descended.

***

'If what you've told me checks out,' said Nabeela to Mr Twining, 'I'll speak to my boss about some kind of deal.'

DI Aftab was on his phone. Pete answered immediately.

'How's it going? Is Inspector Kennedy ok? And we've had a heads up that Emily and Jack might be there somewhere too.'

'The Inspector's here, a bit knocked about. I'll put him on.'

'Hello Inspector,' said Kennedy, 'yes they're both here but it's been a bit like Romeo and bloody Juliet. First they're dead, then one wakes up, wails and conks out again, then the other wakes up and wails. At this moment they're both awake and not wailing but how long that'll last I don't know.'

There was laughter in the background.

Mr Twining looked relieved when DI Aftab relayed the news.

'Looks like your last minute adjustment worked,' said Nabeela.

'It was all I could think of. It didn't seem right to do what King asked.'

'And yet you've probably done it before.'

Mr Twining looked uncomfortable. Nabeela's phone rang.

'Home Secretary,' she said and walked into the glass cubicle to take the call.

***

Down in the yard, Lucy's phone rang.

'It's Jack,' she shrieked, putting it on speaker.

'Hello,' said Emily, using Jack's phone.

'Is Jack ok,' Dil shouted and Emily heard.

'I'm fine in case you want to know,' she said with mock indignation as Lucy put her one speaker, 'and yes Jack's ok. We're both here.'

'We were dead when we got here,' said Jack, chuckling, 'but Inspector Kennedy revived Em and then she shouted at me till I woke up.'

'It's true,' Emily giggled.

'So where are you?' Bina asked.

'BML Partners, Cottenham. We're going for a hospital check-up and then back to the flat. Can you come down? I think we've got to the bottom of the bed mystery but there's other stuff to talk about.'

'Oo yes and we've stuff to tell you,' said Bina. 'Nabeela being SIS, for example.'

'What? So that's who we saw running in with Billy as we were teleported?'

'Yes, we were gobsmacked! Anyway, see you soon. Tomorrow probably.'

Lucy ended the call. Billy had been listening and looked pleased.

'Pity you didn't get here quicker,' said Bina, 'or we might have saved Em and Jack from all that.'

He looked deflated.

'Yes, but honestly we didn't dawdle. The boss drove from Cambridge, don't forget, and she had to negotiate with her boss and the Home Secretary on the way. Convince them that Emily and Jack and you lot weren't on the dark side, unlike Hubbler and several of his staff.'

'I suppose,' said Bina, looking sceptical. 'But how come you know King? What about that friendly exchange before he left?'

'It wasn't friendly. If you must know he killed my mother.'

There was a shocked silence.

'He somehow ingratiated himself with my Mum after Dad died and they were married but he was abusive to both of us. I think it's what made me such an arsehole at school. In the end she died in a car crash that was said to be accidental but I'm pretty sure he arranged it. She'd inherited a lot of money from her parents and I think he had his eye on it all along. Of course her will left everything to him.'

There was another silence.

'What an awful man,' said Bina eventually. 'I don't know what to say. It must have been terrible for you and I'm sorry I've been so antagonistic.'

'You weren't to know,' he said quietly.

***

At Cottenham, Superintendent Gray was relieved that the outcome of the raid was good. DI Kennedy, Emily and Jack were taken to hospital by ambulance and released later after thorough check-ups and, in the Inspector's case, after cuts had been cleaned and dressed. A number of people at BML were arrested including the Managing

Director, Darren and Chris, then released on bail pending further enquiries. Superintendent Gray's bluff paid off and his stock rose dramatically with his men. The Commissioner heard back from the Home Office by mid-afternoon that BML should be closed and sealed until SIS forensic people got there. He was therefore prepared to overlook the Superintendent's unauthorised raid.

***

It was six o'clock in the evening by the time Jack, Emily and DI Kennedy were discharged from Addenbrookes Hospital. A police car came for the Inspector and he dropped Emily and Jack off at the flat via the estate agent's office where Jack picked up a spare key. Emily was still in her pyjamas but had a hospital blanket wrapped around her and borrowed slippers. As soon as they got inside they ran baths in each bathroom and soaked for a while. By half past seven, Jack was feeling better in jeans and t-shirt and Emily was once more in pyjamas, clean ones, and a dressing gown. Jack ordered pizza and they opened a bottle of wine. They sat in silence waiting for the delivery, sprawled on the sofa, TV news in the background, beginning to relax from the tension of the past few days.

'You know what we said before we were transported. Are you still up for it?' said Emily after a while.

'About teleporting? Keeping it out of private hands, Absolutely. Trouble is, being a lawyer King'll probably have it tied up somehow. Anyway, we need to try.'

'Good. And you were also going to say something about where we go from here. What was that about?'

She thought she knew but wanted to hear him say it.

'Er, well, we've been sort of thrown together and been through a lot of stuff and I'd like it to continue,' he coloured slightly, 'I mean, not the stuff we've been through, obviously, but, you know, spending time together…that is if you would too.'

'Jack Wellington you're the most infuriating person I've ever met. I was on my knees beside your corpse begging you not to die having just died myself and been revived and you were the first thought that came into my mind. What do you think that means?'

Jack knew but her response was so strong it made him feel stupid and tongue-tied and he didn't want her to feel he was taking anything for granted.

'That, er, well, er, I'm sure any friend would, er, no I don't mean that, after what's happened you're more than a friend and you're sensible and…'

'Sensible?' She sounded incredulous.

He grinned. 'Yes, not just quite sensible like you say I am and you interrupt and get stroppy sometimes and…'

'Oh,' she screeched, 'so I was being stroppy when I was shouting at you not to die?'

'And,' he continued, ignoring her, 'I really love that.'

'What, you love that I interrupt and get stroppy?'

'Well, not just that, obviously…'

'So what, then?'

'Everything.'

'Everything?'

'Yes.'

'Everything in the world?'

'Well…er…no,' he said, blushing. 'I mean everything about being with you.'

She looked straight into his eyes and he looked back into hers. He felt she was looking straight into his heart and it made him feel scared and giddy. She for her part saw tenderness and respect and, she thought, love.

'I think a hug would be nice at this point,' she said and moved across the sofa to him.

He put an arm round her and squeezed tight.

***

All the police activity at the mill sent the Wilsden rumour machine into overdrive and any number of explanations were posted on social media, ranging from a hostage situation, to a chemical spill, to a fire, to the escape of a deadly virus, so there was some disappointment when DI Aftab released a statement saying that a break-in had been foiled but damage had been done to a getaway car and the inside of the premises. There was only short paragraph in the following day's Bradford Telegraph & Argus.

Bina and Donna went home with Lucy and Dil. Mr Twining was taken into protective custody after providing Nabeela with information about Mr King's activities. He spent the night in a cell at Bradford Central Police Station and when DI Aftab went there to interview him the next morning he was told that two people from SIS had taken him away at four o'clock in the morning.

***

Emily and Jack slept late.

After eating the pizza the previous evening they'd sat together on the sofa staring at the TV in a stupor of tiredness and emotional exhaustion. Emily had quickly fallen asleep, leaning against him, comfortable with her head on his shoulder and his arm around her. Soon he felt himself dozing too and his wound began to ache. He shifted position hoping she would stir, but she didn't, so he gently picked her up, carried her to her bedroom, and put her into her bed. As he pulled the covers over her she had sighed and turned on her side. He could tell she was heading for much-needed deep sleep. He went back to his own room for the same. It came almost at once.

Jack had a call from Nabeela mid-morning.

'We haven't met but Bina's told me a lot about you two and I'd like to have a talk,' she said. 'There are things you should know and things you might be able to tell me.'

She was still in Bradford but would drive back to Cambridge with Bina and Donna and drop them at the flat that evening. Then she would come round the following morning about ten o'clock.

'We've no secrets from them,' Jack said, 'so I hope it'll be ok for them to hear what we talk about.'

'Of course, you make a good team. It'd be nice for Dil and Lucy to be there too. See if you can persuade them to come. I can easily carry four passengers. Billy will come independently.'

'Luce and I were looking forward to some time on our own,' said Dil when Jack called. 'Hang on, I'll ask her.'

'Try to keep me away,' she said when he did. 'There's so much we don't know.'

Later Lucy and Bina agreed that an equally important reason was to find out if Em and Jack were finally an item.

'How could they not be after all this?' said Lucy.

48
More History

Emily and Jack spent a leisurely day. The sun came out and there was a promise of spring in the air but a cold wind whipped across the town and they muffled up for a walk along The Backs. They passed the seat where they had been shot, the yellow police tape now gone.

'When we're rich and famous,' said Jack, 'd'you think they'll put a plaque here saying it was where we were shot?'

'No, it'll say it's where you saved my life.'

She reached for his hand and squeezed. They had a pub lunch, did some shopping and were back at the flat for tea and toast before dusk.

'It's been like a lazy Saturday used to be,' she said later. 'I'd forgotten what they were like.'

They made a big fish pie for that evening, looking forward to seeing the others. Later Emily was browsing clothing websites. She decided on new jeans and checked her bank account but had a shock.

'Account blocked' said a red message across the screen, with a number to call. When she got through after a frustrating wait of hold-on music, she was told someone had claimed back money sent to her in error and although the bank wouldn't return the money without her consent, the account would be overdrawn if it did, so it had been blocked. A letter had been sent explaining the position and the appeals procedure.

Emily couldn't believe it and asked who was claiming the money. 'Clarence & Thirkill' was the reply. She tried arguing but realised the story was too complicated to be accepted by someone in a call centre. She told Jack and his account was the same.

'What are we going to do?'

'No idea,' he said grimly. 'Looks like our dreams of wealth have disappeared with King.'

'Wonder where he is and what he's up to. Probably as we speak he's filling a trunk with Mrs Barton's money and disappearing out of the country.'

'I'll look for a job but I don't want to go back to London.'

The arrival of the others lifted their spirits and there was a lot of hugging and laughing and repartee over wine and the meal, as well as discussion of the events of the past few days. Emily and Jack didn't mention the missing money.

Lucy and Bina were closely watching them all evening to see if they could read if they had become closer. When it came to bedtime Bina said she thought Dil and Lucy should have the second bedroom that she had occupied before. Lucy still had after-effects from the kidnapping.

'Ok,' said Jack. 'The sofabed in the office/snug is a double so if you and Donna don't mind sharing I'll sleep on the couch.'

'Fine by me, said Donna, colouring slightly and exchanging glances with a smiling Bina.

'That's silly, Jack' said Emily. 'You take the other bed in my room. The couch isn't good for your wound.'

It was true.

'Well, if you don't mind,' he said, quickly clearing some plates into the dishwasher to cover his confusion.

Emily noticed, though, and later when she was about to get into bed and he was heading for the bathroom she spoke to him.

'Look, I didn't suggest we share because I expect anything of you. It was just logical and we know each other well enough to share a room.'

'Fine,' he said. 'I think the same.'

'Oh, so you don't want to be my lover?' she said with an sly grin.

'I didn't say that,' he laughed.

'Oh, so you do?'

'I didn't say that either.'

She looked straight into his eyes in a way he found both disturbing and exciting.

'Keeping me guessing, eh?' she said but she thought she had seen the truth.

'No it's just with all this going on…'

'Oh I forgot. You're a man. You can only think of one thing at a time.'

She kissed him on the cheek as he grabbed a pillow to hit her.

***

'Seen the news?' Nabeela said when she and Billy arrived next morning.

'No,' said Dil. 'What?'

They switched on a news channel and looked at their phones. Everywhere it said 'Breaking News: Government Minister resigns.'

'Mrs Latimer,' said Nabeela. 'We found she's secretly been taking money from Anderson in return for approving work permits and research licences for his UK operations, including recommending planning permission for the new Particle Centre. The Home Secretary had a word in the P.M.'s ear and he in turn had a word with Mrs Latimer. She made a deal with him that she'd go quietly if the P.M. prevented any criminal proceedings and her statement this morning says she hadn't realised the burden high office places upon her and her family so she was stepping back from the front line blah, blah, blah. The usual claptrap to keep the Government clean. We suspect, but we can't prove, that she has a stake in an offshore company that will handle commercial exploitation of the Particle Centre's discoveries.'

Emily and Jack exchanged glances.

'That'll be teleporting. A world-changing invention and King will have tied it all up legally so that his and Anderson's noses are deepest in the trough.'

'You could be right,' said Nabeela, 'but I've no evidence – yet. I've found out some history, though. I believe Mrs Barton's letter says that after John Barton disappeared the insurance company eventually dismissed him. I've discovered that his dismissal letter is signed by Anderson.'

'Wow,' said Emily, echoed by the others, 'so they knew each other in those days.'

'Yes, and the Barton family trusts owned the insurance company.'

'Wait,' said Lucy, 'John's family trusts owned the insurance company but John was dismissed? Could they do that?'

'Two separate entities,' said Bina. 'Almost certainly the trustees would leave management of the company to the directors.'

'Yes,' said Nabeela, 'and I get the impression that John wasn't keen to publicise his wealth. Living quietly and working like a normal person kept him in the real world. Very rich people can easily lose touch with it.'

'Where did you find this information?' Jack asked. 'Billy said King stole the SIS file.'

'Yes, we think so but when a file goes missing those on record as having looked at it are asked for their recollections, so some at least of the information is re-recorded. I can't guarantee what I'm telling you is a hundred percent accurate but I don't think it'll be too far from the truth.'

'So did the file mention teleporting?' Emily asked.

'John was an environmentalist, well ahead of his time, and quietly financed projects that he thought would help save the planet. Teleporting was one of them and amazingly it made a lot of progress. Actually, it was as much an act of charity as about the environment. A school friend in Bradford was the son of a German physicist who as a young man had fled from the Nazi regime before the second world war. He became unemployed in a recession around nineteen seventy. John offered him a job looking into teleporting, which he jumped at and was more successful than John had expected.

'Was Anderson involved,' Emily asked.

'Not at the beginning but we think he found out about John's wealth and deliberately befriended him soon after. On a visit to the UK, John took him to see his research facility in Ilkley. The physicist had already moved small objects and insects and was ready for a bigger trial. John wanted to offer himself as a guinea pig but the physicist didn't feel it was safe enough yet. He suggested instead that his research be handed over to a non-profit foundation or university for further development and John agreed.'

'I bet Anderson didn't like that,' said Jack.

'You're right,' said Nabeela. 'He was focussed on the money-making possibilities.'

'So how did he make Barton disappear?' Bina asked.

'King told Jack and I that Barton was the first human being to experience the system but didn't survive,' said Emily. 'It was before King's time, of course.'

'We may never know whether Anderson forcibly disparticled Barton or whether Barton tried it on himself with fatal results. There's evidence that Anderson was in the area at the time, though. I don't think the physicist did it because the file said he was at home that night. However, he was so deeply affected by John's disappearance that he dismantled all the equipment, and closed the facility down. He died soon after.'

'Anderson wouldn't like that either,' said Bina.

'The file just says he was unable to persuade the scientist to keep going and couldn't find anyone else with enough knowledge and experience. That is until King comes on the scene, and manages to get hold of the scientist's notes.'

Billy had been silent.

'I think I know how,' he said.

'Yes I think you do,' said Nabeela.

He nodded.

'The physicist was my grandfather, Professor Klaus Worth.'

'Whaat?' and similar exclamations came from everyone apart from Nabeela, who asked him to explain.

'He died long before I was born but my Dad used to tell me about him and what a good father he was. Just like mine, but he, too, died early. Then King came on the scene and trapped my mother into marrying him. I always thought it was for the money, and I suppose it was, partially, but also it must have been about finding any notes or papers my grandfather had left. I didn't know that until now.'

'Billy,' said Bina, 'It must have been very painful. We all feel for you.'

Everyone agreed. Billy swallowed and nodded. Nabeela finished the story.

'The rest is part supposition, part based on what Twining's told us. Having found the Worth papers, we believe King set up the Wilsden research facility and recruited Twining, who was a physicist specialising in entanglement. He was out of work because he'd published a paper based on data he stole from a colleague at Leeds University and had been dismissed in disgrace. But the papers from King gave him a head start and his system worked fairly quickly, if unpredictably. His first human subject was selected at random. Emily.'

'But it happened to me too,' said Jack, puzzled.

'Yes. Twining said they didn't expect that. He thinks it was maybe a glitch in geo-positioning software or a coding mistake.'

'What about the attempted kidnap after they'd tried it out,' said Emily.

'Twining said they wanted to examine you to see if there'd been any physical changes. He wouldn't say what they might have done to you in the process.'

Emily shuddered. 'Have they tried it since?'

'Yes. Twining's helping us correlate his experiments with missing persons. There've been three hits so far but all the people turned up dead.'

'God,' said Jack. 'Em and I were lucky to survive.'

'We almost didn't,' said Emily.

'When did Anderson reappear?' asked Bina.

'We think King paid for Twining to work on the invention these past ten years but if or when he perfected it, he would need finance to get it working on a commercial scale, so we think Anderson agreed to provide it under cover of the Particle Centre. In return for a share of the profits, of course. King knew from the file that Anderson would be interested. We don't know when King first approached him but it could be as long as ten years ago.'

Before Nabeela left she had a question.

'There's one puzzle I can't solve,' she said. 'Why did King and Anderson want Emily and Jack dead? The only reason I can think of is that they didn't want them telling the story of what happened ten years ago but frankly most people wouldn't believe it if they did.'

'We have no idea,' said Emily, looking at Jack.

'But whatever it was,' said Dil, 'also led to the attack on Bina, and Lucy being kidnapped. They must have wanted it very badly to do things like that.'

'Well, maybe we'll find out in time. By the way, King and Anderson flew to New York this morning. A few years ago Anderson pulled strings to get King US citizenship and a diplomatic passport. He probably paid off some official for it and when it expires there's a chance he might be extradited back to the UK. Don't hold your breath, though. He's a slippery customer.'

After she and Billy had gone, Jack and Emily told the others about their blocked bank accounts.

'I don't think Clarence & Thirkill have the right to do that,' said Bina. 'Can I talk to my boss about it? She might know the legal position better than me.'

49
Money

On Monday morning Bina called her boss and explained the problem. Her boss asked to see Mrs Barton's letter, so Bina consulted Emily and Jack.

'We need to be careful,' she said. 'It won't be good if your being teleported becomes widely known. You'll never hear the last of it from news media and others but Mrs Barton used 'dematerialised' in the letter which more or less gives the game away. My boss will be under a legal duty to keep it confidential, though.'

Emily and Jack hesitated but in the end felt they'd never know where they stood if they didn't allow her to see the letter, so Bina emailed it. Her boss called back later and asked to speak to Emily and Jack. They put her on speaker.

'My name's Jane Pulborough. I'm Bina's boss and Head of Corporate here at Wheatfields, and I've also got Elizabeth Jones with me who's Head of Private Client.'

'Look,' said Jack, interrupting, 'it's very good of you to call but without what's in our bank accounts I'm afraid we have no money at all, in fact we have less than no money, so there's no way we could afford you. But thanks anyway.'

'That's alright, Mr Wellington, our meters aren't ticking, we're not going to charge you for this call. We're doing it because of that dreadful shooting you were unlucky enough to be caught up in, and out of the high regard we have for Bina.'

Emily gave a thumbs up. Bina looked embarrassed.

'Thank you very much,' said Jack. 'And we agree about Bina, by the way.'

'We've looked at Mrs Barton's letter and the first thing I must say is that it may not be easy to get Clarence & Thirkill to unblock your accounts. Of course, you can ask them and they may agree but if they don't you might have to take court proceedings, which would be expensive, and you'd have to prove to the judge that you agreed to solve the mystery of what happened to John Barton, which could be difficult now Mrs Gregory is dead and Mr King is in the USA. Unlikely to return is the word on the street.'

'Oh well,' said Emily, 'I suppose we sort of knew it was too good to be true.'

'Ok,' said Jack, 'we'll ask but if they don't agree there's no way we could afford to take them to court so we'll just resign ourselves to letting them have the money and try somehow to pay off our overdrafts.'

'Well, that may not be end of the story,' said Elizabeth Jones. 'Bina told us you've actually solved the mystery of what happened to John Barton. We don't know the details but we gather several people can verify it, so you may still be in line for the legacy the letter mentions.'

'Whoa,' Dil couldn't stop himself exclaiming.

'The million pounds?' said Emily.

'Yes.'

She and Jack were excited but sceptical.

'I'll believe it if it happens,' said Jack. 'We've thrown a big spanner into Clarence & Thirkill's works so we're not expecting anything good from them. What should we do?'

'Well, get in touch with them and ask, but there may be more to it than meets the eye so I'd be happy to do it for you. No charge, of course.'

Emily and Jack looked at Bina and she nodded.

'That would be great. Thank you again,' they said.

'Fine. I'll do it today.'

She called back late afternoon.

'A surprising outcome. I spoke to Clarence & Thirkill. Apparently the partners, to their great surprise, were contacted and briefed by the Home Secretary yesterday and as a result have officially chucked James King out of the firm. I know the new senior partner. We were at law school together and he's an all-round straight-up guy. He says they apologise for everything, although of course they didn't know what King was up to, and will immediately unblock your accounts.'

'Phew,' said Jack, 'that's a relief. Thank you so much.'

'We're glad he was so helpful but, more than that, they've decided they don't want to carry on dealing with Mrs Barton's will and estate and plan to hand over to a different firm. They'll lose a huge amount of future fees so it's a big financial blow for them but they want to distance themselves from King's activities and minimise the scandal. They're reviewing everything he and Mrs Gregory did and trying to correct anything that's wrong. They say, incidentally, they think King had something on Edith Gregory and was blackmailing her into helping him. Anyway, at the end of the conversation he asked me if our firm would be willing to take over handling the Barton estate. It's a tremendous opportunity for us and I've consulted all our partners and they're happy to agree.'

Bina gave a thumbs up.

'I haven't seen the will,' she went on, 'so I don't know what it says about any bequest to you but we wouldn't want to take on the work without your agreement.'

Jack and Emily were puzzled.

'It's really nothing to do with us,' Emily said. 'We didn't know Mrs Barton well. She just thought we might be able to find out how her husband disappeared.'

'Yes we understand that and the will mentions a lot of charities but we're told you're the only individuals named in it because she had no family. You may be the nearest thing to her next of kin.'

'I hadn't thought of it like that,' said Jack, 'and although I see what you mean, I just think she went to a lot of trouble to make the will so it should be handled by someone who'll simply do as she wanted.'

He raised a questioning eyebrow at Emily.

'I agree,' she said. 'I don't know any other law firms but if Bina's like the sort of people you have, it's ok by me.'

Bina looked embarrassed again and Donna, sitting next to her, stroked her shoulder.

'Thank you very much for that,' said Elizabeth Jones. 'There'll be a lot of files and papers coming our way from Clarence & Thirkill. I'll look at the will as soon as I get it and let you know where you stand.'

Shortly after, Nabeela called Emily and Jack.

'The Home Secretary briefed Clarence & Thirkill and left me to liaise with them to get a full picture of King's activities. My contact there tells me they're handing over Mrs Barton's estate to Wheatfields to deal with. You couldn't be in better hands. I know Liz Jones from University and I've just had a word with her. I thought she ought to know what's been going on as well, so I told her, teleporting and everything. On the phone, a secure line, nothing written down. I think she found it helpful. She promised to keep it confidential but she's under a professional duty to do so anyway and I said that she should avoid discussing teleporting except in conditions of secrecy because you never know who's listening. If I were you I'd do the same. It's sensational stuff and the fewer people who know the better. By the way this is a secure line I've called on.'

After the call Emily and Jack checked their bank accounts. They were unblocked with healthy balances.

'Right,' said Jack, 'dinner's on me. No expense spared. How about that place in Trinity Street I could never afford?'

It was a late and rowdy night with all the pent-up laughter they'd missed for a long time. Later when Jack and Emily were in their beds, had stopped alcoholic giggling and sleep was close, Jack stretched out a hand across the gap between them and she took it.

'You know what?' he said, 'I don't care about a legacy. I'll just glad if we can get back to normal.'

'We?'

'Yes.'

***

It took them all a while to surface next morning but the laughs and conversation of the previous evening continued unabated. Donna went into work expecting to be taken off minding Jack and Emily but DI Kennedy had other ideas and brought her back.

'We want you all protected until we're sure you're out of danger,' he said.

'Surely with King gone it's all over,' said Dil.

'Can't be certain. You've dealt a big blow to him and Anderson which they might not want to take lying down, even though they're in the USA. BML's being closed down and there are rumours of Mitzli reducing or even closing their UK operations. Mrs Choudhry tells me

Hubbler and some other SIS people have been dismissed for gross misconduct and Hubbler's going to be charged with arson and murder. Also, of course, Mrs Latimer's career looks like it's over. So there's a lot of people out there who have reason to dislike you.'

'Was anyone at St Peter's involved?' Jack asked.

'Not as far as I know but I hear the Home Secretary's briefed them and they're running backwards from the Particle Centre. They've announced what they call an unexpected delay and I hear they'll quietly knock it on the head when the news agenda's moved on. Oh and they've dismissed Mitzli as their security people.'

Donna was told to stay with Emily, Jack and Bina, and the Inspector advised Dil and Lucy not to go home until more dust had settled. Towards the end of the afternoon Elizabeth Jones phoned Jack and Emily.

'We've received the first batch of papers from Clarence & Thirkill and I've seen the will. There's some good news for you and I wonder if it would be convenient for me to come and see you? There's quite a bit to go over.'

'So do we qualify for the million?' Jack asked.

'Well the position's not what you might expect after Mrs Barton's letter but I'd rather explain in person. I could be with you first thing in the morning. Is that ok?'

Bina looked surprised but gave a thumbs-up so Jack and Emily agreed.

'You're getting the VIP treatment,' said Bina after the call. 'Normally heads of departments are too important to visit clients unless they're celebs or billionaires and you're not even a client.'

'Sounds like there's some sort of snag about the million, though,' said Jack.

No-one disagreed.

'Good thing we don't care about a legacy,' said Emily that night before they slept.

***

Mrs Jones was younger than they expected, wearing a dark blue suit, yellow blouse and carrying a smart brown leather briefcase. Emily, Jack and Bina were up, dressed and breakfasted by the time she arrived at nine o'clock and the other three, slightly behind, appeared before she got down to business. Jack and Emily had explained they had no secrets from their friends.

'I expect you're wondering what this is about,' she said. 'By the way, call me Liz.'

'Yes, but we'll put your mind at rest right away,' said Jack. 'We're not worried about the million. We just want to get back to normal as soon as possible and get on with our lives. We can't yet because the police are still concerned about our safety but we hope that'll all be cleared up soon.'

'Thanks, but I'm not worried about a negative reaction. At least, not the one you think I might be expecting.'

They were puzzled by the remark.

'Let me tell you about the will first,' she said. 'As you know everything in Mrs Barton's considerable estate was put on hold until it was known whether or not Emily and Jack solved the mystery of what happened to her husband. If they didn't commit to trying, or didn't succeed within a year after her death, the entire estate was to be split between a number of charities. If, within the year, they produced evidence that satisfied the executors they had solved the mystery, a different set of provisions applied.'

'So is that the problem?' Emily asked. 'King's the only executor now Edith's dead and he's left the country. If we contacted him, he'd probably ignore us or just refuse to accept that we've solved the mystery.'

'Just the sort of thing he might try, I gather, but no. Every will has to have executors – they're the people tasked with carrying out what the will says – and the High Court has power to step in where there are none or they've become incapable or unsuitable for some reason. Clarence & Thirkill have insisted, rightly in my view, that they and our firm make a joint application to remove King. We managed to get it listed for an emergency hearing late yesterday in London and I'm pleased to say the judge approved it. He could hardly do anything else with King wanted for criminal offences. The application asked for me and Jane to be appointed instead and that was approved too."

'Wow,' said Bina. 'That's quick work.'

'And a relief,' said Emily. 'Thank you so much.'

'And,' Liz continued, 'I need hardly tell you that what Nabeela's told us more than satisfies Jane and I that you've solved the mystery.'

'That's great,' said Jack, 'and thank you from me too but even so, from what you've said it sounds like the will and the letter don't quite marry up.'

'Well, Mrs Barton wasn't entirely straight with you in her letter.'

Jack and Emily looked at each other.

'I can't believe she ever had even a dishonest thought, let alone ever wrote a dishonest letter,' said Emily.

Jack, Lucy, Dil and Bina nodded.

'I didn't say dishonest. She was only slightly misleading. You may think she can be forgiven when I say that the will doesn't just leave you the legacies she mentioned, it leaves you her entire estate, everything, half each.'

There was a silence as everyone grappled with the implications.

'I don't get it,' said Jack, looking round at the others. 'Half of what?'

Bina understood. 'The whole lot which must be huge. How…?' she said.

'Well, there are all sorts of investments,' Liz, interrupted, 'and I haven't got a full picture yet but a conservative estimate is about eight hundred million pounds.'

She stopped talking as everyone exclaimed and gasped, struggling with the enormity of it.

'Good grief,' said Jack, excited but scared, 'think what we could do with it. Not just for ourselves but other people, too'

'It's so much money it's frightening,' said Emily. 'Like a whole bank full. How will we look after it? I don't know anything about investments and that sort of thing.'

'You won't need to if you don't want. The next thing Jane and I will do – well, me really because she'll continue as Head of Corporate but both of us have to be in agreement about everything – is to draw up an accurate list of assets, have them independently valued, submit tax returns, pay inheritance tax and other normal things. Once we're through that we'll become trustees of all the assets for the two of you. That means all the income and capital is held on trust for you – is yours really – and we'll have to do whatever you tell us. As long as it's not illegal,' she added hastily. 'Eventually we'll need to discuss how you want to handle things for the future beyond that, but it'll be our duty to look after the investments for you unless or until you want to do it yourselves or get someone else to do it. In the meantime if you need money just ask.'

'Wow,' said Dil, laughing, 'imagine that. Just ask for money and you'll get it.'

Lucy giggled infectiously and in seconds they were all laughing, illogically and uproariously. Liz couldn't help joining in.

'I think that's enough for now,' she continued when the laughter died down, 'except for one important thing. Now you're multi-millionaires I strongly recommend you hire security. Once word gets out, and it will despite your best efforts, quite apart from possible enemies you'll become public property, prey for kidnappers, paparazzi and such. I know it from dealing with other big estates. I can recommend a security firm if you like.'

'We've had bad experience with security firms,' said Jack. 'We'll just think about it for now.'

50
Parting

When Liz left, Emily said: 'I need cake.'

They all strolled round to Folds coffee house and indulged her, enthusiastically joining in.

'In a way it's an anti-climax, for you two,' said Lucy. 'One minute you're fighting for your life and the next you've recovered and have so much money that nothing can ever worry you again.'

'I feel it belongs to us all,' said Jack. 'We've all been through such a lot together and Em and I didn't know Mrs Barton any better than you.'

'No it's yours because that's what she wanted,' said Dil, 'but, honestly, I don't envy you. It's a huge responsibility and as well as risks to your security like Liz mentioned, you'll be pestered by people and banks and others, all wanting a share.'

Lucy nodded. 'Dil's right. If I were you I'd keep the full truth and the money as secret as possible, even from your families. It only needs one person to know and news like that spreads like wildfire. If you help people you'll have to do it anonymously or cook up an explanation that doesn't give anything away.'

'You'll find a way through,' said Bina, adding as she caught Lucy's eye, 'and you've got each other.'

It was a fishing expedition. She and Lucy hadn't been able to work out the state of Emily and Jack's relationship. Jack blushed and sneaked a glance at Emily, trying to think what to say, but he was saved.

'Hi, Donna, oh and Emily and Jack,' said Indigo. 'Good to see you. How're you feeling now?'

She had been sitting with others at a nearby table.

'Much better, thanks,' said Jack.

'That's great. Would you be interested in doing a short interview – how things are a few weeks on from the murder attempt and so on?'

'I'd rather not,' said Emily. 'It's taking time to get back to normal.'

Jack agreed.

'Ok, did they find who did it?'

Donna chipped in. 'You'd have to ask Inspector Kennedy but the file isn't closed.'

'Ok, I'll maybe check back with you in a couple of weeks rather than bother him.' A friend hailed her from the door. 'Sorry, got to go. Enjoy.'

'See what I mean?' said Lucy. 'We know what's happened but people like her don't and if they did it'd be big news.'

Dil's phone rang. He looked at the number and stood up from the table.

'Better take this,' he said and hurried outside.

The others carried on talking, until he came back and sat down a few minutes later, looking flushed. They all looked at him expectantly but he said nothing.

'So what was it?' Lucy asked.

'Oh nothing, really,' he said but then a huge smile lit up his face and he jumped to his feet again with a fist pump. 'I've only gone and got that part!' he shouted.

***

Two days later a thick letter from Liz arrived for Emily and Jack with various papers for them to sign. There was also a folder listing all the assets of Mrs Barton's estate. It was staggering. Shares, government securities, whole businesses, land and buildings all over the world. They didn't understand what most of it was but noticed it showed a total value well exceeding the eight hundred million she had previously mentioned.

Near the end of the list in a category headed 'Miscellaneous' there was reference to 'Patent No. GB 93087246 - A novel method of transporting objects.' There was a densely printed four page paper attached, in highly technical language.

'That's it,' Bina exclaimed when she saw it. 'We've never really known why King wanted you dead but I bet this is the answer. It gives you ownership of the technology behind teleporting for twenty years from the date it was applied for which is…' she paused looking at the document '…about ten years ago. Around the time of the bed mystery.'

'What?' said Jack, not quite understanding.

'It must have been owned by Mrs Barton, not sure why, seems a bit peculiar, but anyway it was hers and, now she's died, it's yours. If you thought that list of things you've inherited was valuable, this could well double it. If it works ok and everything.'

'It's so strange,' said Emily. 'We'll ask Liz if she knows how it came about.'

She called later to see if they had any questions and they asked her about the patent.

'Yes, it's odd. You know what a patent is, I take it?'

'Bina says it gives us ownership of an invention.'

'Yes. About ten years ago Mrs Barton bought it at the application stage from the people who'd applied for it, a Mr Twining and an offshore company called Innovative

Transportation AG. Goodness knows why she did it. I'll get our patent department to see if they can work out what it's all about.'

'No, best not to,' said Jack. 'I think we know. It'll be something to do with what we gather Nabeela told you. How much did she pay?'

'About five million according to the file. A tidy sum. Actually there are draft documents suggesting it was about to be transferred back for the same amount but she died before signing them.'

Later they pieced together what must have happened.

'King must have needed the five million to set up and run the research place at Wilsden,' said Bina. 'In return she got the rights to the invention.'

'But it wasn't King's money,' said Lucy. 'How could he do it? Surely it can't have been legal.'

'I expect Mrs Barton left Clarence & Thirkill to handle everything, including where to invest the money. She'll no doubt have signed papers about it without looking at them or at least understanding them. And if she had questioned it King could easily have defended it by saying it was a good investment.'

'It was clever,' said Emily. 'Mrs Barton was a source of money for Twining's research and a safe place to keep what would be an extremely valuable asset if Twining was successful. If he was, Anderson was standing by to finance the commercial exploitation. Her death before re-transferring the patent must have thrown King and Anderson into a panic.'

'Yes,' said Jack, 'and because of it King needed Em and me dead so they and Mrs Latimer or their offshore company or whoever could buy the patent back for five million – a fraction of its real value.'

'They could have made billions,' said Bina.

***

The next morning Dil and Lucy decided to go home.

'We need some time together and then get on with our lives,' said Dil. 'I start rehearsals on Monday, too. But can we talk a lot? We're itching to know how you get on with all this money and the teleporting and stuff. I've got an idea for a film script based on it so I'd like to know what happens next.'

'And we can call Arun or DI Aftab if we have any worries about safety,' said Lucy. 'I agree with Liz Jones that Em and Jack should hire security, though.'

Bina and Donna also had something to say.

'We're moving in together,' said Bina, holding a smiling Donna's hand. 'We're so grateful we've met and just want to be with each other all the time and keep each other safe. Which, of course, we can't because I have the job in London but I can be in Cambridge at weekends and I'll be able to work from home quite a bit too. And who knows what the future will bring?'

'Aw, so happy for you both,' said Emily, hugging them. Jack, Dil and Lucy joined in.

'You've been very discreet,' said Lucy, smiling, 'but Dil and I suspected.'

'Me too,' said Emily.

***

That night Emily was tucked in and propped up on pillows, thumbing her phone, when Jack came to sit on the side of her bed.

'All this money sets us apart, doesn't it? We can't ever be normal again. We don't want to lose touch with Dil and Lucy and Bina and Donna but they'll want to get on with their own lives. We make such a good team when we're all together, whether it's just having fun or struggling to stay alive, but now everything's different.'

'I know what you mean. We're all on different paths and ours has changed dramatically. It's called life and it's down to us to see that we all stay close. We'll have plenty of time to work on it. And as Bina said we've got each other.'

She gave him a stare that made him feel like the world was turning over.

'Yes,' he said, suddenly inarticulate.

'I'd like you to kiss me now,' she said.

About the Author

William Coniston lives in West Yorkshire, United Kingdom. He has been writing all his life but mainly boring legal documents and finds writing fiction much more fun. He welcomes reviews and hopes you will let him know whether or not you enjoyed *Entangled Legacy*.

He has also written and published three scary novels for children 8-13 years:
M.I.C.E. and the Stone (2016)
M.I.C.E. and the Dragon Worm (2017)
M.I.C.E. and the Future (2019)

Printed in Great Britain
by Amazon

64731757R00215